Myths and symbols
in pagan Europe

Myths and symbols in pagan Europe

Early Scandinavian and Celtic religions

H. R. ELLIS DAVIDSON

Syracuse
University Press

Copyright © H. R. Ellis Davidson 1988

Published in the United States of America
by Syracuse University Press
Syracuse, New York 13244-5160

All Rights Reserved

Printed in Great Britain

ISBN 0-8156-2438-7

Library of Congress cataloging in publication data applied for

Contents

List of illustrations

Figures

Plates   *the plates appear between pp.* 16, 17 *and* 48, 49

1a Helgafell, Iceland: drawing by W. G. Collingwood, *Pilgrimage to the Sagasteads of Iceland* (1899), fig. 79.

1b Turoe Stone, Co. Galway, Ireland: Office of Public Works, Dublin.

1c Sanda Stone, Gotland: Gotlands Fornsal, Visby.

2a Cult Wagon from Mérida, Spain: Musée des Antiquités nationales, St Germain-en-Laye. *Belzeaux-Zodiaque.*

2b Top panel of memorial stone from Alskog Tjängvide, Gotland: Antik-varisktopografiska arkivet, Stockholm.

2c Shield from River Witham: J. M. Kemble, *Horae Felales* (1863), pl. XIV.

3a Carved stone from Housesteads, Hadrian's Wall: Museum of Antiquities, Newcastle-upon-Tyne.

3b Carved stone from Vertillum, Coté d'Or, Musée de Chatillon-sur-Seine: Simone Robier, Paris.

4a Stone *stele* with Janus head from Holzgerlingen: Wurttembergisches Landesmuseum, Stuttgart.

4b Wooden figure, Rude Eskildstrup, Denmark: Nationalmuseet, Copenhagen.

Preface and acknowledgements

This study of early religion is the result of many years of exploration into the period before Christianity in North-Western Europe; it is mainly based on the medieval literature of Iceland and Ireland, together with earlier clues from the archaeology and iconography of the pre-Christian period. My first interest in Anglo-Saxon and Old Norse literature and thought I owe to Hector and Nora Chadwick, for the inspiration received in the dim, book-lined study of their old moated house on the Newmarket Road has never faded. This meant that from the beginning I was conscious of links between Germanic and Celtic tradition, since Nora Chadwick was a dedicated scholar in Celtic history and literature, while as a research student I had the privilege of attending Kenneth Jackson's classes in Early Welsh, and later in the fifties those in Old Irish given by Anne O'Sullivan in University College, London. Continued work over the years on various aspects of thought and belief in pre-Christian Europe, and on the way in which oral tradition and folklore can throw light on the attitude of men and women to the unseen world, has convinced me that there is much to be gained by bringing the two areas together. Like the journeys in the folktales, it is one beset by perils and surprises, but seems to offer a worthwhile goal to the discerning traveller. I hope that this tentative effort may encourage others better equipped than I am to follow this path.

One of the problems confronting those who venture to bring together evidence from separate fields is that they are certain to offend those who prefer specialisation within a limited and safer pasture. Spelling alone offers many pitfalls. I have deliberately simplified the spelling of Icelandic names for the benefit of the reader who is not a specialist and may be bewildered by the strange letters, especially as many names, from Odin to Harald Hardradi, are already familiar in a simplified form. Titles and specialised terms however have been given in their Icelandic spelling. On the other hand, I have kept the accents in the Irish names, in accordance with the usual practice of Irish scholars; I am grateful to those who have advised me on this, and only hope I have not let them down too badly.

I owe a debt of gratitude to Dr Emily Lyle and Dr Jacqueline Simpson, for patiently reading the book at an earlier stage, and providing suggestions, comments and general encouragement. Dr Simpson has given me a number of useful references from northern folktales which I was delighted to receive. I would like also to thank Dr Gale Owen-Crocker for her timely encouragement, and those too who showed interest and offered help while I was on visits to Ireland, particularly Professor Bo Almqvist and Dr Patricia Lysaght. Professor Kim McCone has been most kind in giving advice on spelling, while his own work on the Indo-Germanic vocabulary concerned with warrior groups has been a great inspiration to me. To my husband, as always, I am grateful for unfailing interest and practical help, for many enjoyable discussions on visits to remote places, and assistance with proof-reading. I am grateful to those who helped to supply illustrations, mentioned elsewhere. Finally I must thank the Editor and staff of Manchester University Press for the encouragement, helpfulness and patience which they have shown throughout.

Hilda Ellis Davidson
Cambridge, 1987

Introduction

They were in reduced circumstances, yes; and the world (they thought) had grown hard and old and desperately ordinary; but they were descended from a race of bards and heroes, and there had once been an age of gold, and the earth around them was all alive and densely populated, though the present times were too coarse to see it. They had all gone to sleep, as children, to those old stories; and later they courted with them; and told them to their own children.

John Crowley, *Little Big, VI*, 3

Many people, if only through an acquaintance with the works of Wagner, have heard of Wotan or his northern counterpart Odin, and of the valkyries in the hall of Valhalla. Some have come upon the legend of Balder the Beautiful, slain by a shaft of mistletoe, which inspired a long poem by Matthew Arnold and provided the title of one of the volumes of Frazer's *Golden Bough*. Others have heard of the great hammer of Thor, the northern thunder-god, and of the mischievous practices of Loki, the arch-trickster. They may have assumed such tales to be pure entertainment, or the simple legends of a credulous people, not to be taken seriously. Those however who have encountered the conception of the northern Ragnarok, when the gods go down fighting against the giants, and the world of living beings is engulfed by fire and covered by the advancing sea, may appreciate the strength and power of the Scandinavian myths and want to know more of the religious beliefs which inspired them. Are there, for instance, any links between the mythical world of Odin and Thor and that pictured in another rich collection of tales, the doings of the Túatha Dé Danann of Ireland, the figures of Lug and the Dagda and their dealings with kings and heroes? Is it possible, as Dumézil believed, to fit these Norse and Irish legends into a general pattern of Indo-European religious beliefs, extending back far into prehistory? The answers to such questions depends on how much evidence can be found for religious practices and the conception of a supernatural world existing as a background to the old tales.

I

The Celts, Germans and Vikings, names given to various peoples of north-western Europe by those who suffered from their attacks, seem each in turn to have been possessed by boundless energy and vigour, bringing them out of their homelands to cause trouble in many parts of Europe. There are links between the cultures of these peoples, and striking resemblances between the religious symbols which they used and their pictures of a supernatural world. Although there are enormous gaps in our knowledge, traces of their beliefs survive in their art and in later literature, while glimpses of their religious ritual have been revealed by archaeology and the descriptions left by foreign observers. The Scandinavian Vikings were not converted to Christianity until about AD 1000, and so it is from their records that most of our information about gods and sacred places and supernatural realms is derived; the last flowering of Germanic religion can be found in the Viking Age. When in the late ninth century men from western Norway and other areas of Scandinavia moved out to Iceland, an island empty of inhabitants except for a few Irish hermits, they built up a religious system there of much the same pattern as that of Germans and Celts centuries earlier. They appealed to Thor and Freyr, powerful deities of the sky and of fertility, to guide their little wooden ships to land and show them where their new homes should be built. They sought out holy places in the new country, rocks and hills to replace the ancestral burial mounds, a volcanic cleft to mark the place of their law assembly under the protection of the gods, and fields, waterfalls and strangely-shaped stones for new cult places. They made shrines to house the figures of their gods, uprooting carved pillars associated with them from buildings in Scandinavia to set up again in Iceland, and held regular feasts in honour of their deities. Records of the doings of the early settlers, as remembered and set down in the *Book of the Settlement* (*Landnámabók*) in the twelfth century, show us a religion closely linked to the land itself, and adapted to the life of the men and women who established themselves in the inhospitable northern island.

The landscape of much of Scandinavia and certainly of Iceland is majestic, bleak and powerful. Men were threatened by storms, treacherous seas, cold and long winter darkness, and it was a precarious business keeping animals alive through the long winter months and building up a secure livelihood. The myths which have come down to us in early Icelandic literature match this natural background in their vigour and power. They reflect an awareness that the little sheltered areas of habitation slowly built up by men were overshadowed by beings and forces far stronger than they. There is a spirit of resolution in the myths, a determinaton to fight on whatever the odds might be, to stand upright

2

to meet approaching fate, and if necessary to go down fighting. If we begin from the standpoint of these northern myths and legends, where the bright gods of Asgard are continually threatened by giants and monsters from a world of cold and darkness, we can perhaps work back to discover something of the religious pattern in the beliefs of Germans and Celts at an earlier period.

Clearly the emphasis must have varied according to the background against which warrior bands, hard-working farmers and adventurous seamen lived out their lives. A working religion develops out of men's needs and ways of life, and the natural world in which they find themselves determines the images which they use for supernatual powers and their picture of the Other World. A Celtic chief in a Scottish hill-fort would have a different world-view from one settled in Galatia in Asia Minor, and a Viking captain in the cold northern seas might not share the outlook of a Germanic leader confronting Roman legions in the mountains and forests of central Europe. But on the whole it seems probable that a man from Iceland or Sweden in the tenth century AD who was still worshipping the gods of his forefathers would not have felt in unfamiliar surroundings had he been transported into a religious ceremony of the Germanic or Celtic peoples some ten or more centuries earlier. Details of ritual and imagery and the names of gods and goddesses might vary according to locality and date, but the sense of the powers governing man and the natural world remain recognisably the same.

The origin and movements of the people whom we think of as the Celts remain elusive. Few of the ancient Celts are likely to have thought of themselves as such; it was the Greeks and Romans who called them Keltoi and Celtae, Galatai and Galli. The Greek form *Keltoi* goes back as early as 500 BC, and may have been a corruption of the name *Galatai*, the Galatians. *Galli* also may be a shortened form of this.[1] We know that these peoples were bands of nomadic warriors of various ethnic traditions causing considerable problems to the Roman Empire in the last centuries before Christ. The term *Celtic* came into modern use when interest in the early Welsh and Irish languages developed in the sixteenth and seventeenth centuries. It was discovered that there were two groups of 'Celtic' languages in the British isles, known as Q Celtic or Goidelic and P Celtic or Brythonic. Those spoken in Ireland, Scotland and the Isle of Man belong to the first group, in which the sound 'q' in Indo-European survived as 'k'. In Wales and Cornwall and Celtic areas on the Continent, however, the sound 'q' was replaced by 'p': Thus in Irish the word for head is *cenn* and in Welsh it is *penn*. The Q form of Celtic is the earlier, and Celts from Ireland evidently carried this into

3

Scotland and Man, while the change from *q* to *p* in Wales and Cornwall must have taken place after the Celts arrived there from the Continent in the fifth century BC. The date when the Celts first became a recognisable people with their own language is not known. About the sixth century BC there are references in written sources to roving warrior bands in the region round Czechoslovakia, Hungary, Austria, Switzerland and southern Germany. From here they expanded in various directions, so that for a time the Celtic language was spoken in Gaul, the Iberian peninsula, and as far as the Black Sea and Asia Minor, as well as in the British Isles. But these early people left no written literature behind them, and except in the British Isles and Brittany our knowledge of Celtic is limited to personal and tribal names, placenames, and occasional words quoted by ancient writers.

The word *Celtic* also came to be applied to a certain type of art. Sir Augustus Franks of the British Museum was the first to use it of the culture of the early Iron Age in western Europe. Outstanding discoveries at Hallstatt in Austria and La Tène in Switzerland led to the recognition of this culture,[2] which seems to have flourished from about the eighth century BC to the second century AD in Europe, and continued later than this in the British Isles. In 1846 the director of the salt mines at Hallstatt discovered an enormous cemetery beside Lake Hallstatt, where the mountains rise steeply from the shores. The earliest graves are thought to go back to about 700 BC, and traces were found of the people who had worked in the mines there, since fragments of their clothes, food, iron tools and simple possessions were preserved in the salt. A flourishing local industry had existed there, and the rich folk who prospered from it were buried in elaborate graves in the cemetery nearby. Both men and women were laid in wooden chamber graves, with wagons, riding gear, ornaments drinking vessels and food, as though they were intended to enjoy an existence of luxury and feasting in the Other World. In the same 'Hallstatt' period, impressive carved figures of stone were set up in Celtic territory, which might represent gods or ancestors. The craftsmen of this period were skilled in metal working, and used a decorative style which shows the influence of foreign art. Some objects appear to possess religious significance; there is for instance the so-called cult wagon of Strettweg, from a burial mound near Graz in Austria, which consists of a small wheeled platform on which a group of human figures and a stag are set. There is a large female figure in the centre who has the appearance of a goddess, while the stag could be a sacred and possibly a sacrificial animal.

The second major discovery of a Celtic site was made at La Tène, at the point where the Canal de la Thièle enters Lake Neuchâtel in north-east Switzerland, and this is believed to date from about 100 BC.[3] In 1858 the water levels were lowered and the remains of ancient timbers revealed. Around these were many objects, either thrown into the water as votive offerings or possibly overwhelmed in a flood (p. 63 below). What is now known as the La Tène period began about 500 BC with a change in funeral customs. Instead of the wagons of the Hallstatt period, two-wheeled chariots were provided for dead chieftains, who wore long swords in ornamented scabbards. In this period the art of the Celtic peoples developed into a new style of striking originality and power. It became freer and more fluid, with winding, sinuous patterns, although the discipline of the earlier geometric style was retained. Foliage patterns, spirals and tendrils were interwoven with popular motifs from Mediterranean art like crescentic and trumpet shapes. Human faces and heads were introduced into the designs, sometimes peering out of the patterns, sometimes distorted into monstrous shapes. Birds and animals might be realistically or fantastically treated, particularly bulls, boars and ducks. There were carved stone heads which suggest divinities, and recurring symbols on pillars and stones. This brilliant art declined in Italy and Gaul when heavier, naturalistic Roman styles came into fashion, but flowered anew in the British Isles, where some of the finest Celtic masterpieces were produced. Even after the coming of Christianity, the traditions of Celtic art continued to influence metalwork, carved stone crosses and illuminated manuscripts.

The Germans first came into prominence in Europe in the first century AD, although the term *Germani* was in use about a hundred years earlier and appears originally to have been a Celtic tribal name. Tacitus in *Germania* claimed that it was the name of one tribe which gradually came into general use, and it was generally held to be linked with the Latin *germanus* (brother). Because of the ambiguity of this term 'Germanic', many English scholars have preferred to use 'Teutonic' for this group of peoples. The adjective *Teutonicus* was a latinised form of OE *þeodisc* from *þeod* (people/nation), a term applied by the Goths to themselves and their language; the earlier form **teuta* may originally have had the meaning 'power' or 'strength'.[4] What the Romans knew as Germania was the area between the Rhine and the Danube, extending possibly as far as the Vistula, and including in the north Denmark and the southern parts of Norway and Sweden. As was the case with the Celts, people living in this wide and sparsely populated area were unlikely to have thought of themselves as Germans; it was the collective name used by the Romans for the barbarians beyond the Rhine. Julius Caesar came into contact with these tribes, and the Romans paid heavily for their attmepts to bring them under control. He wrote his brilliant account of his campaigns in Gaul in the mid first century, equating the Germans with the peoples living to the east of the Rhine, while the Celts were to the the west of it. This seems to have been an oversimplification of a complex situation, perhaps due to his ignorance of the languages spoken by many of the tribes, or to a desire to justify his military advances for political reasons. Certainly some of the tribes which he called German are now thought to have been Celtic-speaking peoples. It seems that there was no fundamental difference between the two except that of language, and as Powell pointed out,[5] the many resemblances between them in religious practices, social organisation and vocabulary may have been derived from a common ancestral source. But in spite of this, and the fact that they were in contact with each other for considerable periods, the difference in language must reflect a distinct separation between the two sets of peoples.[6]

It is not clear at what period the original Germanic language from which modern German, Anglo-Saxon and consequently English, Dutch, Frisian and the Scandinavian languages are derived came into general use; it was probably at some time in the course of the first five centuries BC, although some would say earlier. Nor do we know in what region it was first developed. It seems to have originated east of the Elbe and then spread westwards as tribes from that area conquered and settled land beyond the river. By the fifth century AD it was spoken over most of the Elbe basin. Further east Teutonic languages of the Gothic type were spoken, but most of this region was later overrun by Slav peoples. Considerable dialectical differences (High and Low German, Dutch, Old Saxon, etc.) developed by the eighth century AD, while the Scandinavian languages became a separate group. Typical 'Germanic' objects can be traced back into the period before Christ, and 'Germanic' culture seems to extend back into the early Iron Age. The term 'Germanic' came once more into general use in the nineteenth century as a comprehensive term for the whole group of peoples and languages, replacing 'Teutonic', or sometimes used as a sub-division of it.

What is known of the Germanic tribes is that they moved out of the area between the Rhine and the Vistula in various directions in the fifth and sixth centuries AD, just as earlier the Celts had spread out from their original homeland. Finally the Germanic peoples overran and destroyed the Roman Empire. The best known of these tribes are the Franks, who settled in Gaul; the Visigoths, who invaded Italy, captured Rome and later moved into Spain; the Ostrogoths, who settled in Italy; the Alamanni, in south Germany and Switzerland; the Langobards, who took over northern Italy; the Burgundians in eastern Gaul; and the Vandals who finally crossed to north Africa. In the fifth century a mixture of tribes generally known as Angles and Saxons came to England and settled in the south and east, driving much of the Celtic population westwards into Wales and Cornwall. Our knowledge of tribal groupings however is limited; the precise movements of many known tribes are far from clear, and there are a number who could be either Celts or Germans, since we do not know what language they spoke. There is no other simple way to distinguish them.

In spite of the threats which they posed, the Mediterranean peoples were fascinated by the Celts and tended to idealise them as noble barbarians, led by druids possessing the secrets of ancient wisdom. In the same way the Romans regarded the troublesome Germans with both fear and admiration. An invaluable account of their way of life, 'On the origin and geography of Germania', now generally known as the *Germania*, was written by the historian Tacitus in 98 AD. This was partly based on information from the twenty lost books of the Elder Pliny on the German campaigns, a most regrettable loss, since Pliny had served on the both the Upper and Lower Rhine and knew the Germans well. Although doubts have been cast on the reliability of Tacitus, evidence from archaeology has increasingly confirmed the picture which he gave of Germanic life and culture. Admittedly his work is slanted in order to show up the greed and corruption of Roman society in his time, since he contrasts it deliberately with the simple, healthy existence of the barbarian peoples. Yet it can be claimed with some justice that his book remains 'the best of its kind in antiquity, perhaps in any age'.[7]

Tacitus found much to admire in the courage, loyalty, toughness and simple family life of the Germanic warriors, and yet he was by no means blind to their shortcomings. He admitted their ignorance, their excessive love of drinking, and a fatal tendency to quarrel among themselves, and this picture is very similar to that which an earlier historian left of the Celts about a century before. Posidonius was a Stoic philosopher writing in Greek, and his history is now lost, but several later writers quoted from his material, so that much of it can be reconstructed.[8] He left an account of the Celts, stressing their passion for feasting and for elaborate ornaments, the vanity and boastfulness of their champions, and their extreme touchiness, continually leading to conflict. But he made it clear that these weaknesses were linked with more praiseworthy qualities, those of endurance, courage and considerable fighting skill. The Celts and Germans had clearly much in common in their way of life, and in both their strengths and their weaknesses.

The third set of barbarians from northern Europe who raided and robbed the richer and more settled lands to the south were Scandinavians, generally known as Vikings, of the same stock as the northern

Germans. They were called Northmen by contemporaries, but the term Viking (*vikingr* in Old Norse) used by monkish chroniclers came to denote pirates and raiding bands who attacked monasteries and had no respect for churches. The term probably comes from *vik* (bay/ fiord), and 'to go a-viking' meant to sail out from home to seek fame and wealth by fighting, trade or piracy or a mixture of the three. Consequently the period when the Scandinavians were most active outside their home-lands, from the mid eighth to the mid eleventh centuries, is generally known as the Viking Age. By the eighth century the men who inhabited Norway, Sweden and Denmark were building seagoing ships of un-rivalled excellence, and forging fine, reliable weapons. In their vigour and ruthlessness they were in no way inferior to the Germans and Celts who preceded them. In the Viking Age, Scandinavian pirates, adven-turers, traders and warrior bands, fighting either independently or as mercenaries, penetrated from one end of Europe to the other. They attacked and terrorised the very peoples who had behaved in the same way centuries earlier, such as the Anglo-Saxons, the Franks, and the Celtic inhabitants of Scotland, Wales and Ireland. The Vikings found a few areas in which to settle permanently, such as Iceland, Orkney, Shetland and the Faroes, as well as parts of northern and eastern England and Normandy, but over most of Europe their dominion proved no lasting one.

These Scandinavians were superb seamen and good fighters, loyal to their chosen leaders and ready to die in their defence. At the same time they are described as touchy and quarrelsome, overfond of drinking, and too independent in spirit to build up large, well-disciplined armies. They operated mainly in small bands, continually forming loose al-liances which soon broke up again. They were able to endure appalling conditions of cold and hardship, and were shrewd and knowledgeable traders, ready to go far into inhospitable regions if there seemed a chance of gaining silver and winning valuable booty. There were gifted poets and story-tellers among them, and they had a gift for communicating with those of other languages and cultures. They much enjoyed legal arguments and the complexities of word-games and genealogies. What we know of their character and mode of life is similar to that of the Celts and Germans before them, and indeed they were of the same stock as the Germanic tribes of northern Europe. But while the continental Ger-mans and Anglo-Saxons were converted to Christianity fairly early, the Vikings continued to hold on to their old religion for some centuries after the Christian church was well established in neighbouring kingdoms.

Like their Celtic predecessors, the Germans and Scandinavians

8

produced smiths and craftsmen of distinction, and were excellent workers in wood and metal. Much surviving material comes from pre-Christian graves, for at certain periods splendid possessions were left in graves of both men and women of the ruling class. Rich burials from what is known as the Migration Period, from about the third to the sixth century AD when the Germans were on the borders of the Roman Empire and settling in new territories, have been excavated. It was a prosperous period in Sweden, where elaborate cremation ceremonies were held for the kings of Uppsala, and other leaders were buried with fine weapons, shields and helmets. Extensive cemeteries of the continental Germans have been discovered, some holding hundreds of cremation urns and others made up of inhumation graves, and burial mounds of kings and local leaders have yielded up splendid treasures and given indication of impressive funeral ritual. From the seventh century onwards there were rich ship burials in East Anglia, Norway and Sweden, and the possibilities of an undisturbed ship-grave of a rich leader became apparent when one of the mounds at Sutton Hoo in Suffolk was opened in 1939. This is now known to have formed part of a cemetery of considerable size, and more discoveries are expected there. Another outstanding grave was that of King Childeric of the Franks, but the treasures taken from it were unfortunately stolen from a museum in Paris after their discovery in the late seventeenth century.

Wood seldom survives in the earth except in unusual soil conditions, as in the Alamannic cemetery of Oberflacht in West Germany, and the ship-grave at Oseberg in south Norway. In both these cases the rich variety, skilled craftmanship and elaborate symbolism of the carving on the wooden objects found indicate how much may have been lost in other rich burials. Elaborate ritual objects were sometimes abandoned along with vessels, ornaments and weapons in the northern peat bogs or lakes, as happened in the case of the Gundestrup cauldron in the Iron Age, and the pair of gold drinking horns from Gallehus in Denmark. The decoration on such objects may tell us something of the mythology of the people who used them. So too may amulets once worn for luck and protection, such as the golden bracteates popular in the Migration Period, while carved stones raised in memory of the dead may give some indication of beliefs. A fine series of picture stones on the island of Gotland set up in the Viking Age and earlier are covered with scenes and symbols. Some figures apparently representing the gods have survived in Northern Europe, roughly carved in wood or in the form of small metal amulets. In spite of a delight in abstract art and complex patterns, the Scandinavians occasionally produced vigorous narrative scenes carved in wood or stone. There is reason to think that this form of art

9

found wide expression not only in wood-carving but also in weaving and tapestry; a roll of embroidered wall-hangings found in the Oseberg ship revealed after years of patient restoration supernatural figures and processions of what appear to be gods and heroes.

The influence of other art styles and religious symbolism from Christian art can be seen in the work of the Celtic and Germanic peoples. Celtic sculptors in Gaul and Britain produced native figures of their local deities in imitation of the Roman manner, often with titles and inscriptions in Latin which are a source of information about the types of god they worshipped. At the close of the Viking Age, myths and symbols from the pre-Christian past were employed to decorate monuments raised over the Christian dead, so that Thor and Odin and the ancient World-Serpent are found in association with the cross of Christ. New evidence of this kind is still being discovered in northern England, where Scandinavians settled in the tenth century and were soon absorbed into the Christian church, in the form of carved stones set up to commemorate the newly converted.

Neither Celts, Germans nor Scandinavians appear to have built elaborate temples and sanctuaries, except in Celtic areas where classical fashions were adopted, such as in the south of France, or in Romanised towns like Colchester and Bath. Such religious art as we possess is mainly restricted to graves and monuments, figures representing supernatural beings, religious or lucky symbols on ornaments, weapons and objects of daily use. There are runic inscriptions from Germanic or Scandinavian territory which belong to the pre-Christian period, but these are not easy to interpret. In discussing the religion of these early peoples of north-western Europe, it has been customary to turn to legends of gods and heroes in the early literature of Ireland and Iceland to fill the gaps in our knowledge. These were written down in Christian times, although a few surviving poems in Old Icelandic on mythological subjects were composed before the conversion to Christianity. Most of the written sources, however, were put together or edited by Christian monks and scholars at various times, in some cases long after the old faith had been abandoned by the people. In Iceland, from which most Old Norse literature is derived, our earliest sources are poems, some attributed to the 'skaldic' poets attached to the courts of Norwegian kings in the period before the establishment of Christianity. The mythological poems of the *Poetic Edda* come from a thirteenth-century manuscript book, the *Codex Regius*, although some may be considerably earlier than this. Prose records of early Iceland, such as Ari the Learned's 'Book of the Icelanders' (Íslendingabók) and the elaborate 'Book of the Settlements' (Landnámabók), giving information about the first families settled in Iceland, do not go back beyond the twelfth century, although they may record older traditions. As for the rich body of prose sagas, most of these belong to the thirteenth or fourteenth century. There is little early material from the other Scandinavian countries, apart from a few Latin works and the late twelfth-century history of Denmark in Latin by Saxo Grammaticus. The invaluable account of Norse mythology derived from early poetry and oral tradition by the gifted Icelander Snorri Sturluson is roughly contemporary with the work of Saxo. In Ireland the Christian church was established much earlier, by the fifth century, although from about the seventh century onwards Irish monks were absorbing and recording pre-Christian traditions in the tales making up the great manuscript collections of various dates, and the poems included in the tales. However, this wonderful material has been mixed with later speculation, Christian learning and antiquarianism, and many supernatural beings transformed into human heroes and heroines.

This is why the art of the pre-Christian period, shaped and handled by those who accepted the old beliefs, is in some ways a more direct link with the religious past than the recorded literature. But indeed we have to seek out whatever clues are available, and not limit ourselves to any one type of source material. It is no easy task to build up a convincing picture of beliefs and practices from scattered hints, echoes and chance survivals. Only by critical evaluation of evidence from a wide field and by bringing different types of material together is it possible to find a perceptible pattern in the religion of these early peoples.

Much of their religion was concerned with battle ritual, which is hardly surprising, since Celts, Germans and Vikings were all warrior peoples in a period of expansion. It was also closely associated with the natural world, of which they were very much aware. They did not regard this as something inanimate or wholly separate from themselves; as Henri Frankfort pointed out: 'For modern scientific man the phenomenal world is primarily an It; for ancient – and also for primitive – man it is a Thou'.[9] They revered their dead ancestors beneath the earth, and particularly their kings and founders of families. They practised various means of divination, observing movements of birds and animals, fire and water. They relied on supernatural powers ruling sky, earth and sea to bring them strength and luck and to protect them from hostile forces, which they pictured as giants, monsters or destructive goddesses. Certain symbols had particular meaning, remaining potent through the centuries. The heads of warriors possessed special power, as did the remains of the noble dead within their mounds. The sacred drink of the gods giving immortality and inspiration was a favourite motif, and

11

the axe-hammer of the sky-god, warding off cold and chaos, another effective symabol. Vigorous male animals such as horse, stag, bull and bear, together with ruthless birds of prey like the eagle and raven were seen as special manifestations of supernatural power. The centre of their universe was pictured as a great tree or pillar, and they laid emphasis on the creation of the worlds surrounding this and foresaw their ultimate destruction.

Such symbols and motifs were absorbed into religious ritual. Feasts in honour of the gods marked out the course of the year and were held to promote success in war and good harvests. Men and animals were offered as sacrifices, and objects thrown into water or hung on trees as gifts for supernatural powers. Such practices established a mysterious yet familiar background of contact with the Other World. All this inspired their art and left an imprint on their legends. Long after the Christian church had been firmly established, story-tellers and artists turned back to the old ways of thought for inspiration and imagery.

We shall be concerned with the exploration of this rich world of tradition and belief, tracing the main outline of man's relationship with the natural world and with supernatural powers. It extends back into a time long before the northern myths were recorded in writing in the Middle Ages. An underlying pattern can be made out in spite of local variations and changes due to altering modes of life and the fragmentary nature of the evidence. The basic religious traditions of our ancestors in north-western Europe were accepted over a long period of time, and we should surely approach their world picture with respect as well as curiosity and make some attempt to understand it. It may be that by following the working of men's minds in the past we may learn more of our complex reactions to our own world, while gaining insight into the realms of imagination, imagery and spiritual perception once open to the barbarian peoples who inhabited north-western Europe.

I   Holy places

Jacob woke from his sleep and said 'Truly the LORD is in this place, and I did not know it . . . How fearsome is this place! This is no other than the house of God, this is the gate of heaven.'

Genesis 28, 16–17 (*NEB*)

Every religion must have its holy places, affording a means of communication between man and the Other World. Sometimes as in ancient Egypt and Jerusalem this was essentially the great temple, where kings and priests could conduct ceremonies, make offerings, learn the will of the god, or enquire into hidden things, with or without a congregation. Among the Celts and Germans there seem originally to have been few permanent and elaborate temples used as meeting places for worship and sacrifice. In spite of the rigours of the climate, the place where men sought contact with the supernatural powers was for the most part in the open air. The resorting to holy places was something which could be witnessed by outside observers, often arousing interest and curiosity. Thus in the works of Greek and Latin writers we hear repeatedly of sacred woods and groves, sanctuaries in forest clearings and on hilltops, beside springs and lakes and on islands, and of places set apart for the burial of the noble dead.

1 Sacred landmarks

When the Scandinavians came to settle in Iceland in the late ninth century, certain natural sites were chosen by them as areas of sacred space. It may be noted that these were not marked by permanent buildings, or even enclosed by walls or obvious boundaries. An impressive example of the simplest type of holy place is Helgafell, on the peninsula of Snæfellness in western Iceland (Plate 1a). This is described in one of the Icelandic sagas as a place of great sanctity, venerated by one of the early settlers from Norway, Thorolf of Mostur. It remains today as a landmark, visible from many miles away, as at the time of the Settlement. Helgafell is a small natural outcrop of rock, resembling in

13

shape a long burial mound, with the little church close beside it. From its top there is a superb view over islands, mountains, glaciers and the winding coastline, and on a clear day it is as if one stood upon a stage or sat in the famous seat of the god Odin overlooking the whole rich world of land and water. The saga in which Helgafell is mentioned is *Eyrbyggja Saga* (4), one of the finest of the family sagas, the story of the outstanding men who lived on Snæfellness in the early period of the Settlement. It was composed in the mid thirteenth century, and may have been written at the Augustinian house at Helgafell, which moved there from Flatey in 1134.[1] From early Christian times Helgafell was one of the intellectual centres of western Iceland; it was here that the famous historian, Ari Thorgilsson the Learned, was born in 1067/8, and there was a considerable library there in the early twelfth century before the arrival of the monks.

In view of this, there seems little reason to doubt the local tradition preserved in the saga of the importance of Helgafell as a holy place which had to be kept free from pollution, and on which men and beasts were safe from injury, because no violence could be committed on the hill. It was said that no man should look on it unwashed; this would be impossible to avoid when the hill was visible over so wide an area, but MacCulloch is no doubt right in interpreting the verb used, *líta*, as meaning to turn towards it in prayer and supplication.[2] It was said also that Thorolf believed that he and his family would pass into Helgafell when they died, so that the rocky hill was seen as a possible entrance into the Other World, and also as a dwelling for the dead. From one side the hill resembles a house with a door, strengthening the parallel with a burial mound where the dead is brought to join his ancestors (p. 115 below).

Of a different nature is the meeting place of the Althing, the Law Assembly for the men of Iceland, deliberately selected in the tenth century by Ulfljot's brother Grim, after Ulfljot returned from Norway with a code of laws for Iceland.[3] According to Ari the Learned, he chose this site after exploring all Iceland, and once more it is not difficult to see why he felt that this particular place was suitable. It is formed by a natural volcanic rift in a large sunken valley, where the swift-flowing river (*Öxará*) runs into a large lake. A line of sinister twisted rocks provides an impressive background and natural sounding board, which would have been effective when a section of the laws was recited every year at the 'Law Rock' by the Speaker or Lawman who presided over the Assembly. In front stretches an open plain, providing ample room for representatives from all over Iceland to set up their 'booths', small shelters of turf and stone tented over, when they came at Midsummer to attend the Althing. Two weeks were spent there each year by the landowners who made up the assembly, together with friends, kinsmen, followers, traders and hangers-on who accompanied them. The site was reasonably accessible, within easy reach of the popular inhabited areas in the south and west and with possible routes to the more distant parts of the island, the furthest of which could be reached within two weeks' journey on ponies. There were suitable sites where the various courts could meet, and wood was available for fires together with pasturage for horses. It was said that the Icelanders even went to the trouble of diverting the Axe River into a new channel in order to provide a good water supply.[4] There is no reference to temples of any kind at Thingvellir, and no archaeological evidence for such buildings has been found. The Althing continued to be held here throughout the period of the Commonwealth and after Iceland came under the rule of Norway in 1271 and of Denmark in 1380. In 1798, when its importance and power had declined, it was finally moved to Reykjavik.

When the meeting at Thingvellir was the most important event of the year for the Icelandic state, the Lögrétta, the adminstrative and judicial

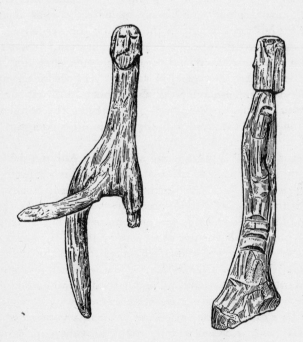

1 Phallic figure from Broddenbjerg, Jutland, and female figure from Ræbild, Himmerland, both in wood and about 63 cm in height.

assembly, would assemble in the space in front of the Law Rock, the point where part of the Law was regularly recited. Buildngs were set up there in later times, but in the Viking Age the various courts seem to have had no permanent location. The purpose of the Althing was the recital of the laws, the making of changes in the law system, the hearing of cases and judging of disputes brought from the four quarters of Iceland, each of which had its own small Thing place. It was at Thingvellir that the decision was taken to accept Christianity as the religion of Iceland in the year 1000. Everything concerned with the law was under the rule of the gods, making the place of assembly a hallowed one. The Althing opened on Thursday, the day sacred to Thor, the sky god. Sacrificial feasts were held there, and in the early days there was a ban on the carrying of arms when the Thing was in progress, even if this was not always enforced.

Thingvellir still remains a place of pilgrimage for Icelanders, and visitors are always taken there. It is no sheltered site, but lies open to strong winds and blizzards and even sandstorms at all times in the year. The sense of wide distances and far views of lakes and mountains give it something of the same numinous quality as is possessed by Helgafell. These two sacred places of the Viking Age have no need of monuments or permanent buildings to render them memorable. Undoubtedly holy sites of this kind have been used by men from very early times, and many well-known Celtic and Germanic ones had been in existence as burial or cult places in the Bronze Age or earlier still. Bronze Age burials were found on the Hill of Tara in Ireland, and beneath the artificial hill raised by Norse settlers as a place of assembly on the Isle of Man. There are similar examples in Gaul, such as a cult place at the spring of Grisy, important in Roman times and apparently in use since the neolithic period.[5] In Iceland however there were no previous settlers whose graves might mark sites as holy ones, and we have the rare opportunity of learning something of the process of hallowing a place in a new territory, with the whole of the island from which to choose.

2 Images of the gods

Tacitus wrote of the Germanic peoples in the first century AD in *Germania* (9): 'The Germans do not think it in keeping with the divine majesty to confine gods within walls or portray them in the likeness of any human countenance. Their holy places are woods and groves, and they apply the names of deities to that hidden presence which is seen only by the eye of reverence' (Mattingly's translation). According to this, images of the gods were not common among the Germans, the inference being that in this they differed from the superstitious Romans

16

1 *Symbols of the sacred.* *Top* Holy hill of Helgafell in Iceland; *left* Turoe Stone,
Co. Galloway, Ireland, symbol of the centre, Third to first century BC; *right*
Sanda Stone, Gotland, showing whirling disc, central tree and ship of the
dead, fifth century AD.

2 *Animal symbols.* *Top* Small cult wagon from Mérida, Spain, depicting a boar
hunt, second to first century BC; *left* Panel from memorial stone, Alskog,
Gotland, showing eight-legged horse of Odin and welcoming valkyrie, eighth
century AD; *right* Shield from River Witham, showing outline of boar from
lost mount, second to third century BC.

with a multiplicity of temples and statues of countless deities. Tacitus had in mind the sacred groves mentioned by other writers, and these, like Helgafell, were apparently free of buildings and images. In any case he would probably have discounted rough wooden figures such as are mentioned by the poet Lucan in his description of a Celtic sanctuary near Massalia in southern France, in *Pharsalia* (III). This was destroyed by Julius Caesar in the first century BC, and Lucan mentions 'dark springs' and 'grim-faced figures of gods, uncouthly hewn by the axe from the untrimmed tree-trunk, rotted to whiteness'. Wooden figures which would answer well enough to Lucan's description have survived from northern Europe and the British Isles. One from Broddenbjerg in north Jutland is roughly shaped from a forked piece of oak, with little carving except to provide it with a mask-like face and to turn a projecting branch into an enormous phallus. This figure was mounted on a heap of stones and found in association with pots of the early Iron Age, in a place not far away from finds dated to the Bronze Age, which suggested that it was used as a cult site over a long period.[6] A more realistic figure comes from a peat bog at Rude Eskilstrup in Sjælland (Plate 4b). This is about 41 cm high and carved with some skill. It depicts a seated male figure with an arresting bearded face and large eyes, wearing a cloak and a threefold neck-ring in the style of the post-Roman period, who holds some unidentified square object in his lap. Such a figure could represent either a Celtic or a Germanic deity, and it has been suggested that the seated figure in the cloak is Wodan, but there is no clear indication of this.[7]

Without related finds it is impossible to date such figures from their style, and they may have been set up in remote places as late as the Viking Age. Particularly impressive are two roughly carved in wood, slightly taller than human, found in a peat bog at Braak, Schleswig.[8] They represent a man and woman with sockets for arms, although the arms are lost, and pebbles were probably used for their eyes. They could be either deities or ancestors, but recent pollen analysis suggests a much later date in the Viking Age, and they might have been erected by Slavs living in this area. Close to these wooden figures was a hearth with carved stones and fragments of pottery, indicating that this was a cult place, one perhaps used by different peoples in turn over the centuries. A considerable number of carved wooden figures, skilfully worked, come from Celtic territory,[9] although these must represent only a small portion of those which once existed. Some, like a series of human figures found at the source of the River Seine, were apparently left as votive offerings by pilgrims who came there for healing. Others, like what seems to be the figure of a woman from Ralaghan, Country Cavan, in

17

Ireland, made from bog oak, may originally have stood in cult places or small shrines (Fig. 1).[10]

There is a detailed account from the tenth century of ceremonies connected with such wooden figures. An Arab diplomat and scholar, Ibn Fadlan, who had a lively interest in strange peoples and their religious customs, was sent on a mission from Baghdad to Bulgar on the Middle Volga in 921. His task was to instruct the king of the Bulgars in the Islamic religion, and while he was in the town he became interested in the Rus, Swedish merchants who had come to the Bulgar capital to trade and who lived in the merchants' quarters on the other side of the river. He was curious to know about their practices, and described a group of crude wooden figures they had set up;[11] these consisted of ' . . . a long upright piece of wood that has a face like a man's and is surrounded by little figures behind which are long stakes in the ground'. A Rus trader who arrived at the station would make offerings of bread, meat, leeks, silk and beer to the main figure, praying that his Lord would send rich merchants in his way who would pay a good price for the wares which he had brought. If his prayer was granted, he would kill sheep and cattle as an offering, leaving some of the flesh beside the wooden figures and setting up the heads of the slaughtered beasts on the wooden stakes. If things did not go as he wished, he would then turn to the smaller figures and ask their help; Ibn Fadlan was told that these were the sons and daughters of the god. Possibly they were lesser deities recognised by the Rus, who were Scandinavians, probably from Sweden, coming to trade in eastern Europe.

Since most images were of wood, few have survived in the earth. There are a few impressive ones in stone from the early Celtic period, carved with restraint and power. One of these stood in a burial ground containing several graves at Hirschlanden near Stuttgart, and probably goes back to the late sixth century BC,[12] It represents a naked warrior with a neck-ring, belt and dagger, wearing a pointed hat on his head; this is an agreement with statements by classical writers that the Celts were accustomed to fight naked (p. 89 below). The figure is almost life size, standing 1.5 m high, and might represent either the hero buried in the tumulus or some supernatural guardian. Certainly this erect, menacing form must have evoked a feeling of awe and memories of the famous dead. A second and larger figure comes from Holzgerlingen in the same area,[13] and could be of about the same date, although the style is different (Plate 4a). This stands 2.3 m high, and has two faces like the Roman Janus; it depicts the upper half of a human figure rising from a square pillar, perhaps a stone version of wooden figures carved in this way. The strange curving crown above the face possibly represents

18

horns, and this seems more likely to be a cult image than a memorial to the dead man in the grave; the stern remote features would be fitting for the image of a god.

3 Mounds and standing stones

There were more abstract monuments set up at times in sacred places. The great burial mounds of kings were themselves important symbols and a possible means of communication with the Other World. Those of Old Uppsala in Sweden consist of three huge mounds, with a large number of lesser ones clustered round them, and these were raised over cremation burials of the Migration Period preceding the Viking Age. Some Swedish mounds had flattened tops with a slight slope, suggesting a stage on which action would be visible to those standing below. According to Norse literary tradition, the burial mound was a place on which kings and seers might sit in order to obtain wisdom and inspiration (p. 130 below). The mound also served as a centre from which the king could make announcements to the people, from which new laws could be proclaimed, and on which a new ruler could be installed. An example of this is Tynwald Hill on the Isle of Man, where the Manx Parliament still assembles at Midsummer. It is a stepped mound, with a place on top for the reigning monarch, usually represented by the Lieutenant-General, accompanied by Bishops and Deemsters, while the three lower tiers are for members of the House of Keys, representatives of local authorities, ministers of the churches, and so forth. The mound was raised by Norse settlers who arrived in the ninth century, and it is an artificial hill set up on the site of an earlier burial mound of the Bronze Age.

In Irish tradition also mounds form part of the assembly place, and in the tales there are instances of visions or strange adventures befalling those who sit on mounds near the courts of kings. There was a close link between man and the supernatural world by way of the burial mound, since it was into such mounds that the gods of pre-Christian Ireland, the Túatha Dé Danann, were said to retreat after the coming of Christianity. The dwelling of the Dagda was at New Grange, a great prehistoric burial mound near the river Boyne (p. 127 below). At the festival of Samain on 1 November, the beginning of winter, it was believed that the way to the Other World lay open, and there are many tales of living men entering the mounds or of visits by the dead to the living on that night.

The stone figure of Hirschlanden stood upon a burial mound, and in Scandinavia carved stones were sometimes placed on them. Flat, rounded stones, difficult to date with any accuracy, survive in Sweden, and one of these, from Inglinge Howe near Växjo, is elaborately decorated. This formerly stood on a tumulus, and was known as 'The King of Värend's Throne'.[14] It is not known whether such stones were intended for seats or whether they were rolled down the mound on some ritual occasion, as wheels were rolled down hills at midsummer.

Another type of decorated stone associated with holy places is the domed or pyramid-shaped stone, of which an outstanding example is that outside Turoe House, County Meath, in Ireland (Plate 1b). This was brought from its original position on the north side of a circular 'rath' or earthwork dating back to the first century BC, and may have been set up as early as this. It is decorated with asymmetrical curving patterns in the La Tène style, and other examples, less well-preserved, have been found in Ireland. It has been claimed that these show a complex division into four parts, comparable to the patterns on an earlier stone from Kermaria, Finistère, of roughly pyramid shape.[15] The Turoe stone bears a striking resemblance to the Omphalos at the shrine of Apollo at Delphi, and these northern stones may have served a similar purpose, symbolising the navel or centre of the earth. At Uisnech, a sacred place roughly in the centre of Ireland, where the druids were said to meet, there was the stone known as the 'Stone of Division', which according to Geraldus Cambrensis was 'the navel of Ireland, as it were, placed right in the middle of the land'.[16] Uisnech as well as Tara could be regarded as a traditional centre, and the two are described in one Middle Irish source as being like two kidneys in one animal.[17]

Yet another famous stone was Fál, called the Lia Fáil or 'Stone of Knowledge', which was on the Hill of Tara. This is called a 'stone penis', and is usually assumed to be the pillar with the rounded top which is still on the hill, although Keating thought that the original stone ahd been taken to Scotland.[18] The tradition preserved in twelfth century literature was that this was a stone of inauguration, which roared under the feet of the man destined to be king, or, in an earlier acccount,[19] gave a screech when the king drove past it in his chariot, while two flagstones opened to allow the king to pass between them: 'And there were two flag-stones in Tara: 'Blocc' and 'Bluigne'; when they accepted a man they would open before him until the chariot went through. And Fál was there, the 'stone penis' at the head of the chariot course; when a man should have the kingship of Tara, it screeched against his chariot-axle so that all might hear'.[19] While there appears to be some confusion in the traditions between the standing stone and a flagstone on which the new king stood, it is clear that ancient stones formed an important part of the holy place and that they were associated with the choice and recognition of a king. The stone from Scone taken by Edward I from Scotland to Westminster Abbey is another example, and there are others from various tribal centres.[20] Similar stones existed also in Scandinavia. A Danish chronicle refers to the Danærigh near Viborg, used by the men of Jutland when they proclaimed a new king, while Olaus Magnus mentions the Morasten near Uppsala, said to be a 'huge and rounded stone' on which the Swedes raised their chosen ruler.[21]

The association of the holy place with the choosing of a king is in accordance with the importance of Thingvellir in Iceland as the site of the main assembly where the law was proclaimed, although there was no king to be inaugurated there. Men from the four quarters met at Thingvellir, and there was a plan of the places they were entitled to occupy in front of the Law Rock. Thingvellir was not the geographical centre of the island, for a true centre would be in the lava desert, but it was the symbolic one, with roads leading to it from every direction. Like Thingvellir, Tara in Ireland is superbly situated, with wide views on every side over the central plains: 'It is this feature of the Hill of Tara', O'Riordain wrote in his description of the site, 'which never fails to impress'. One medieval poem described Tara as the central square of a gaming board: 'Tara's castle, delightful hill, out in the exact centre of the plain'.[22] However it is far from being the true centre of Ireland, and once more what we have is a symbolic centre, surrounded by the four kingdoms of Ulster, Connacht, Leinster and Munster. Plans for the seating of the hall at Tara are given in two manuscripts, the twelfth century Book of Leinster and the fifteenth century Yellow Book of Lecan; late though these are, they preserve memories of a careful plan, and it seems possible that the whole country was reproduced in the layout of a central hall with four provincial halls ranged around.[23] The pattern of four divisions round a central point is found in both Iceland and Ireland, and Müller claims that this is a fundamental pattern in both Germanic and Celtic tradition.[24] Another centre was the place where the Druids met in Gaul, described as 'the centre of all Gaul' by Julius Caesar, but in fact somewhere near Chartres (p. 26 below). Here, as at Thingvellir, disputes from the regions round were said to have been brought for settlement.

4 The pillar and the tree

A pillar was an important feature of some of the holy places of the Germanic peoples. The Saxons had a high wooden pillar called Irminsul at Eresburg, thought to have been Marsberg on the Diemel, although other suggestions have been made, and this was cut down by Charlemagne in 772.[25] The historian Widukind associated such pillars with Mars and stated that their position was chosen to represent the sun. Irmin is thought to be the name or title of a god who could be identified with Tîwaz, as an early Germanic deity associated with the sky. Another medieval writer, Rudolf of Fulda, described Irminsul as *universalis columna quasi sustinens omnia*, a universal pillar supporting the whole. There is some indication of pillars raised by the Anglo-Saxons in pre-Christian times. At Yeavering in Northumbria a wooden building which may have been a pre-Christian temple was set up close to what had been a holy place of the Celtic people of Bernicia.[26] It was clearly a site of ancient sanctity, since a Bronze Age tumulus had stood there earlier, as well as a stone circle of early date. A tall wooden post was set up on the mound, and near the temple building there were indications that a huge shaft had been sunk into the ground. While it cannot be assumed that all wooden pillars and isolated shafts were erected for the same purpose, they appear to have been frequent features of holy places (p. 27 below).

There may be a link with so-called Jupiter Pillars or Columns form Gaul, erected in the Roman period, which are found especially around the Moselle and the Middle Rhine and in the Vosges.[27] One of these, at Cussy, still stands in its original position near the source of the river Arroux, and the figure of Jupiter on this faces the rising sun. The pillars are carved in the classical style, and sometimes have figures on the base representing the four seasons and the days of the week, apparently asociated with the sun's journey thoughout the year. They are also connected with water; Jupiter, sometimes standing and sometimes on horseback, is often shown dominating a water-monster, and the pillars seem usually to have been near a spring or river. In spite of their sophisticated style of decoration, they appear to have been erected in continuation of the Celtic tradition of raising monuments in a sacred spot, beside a burial place or a spring, associated with the sun, water, and healing. The Jupiter pillars were in honour of the god of the sky, evidently set up to invoke his blessing and protection for the local community, and the representation of him as a rider must be Celtic in origin. The columns which survive are sometimes in sites which appear to have been small native hamlets, although it must have needed someone of wealth and cosmolitan tastes to erect such great monuments carved in elaborate classical style. We know that a few were erected in towns at public expense, but others were in remote districts where there must already have been sacred places.

A particularly interesting example is that of the restored pillar from Hausen-an-der-Zaber, now erected in the museum at Stuttgart. This was set up by Caius Vettrius Connougus about 200 AD in fulfilment of a vow, presumably on his estate. The shaft of the pillar is covered with oak leaves and acorns, and there are four female heads representing the seasons on top, while it is surmounted by the figure of Jupiter as a rider overcoming a giant. This emphasises the link between the sky god and the oak, and his influence over the course of the year; Maximus of Tyre in the second century AD (*Logoi* 8, 8) stated that the Celtic image of Zeus was a high oak tree. A second, even larger pillar, unfortunately incomplete, shows the battle between gods and giants, with Jupiter, Mars, Vulcan and Hercules taking part. This is of some interest in view of the traditional battle between the gods and a giant race in both Celtic and Germanic sources of a later date (p. 192 below).

The description of Irminsul as *universalis columna* is paralleled by the image of the World Tree, Yggdrasil, one of most powerful symbols in Norse mythology, said to stand at the centre of the worlds of gods and men (p. 170 below). Among Scandinavians of the Viking Age a tree appears to be the main symbol of the central pivot of the universe, but the so-called 'high-seat pillars' of wood which formed the main support in the centre of halls and sanctuaries might be viewed as a northern version of the Germanic pillars raised in holy places. In the literary sources such pillars are associated with the god Thor, and were said to have been taken by early settlers to Iceland from their homes in Norway, so that they could be set up in the new environment. There are also legendary tales of royal halls with a living tree in the centre of the building, and trees may have been sometimes used in this way, as in the Old Manor House at Knaresborough in North Yorkshire and the hall of Huntingfield in Suffolk.[28] In the late saga of the hero Sigurd the Volsung, a tree is said to have formed the central support of the royal

2 Upper part of Jupiter pillar from Hausen-an-der-Zaber, now erected at Stuttgart Museum.

23

hall of his grandfather, King Volsung. It was from its trunk that Sigurd's father Sigmund pulled out the sword which Odin had driven into it and which no one else could remove; this was kept as a family treasure and after it had been shattered in the battle in which Sigmund fell, it was reforged and used by his son Sigurd to slay a dragon.[29] A parallel may be found in the tale of young Arthur drawing out the sword Excalibur from a stone in the churchyard and so proving himself the lawful king.

According to the picture of the ash Yggdrasil in the poems of the *Edda*, its great trunk marked the centre of the cosmos and its branches stretched over all lands. Beneath it was the assembly place of the gods, and the nine worlds of gods and men and other beings were ranged around it, as the kingdoms of Ireland were ranged around Tara and the four quarters of Iceland around Thingvellir. In Iceland there were no large trees, so that the concept could hardly have originated there, but in the great oak-forests of Germany, Scandinavia and Anglo-Saxon England the symbol of a mighty tree marking the centre and forming a link between man and the gods was a natural one to use. A sacred grove was often a feature of the holy place, as at Uppsala in Sweden. Adam of Bremen (IV, 28) in the eleventh century describes sacrifices there and claims that bodies of men and animals offered to the gods could be seen hanging from trees. A thousand years earlier Tacitus in *Germania* (39) describes the sacred grove of the people of the Semnones, 'hallowed by the auguries of their ancestors and by immemorial awe', where the offering of a human victim marked the beginning of the assembly of the tribes from this area. They believed the grove to be the 'cradle of the race and the dwelling-place of the supreme god', so that it evidently represented for them the place of creation. Here the god worshipped seems to have been Tîwaz, the sky god, but the goddesses might also be worshipped in such sacred groves. Traces of a wood survive near the sanctuary of the goddess Nehalennia at Domburg in Holland,[30] and Tacitus knew of a grove on an island in Denmark sacred to the goddess Nerthus (*Germania* 40).

Many Celtic names for sanctuaries incorporate *nemeton*, which meant a clearing open to the sky;[31] examples are *Drunemeton* in Asia Minor, the oak grove where the Galatians met, according to Strabo, and *Aquae Arnemetiae*, now Buxton in Derbyshire, with its thermal springs. It was in a sacred grove on the island of Anglesey that the druids defied the Romans, according to Tacitus (*Annals* XIV, 30), and had their sacred trees destroyed. Anglo-Saxon placenames based on the name *Thunor*, the sky god, incorporate in some cases the word for a wood or a clearing, *leah*, as in Thunderley and Thundersley in Essex.[32] There were sacred

24

trees in continental sanctuaries, since we hear of Christian missionaries
cutting them down, while in the Viking Age the Irish king Brian Boru is
said to have spent a month wreaking destruction on the sacred wood of
Thor near Dublin.[33] Memories of sacred trees at holy places can also be
found in Irish literature, and the ancient tree known as the *bile* was
apparently a usual feature of the site where the inauguration of the king
took place, the sacred centre[34] (p. 179 below).

As the centre of the cosmos, the sacred place was linked with creation
legends; it was also a spot where communicaton with the powers of the
Other World might take place. In the *Annals* of Tacitus (XIII, 8) there
is a reference to two tribes battling for possession of a sacred place beside
a river, which they believed was especially close to heaven, 'so that men's
prayers received ready access'. This was a place where salt could be
obtained, and therefore presumably of economic value, and indeed this
may have led to its reputation as a sacred area because of this
inexplicable gift from the gods who could grant wealth and prosperity.
The two opposing tribes who lived on either side of the river were
prepared to offer huge and extravagant sacrifices if they could gain
possession of it (p. 62 below). It was appropriate that the sacred centre
should be the place where kings were chosen and proclaimed, and where
the law was recited. It was a ritual and symbolic centre, not to be taken
in a literal sense; men would be well aware that there were many other
sacred places besides their own for which similar claims were made. But
the place where there was communication with the gods, kept alive by
ritual and sacrifice, served for the community as a model of the original
centre, set up at creation when order emerged from chaos.

Communication with the Other World in such a place extended both
upwards and downwards. The lightning which can strike and even fell a
mighty oak was taken by Germans and Scandinavians as a powerful
symbol of divine power descending in fire. This developed into the
many-sided symbol of the axe-hammer of their god Thor,[35] which could
shatter rocks, leave dents in mountains and control the monsters of
chaos. The link between the pillar and the rising sun might be another
aspect of this link, since it connected earth and heaven. The journey of
the sun signified the sequence of the year, with its recurring renewal
of life and bringing of harvest. It is not surprising to find the symbols
of seasons and months on the Jupiter columns.

There was also a link with the depths of earth and of water. This can
be seen in the importance of the spring or well, continually found in or
beside holy places. Some of these possessed medicinal qualities, but
others are only sources of pure water. In Scandinavian tradition the gods
had their own holy spring by the World Tree, the place of assembly, and

its waters brought inspiration and knowledge to those who drank from it. It was known as the Well of Mimir, and it was said that Odin cast his eye into its waters as an offering in return for a drink which would reveal the future. Irish tradition also preserves the memory of a spring, known as the Well of Segais, or Connla's Well, which also was seen as a source of knowledge and inspiration. Bubbles formed on the streams which flowed from it, while nuts dropped into the water from the hazel tree above, and the salmon eating them could pass on special gifts if they in turn were eaten by men when they swam down the rivers originating from the well.[36] There were many Celtic sanctuaries at the sources of rivers or beside lakes, and offerings were regularly thrown into water.

Among Germans and Scandinavians offering places also included the shores of lakes and waterfalls (p. 131 below); one early settler in Iceland was said to worship a waterfall and to have flung offerings of food into it (p. 104 below). Clefts going down into the earth were also seen as a means of communication with the underworld, and caves might serve the same purpose. The famous St Patrick's Purgatory on an island in Lough Derg in Ireland still attracts many pilgrims, and was clearly viewed in earlier times as an entrance to the underworld. Those undergoing the demanding discipline of the pilgrimage now gather in a chapel, but in former times they were shut up for hours in the cave, where they had to go without sleep or food through the night and so endure something of the torments of purgatory for their souls' welfare. 'With the fall of night', wrote a twentieth century pilgrim, 'the world slipped away. We seemed to stand in a dim place where two worlds meet.'[37]

If a natural feature did not exist, it was possible to provide an artificial link with the supernatural world. A number of Celtic enclosures believed to have been sacred places had deep shafts like wells dug down into the earth, in which offerings were placed. Human and animal bones have been found, and in some shafts human beings have been buried with dogs. Groups of pits of this kind have been found both in Britain and on the Continent, for example at Newstead and Maryport and over a large area round Chartres, which may have been the centre where druids once met, mentioned by Julius Caesar.[38] Carved wooden figures have also been recovered from such shafts, and at St Bernard in La Vendée a cypress sapling 4 m in length; this has led to the suggestion that the panel on the Gundestrup Cauldron showing a line of men carrying a tree represents and offering of this kind. A shaft recently excavated at Deal in Kent went down about 2.50 m to finish in an oval chamber, in which a figurine of chalk was found, consisting of a block ending in a long slender neck and well-carved face of typical Celtic type. Footholds

26

in the chalk indicate that access to the chamber was possible, and it may have served some ritual purpose.[39]

The Gundestrup Cauldron itself seeems to have been an offering to the powers of the underworld, since it had been dismantled and set on the ground in an area of bog; other ritual objects found in Denmark appear to have been deposited in this way. The Scandinavians also threw offerings into lakes, and vast numbers of objects have been recovered from a dried-up lake at Skedemosse on the island of Öland in the Baltic, as well as from famous sites in the peat like Nydam and Vimose (p. 62 below). There are close parallels in the sacred pools of the Celtic peoples, such as the Iron Age site at Llyn Cerrig Bach in Anglesey.

5 The enclosed sanctuary

While unfenced areas and natural features of the landscape might be regarded as holy places, the need to provide an enclosed space, a *temenos* or sacred precinct, was often felt. It might enclose figures of the gods or sacred objects, or provide an obvious boundary around holy ground, separating it either temporarily or permanently from the normal world. Examples of this from the Viking Age suggested by Jacqueline Simpson are the ropes enclosing a court of law, the careful marking out of the area in which an official duel was fought, the squares on the floor used by a wizard calling up the dead (p. 149 below), and the stone settings placed round graves. The earliest enclosures for sacred places appear to have consisted of an earthwork or ditch to mark off the area in which worship or special rites took place. Such enclosures might be square, rectangular or circular in shape, and might contain such features as ritual shafts, springs, hearths, pillars, standing stones or monoliths.

The Goloring near Coblenz is an example of a huge circular enclosure as much as 190 m in diameter, possibly dating back to the sixth century BC. It had a large posthole in the centre which could have held a post 12 m high.[40] At Libernice near Kolin in Czechoslovakia there was a large rectangular enclosure 80 m by 20 m, marked out by a ditch. Inside remains of children and animals were found, as well as a skull, and there were traces of an artificial platform and pits holding bones and pottery fragments. In the area where offerings seem to have been made, a stone in the shape of a rough pyramid about 200 cm high had stood with its base deep in the earth, until at some time it was deliberately overturned and moved out of position. In the centre of the enclosure was the grave of a middle-aged woman, who it was suggested may have been a priestess. She wore jewellery of the La Tène period, and there were also two huge neck-rings of bronze which could have been used for figures of gods or heroes. The date of the grave was estimated at about the third century BC.[41] Many enclosed sites are known in Britain and on the Continent, and some were used over a long period. At Uley Bury in Gloucestershire there was a sacred place close to the great hill fort which was in use for as much as eight centuries. It was first enclosed by a ditch, then by a palisade, and it contained votive deposits, infant and adult burials, and isolated postholes. Buildings were set up there in the Roman period, and a recognisable shrine dedicated to Mercury built in the fourth century AD.[42] It is possible that the so-called Banqueting Hall at Tara was in fact a ritual enclosure, a parallelogram about 229 m long, of the type known as a *cursus* found on other sites of the Celtic Iron Age.

Small shrines or temples were set up in many existing enclosures during the Roman occupation. The earliest of these were of wood, and some seem to be pre-Roman in date, but later more permanent buildings of masonry were erected, to meet the needs of more sophisticated worshippers.[43] The enclosing wall with gates became an important feature. At Lhuis in Gaul, where a temple was set up with inscriptions to Jupiter and the goddesses, votive plaques were discovered which showed that portions of the wall round the temple had been built by grateful donors who had found healing there.

In southern France, elaborate shrines with stone carvings existed before the advent of the Romans, due to the influence of Greek and Italian merchants and settlers.[44] Carved figures in stone show Mediterranean influence, but have been produced by native craftsmen. At Roqueperteuse, north of Marseilles, there was a great stone portico supported on three stone pillars, with niches to hold skulls or severed human heads, and a carving of what is thought to have been a great bird of prey was set on the stone lintel. Another piece of carved stone depicted a pair of human heads facing opposite ways, and between them was what seems to be the beak of a great bird. Some of the stones were painted, and there were red, white and black horses on the lintel, with traces of fishes and foliage. In front were five stone figures which also showed signs of paint, and these were represented sitting cross-legged in Celtic fashion. At Entremont, an important sanctuary of the Salluvii, dating from the third century BC and finally destroyed by the Romans in 124 BC, there was a sacred way leading to the sanctuary which had been lined with lifesize figures of men and women carved in stone, some cross-legged as at Roqueperteuse. A reused pillar in the sanctuary had carvings of human heads and niches for holding skulls, and a number of skulls were recovered beside it. Another carved stone showed a mouthless head in an oval frame, with two sockets for skulls, one on either side. The Celtic Salluvii had made use of an earlier sanctuary which already had carved pillars, and they set up another building beside the sacred way which held a number of skulls nailed to stakes set on a wooden platform.

The statues and stone carvings in these temples give some idea of the artistic skills of these people, particularly now that they can be compared with wooden figures found more recently in Gaul. The carving shows both vigour and variety, and gives some idea of how elaborate these sanctuaries could have been before the arrival of the Romans. It includes realistic human figures and fantastic powerful creations like the 'Tarasque' of Noves, another holy place in Provence overrun by the Romans. This is a sinister wolf-like monster, with a scaly back like a dragon; it may be a symbol of devouring death, since it is crunching a human arm in its mouth and holding a human head under each of its front paws. The emphasis on the severed head in these sacred places is a recurring feature in Celtic religious symbolism and ritual (p. oo below).

Elaborate temples erected after the Roman conquest in Gaul and Britain are less barbarous and more sophisticated in design. Considerable efforts were to cater for the needs of visitors and to attract distinguished pilgrims. In AD 310 the Emperor Constantine visited a temple in Gaul, described as 'the most beautiful in the world', and there had a vision of himself as Apollo, receiving a wreath of victory and the promise of a reign of thirty years.[45] The wide views from some of these temple complexes, a marked feature of Celtic holy places, made them attractive places to visit. Some were used for healing, and attracted may seeking cures, as is clear from the inscriptions and votive offerings found there. One form of offering was that of models of various parts of the body where healing had taken place, and another of human figures which show the nature of the disease which afflicted the patient. The most valuable find of this kind was a collection of about two hundred wooden figures from the temple of Sequana, the goddess of the source of the Seine, which were discovered in 1963.[46] They were made about the first century AD, and in some cases earlier, before the erection of Roman temples on the site; they are carved with skill and artistry and are very varied in character. They were dredged out of what is thought to have been a ritual bathing pool within the sanctuary, where they had been carefully laid out in rows, perhaps at the dedication of the Gallo-Roman shrine. The methods of healing practised in such sanctuaries included drinking and bathing in the water, as at spas in later times, and also incubation, healing by means of dreams received by the patient sleeping in the temple. Inscriptions left by grateful pilgrims shows that this was practised in Gaul, and Miranda Green suggests that it may have been used at the temple of Sequana and also at Lydney on the Severn.[47]

The use made of striking natural features which formed part of the landscape is illustrated by the temple of Sulis Minerva at Bath.[48] Here the natural hot springs which led to the choice of the site as a holy place were enclosed in a temple in the Roman period, and even roofed in by a considerable feat of engineering. Pilgrims were able to enter the temple and approach the place where water gushed out from a stone arch, and could then drink from it and throw in offerings. The mist and steam rising from the stone cavern from which the hot flood poured must have made it a memorable place, and many rich gifts were left by the visitors. When the site was excavated in the nineteenth century, treasures found included jewellery, a set of thiry-four inscribed gems, rich metal vessels and large numbers of coins. The finds included a piece of lead with a vindictive prayer: 'May he who carried off Vilbia from me become liquid as water'. This was written backwards, with a list of possible names of the guilty party, and there are other examples of curses of this kind being found among votive offerings. As well as the temple buildings, a set of luxurious baths was added in the first century AD; they were in use until about the fifth century, and probably inspired the poem known as 'The Ruin' in the Exeter Book, composed by an Anglo-Saxon poet. Another example of the use of a natural feature in a Romano-Celtic temple is at Triguères (Loiret) in Gaul, where the *cella* or central sanctuary was almost filled by a menhir, an enormous stone which projected over the rear wall into the ambulatory beyond.[49]

A typical temple of the Romano-Celtic type, however, would not be on such a grand scale as that at Bath. It would consist basically of two concentric units; the inner sanctuary or *cella* where a cult object or figures of deities might be placed, and an ambulatory outside this, encircling most of the building, which could be used for processions. The *cella* might be of considerable height, in the form of a tower, and could be square, rectangular or circular in shape. The roof of the ambulatory would be lower than that of the *cella*, and it might be left open at the side, enclosed only by a low wall with pillars to support the roof. Although it used to be assumed that such temples belonged to the period of Roman occupation, it is now known that a number existed before this both in Gaul and Britain.[50] There was a pre-conquest temple at Heathrow in southern England, now under the airport; this was a massive timber building 6 × 5 m, with a colonnade surrounding it. Another example of an early temple is at Tremblois in Gaul, where a series of buildings succeeded one another on the same site.[51] Since the earliest temples were of wood, many may have been missed by excavators, for it is difficult to be sure whether a small structure of this kind was built for secular or religious purposes. Some of the shrines of the Romano-Celtic period were little more than sheds set up on private estates, or chapels forming part of private houses.

The Germanic peoples were less affected by Mediterranean fashions or by the demands of foreign worshippers, and they do not seem to have progressed beyond the erection of wooden buildings. In Bede's story of the conversion of Northumbria (*History* II, 13), he refers to 'altars and shrines' of the idols, and to enclosures surrounding them. The High Priest is said to ride over to the idols and profane the temple by throwing a spear into it, but it is not clear whether Bede pictures the idols inside the temple or not. The inference is that these structures were wood, since they burned easily. A seventh century building near the royal hall of Yeavering in Northumberland is a possible example of a wooden temple of considerable size in the Anglo-Saxon pre-Christian perod.[52] It measurements were 11 × 5.5 m and it had inner walls of wattle and daub strengthened on the outside by timber. It was rectangular in plan, with doors in the centre of the two long walls. A second building in line with this may have served as a kitchen where the sacrificial meals were cooked, and there was an area where the cattle may have been killed, as there were animal bones there but no skulls. Inside the possible temple, there was a pit beside the east wall filled with bones, together with many skulls of oxen, sufficient to overflow the pit and form a pile against the wall. There were three post-holes within the building, but the posts had been removed from them and the holes filled with stones; this might mark alterations made to the building after the acceptance of Christianity.

There are descriptions of fairly elaborate temples in Scandinavia in saga literature, but these were written relatively late, and may have been influenced by accounts of pagan temples in the Old Testament or Virgil, or by familiarity with large medieval churches of stone. Up to now archaeological research has failed to establish the existence of any large building used as a temple, or outlines of such buildings under churches.[53] The most convincing evidence for a pre-Christian sacred site is at Mære on Trondheim Fjord, where an important sanctuary is known to have existed in the Viking Age.[54] The medieval church there originally stood on an island, and traces of earlier buildings were discovered beneath it. The earliest appeared to date back to about AD 500, and was marked by post-holes which held the main pillars of the building. These had signs of burning at the bottom, and a number of tiny pieces of thin gold foil of the type known as *goldgubber* in Denmark were found.[55] Such tiny pieces of gold usually depict two figures, a man and a woman, who face each other and are sometimes embracing, or may have a leafy branch between them (p. 121 below). They are usually found in sets, on house-sites and not in graves, and are believed to be associated with the deities of fertility, the Vanir of Scandinavian mythology. It has been thought that they symbolise the marriage of god and goddess, and that they may have been used at weddings, or to bless a new home; in this case, it appears, they were used in the rite of hallowing a temple building.

The temple at Mære was presumably of wood, and the same is true of the famous temple at Uppsala, described in Adam of Bremen's eleventh century history as a splendid building with a roof of shining gold. No clear plan of a pre-Christian shrine has been found under the church there, although Sune Lindqvist discovered traces of an earlier building and a few post-holes which could have belonged to a temple. The reconstructed Uppsala temple model to be seen in Scandinavian museums was based largely on the ground plan of a Wendish temple at Arcona, destroyed by the Danes in the twelfth century and described in detail by Saxo Grammaticus, which was reconstructed by Schuchardt in 1921.[56] It was once thought that the term *hof* which occurs in many Icelandic placenames indicated the existence of a former temple, but it has been shown by Olsen that many of these names were based on the assumptions of local antiquarians in later times. In 1908 a building was excavated at Hofstaðir in north-eastern Iceland; the ground plan was thought to be an example of a large temple, and is shown as such in many books on the Viking Age. It seems however more probable that this was the hall of a farmhouse used for communal religious feasts, perhaps that of the *goði* or leading man of the district who would preside over such gatherings, and there was no indication that it was erected purely for religious purposes.

Individuals in Scandinavia evidently set up small shrines for their own use, as Thorolf of Helgafell is said to have erected a 'temple' for Thor near his own house in Iceland, where the sacred ring of the god and a bowl used for sacrifices were kept. However such temples appear to correspond to the small shrines of Celtic areas rather than large temple buildings of the Roman type or halls where a number of worshippers or pilgrims could collect. A farm called *Hof* may have been a place where ritual celebrations were held at regular times when the annual feasts took place, cattle were killed, and men met to do honour to the gods.

There is not much indication that healing was associated with holy places and shrines among Germans and Scandinavians. Something of the kind, however, appears to have been linked with cult places out of doors and with burial places. Those in tales who sleep on burial mounds sometimes have dreams which bring inspiration or healing, and the implication appears to be that it is the dead within the mound who communicates with the sleeper (p. 130 below). It was claimed that Freyr, the god associated with the earth and burial mounds, could send dreams and visions to men. There are tales also of men consulting both Freyr and the sky god Thor when an important decision had to be reached, such as whether to leave Norway for Iceland; such consultations might take place in the shrine of the god, in the hall of a house, or perhaps out of doors beside a mound, a sacred tree, or a great stone. As preserved in the literature such traditions are fragmentary and confused, and there is less emphasis on healing than on urgent warnings, the revelation of future events, or good luck in hunting and fishing, but there are hints that indicate it was not wholly forgotten.

Even if temples were usually small impermanent structures, this does not rule out the possibility that rich carvings in wood, fine hangings and great treasures in the form of splendid vessels or ornaments for the figures of the gods might be preserved in them. When Charlemagne

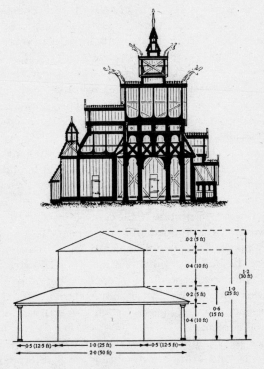

3 *above* Section drawing of stave church of early thirteenth century from Gol, Hallingdal, Norway, now in Bygdöy Museum. *below* Typical Romano-Celtic temple with suggested proportions.

33

destroyed the Irminsul in the eighth century, he is said to have removed much gold and silver from the sacred place. A superb treasure was found at Petrossa in Romania in 1837, which included gold vessels, a great jewelled collar, and some splendid brooches, one an enormous one in the shape of an eagle. These are thought to have been the work of Gothic craftsmen and to have come from a sanctuary, perhaps hidden for safety during the aproach of the Huns. Objects like the Gundestrup Cauldron were carefully dismantled and deposited in the Danish peat-bogs, and these seem likely to have been the property of some sanctuary of the gods, which might be stored there and brought out for special festivals.

While so far there is little definite evidence for early shrines among the Germanic peoples, the wooden stave churches built in Norway between the eleventh and thirteenth centuries may provide a possible clue as to what kind of sacred buildings were set up there in pre-Christian times. As many as thirty-one stave churches survive, some in remote parts of Norway and others now in open-air museums, and they are strikingly different in appearance and construction from early churches of brick or stone in England and Germany. The earliest Norwegian churches had their pillars and walls set in the ground and packed round with stones, and consequently they could not survive for long. Those built in the twelfth century, however, rest on 'groundsills', formed of four massive lengths of timber set to form a square. From these a series of 'masts' or wooden pillars rise to support the walls and roof, rounded at the foot like the masts of a ship.[57] In a small 'one-mast' church, two pieces of timber are laid crosswise over the sill, and a single central pillar rises from the crossing. In larger churches, masts are placed at the four corners of the sill, while in a 'many-masted' church like that of Borgund the 'sleepers' forming the sill are arranged to form a square inside a rectangle, and the masts are set round the square. At Borgund there are as many as six different levels from the ground to the central tower, and a series of roofs of different heights are grouped around the central sanctuary. As in the case of the Romano-Celtic temple, an ambulatory (*svalgang*) runs round the outside of the building. This is usually enclosed by a low wooden wall topped by an arcade, so that it is open to light and air. It was used for processions moving clockwise round the church, as well as for depositing weapons during the service, and for transacting business and making formal agreements.

The earliest stave churches have rich and often fantastic carvings on doors and walls, and grim, sinister heads set at the points where the pillars touch the roof, recalling ancient gods and monsters rather than Christian symbols and markedly different from fantastic heads of Anglo-Norman churches.[58] Outside dragon shapes protrude from the gables

34

like figure-heads from a ship. Indeed there is an obvious link between the construction of the stave churches and the techniques of ship-building, as was pointed out by Lorenz Dietrichson: 'A row of arches, upside down, is placed between different rafters, just as it was between the ribs of a Viking ship. In the ship these ribs were ot attached to the keel, and similarly the rafter arches and the beams are separate from the ridge beams in the church ... The entire church is strengthened throughout by elbow joints and brackets, just as the Viking ships are.[59] Inside the churches it is dark and mysterious, and the fact that the roof rises in the centre gives an impression of narrowness and height, drawing the gaze upwards. A building of this kind would emphasise the centrality of the sacred place, while the series of different levels would be in accordance with the picture of the world of gods and men and supernatural beings grouped vertically and horizontally around the World Tree (p 171 below).

It is clear that sacred buildings in various parts of Celtic and Germanic territory developed in different ways according to outside influences and the building materials and skills available. They were raised to house figures of the gods and cult objects, for the making of private offerings and consultation of the supernatural powers, not for congregational services and large assemblies. They would be visited by the faithful, and the processional way round the building would make it possible for visitors to view sacred objects without entering the sanctuary. The treasures stored in the temple sometimes necessitated a wall or fence to enclose it, and this also served to mark off sacred space. Communal feasts and rituals in which the neighbourhood took part, however, would normally be out of doors or in suitably large buildings where feasts could be prepared, as in the hall of a king or local landowner. In spite of occasional encircling walls, it is essential to see the sacred place as something not set apart from the ordinary secular world, but rather as providing a vital centre for the needs of the community and for the maintenance of a kingdom. It offered a means of communication with the Other World, and was regarded as a source of power, inspiration, healing and hidden knowledge. One or more deities might be revered in the shrine or cult place, and through them men might get in touch with the underworld or with the world of the sky. Law and order essential for the established community was centred in the holy place, and sanctuaries like Tara, Uppsala and Thingvellir might serve as microcosm and map of the entire kingdom.

II Feasting and sacrifice

> The big ram ... I sacrificed on the beach, burning slices from his thighs as
> an offering to Zeus of the Black Clouds, the Son of Cronos, who is lord of
> us all. But Zeus took no notice of my sacrifice; his mind must already have
> been full of plans for the destruction of all my gallant ships and of my
> trusty band. So the whole day long till sundown we sat and feasted on our
> rich supply of meat washed down by mellow wine.
>
> *Odyssey*, IX (Rieu's translation)

In the holy places of Celts, Germans and Scandinavians regular rituals
were organised to renew and strengthen communication with the
supernatural world. The communal feast which included the hallowing
of ale or mead to the gods was of major importance, and the sacrifice of
living creatures was linked with this. Animals had to be slain, and meat
and drink shared with the powers in whose honour men came together.
There might also be offerings of booty taken in war, sacred animals, part
of the harvest, or perhaps food and drink set aside as a token gift to the
supernatural beings from whom help was awaited. Such sacrifices, as
well as the killing of victims, might take place on private occasions or at
special times of crisis and danger, but always sacrifice formed an
essential part of the communal feast held regularly in honour of the
gods.

To some extent sacrifice may be seen as a contract between god and
worshipper. The Scandinavian merchants on the Volga, according to
Ibn Fadlan (p. 18 above) made offerings of food and cattle to wooden
figures set up outside their houses, and hoped in return to receive the
luck which would bring good trading. When other Rus traders went
down the Dnieper to Byzantium, always a dangerous enterprise, we are
told in a tenth century Greek account[1] that when they reached St
Gregory's Island in the lower river, they would sacrifice cocks as a
thank-offering. The poultry had presumably been taken with them for
food, and they drew lots to decide which to offer in sacrifice, which to eat
themselves, and which to keep alive. The idea of consulting the gods

36

themselves when choosing a victim for them is frequently encountered in reviewing the evidence for sacrificial practices. There were no figures of gods on St Gregory's Island, since this was foreign territory, but the offerings were placed round an enormous oak, a famous tree which survived into the nineteenth century. In this case the main deity may well have been Thor, god of the sky and said to assist travellers, who was associated with the oak. Later in the mid tenth century a Spanish Jew from Cordova left an account of what is thought to be the market town of Hedeby in Denmark, where few of the inhabitants were Christian.[2] He described their way of life with fastidious distaste, noting that they ate much fish, threw unwanted infants into the sea, and sang in gruff voices like growling dogs. He observed that among them sacrifice and feasting went together: 'They hold a feast where all meet to honour their god and to eat and drink. Each man who slaughters an animal for sacrifice – ox, ram, goat or pig – fastens it to a pole outside the door of his house, to show that he had made his sacrifice in honour of the god.'

1 The fixed festivals

While sacrifices might be made on special occasions, such as the arrival at a holy place, the setting up of a new house, victory in battle, the opening of the Assembly, or the death of a king, and might also be carried out by private individuals, there were regular feasts in which all the community took part. The fixing of these must have come about long before any formal calendar was in use, although by the first century AD the Celts in Gaul seem to have possessed an elaborate one. The Coligny Calendar, on fragments of bronze plate found at Ain in France in 1897, covered roughly five solar years of twelve months each, with two additional months to adapt the lunar year to the solar one.[3] Months and certain days are classified as either auspicious or inauspicious. This calendar was probably for the use of the learned men of the community, enabling them to work out dates of feasts. Before such calendars existed, the feasts were presumably at the points of the seasonal round important for farmers, herdsmen, hunters, fishers and warriors, and could be roughly reckoned by observation of the moon or the planets.

The Celts and Germans used the half-year as the basic unit of time. In Iceland the *misseri* (from *miss*, alternation) were summer and winter, each season twenty-six weeks in length, and the beginning of each was marked by feasting and religious ritual. The passage of time was by counting winters and nights. Julius Caesar (*Gallic War* VI, 18) noted that the Gauls held that night came before day, and kept to this when celebrating birthdays and the beginning of a month or a year, just as for us Christmas begins on Christmas Eve. Tacitus reported similarly of the

37

Germans in *Germania* 11: 'They do not reckon time by days, as we do, but by nights. All their engagements and appointments are made on this system.' This way of reckoning seems to have been common among agricultural and hunting peoples without exact calendars over a large part of the world.[4] The two half-years of the Icelanders made up a year of 364 days, and this meant that there would gradually be a shift of seasons as time passed. The long winter darkness made this very noticeable, and Ari tells how men realised 'by the course of the sun that the summer was moving backwards into the spring'. This caused consternation, as he tells us in *Íslendingabók* (4), and one night Thorstein Surt, the grandson of Thorolf of Helgafell (p. 18 above), had a dream. He thought that he was at the Law Assembly during the annual summer meeting at Thingvellir, and was the only one there awake; then he fell asleep when all the rest stayed awake. Ari interprets this as signifying that when Thorstein addressed the Thing, everyone would be silent, and when he stopped they would applaud. It might, however, have an additional meaning: by reckoning seasons wrongly, they had come to be active when they should be inactive and vice versa, but Thorstein alone knew a way to remedy this. He suggested that an extra week be added to the year every seventh summer, thus setting the calendar to rights, and the idea was enthusiastically received and became part of Icelandic law. It is interesting to note that the determination of time and dates was part of the responsibility of the Althing, and that the Lawspeaker proclaimed the *misseristal* (reckoning of the seasons/calendar) for the coming year at the close of the Assembly.[5] Thus the reckoning of time was originally seen as under the control of the gods.

In the course of the solar year, the Celtic peoples had three main feasts. *Samain* on 1 November, marked the beginning of winter and opening of the new year, and the word is usually taken to mean 'end of summer'.[6] At this time animals which could not be kept through the winter were slaughtered, so that it was a convenient time for feasting. Samain was regarded as a period of danger, since it was the boundary between the seasons, when the way to the Other World lay open and the dead had encounters with the living. It is said in the opening of 'The Adventures of Nera': 'The fairy mounds of Erin are always opened about Samain'. Various rites were practised to discover what the year would bring to the community and to individuals, and echoes of this are still found in the observance of Hallowe'en in the British Isles. The other main festival was *Beltene* on 1 May, at the beginning of summer, which in Christian times continued to be marked by the lighting of bonfires and various rites to ensure fertility among the herds and bring a good harvest. There were also two quarterly festivals on 1 February and

1 August. *Imbolg* in February was associated with the goddess Brigantia and later with St Brigit. The name indicates a connection with milking, but may also have had ancient associations with purification.[7] Cormac in his *Glossary* explained it as meaning 'Sheep's milk', thus alluding to the beginning of the lambing season, but this can hardly be correct. The date was an important one in the year, for as well as lambing there were preparations for spring sowing, while farm workers were hired for the coming season, fishermen took out their boats after the winter, and on the coast seaweed was gathered to fertilise the crops and people gathered shellfish. St Brigit was said to travel about the countryside on the eve of her festival to bestow her blessing on the people and their animals.[8] This could well have been a festival in which women played an important part. At the festival of *Lughnasad* in August, the emphasis was on the beginning of harvest, and in pre-Christian times this was associated with the god Lug. Maire MacNeill in her detailed investigation of this festival has shown how it continued to be observed into recent times in Ireland by expeditions to wells and hilltops, by the holding of fairs and general rejoicing. All these festivals included various ceremonies and rites to bring luck, protection and blessing in the coming season, and there were various methods of foretelling what the future was to bring.[9]

The Germanic winter started in autumn with the 'winter nights', three or more days in late October; in Iceland this was the period between 11 and 18 October. The plural expression implies some vagueness about the exact date, and it was probably kept as a period of feasting rather than as a single festival. The equivalent summer period began in April, in Iceland as *sumarmál* (summer time) between 9 and 15 April. In the Viking Age this was the time to seek for good luck in raids and expeditions, after men had been at home for the winter. There was also the midwinter feast known as Yule, which came to be identified with the festival for Christ's birth in Christian times. This was the time of the winter solstice, when little could be done out of doors. Tacitus in the first century AD declared in *Germania* (26) that the Germans had only three main seasons, winter, spring and summer, since they had no fruit harvest in the autumn like the Mediterranean peoples. Similarly in the thirteenth century, Snorri in *Ynglinga Saga* (8) mentions three main feasts in Scandinavia before the conversion: one at the beginning of winter, when men sacrificed for plenty, one at mid-winter for the growth of crops, and one in summer for victory. There might be other times when regular feasts took place, depending on local conditions, but the three main ones seem to have made up the established pattern over a large part of north-western Europe. Grimm in *Teutonic Mythology*[10] wisely observed that the further north men lived, the more important the distinction between light and darkness, with emphasis on the shortest day in mid-winter, amd Procopius noted that the men of Thule, in the far north, held their main feast when the sun was first seen from a mountain top after the long period of winter darkness.[11]

The holding of a feast was always a matter of pride and reputation among kings and leaders. In the first century BC Posidonius wrote of a certain Celtic chief, Louernius, that he made generous gifts of gold and silver to his followers,[12] and built a square enclosure for feasting one and a half miles each way. He had filled '. . . vats with expensive liquor, and prepared so great a quantity of food that for many days all who wished could enter and enjoy the feast prepared, being served without a break by the attendants.' This implies a period set apart for feasting by the whole community rather than a particular entertainment when guests were invited to the king's hall, and some of the enclosures found in sacred places may have been used in this way. The heroic poetry of north-western Europe is full of praise for generous rulers who provided rich hospitality in the mead hall, but the sacrificial feast can be distinguished from banquets in general because at this men partook of animals sacrificed to the gods, and drank mead and ale in the gods' honour. They met to renew their contract with the supernatural world, and to ensure good luck for the coming season, and this was something for the whole community to share in and not for selected guests. Games and contests might form part of the feast, which could last for several days. The essential element, however, was eating and drinking together, and there may have been occasions when strangers were not admitted. This seems implied in an account of the poet Sigvat's journey through Sweden in the early eleventh century, when the Norwegian king sent him on a mission concerning marriage with the king of Sweden's daughter.[13] By this time Norway was officially Christian, but the Swedes retained their old religion, and Sigvat had a difficult journey. It was late in the autumn, and many householders, including one man renowned for hospitality, refused to allow him inside their houses. We have Sigvat's own verses describing this, and it is on these that Snorri has based his story. At one farm called Hof, the poet declared that he was unable to thrust his nose inside, and could get scarcely a word out of the people but was turned away because they declared that the hall was 'hallowed'. At the next farm the housewife forbade him to enter, because they were holding álfablót (sacrifice to the elves), and feared the anger of Odin if he were allowed in: 'She thrust me away as if I were a wolf', he complained. It is true that St Olaf's poet was a Christian, which might account for the hostility, but the implication is that the doors were barred to strangers once the feast had begun.[14]

2 Ceremonial drinking

The drinking of wine, ale or mead was of ceremonial importance at all feasts, and it seems to have been this which 'hallowed' the hall when men met for sacrifice. Among the Celts, splendid drinking vessels, jugs, flagons and horns are frequent in rich graves from the Hallstatt period onwards, and it has been said with truth that we owe much of our knowledge of Celtic art to Celtic thirst.[15] Traces of liquid were sometimes left in these which on analysis proved to be beer or mead, and since a number of vessels were often included in one grave, the symbolic meaning appears to be that of a feast in the Other World rather than a supply of nourishment for the single occupant. While some vessels were of foreign workmanship, like the enormous bronze crater in the grave of the 'Princess of Vix' from the sixth century BC,[16] many magnificent examples were made by Celtic craftsmen. Superb flagons like one from Dürrnberg in Austria (early fifth century BC)[17] or the matching pair from Basse-Yutz in Lorraine (late fifth/early fourth century BC)[18] may well have been made for religious feasts, in which kings and nobles would certainly take part. Their ornamentation has been inspired by the Celtic view of the world of gods and monsters, and fantastic creatures creep up the handle, adorn the lid, or perch on the shoulder. In a chieftain's grave from Hochdorf in Austria (sixth century BC)[19] there was a set of nine drinking horns on the wall of the burial chamber, and a cauldron from Greece which had held mead. The use of horns in the heroic past was remembered in Irish literature. In the 'Colloquy of the Ancients', St Patrick asks whether men used horns, cups or goblets in the old days, and Caílte replies that Finn had three hundred and twelve gold drinking-horns, which held an enormous amount of liquor, and gives a list of some of their names.[20]

The Germans also drank from horns on ceremonial occasions, according to Julius Caesar, setting particular value on the great horns of the aurochs, which could only be obtained by hunters of great skill and courage (*Gallic War* VI, 28). These they adorned with rims of silver and used at their most splendid feasts. Horns were still in use at the Norwegian court until the end of the Viking Age. According to Snorri Sturluson, it was Olaf the Quiet in the eleventh century, an enthusiast for modern innovations, who replaced them by cups which could be filled at table: 'King Harald [*Hardraði*] and former kings had been accustomed to drink from animal horns and have the ale taken round the fire from the highseat.'[21] A magnificent pair of gold drinking horns of Germanic workmanship, one bearing runes which indicate a date about the early fifth century AD, was discovered near Gallehus in North

41

Schleswig in the eighteenth century, then part of Denmark.[22] They were treasured for a while after the discovery of the second horn in 1734 and even used at the king's court, but in 1802 they were stolen and melted down before the thief was caught. A series of decorated rings fitted over the horns, and on these human and animal figures were depicted, engaged in various activities such as dancing, riding, shooting with a bow, ball-playing and acrobatics; there were also men with animal heads, warriors in huge horned helmets, and a three-headed giant. It is not possible to interpret the scenes with certainty, but they suggest seasonal rites and might represent sports and ritual actions at a feast. Horses are shown on both horns, and one has been pierced by an arrow while next to it a woman is shown carrying a horn, so one possibility is that the horns were intended to be used at the horse sacrifice (Fig. 4).

Another pair of large ceremonial drinking horns formed part of the royal treasure from the ship-grave at Sutton Hoo, and the rims and tips of silver-gilt have survived. These are of seventh century date, and were evidently intended for communal drinking.[23] In the Anglo-Saxon poem *Beowulf* (612–14) the drinking ceremony in a Danish king's hall is described: the Danish queen first carried the cup to the king and then bore it round to the chief warriors in the hall. She uttered a formal speech as she handed it to the king, and again when she gave it to Beowulf, the visiting champion, and as he received it from her he solemnly pledged himself to do battle against the monster Grendel on the king's behalf. However in spite of many references to feasting and drinking, there is no mention of drinking horns in the poem, and in the Christian period they were presumably replaced by cups and glass drinking vessels.

The hallowing of wine drunk to the gods, an essential part of the sacrificial feast, continued in the form of a toast or *minni* which was drunk at the meetings of the medieval guilds held in Scandinavia in Christian times.[24] The expression 'to drink a feast' was used when referring to the holding of a guild meeting, and it may be noted similarly that the word for feast (*symbel*) is used in *Beowulf* (619) of a drinking cup.[25] It was customary to drink three main toasts at a guild feast. The Gothland Karin's Guild, for instance, drank to Christ, St Catharine and Our Lady, while the Swedish Eric's Guild to St Eric, Our Saviour and Our Lady. Snorri tells us that three toasts were drunk at the funeral of Harald of Denmark, who had been converted to Christianity, and these were to Christ, to St Michael and to the memory of the dead king.[26] He also mentions three toasts drunk in pre-Christian times: at Lade, Jarl Sigurd drank to Odin for power and victory, and to Njord and Freyr for peace and good seasons, while a third toast was to the memory of dead ancestors.[27] On such occasions the Jarl presided at the feast, and hallowed the drink with appropriate words before the horns were carried round the hall.

There are many Icelandic tales of the mystery and magic of drinking horns, which like the Irish ones were often given names. Olaf Tryggvason was said to possess a pair called the Hyrnings, and another called the Grims. The latter came to him as a gift from the legendary

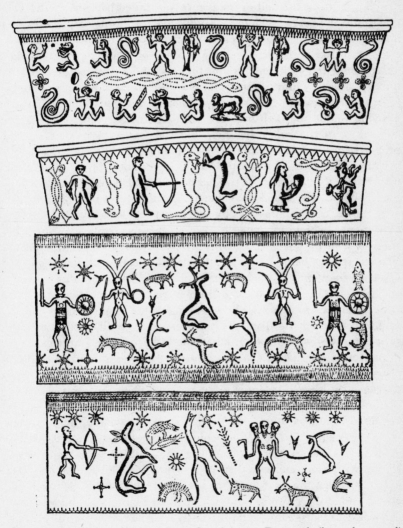

4 Panels from two gold horns from Gundestrup, Denmark (later destroyed), from drawing of 1734.

Gudmund of Glasisvellir (p. 185 below), ruler of a supernatural realm who was hostile to Christianity. When the horns were blessed in Christian fashion before Olaf drank from them the men who brought the horns were furious.[28] A late legendary saga describes an enormous horn called Grim the Good, and this had a man's head on the tip which was said to speak and foretell the future.[29] A well-known tale of the god Thor in the *Prose Edda* describes how he struggled to empty a huge drinking horn in the hall of the giants, but failed because the tip went down into the ocean. The name Grim given to horns emphasises their link with Odin, since it is one of his many names. The brewing of ale was also associated with him, and the mother of Starkad, one of Odin's heroes long remembered for his bravery and evil deeds, vowed her unborn child to Odin in return for the god's help in a brewing contest with other women.[30] In *Ynglinga Saga* all the gods helped with the brewing of the mead drunk in the Other World. When the warring companies of the gods, the Æsir and the Vanir, made a truce, they prepared mead in a huge vessel as a pledge of their agreement, each spitting into the bowl to ensure the fermentation of the liquid.[31] The fact that in the late days of the old religion toasts were drunk to both the Æsir and the Vanir may partly account for this myth, but the importance of the brewing by both parties as a symbol of their agreement – which was never broken – remains significant. The giants tried to steal the mead, but Odin recovered it and brought it back to Valhalla (p. 175 below). The tradition of his escape with it in eagle form was used frequently in the imagery of the early poets, and this may be an ancient tradition, going back to Indo-European times.[32]

Celtic and Germanic tales both emphasise the importance of the great cauldron holding the drink for the feast, and dwell on the unending supply of life-giving mead or ale in the Other World. Large cauldrons have been found in Celtic graves from the Hallstatt period onwards and also in Germanic graves. In the Latin *Life* of St Columbanus, written in the seventh century, there is a tale of how when the saint was in the region of the Alamanni in Switzerland, he came upon a group of men clustered around a huge vessel which they called *cupa*, holding about twenty measures of beer. They told him that they were offering it to Wodan, but the saint approached the vat and blew on it, causing it to shatter with a loud noise so that the beer was lost.[33] A similar episode in a different setting is found in a tale of St Vedrastus, who once accompanied the Frankish king Chlothar to a banquet. This was in the early days of Christianity, and the festival ale had been tactfully divided into two portions, one hallowed according to the heathen custom and the other set apart for Christians. Vedrastus would not accept this, and he made the sign of the cross over the hallowed vessel, whereupon it burst, and the heathen who were about to drink from it were converted by the saint's display of power.[34] These stories can be recognised as Christian propaganda, but they indicate how feasts were conducted.

There are references in early Irish literature to the inexhaustible cauldron of mead in the Other World. Such a vessel is said to be inside the *sid* or fairy mound:

> A vat of intoxicating mead
> was being distributed to the household.
> It is there yet, its state unchanging –
> it is always full.[35]

Such vats were said to stand in a crystal bower in the otherworld island in the tale of 'The Adventure of Art': 'Fair was the site of that bower, with its doors of crystal and its inexhaustible vats, for though everything be emptied out of them, they were ever full again.'[36] The image passed into Christian poetry, and a poet of the tenth or eleventh century declares: 'I should like to have a great ale feast for the King of Kings; I should like the heavenly host to be drinking it for all eternity.'[37]

Such a picture may be compared with that of the unceasing supply of mead in the hall of the god Odin, who feasted his heroes in Valhalla each evening when the day's fighting was over. In one poem, *Grímnismàl* (25), it is said that the mead comes from the udders of the goat Heidrun who fed on the World Tree. The importance of the drinking in Odin's hall is emphasised by the popularity of the symbol of a woman offering a horn.[38] She is shown on a number of stones of the Viking Age set up as memorials in Gotland, and there she is greeting a warrior who is arriving at Valhalla. A similar figure was used as an amulet in Sweden, for an example was found in the cemetery at Birka, and she appears again on carved stones of the tenth century in northern England. Poems of about the same date mention the valkyries bearing mead to kings entering Valhalla (p. 92 below). The image may go back earlier than the Viking Age, since a woman carrying a horn appears on one of the gold drinking-horns from Gallehus, dated to the fifth century AD (p. 43 above).

3 The sacrificial meal

The second cauldron at the feast was that in which the meat was cooked, and as with the mead, supplies of this in the Other World feasts would never run out. The Irish Dagda possessed a cauldron of plenty, and it was said in 'The Second Battle of Mag Tuired' that none went away from it unsatisfied. In such a cauldron, a pig might be cooked for the feast, or a bull or an ox boiled, although sometimes the meat was roasted over the fire:[39] 'A pig perpetually alive and a roasted swine and a vessel with marvellous liquor, and never do they all decrease.' The god Manannán who ruled in the Land of Youth had a supply of pigs which could be devoured and then restored to life to be cooked anew on the morrow.[40] Again there is a parallel in the account of the hospitality in the hall of Odin, where the boar Sæhrimnir provided the warriors with an unending supply of pork; it was said in *Gylfaginning* (37) that it was 'boiled every day and comes to life each evening'.

Food was placed in both Celtic and Germanic graves from an early period, and tough cauldrons suitable for cooking over a fire as well as more fragile ones to hold liquor have frequently been found; one from Sutton Hoo, for instance was big enough to hold a sheep. The heating and cooking of meat on the hearth was in itself an image of the link between man and the Other World. Fire and cooking are constantly emphasised in the Fenian tales, while 'fire-dogs' to hold the logs in place, with horned heads of bulls, found in chieftains' graves of the La Tène period, are likely to have possessed ritual significance.[41] In individual graves of the earlier Hallstatt period there were sets of plates and dishes, as if for a dinner party, and this practice is continued in the so-called 'pottery graves' of Jutland in the early centuries AD.[42] The Other World cauldron is associated with the idea of resurrection, for not only the unfortunate boar, doomed to be slaughtered and cooked daily, but other animals also might enter the cauldron and yet be restored to life. It was said of pigs in the Irish tales that 'if their bones were kept without breaking or gnawing, they would survive alive every day'.[43] A popular legend about St Patrick tells how he brought back a bull to life when its bones were collected and placed on the hide,[44] while the Scandinavian Thor did precisely the same with his goats, cooking them for supper and then resuscitating them when the bones were placed on the skin by raising his hammer over them.[45]

There is a tradition that warriors plunged into a magical cauldron might return to life in the same way. This happens in the Welsh tale of 'Branwen Daughter of Llyr' in the *Mabinogion*, which shows signs of Irish influence; here a dead man thrown into a cauldron which was brought from beneath a lake rises next day as good a fighting man as before, 'save that he will not have the power of speech'.[46] An Irish tale with a strong Christian element, 'The Death of Muircertach mac Erca', contains an episode in which an enchanted feast of pig's flesh and wine was provided for warriors who had fallen in battle but who were recalled to life; and this is represented as the evil deception of an enchantress. The raising of dead warriors to fight anew is a familiar theme also in

Norse literature, and is not confined to accounts of Odin's realm of Valhalla, but may take place also within a burial mound. It was a familiar motif in the Viking Age, and possibly one of considerable antiquity; among the many different interpretations of the panel showing marching and riding warriors on the Gundestrup Cauldron, one is that a man is being placed in a cauldron in order to restore him to life to fight anew (Fig. 5).

It appears that the leaving of food and drink in the graves of Celtic and Germanic dead was based on something more than a crude notion that they needed nourishment after death. The cost and effort involved in providing splendid vessels for food and drink reached vast proportions in certain periods, and the custom continued in varying degrees throughout the pre-Christian period. In the elaborate arrangements for a feast for the rich and powerful dead, we seem justified in seeing the symbolism of the Other World banquet with its implication of renewal of life. The more pathetic provision made for poorer folk in the form of an egg or two or a small piece of meat, along with a vessel of beer, might also be viewed as a hopeful offering, implying in a vague way some kind of continuing life in the next world. This must at least be counted as a possibility among peoples to whom the feast and the hallowing of food and drink represented one of the most important means of communicating with the gods.

The chief cult animals whose meat was used for the sacrifical feast were the boar, the bull and the horse. Pork was popular among the Celts from early times, and the herding of swine played an important part in farming both on the Continent and in the British Isles.[47] The use of the

5 Panel from interior of Gundestrup Cauldron, showing ritual scene and lines of warriors.

pig as a religious symbol may account for the prominence of swineherds in the Irish tales, and their association with Other World wisdom. Posidonius described the fierce competition between warriors in the second century BC for the best cuts from the carcase of the boar provided for the feast. As with the seats for the guests, there were strict rules of precedence when the boar was carved, and the finest or 'champion's portion' of the roast meat was much coveted as an honour: 'In former times when the hindquarters were served up, the bravest hero took the thigh piece, and if another man claimed it they stood up and fought in single combat to the death.'[48] Competition for the champion's portion and also the right to carve the boar, claimed by the foremost warrior present, was still remembered in the Irish tales, particularly in 'Bricriu's Feast' and 'Mac Da Thó's Pig'.[49] Bricriu inflames the warriors with his challenge: 'Yonder you see the champion's portion ... let it be given to the best warrior in Ulaid', whereupon the names of three outstanding heroes present are shouted out, and in a moment they are contending in furious combat: 'The three heroes rose out into the middle of the house with their spears and swords and shields: and they so slashed at each other that half the house was a fire of swords and glittering spear edges, while the other half was a pure-white bird flock of shield enamel.' In Mac Da Thó's hall, Cet son of Magu takes it on himself to do the carving, and though various warriors challenge him he silences them all with references to his superiority in the past, until at last Conall Cernach arrives with the head of Cet's brother in his wallet and drives him away from the pig: 'Cet left the pig then, and Conall sat down to it, saying "On with the contest!" The Connachta could not find a warrior to equal him ... Conall then began to carve the pig.' Lists have survived telling how the joints were allotted, and there is general agreement that the most distinguished guest received cuts from the leg, while the head was reserved for the charioteer.[50]

Bones and heads of pigs are found in graves in the Celtic areas, and many boar figures in stone or metal. Some of these might be accounted for by the fact that the boar was the symbol of the Twentieth Legion in the Roman army and so was frequently found on Roman sites, but the typically Celtic beasts are recognisable as spirited and vigorous fighting animals, appropriate symbols for warriors.[51] Boars might be placed on swords and shields (Plate 2c), and warriors wore them as crests on helmets, as can be seen from the Gundestrup Cauldron; they appear on the same panel where marching warriors are shown carrying the *carynx* or war-trumpet, which ended in a boar's head.

A boar for the feast had first to be caught and killed, and this might prove a somewhat perilous enterprise, since according to Strabo (*Geo-*

3 *Hooded men and Mother Goddesses. Top* Three *Genii Cucullati* on a stone from Housesteads on Hadrian's Wall. *beneath* Three goddesses with child, scroll of destiny (?) and bowl, from Vertillum in southern France.

4 *Ancient deities. Left* Stone figure with two faces and leaf crown from Holzgerlingen, Württemberg, over 2 m in height, sixth to fifth century BC?; *right* Wooden figure from Rude Eskildstrup, Denmark, with long robe and neckring, holding square object in lap, 41 cm in height, fifth century AD?

graphy IV, 4, 3) even the ordinary pig bred by the Celts was noted for its height, ferocity and swiftness, sometimes proving a match for a wolf (Plate 2a). There are accounts of boar hunts in both Welsh and Irish literature in which the strength and fury of the quarry reach mythological proportions, as in the description of the Twrth Trwyth in the *Mabinogion*, and the wild boar of Benn Gulbán in 'The Death of Diarmait'. Evidently many such tales were known, since on one occasion Finn recites to his hound a list of great boars killed on expeditions in the past.[52] In the Welsh Triads there is mention of a gigantic sow called Henwyn (Ancient White One), one of seven pursued by Arthur.[53] She brought forth wheat, barley grain and bees on her journeyings, and seems to symbolise the other aspect of the pig, that of fertility, while the grain and honey suggest the drink brewed for the feast. On the other hand, she also gives birth to dangerous creatures associated with slaughter, a wolf, a fierce eagle and a cat. In Spain, large figures of boars in stone were set up by the Celto-Iberians beside their hilltop settlements, perhaps intended to bring prosperity to their herds of pigs.[54] One strong indication of the association of the boar with a Celtic deity is the small figure in sandstone from Euffigneix in France.[55] This is a male figure wearing a neckring, with a fine crested boar carved on his chest, and a large staring eye on one side of the body. It stands 30 cm in height and seems to have been set up with the lower part of the stone in the earth. The estimated date is the first century AD.

Joints of pork and the heads of pigs have been found in Germanic graves of the pre-Christian period. One early cremation urn from Saxony had a boar on the lid,[56] and the boar seems to have had some association with the dead in the fifth and sixth centuries AD. It was also a favourite symbol for kings and warriors, and two magnificent shoulder-clasps from the Sutton Hoo treasure are decorated with two crested boars which form an intricate and effective pattern. There are boars on the eyebrows of the helmet from the same grave, throught to have been of Swedish craftsmanship, and boars were certainly popular in Sweden in the Vendel period, from about AD 600 to 800. Helmet plates from the ship graves at Vendel show warriors with immense boar crests on their helmets, and one man wearing what is almost a boar mask, with huge protruding tusks. The early kings of Uppsala are said to have had great boar helmets as treasures, with names like *Hildisvín* (Battle-Swine). One complete small boar crest on a helmet has survived from a seventh century grave at Benty Grange in Derbyshire; the boar is about 9 cm long, elaborately made with gold spots for bristles and tiny garnet eyes.[57] In the poem *Beowulf* the boar is said to protect warriors who wear it on their helmets, and to keep guard over their lives (305–6),

49

while Beowulf himself wore a boar helmet which it was said no sword could pierce (1453-4). There is an Anglo-Saxon sword with three boar figures stamped on the blade, a parallel to the Celtic example.[58] Another instance of the link between the boar and warfare is the name given to the wedge formation in battle, the Roman *cuneus*, known to Germans and Scandinavians as *caput porci* (boar's head) or *svínfylking* (swine formation).[59]

A man receiving the horn at a feast might make a solemn vow before drinking from it, and in one of the legendary Icelandic Sagas, *Hervarar Saga* (10), as well as in a prose note added to the Helgi poems in the *Edda*, a vow of a similar kind is made with a hand placed on the sacrificial boar. If this was based on actual practice, it was presumably made on the carcase of the boar brought into the hall for the feast. The word used of the boar in the saga is *sónargǫltr*, literally 'boar (*gǫltr*) of the herd', and the boar sacrifice had the name *sónarblót*, and was said to be associated with divination.[60] The boar on which men made vows was said to be offered to Freyr, and a golden boar is known as a symbol of the Vanir deities, Freyr and Freyja. Snorri in *Skáldskaparmál* (33) describes this as one of the treasures of the gods, forged in precious metal by the dwarves and adorned with bristles of shining gold: 'He could run through air and sea by day or night, outdoing any horse, and however dark the night or the realms of blackness, there was ample light in his path from the shining of his bristles'. The little boar on the Anglo-Saxon helmet from Benty Grange has his bristles picked out in gold, and as Miranda Green points out, it is the dorsal bristles, rather than the tusks, that are emphasised in Celtic iconography when the boar is represented.[61] She suggests that this might be to stress the ferocity of the beast, but it might also be based on the link between the boar and the sun. The realm of blackness was the underworld, and the boar could carry the goddess Freyja there when she wanted to gain special knowledge, as we learn from the poem *Hyndluljóð* in the *Poetic Edda*; here her human lover Ottar takes on the form of her boar so that she can take him down with her to learn the names of his ancestors. After discovering his genealogy, Ottar drank the ale of remembrance, which may imply a link between the boar and the *minni* drunk at the feast in honour of dead ancestors, and thus with the Vanir deities also. In his rapid journey through the sky into the lower world, the boar shining so brilliantly must surely be a symbol of the travelling sun.

The boar has remained a traditional dish at Christmas in parts of Sweden and Denmark up to recent times, and in Scania a salted pig's head with trotters and tail used to be placed on a flat loaf, and kept until the first ploughing after Christmas, when it was shared between the ploughman and his horses.[62] John Aubrey mentioned the boar's head as a popular Christmas dish in England until the early seventeenth century, and it continued to be introduced in a special ceremony at Queen's College, Oxford, a custom going back at least as far as the fourteenth century.[63] At a more popular level, a boar's head was wrestled for and afterwards eaten in a public house at Hornchurch in Essex in the nineteenth century.[64] Thus the tradition of a link between the boar and the midwinter feast continued in folklore and popular tradition over a long period, even if it might be difficult to prove continuity for such customs from pre-Christian times.

The bull was an important cult animal in northern Europe, and also in Mediterranean countries from a very early period. Its head was a favourite symbol on metal cauldrons of the Roman period in Denmark and Britain. [65] There is a vigorous scene on the base of the Gundestrup Cauldron which shows a man with dogs attacking a bull, and this corresponds with the description by Julius Caesar (*Gallic War* VI, 2) of the hunting of the great bull, the aurochs, by young Germans, who used to trap the animal in a pit and then go down to kill it as a test of valour. It may also be noted that the great 'standard' from the Sutton Hoo ship grave has four bulls' heads on the corners, presumably chosen because of symbolic significance. Celtic figures of bulls, particularly those from Gaul, are often depicted with three horns, presumably to emphasise the horned head as a power symbol, while knobs placed on the ends of the horns may be another expression of this, or to emphasise a link with the Other World.[66] It seems that the bull, like the boar, might be associated with the sun, and a metal mount in the form of a bull's head from the grave of the Frankish king Childeric had a sun-symbol on the forehead, the place where a third horn could be set.[67]

The slaying of the sacrificial bull, like the boar, could provide an opportunity for divination. The Irish *tairbfeis* (bull feast) was said to include the eating of the bull's flesh and drinking of the blood, after which the man who had partaken would sleep on the bull's hide in order to dream of the future king (p. 143 below). As there were mighty boars from the Other World, so too there were legendary bulls of enormous strength and power. The celebrated Brown Bull of Cúailnge died after conquering his rival, Findbennach (White-Horned), and these two splendid and terrible beasts are said to be swineherds from the *Síd*, reborn in animal form.[68] There are a number of Welsh and Irish tales in which Otherworld cattle emerge from a lake or come out of a fairy mound; they are usually white with red ears, a type of early British cattle still preserved in a few places in Britain. A similar tradition is preserved in Scandinavian folktales; one from Denmark tells of a merwoman whose cattle used to come out of the sea to graze, and these were coralled by the local people, who demanded a ransom for them. The merwoman paid this, but she took her revenge by telling her bull to churn up the sand and ruin the fields, while she paid the people in fairy gold which did not last.[69] There are also examples of cattle in Norwegian folktales who come out of the mountains, and in *Eyrbyggja Saga* (63) we have the tale of a sinister grey bull whose offspring caused the death of the farmer Thorodd. This is an interesting example, since the bull was born to a cow which had licked the ashes of the fire which burned the body of the evil character Thorolf, who had been active after death; it is possible that we have Irish influence here. In another major saga, *Laxdæla Saga* (31), a supernatural woman refers to a sagacious bull which was able to find grazing for the other cattle in winter as her son (p. 138 below). This bull had two extra horns, one of which is said to have grown out of his forehead and then curled down below his eyes, and this he used for breaking the ice in winter, so that here we have an independent piece of evidence for the link between the extra horn and the powers of fertility.

Cattle formed a major source of food for the Germanic peoples. When Bishop Mellitus came to England in 601, Bede tells us that he was directed by Pope Gregory to replace the pagan feasts at which men sacrificed to devils by some kind of 'devout feasting' suitable for Christians to take part in. This was to take place outside the new churches, and those who came to the feast could put up temporary wooden shelters, according to the *Ecclesiastical History* (I, 30). Stow in the sixteenth century reported a find of a heap of ox-skulls on the south side of St Paul's in London, and assumed that a Roman temple had stood there, but these might have been relics of Anglo-Saxon feasts of the kind mentioned by Gregory. A huge heap of such skulls was found at Yeavering, in the building thought to be a temple (p. oo above), and another collection is recorded from Harrow Hill.[70] Such piles of skulls could represent cattle killed at a series of feasts over the years, a grisly record like the great turtle shells kept as records of Victorian banquets. Occasional ox-skulls are reported from Anglo-Saxon graves, and there are examples of ox-skulls or whole cattle buried in Celtic areas, both in burial sites and as ritual deposits.[71]

When a traveller in Denmark in the Viking Age saw cattle hanging up outside the house in which sacrifices had taken place, this probably means that the meat was eaten at a feast, while the hide, perhaps with the head, horns and hooves attached, was set up as a record (p. 37 above). This was a practice which can be traced back to very early times in northern Europe, and it has been kept up by some of the peoples of the Steppe within recent memory. As late as 1805 the hides of horned creatures killed were presented to the church in one remote district in Sweden until the bishop objected to what appeared to him to be a heathen custom, while the Lapps used to offer the hides of reindeer to the churches in the early days of their conversion to Christianity.[72]

The bull sacrifice in Viking times appears to have been associated both with Thor and with the Vanir deities of fertility. A bull was reputed to have been sacrificed at the annual Assembly at Thingvellir, over which Thor presided as guardian of law, and the sacred ring on which oaths were sworn was immersed in the blood of the sacrificed animal.[73] In *Viga-Glúms Saga* an ox was offered to Freyr in an attempt to gain his support, and Freyr gave a sign that he accepted the sacrifice, with disastrous results for the fortunes of the hero (p. 138 below). According to *Egils Saga* (65) the winner of an official duel sacrificed an ox to the gods as a thank-offering for victory. However in Scandinavia in general the stallion seems generally to have replaced the bull as a symbol of power and virility.

The horse in its turn was an animal which could be associated with the journeying sun, and it was an important religious symbol in the North from the Bronze Age onwards, A horse could carry a departed hero to the realm of the dead, and is shown doing this on many of the memorial stones set up in Gotland in the Viking Age. Like Freyr's boar, Odin's horse travelled swiftly through the sky and down into the realm of death. In the first century AD, the sacred horses of the Germans were held to understand the will of the gods more clearly than their priests could do, according to Tacitus, so that they were used for divination (p. 150 below). The Celts seem to have associated horses with the gods in the pre-Roman period, since they were shown along with birds of prey in the great sanctuaries of southern France (p. 28 above). The cult of a goddess Epona (Divine Horse) flourished in eastern Gaul and on the German frontier, and was known in Britain; the goddess is shown with horses and foals, sitting astride or riding side-saddle or seated with a horse on either side of her. She has been identified with Macha in the Irish tales, a woman from the Other World able to outrun the king's fastest horses, and also with the Welsh Rhiannon.[74] Like the boar and the bull, the horse was a powerful symbol both for fertility and for warfare.

The impressive White Horse cut in the chalk hillside at Uffington in Oxfordshire has been claimed as a Celtic monument, because its curved shape resembles the fantastic horses on Celtic coins. However there is no proof that this figure existed before the arrival of the Anglo-Saxons, and its present shape can scarcely be deliberate, since the original outline is distorted by water draining down the slope. It has been claimed that

53

earlier traces of a more realistic horse can be made out below the present one.[75] A white horse outlined on the chalk hill might be expected in either an Iron Age or an Anglo-Saxon setting, since the horse served as a powerful religious symbol for both peoples.

It seems that horse sacrifice was more developed among the Germanic peoples than the Celts. Horses were not included in the wagon burials of the Hallstatt period, although the harness might be left in the grave. They could be sacrificed with their riders after a victory (p. 62 below) but do not seem to have regularly formed part of the sacrificial feast. Only one horse tooth was identified at Llyn Cerrig Bach, the lake in Anglesey into which offerings were thrown, although admittedly this collection of bones was not thoroughly examined.[76] References to horses on stakes are found occasionally in the Irish tales, which might be a memory of horse sacrifice, and there is one late account of the killing of a white horse in the writings of Giraldus Cambrensis.[77] He declares that he heard of a tribe in Ulster which celebrated the inauguration of a new king by a strange and shocking ceremony. The king entered on all fours in the presence of the people, approached a white mare and acted the part of a mating stallion. The mare was then killed, and the flesh cooked in a cauldron; the king bathed in the broth, drank from it, and ate some of the flesh. There are some grounds for taking this account seriously, although it seems improbable that such a ritual could take place in Christian Ireland in the twelfth century. There are noteworthy parallels: the bull sacrifice, when a man drank or bathed in the broth, the horse sacrifice in Norway in the Viking Age, when the king was required to partake of the broth in which the horse was cooked (see below), and the Hindu rite of the *asvamedha* in India.[78] This is the subject of a hymn in the *Rigveda*, for which we possess a Brahmanical liturgical commentary; the queen is said to approach a stallion which has been sacrificed, representing the universe, and simulate the act of copulation with it. It is possible that Giraldus was here using some oral tradition, remembered vaguely from the past, and it is even conceivable that this was influenced by memories of the horse sacrifice performed by Vikings in Ireland.

In German and Scandinavian countries horses were killed on many occasions as part of the funeral ceremony, for there are a number of horse skeletons at the great ship-burials of Norway and Sweden, and horses were buried in many pre-Christian cemeteries on Germanic territory. Ibn Fadlan's account of a ship-funeral on the Volga in the tenth century (p. 18 above) includes the killing of two horses, which were first made to gallop and then cut to pieces with swords and thrown into the ship which was to serve as a pyre for the dead chief. A horse might be buried with the dead either in the same grave or separately, and could be seen as a necessary part of a warrior's equipment. However a detailed survey of horse-burial during the first millenium AD in Prussia and Sudovia made by Jaskanis in 1966 shows the danger of generalisation in such matters, since among horse-breeding peoples who lived in the same area it was possible to sacrifice horses in a variety of ways at the funeral. They are found in both cremation and inhumation graves, and in a number of cases those buried with horses were neither warriors nor people of wealth and importance. The horses might be buried in separate graves, sometimes in one section of the cemetery, and some were killed before burial, others apparently buried alive. Sometimes only heads or teeth were found, or part of a horse harness without the animal. Jaskanis emphasises close similarities between German, Scandinavian and Baltic material, and parallels among the nomad peoples of the Steppe, but it is clearly impossible to draw neat conclusions from the wide variety of practices. The increased popularity of horse sacrifice in the Viking Age may be due to influences from eastern Europe.

Horses certainly formed part of ritual feasts held at Skedemosse on the island of Öland in the Baltic in the third and fourth centuries AD.[79] This site was once a lake, and a vast number of objects had been thrown into the water. It seemed from traces of scorched earth, charcoal and burnt bones that fires were lit on the shore of the lake and feasts held there, after which the remains were tipped into the water. The largest number of bones, about thirty-five per cent, were those of horses, with smaller numbers from cattle, sheep and goats, and a small number from pigs, deer and dogs. Animal remains from contemporary settlements on the island, however, give a different picture; here the animals most used for food were sheep and cattle, and horses were comparatively rare. At Skedemosse hides, heads, legs and tails of horses and cattle were sometimes found together, as if set up for cult ceremonies (p. 52 above). The name Skedemosse is thought to be formed from *skeid*, which could be used either for a fight between stallions or a horse-race, and it has been suggested that races took place on the long ridge near the lake, or that horse-fights were held there, to decide which animals should be killed and which kept for breeding. No signs of blows were found on the bones, and the animals may have been stabbed to death.

The *Heimskringla* of Snorri Sturluson has a description of a horse sacrifice at Trondheim in the saga of Hakon the Good (14), in which the Christian king was forced to take part against his will. The source of Snorri's information is not known, but the account is a fairly detailed one. The king had been brought up in England as a Christian, and his usual practice at feasts was to eat privately with a few companions, but on this occasion the people insisted that he take a full part. They wanted him to sacrifice for good seasons and peace as his fathers had done, and he was forced to comply. Sigurd, the Jarl of Halogaland, presided, and hallowed the first bowl in the name of Odin. The king made the sign of the cross over it, but the Jarl tactfully explained that he was making the hammer sign in honour of Thor. On the second day the horse sacrifice was prepared, and when the king refused to eat the meat or drink the broth, Sigurd urged him to touch the greasy handle of the cauldron with his lips, but the king put a linen cloth over it before doing so, and the people were not satisfied. Later the midwinter feast took place, and again a horse was sacrificed; this time the king agreed to eat a little of the liver and to drink from the *minni* bowls. It was evidently important that he should consume some of the blood of the slain horse, since on this the wellbeing of the land depended. In spite of his Christian scruples, Hakon was a popular king, for the land was prosperous during his reign; in the poem composed at his death in 961 he was warmly praised for the respect he had shown to the holy places, and was represented as being welcomed as a hero into Odin's hall after his last battle.[80]

4 Varieties of sacrifice

Other animals were certainly sacrificed, but were not of the same importance in the sacrificial feasts. Rams and goats were said to be offered to the gods at Hedeby (p. 37 above); goats, whose bones cannot always be distinguished from those of sheep, were no doubt popular as an inexpensive form of sacrifice, and the tale of Thor's goats eaten for supper and then restored to life by the hammer of the god (p. oo above) suggests an established tradition of goat sacrifice. A goat's skull was found in a special grave at Yeavering, at the entrance to hall A4, and it may be noted that the British name Yeavering would mean 'Hill of the Goats'.[81] The ram was a significant figure in Celtic art over a long period, and some deities are shown with rams' horns, while ram-headed serpents are a favourite motif, an example of the linking of symbols for fertility, healing and the underworld.[82]

The stag may have served as a sacrificial victim in forest areas, and its importance in early times is indicated by the small bronze wagon from a grave mound at Strettweg in Austria, depicting what could be a ritual hunt, with a central figure of a goddess towering above riders, and escorting two stags. Cunliffe suggests that such processions on small wagons were symbols of the death journey,[83] and certainly the hunt is used in funeral symbolism both in Mediterranean areas and in northern Europe up to the Viking Age. In the later Middle Ages kings and nobles delighted to hunt the stag, and there was an elaborate ceremonial connected with its slaying, but little is known of its importance as a cult animal in pre-Christian times. The tradition of the king's hall, Heorot (hart) in *Beowulf*, decorated with antlers, and the little stag on the royal whetstone sceptre from Sutton Hoo, possibly of Celtic origin (p. 128 below) point to the stag as a possible royal symbol.

Dogs appear to have had much significance for the Celtic people, so much so that Miranda Green places them together with horses and bulls as one of the three most important domestic animals with a sacred significance.[84] The dog is associated in Mediterranean areas with healing, hunting and death, and these rules seem to have been recognised by the Celts, and also to a lesser degree by the Germans and Scandinavians. Dogs were linked with the Mother goddesses, and in particular with Nehalennia; in the many representations found at her two shrines in Holland, she invariably appears with a dog as her companion. Dog figurines have been found at various Celtic shrines, as at Lydney.[85] and votive figures of children with dogs, perhaps for sacrifice, come from healing shrines. There are dog skeletons in ritual shafts and deposits, and similar evidence for sacrifice from Germanic territory, the most elaborate example being from Mannhagen in Holstein, where the skulls of twelve dogs were found with the skull of a horse and that of a man.[86] Dog skeletons, sometimes several at a time, are found along with those of horses and cattle in the great Scandinavian ship-burials of the Viking Age, and both large hunting dogs and smaller breeds in individual graves.[87] In Irish tradition there was a close link between the guarding or hunting dog and the wolf, both being used as symbols for young warriors.[88] In Scandinavian myth and legend the dog is the guardian of the underworld , and one reason for putting a dog into a grave might be to provide a guide for the dead. The baying of the dog Garm provides a kind of chorus for the events leading to Ragnarok in the poem *Vǫluspá* (p. 190 below), and again it is hard to distinguish between Garm and the wolf Fenrir, who breaks loose at the time of destruction; it may also be noted that a dog or a wolf appears on a number of Gotland memorial stones of the Viking Age depicting the arrival of a dead hero in Valhalla.[89]

Birds offered a cheap and convenient form of sacrifice, as when cocks were offered by Scandinavian merchants on their way to Byzantium (p. 36 above). Remains of birds have been found in cremation urns and inhumation graves from the Bronze Age, and bird skeletons were included in the great ship-burials of the Viking Age, The symbol of water-birds such as ducks and swans, and of wading marsh-birds was important for early Celts, and they play a prominent part in the art from the Hallstatt period, and in the Bronze Age preceding it. The symbol of the bird of prey was also one of significance for the Continental Celts, emphasised in the pre-Roman sanctuaries of southern France (p. 28 above). The raven and crow in particular were associated with Lug and the war goddesses in art and later literature; in one Irish tale Cú Chulainn kills one black bird out of every flock when seeking to avenge himself on Cú Roí.[90] The war goddesses themselves could appear in the form of crows or ravens, and here we have a parallel with the Norse valkyries (p. 96 below). Ravens and hawks were closely associated with Odin, and cocks sacrificed at Lejre, according to Thietmar of Merseburg, were substituted for hawks. Birds, like the main cult animals, were linked both with battle ritual and with fertility rites, and observation of their cries and movements was one method of learning the future (p. 86 below).

The shedding of the blood of the victim formed an important part of the sacrificial rite, and the term *rjóða* (redden) occurs frequently in Icelandic poetry in connection with sacrifice. In *Hyndluljóð* (10) a sacrificial place called a *hǫrgr* was set up by a worshipper of Freyja out of doors, and this was said to have been reddened with blood until it shone like glass. The word used for the blood of the sacrifice was *hlaut*, and this in the account of the horse sacrifice at Trondheim (p. 55 above) was sprinkled on walls and altars, splashing those at the feast. In *Eyrbyggja Saga* (p. 32 above) Thorolf kept a bowl of *hlaut* in Thor's shrine by Helgafell, and blood from this was sprinkled on the walls. It has been suggested that this was based on the use of holy water in Christian churches, but an instructive parallel may be seen in the customs of bear-hunters in southern Scandinavia and Finland. As late as the nineteenth century the hunter would sprinkle himself and his family with the blood of the slain bear, and put some of it on his house and the trees around, while the hunters also drank some of the warm blood; Ström notes that the blood of slain oxen was put into coffee in more recent times.[91] These appear to have been protective measures, to avert the ill-luck which might otherwise be brought on those responsible for the slaying. In an early *Life* of King Olaf Tryggvason, the heathen Swedes are mocked at because they lick their offering bowls, suggesting that it was felt important to consume the blood of the sacrifice.[92] Such blood was frequently said to have been used to redden runes in order to discover the will of the gods (p. 148 below).

5 Human sacrifice

Besides the regular feasts which marked the course of the year, there were gatherings held at longer intervals, when a more impressive sacrifice took place and human victims as well as animals were sacrificed. These might be on special occasions such as times of danger, as a thanksgiving after victory, or at the funeral of a king. In the eleventh century Adam of Bremen in his history (IV, 27) refers to a sacrifice of animals and men held every ninth year at Uppsala in Sweden, when the bodies of the victims were afterwards hung on trees by the temple:

It is the custom moreover every nine years for a common festival of all the provinces of Sweden to be held at Uppsala. Kings and commoners one and all send their gifts to Uppsala, and what is more cruel than any punishment, even those who have accepted Christianity have to buy immunity from these ceremonies. The sacrifice is as follows: of every living creature they offer nine head, and with the blood of those it is the custom to placate the gods, but the bodies are hanged in a grove which is near the temple; so holy is that grove to the heathens that each tree in it is presumed to be divine by reason of the victim's death and putrefaction. There also dogs and horses hang along with men. One of the Christians told me that he had seen seventy-two bodies of various kinds hanging there, but the incantations which are usually sung at this kind of sacrifice are various and disgraceful, and so we had better say nothing about them.

This festival was said to last for nine days, with one human victim offered daily along with one of each species of animal or bird. It might be expected that the total of victims would be nine times nine, or eighty-one, but perhaps Adam's informant was counting only the animal victims when he gave a total of eight times nine. The sacrifice was made at the beginning of summer, the time traditionally associated with offerings made to Odin in return for victory in the coming season. Thietmar of Merseburg, unfortunately not a very reliable informant, wrote later of a similar sacrifice held at Lejre in Denmark every ninth year, and gives a figure of ninety men offered along with horses, dogs and cocks 'to the power of the Underworld'.[93] Thietmar may simply have been echoing Adam of Bremen, but evidently knew of some tradition of multiple sacrifice connected with Odin and the underworld. Occasional glimpses of gruesome sacrificial places in which much killing had taken place are afforded by the Greek and Latin historians. Tacitus describes the visit of Germanicus to the Teutoburgian Wood where Varus and three Roman divisions had been wiped out by the Germans some years earlier (*Annals* I, 61):

The scene lived up to its horrible associations ... A half-ruined breast-work and shallow ditch showed where the last pathetic remnant had gathered. On the open ground were whitening bones ... Fragments of spears and of horses' limbs lay there – also human heads, fastened to tree-trunks. In groves nearby were the outlandish altars at which the Germans had massacred the Roman colonels and senior company-commanders.

59

Survivors of the catastrophe told ... of all the gibbets and pits for the prisoners. (Michael Grant's translation)

Among the Celts also we hear of mass sacrifices organised by the druids, and Diodorus (V, 61) refers to special sacrificial ceremonies held every five years.[94] Posidonius mentioned the slaughter of human victims, and how those who presided over the ritual observed the last convulsions of the dying, an important method of divination (p. 63 below). It seems likely that Germans and Scandinavians relied on information learned from their strangled victims in the same way, since in a verse of the poem *Hávamál* Odin claims that by his skill in runes and magic spells he could cause a hanged man to walk and talk with him. Valuable knowledge, it appears, could be acquired from a man who died a violent death.

Accounts by Strabo and Julius Caesar also mention large figures of wickerwork into which victims were placed to be burned. Strabo (IV, 4) describes such a construction as 'a colossus of straw and wood', into which cattle, wild animals of various kinds and human victims were thrown, adding that the ashes helped the growth of crops. Caesar (*Gallic War* VI, 16) refers to '... figures of immense size (*immani magnitudine simulcra*) with limbs woven out of twigs, filled with living men and set on fire so that the victims perished in a sheet of flame'. Strabo probably got his information from Posidonius, and he does not make it clear whether the victims were burned alive, but Caesar has no doubts about this. It is difficult to know how to interpret these horrific accounts. It would not be easy to make a great upright wickerwork figure such as seventeenth century antiquaries pictured,[95] and keep it upright while it burned. It was suggested by scholars studying the origins of the Wilmington Giant in the last century that this or some similar hill figure was known to Caesar and that he had heard reports of the burning of victims associated with it.[96] No signs of burning in or near the figure have been discovered, however, in recent investigations, and there would be practical difficulties in its use as an enclosure for victims. Some kind of upright wickerwork construction, on the other hand, might have been used if the sides were covered with incendiary material, as was done in the French Pyrenees at the midsummer ceremonies at the end of the last century. One is described as about 6 m high, 'shaped like a mummy or perhaps a cigar set on end', and an Englishman who watched the ceremony of the Brandon in Basque country in 1890 was told that in the past snakes, toads and even apes had been put into it, and thrown back into the flames when they tried to escape.[97] Frazer gives similar examples from this area and other parts of France, and mentions cases of cats burnt in wicker cages in the same horrible manner, in the midsummer bonfires.[98] Sometimes the carcase of an animal was burnt after killing it, as was done sometimes with an ox or bull at the summer festival in Ireland.

Burnt sacrifices of some kind certainly seem to have taken place among both Celts and Germans. Julius Caesar (*Gallic War* I, 47) left a circumstantial account of a narrow escape from death by a young man well known to him, Valerius Procillus, who was captured by the Germans after being sent as an envoy to Ariovistus, and treated as a prisoner of war. Lots were cast three times to decide whether he should be burned to death immediately or reserved for a later sacrifice, but luckily for him the result was against instant death, and later during a Roman attack he escaped in the confusion and was able to rejoin his own men.

Both Celts and Germans are represented as taking men found guilty of crimes to be offered as sacrifices, together with captives taken in war and slaves. According to Strabo (IV, 4) the druids acted as judges in cases of murder, and if many men were found guilty of death, this was thought to ensure a good season, since it meant there would be plenty of victims for sacrifice. Julius Caesar (VI, 16) confirms this: 'They believe that the execution of those who have been caught in the act of theft or robbery or some crime is more pleasing to the immortal gods; but when the supply of such fails they resort to the execution even of the innocent.' (Loeb translation) The practice of using wrongdoers for sacrifice is recognised also in Norse literature. According to Snorri, King Olaf Tryggvason threatened to introduce new sacrifices if the people refused to give up the old religion, and his victims, he declared, would not be slaves or criminals, as was customary:[99] 'I shall not choose thralls or evildoers, but those selected as a gift for the gods will have to be the most distinguished men.' In *Kristni Saga* (12) it is again stated as a recognised fact that 'the heathen sacrifice their worst men'. Although these are late Christian sources, they show how heathen sacrifice was remembered in Scandinavia.

It is not easy to determine from the archaeological evidence whether men have been deliberately sacrificed, or condemned to death by their fellows without any appeal to the gods, and Ström and others have doubted whether criminals were ever sacrificed in Germany.[100] Isolated bodies of men and women have been found in the peatbogs of Denmark and northern Germany, and in some cases the victims have been bound, mutilated or blindfolded, or have nooses round their necks, but Ström has argued that these could be victims of vengeance or summary justice rather than offerings vowed to the gods. Amira, on the other hand, argued that later penalties imposed on criminals, such as hanging, were sacrificial in origin.[101] A survey of the bodies from the peat bogs shows us that it is dangerous to select and generalise, for it is highly unlikely that the reasons for the killings were the same in every case. Struve sensibly argued that the dead should not be assumed to be sacrificial victims unless they were accompanied by animal bones, signs of burning, and other indications that the killing may have been a ritual one, in a spot dedicated to supernatural powers.[102] It is obviously difficult to draw a firm line between executions and sacrifices, since certain crimes, such as sacrilege, were held to provoke the anger of the gods. Accounts of Christian missionaries on the Continent being put to death for cutting down holy trees or baptising in sacred springs give some ground for regarding such executions as cases of sacrificial killing, for in some cases the victims were chosen by lot so that the gods could decide which of the Christians should die (p. oo below).

When captives were taken in war, a proportion of them might be offered as a thanksgiving for victory, sometimes in fulfilment of an earlier vow. In extreme cases a considerable number of men seem to have been put to death. Tacitus (*Annals* XIII, 57) gives an outstanding example in an account of fighting between two Germanic tribes, the Hermundari and the Chatti, over possession of a tract of land beside the river which divided their territories, regarded as a holy place (p. 25 above). They vowed to sacrifice their enemies to Mars and Mercury, the Germanic equivalent of which would probably be Tîwaz and Wodan. When the Hermundari were victorious, they felt bound by their vow to sacrifice 'the entire beaten side with their horses and all their possessions'. This was early in the first century AD, and in the fifth century Orosius (V, 16) ascribes similar behaviour to the Cimbri, a tribe from Jutland who may have been either Celts or Germans, in 105 BC: 'In accordance with a strange and unusual vow, they set about destroying everything which they had taken. Clothing was cut to pieces and cast away, gold and silver were thrown into the river, the breastplates of the men were hacked to pieces, the trappings of the horses were broken up, the horses themselves drowned in whirlpools, and men with nooses round their necks were hanged from trees.'

In spite of such vivid descriptions, such accounts might not carry conviction were it not for convincing evidence from the deposits in the Danish peat-bogs, where objects have been well preserved in votive deposits of the Roman and Migration periods. Piles of valuable booty, including weapons and armour, were found arranged in some kind of order, and human as well as animal bones indicate that living victims were sometimes offered in the way early writers describe. Weapons and other objects were deliberately damaged by being bent or burned before being laid down in the marsh or thrown into pools. At the major offering places such as Nydam and Skedemosse on Öland repeated offerings seem to have been made, representing the spoils of several battles. These might be mixed, as at Skedemosse, with offerings of food or a share of the communal feast. Sometimes, as at Illerup in Denmark, we seem to have a single deposit of the arms of about seventy warriors, presumably from one battle.[103] At Ejsbøl one area seemed to represent the equipment of a whole warrior band, as at Illerup, while another had objects suggesting a date of about a century later, and there were also some non-military offerings. Sometimes, as at Nydam and Ejsbøl, remains of swords of outstanding quality seem to have been set apart from the rest.[104] Evidently there was considerable variety in the way in which the offerings were made, and the length of time for which a special area was in use. The main period for such votive offerings was from the third to the sixth century AD, and in some cases we do not know whether those who made them were Celts or Germans. Julius Caesar in his *Gallic War* (VI, 17) describes offerings of a similar kind made by Celts in Gaul:

> To Mars, when they have determined on a decisive battle, they dedicate as a rule whatever spoil they may take. After a victory they sacrifice such living things as they have taken, and all the other effects they gather into one place. In many states heaps of such objects are to be seen piled up in hallowed spots, and it has not often happened that a man, in defiance of religious scruple, has dared to conceal such spoils in his house or to remove them from their place, and the most grievous punishment, with torture, is ordained for such an offence. (Loeb translation).

It is doubted now whether the finds from La Tène (p. 5 above) were an offering of this kind, as the objects may have been lost in a flood. A number of weapons and belongings of fighting men, however, were recovered from Llyn Cerrig Bach in Anglesey in 1943,[105] and seem to have been thrown into the water about the first century AD. Other weapon finds were made in the nineteenth century, but unfortunately only the valuable objects were kept and there is no record of how they were deposited. More recent work on such finds is of great value in telling us more about these sacrifices, and how they may have been linked, as at Skedemosse, with communal feasting.

The proportion of captives sacrificed after a battle evidently varied, and some attempt was made to discover the will of the gods as to how many should die, as in the case of Valerius Procillus (p. 61 above). Part of the value set on sacrifices of men and animals depended on their use in divination rites, since men attempted to discover what the future would be by observation of the death of the victim or by examination of the

63

corpse after death. Procopius in the sixth century (VI, 15, 24) stated that in Thule, which is presumably Scandinavia, the most valuable sacrifice was judged to be that of the first captive taken in battle, who would be put to death by hanging, impaling on thorns, or some other unpleasant method. The significance of this rite must have been to discover what the result of the battle would be by the manner in which the victim died. Hanging was one way of disposing of the victim, particularly among the Germans, and in the Viking Age it was a method of sacrifice associated with the cult of Odin. Strabo (IV, 4) refers to the impaling of victims by the Celts, and Dio Cassius (62) mentions the cruel treatment of Roman ladies by Boudicca, who had them impaled in the temple as offerings to a goddess. The Cimbri, generally thought to be a Celtic tribe, staged a gruesome divination ritual when prisoners of war were brought into the camp, according to Strabo (VII, 2, 3). They were met by priestesses, grey-haired women in white robes, who consecrated them for sacrifice, and then were hung up above an enormous bronze bowl. One of the women climbed a ladder and cut the throats of the victims with a sword, so that the blood flowed into the bowl and she could judge from observing it what the result of the fighting would be. Other prisoners were disembowelled, presumably for the same reason. Tacitus, describing Boudicca's revolt of AD 61 (*Annals* XXX, 30) remarks that it was a part of the native religion 'to drench their altars in the blood of prisoners and consult their god by means of human sacrifice'.

Lots were sometimes taken to decide which prisoners should die, as with the cocks which Scandinavian merchant-adventurers took with them on their journey down the Dnieper to Constantinople (p. 36 above). Such a practice was described to Julius Caesar by one of the victims who escaped (p. 61 above), and there are other examples to be found in literary sources. In the eighth century *Life* of St Willibrod, the Christian missionaries in Heligoland were threatened with death after the saint committed sacrilege by baptising men in a holy spring and killing sacred cattle. Lots were cast three times a day for three days to decide the victims, but the saint himself escaped with his life (III, 47). A letter of Sidonius deplores the cruel custom of Saxon pirates, who would offer one prisoner in ten to the god of the sea as a thank-offering for a successful voyage. He admits however that they feel pledged to make their offering in fulfilment of a vow: 'These men are bound by vows which have to be paid in victims. They regard it as a religious act to perpetrate their horrible slaughter. This polluting sacrifice is in their eyes an absolving sacrifice.'[106] It is evidently necessary to take into account the fulfilment of a solemn vow among the other reasons which prompted human sacrifice.

When criminals or prisoners were not available, slaves might be used as victims, and archaeological evidence gives the impression that they were occasionally killed at funerals in the Viking Age and buried along with a master or mistress. Ibn Fadlan's well-known account of the sacrifice of a slave girl on the Volga in 921[107] tells how one of the slaves volunteered to die, and for the period before the funeral she was treated with great honour, as if she had been the wife of the dead man. The Scandinavians on the Volga whom he encountered may have been influenced by Turko-Tatar or Slavonic customs, and it seems unlikely that the old woman called the Angel of Death, who presided at the killing of the girl, could have been a Scandinavian, brought into Russia by the merchants. The victim on this occasion, however, was killed by strangling and stabbing at the same time, a form of death associated with Odin, while the account of the burning of the ship at the cremation funeral and the ceremonial which Ibn Fadlan describes is in agreement with what we know from archaeological records of ship-funerals in the North. The great ship-burials from Norway and Sweden give indication of elaborate rites in which various animals were killed, while the Oseberg ship contained the bodies of two women, one of whom is assumed to have been an attendant on a lady of rank and importance. Sometimes in Viking Age graves and also in graves of the early Anglo-Saxon period in England a second body has been found lying in a grave as though thrown in with little ceremony, and there are occasional references to slaves killed at funerals in Iceland in *Landnámabók*.[108]

Although children's graves are sometimes found in enclosures marking holy places, there is little evidence in the literature of either Celts or Germans sacrificing children to the gods. The exposure of unwanted infants at birth, or the throwing of them into the sea (p. 37 above) has no clear connection with sacrifice; it was a recognised form of keeping down the population and probably of disposing of the offspring of slaves. There are references to the sacrifice of children to a pagan idol in Ireland. The idol is called Crom Cruach and the sacrificial rites are referred to in the *Dindsenchas* (IV, 18–23):

> For him ingloriously they slew their wretched firstborn with much weeping and distress, to pour out their blood round the Bent One of the Hill.
> Milk and corn they used to ask of him speedily in return for a third of their whole progeny; great was the horror and outcry about him.

This seems, however, to be little more than an antiquarian fantasy, and the picture of child sacrifices could have been based on Biblical traditions about the god Moloch.[109] Old Norse literature also has references to kings and leaders sacrificing their sons in order to win a favourable response from the gods. The extreme example is that of Aun of Uppsala, said to have reigned for a long period in Sweden as a result of the policy of sacrificing a son to Odin every ten years. Snorri tells the story in *Ynglinga Saga* (25), but the poem about Aun which he quotes has no reference to sacrifice, only to Aun's extreme old age when he died.

It is implied in both Irish and Norse sources that kings were offered to the gods before the coming of Christianity. A number of legendary kings in Scandinavia are said to have been put to death because the harvests were bad, and some of these were burned in their halls. Others are described as perishing by strange and violent deaths. An Irish king, Muircertach, was said to have been drowned in a cask of wine while his enemies set fire to the hall.[110] Similarly the Swedish Fjolnir, a descendant of Freyr ruling in Uppsala, is said to have drowned in a great vat of mead; his death is briefly mentioned in a poem, and Snorri seems to have elaborated this into a circumstantial tale of how after heavy drinking the king got up in the night to relieve himself and fell through the floor into a vat below.[110] Dumézil claimed that the three forms of sacrifice by hanging, stabbing and drowning were associated with three types of gods, but the evidence for this is not very convincing.[111] Complicated deaths from more than one cause may be introduced as the unexpected fulfilment of a prophecy, a well-known folktale motif; the extreme example of this being the slaying of Lleu in the tale of Math in the Welsh *Mabinogion*. Since he could not be slain either in a house or out of doors, either on horseback or on foot, he met his death with one foot on a cauldron with a roof above it and the other on the back of a goat. Such traditions however may be viewed as puzzle tales, some of which have a didactic Christian meaning and tell how a ruler who had broken the Church laws is finally punished,[112] and they can hardly be relied on as echoes of pagan practice. There is however a well-established record of victims sacrificed to Odin being strangled and stabbed at the same time. There seems also a possibility that death by drowning, a sacrifice to the waters, was once a form of sacrifice linked with the gods of fertility.

It is necessary to remember that in dealing with this kind of evidence we are concerned with confused material from poetry and legend which may also have been worked on afterwards by learned writers or romancers. This also applies to accounts in later writings of a king being put to death by the carving of a 'blood-eagle' on his back as a sacrifice to Odin.[113] Each separate source must be examined on its own merits before reaching a general conclusion, and we must be cautious in accepting such material as reliable evidence for pre-Christian practices. There are episodes in Irish tales of a king being killed by a spear at the assembly at Tara, but this gives us no reason to assume that the king was therefore ritually killed there at regular intervals. Kings were frequently murdered by their enemies or rivals, and it might sometimes be felt expedient to sacrifice a king in return for victory or to end a series of bad harvests. In *Ynglinga Saga* (15) Snorri tells us that this is what happened to the Swedish king Domaldi:

> The first year [of the famine] they sacrificed oxen, and there was no improvement in the harvest. The next autumn they sacrificed men, but the harvest was as before or even worse. And the third autumn many Swedes came to Uppsala when the sacrifice was to take place. The chiefs took counsel then, and decided unanimously that the famine must be due to their king Domaldi, and that they must sacrifice him for a good season and redden the altars with his blood, and this they did.

Snorri's evidence for this is apparently a poem by Thjodolf, and the verse which he quotes states that all this happened 'long ago'. The poem, composed in the ninth century, confirms Snorri's presentation of the killing of the king as an unusual act, brought about by desperation at a series of crop failures:

> Eager for harvest
> the Swedish people
> offered up their king . . .

One story long remembered in both Iceland and Denmark is that of the sacrifice of King Vikar, who was singled out by the casting of lots when he had decided to offer a human sacrifice in return for a favourable wind.[114] When he was selected, he decided to make it a mock sacrifice, in which he arranged a simulated hanging from a tree and stabbing with a spear. However through the prompting of Odin, a dedicated follower of the god, Starkad, made sure that the killing was a genuine one, and that the king was hanged and stabbed at the same time. Again, however, the event is singled out as an exceptional occurrence, and it was indeed regarded as one of Starkad's great crimes that he slew his king and leader. There is no indication in this or other tales that a regular ritual sacrifice took place after the king had reigned for a certain number of years.

Indeed from the rich field of evidence available, the pattern which emerges is that sacrifice at a feast was a regular feature in every community, and the killing of animals and human victims also a possible expedient in times of danger, when there was urgent need for help and protection from the gods. In the Norse poem *Hávamál*, which gives counsel to the man who wishes to prosper on earth, he is urged to visit the friend whom he trusts regularly, to share his thoughts and plans with him, and to exchange gifts with him as a token of their friendship. This might also summarise the relationship of men with their gods; if they trusted them, they needed to frequent the holy places, seek help and guidance, eat and drink in their honour and make regular offerings in return for luck and protection. Success against one's enemies and the gaining of sufficient food to maintain oneself and one's family were the two essential requirements in the precarious lives of the warrior peoples of north-western Europe, and it was these basic needs which prompted their sacrificial rituals. In return for victory and good harvests they must be prepared if necessary to make costly offerings, and promises made to the gods must be kept when their prayers were granted. The gods were honoured and perhaps held to be strengthened by the brewing and drinking of the festival ale, and by the slaughter of victims whose blood would bring new potency to the holy places. Also the means of communication with the Other World which sacrifice provided enabled men to obtain some of the hidden knowledge the gods possessed. The killing of sacrificial victims was associated with omens and divination, and one purpose of the sacrificial feast was to learn what was in store for the community in the coming season.

The organisation of sacrifices must have depended largely on the power of the priesthood, since it might include elaborate ceremonial and impressive ritual. The account of a ship-funeral in the tenth century which has survived by chance through the presence of Ibn Fadlan on the Middle Volga gives some indication of how elaborate and moving such rituals may have been (p. 65 above). It is noticeable that women often play an important part in the actual slaying of the victims and in the interpretation of omens, both in accounts of ceremonies among the Celtic peoples and in the Viking Age. There is not much evidence for a strong organised priesthood in Scandinavia by the tenth century, and little indication of much human sacrifice in the Viking Age, although in certain centres such as Uppsala sacrifices continued until the end of the pagan period. Out of the established ritual of the offering of living creatures in sacrifice arose a series of powerful and varied religious symbols, which enriched Celtic and Germanic art. Sacrificial rituals held the community together, gave men certain fixed points in the year to which to look forward, and enabled them to meet in time of need and to unite in thanksgivings for benefits received. Complex and scattered although the evidence may be, there is no doubt of the significant part which sacrifice played in the early religion of north-western Europe up to the acceptance of Christianity.

68

III The rites of battle

When I stand in the midst of the battle,
I am the heart of the battle,
the arm of the warriors,
when I begin moving at the end of the battle,
I am an evilly rising flood,
when I follow in the wake of the battle,
I am the woman (exhorting the stragglers):
'Get going! Close (with the enemy)!'

Hymn of the goddess Inanna
(Jacobsen, *The Treasures of Darkness*, p. 137)

Clearly the elaborate sacrificial ritual of the Celts and Germans was not prompted solely by a desire for fruitful crops and prosperity at home. A large proportion of their rites appear to have been used to obtain luck in battle and victory over their neighbours. This is hardly surprising for peoples famed for their achievements in war and successes in raiding and plundering, in times when competition for land and rivalry between tribes posed constant threats and problems. The feast held regularly at the beginning of summer seems to have been associated consistently with sacrifices for victory in coming campaigns, at the time of year when raiding parties set out, invasions were planned, and viking fleets took to sea. Part of the offerings laid out in holy places or thrown into sacred lakes was made up of booty taken in battle, which was voluntarily handed over to the powers held to govern victory in war. In the Viking Age, men put great trust in battle ritual and consultation of omens to tell them when to fight and what the results of an encounter would be. There were many spells available for warriors in tight places, like those mentioned in the poem *Hávamál* in words attributed to Odin:

I know a third: if I should have great need of shackles to put on my adversaries, I can blunt the edges of hostile weapons, and their blades and staves will do me no harm. (148)
I know an eleventh: if I lead my old friends to battle, I will chant

beneath my shield, and they will go forward with power, safe into battle and safe out of battle again; they will come away free from harm. (156)

Many stories in the Icelandic sagas illustrate the need for such battle magic. An outlaw fighting valiantly against odds in Iceland, for instance, was seized with momentary paralysis so that he could not use his limbs. This meant that the dreaded 'shackles', held to be the result of hostile magic, had taken hold on him, as described in *Harðar Saga* (36): 'Then 'war-fetters' (*herfjǫturr*) came upon Hord, and once and a second time he cut himself free. The war-fetters came upon him a third time, and now the men managed to hem him in and he was surrounded by a ring of enemies.' Such tales are linked with the traditions of battle-spirits and war-goddesses, to be considered later. Norse literature has preserved also a wealth of legends associated with the spear and the sword, and the splendid exploits of Odin's heroes. Battle magic cannot be kept distinct from the worship of the gods, or from the practice of sacrifice. This aspect of religion was sufficiently important to leave an indelible mark even on the literature of medieval Iceland, where there were no kings to keep up the cult of Odin, no standing army or regular training of warriors. We should know much more about battle ritual had there been the same enthusiasm for recording tales and poems in Norway, Sweden and Denmark, and if more than a single fragment of an heroic poem, *Hildebrandslied*, and one early battle spell had survived from Germany.

Weapons and armour recovered from graves or places of offering in Germanic and Celtic territory bear many symbols based on beliefs concerning luck in battle, and these show a marked continuity from the Iron Age to the Viking Age. They are such as were held to afford protection to the wearer and user, to invoke the aid of supernatural powers, strengthen a warrior's arm and give him courage, as well as guide his instinctive reactions at the time of testing. The chief cult animals offered in sacrifice – boar, bull and stallion – were all powerful fighters and were associated with the battlefield, while so also were wolves and ruthless birds of prey who feasted on the dead. Powerful deities were invoked and feared for their dominion over the fortunes of war. Funeral monuments to leaders killed in battle and poems describing the fall of heroes are particularly vivid in evocation of mythological beliefs linked with battle ritual. Memories of supernatural figures linked with fighting, still charged with something of their former power, give strength and imaginative vigour to the legendary tales of Ireland and Iceland. They indicate how important this aspect of religious ritual must have been in the days when Celts, Germans or Vikings presented a constant threat to their neighbours.

1 The taking of heads

From accounts going back to the second century BC it is evident that the pursuit of enemy heads was something in which Celtic warriors exulted. Posidonius is very definite about this:[1]

> They cut off the heads of enemies slain in battle and attach them to the necks of their horses. The blood-stained spoils they hand over to their attendants and carry off as booty, while taking part in a triumphal march[2] and singing a song of victory; and they nail up these first fruits upon their houses, just as do those who lay low wild animals in certain kinds of hunting. They embalm in cedar-oil the heads of the most distinguished enemies and preserve them carefully in a chest.

This is something distinct from sacrifice, and there is no mention of dedication of the heads to the gods. The customs here described might be seen as an initiation test for young warriors, an attempt to gain power by possessing the head of a courageous enemy, or simply the proud parading of a trophy, since the comparison is made with the setting up of the heads of animals. On certain Roman monuments such as the Arch of Orange (probably erected in the first century BC) Celtic warriors are shown with human heads hanging from their saddles, as described above, and Reinach claimed that some are also carrying scalps.[3] The Romans are said later to have forbidden the practice.[4] A mounted warrior holding a head is shown on a carved stone in the Entremont

6 Pillar from Celtic sanctuary at Entremont, Provence with carvings of human heads.

sanctuary, and the repeated emphasis on severed heads in sacred places certainly suggests some religious basis for their preservation.

At Entremont in particular the statues of what Benoit assumes to be ancestors in the sacred way were depicted in the squatting position, with an iron weapon, perhaps a thunderbolt, in the right hand, and the left hand placed on top of a severed head, with closed or half-closed eyes. Similar heads were carved on pillars, and other pillars had a skull-shaped niche with a hook inside on which a skull might be suspended.[5] Twenty skulls found in the sanctuary or on the sacred way seem to be trophies, probably the result of battles with the Romans, who finally destroyed the site and left it in ruins. Livy (X, 26, 11) stated that skulls were sometimes decorated and used for solemn libations in the temples of the Celts, while according to Posidonius the heads of valorous enemies were so highly valued that the owner of such a treasure might boast that he had refused to sell it for its weight in gold.[6] The head appears to have been regarded as an object of power, bringing luck and strength into a house or increasing the holiness of a sanctuary. A further reason for valuing a severed head might be its association with the practice of divination, suggested by the part played by speaking or singing heads in Irish tales.

The veneration of the human head as the seat of consciousness and wisdom and as the representation of a deity seems to have been important for the Celts from early times. It might be viewed as a development from the abstract symbolism of the Bronze Age in the North.[7] A pillar from Pfalzfeld in Germany of about the fourth century BC is thought originally to have had a carved head on top, a mask-like face with a 'leaf crown' like a smaller example from Heidelburg.[8] Later in the La Tène period heads and faces are included in the decoration of coins, bowls and weapons.[9] Severed heads on chains with a larger head which might represent a deity appear on coins of the pre-Roman period in Gaul. There are many surviving stone heads, some of considerable size, and in many cases the eyes are closed, as if severed heads were the inspiration behind them. Some stone heads have two or three faces, and as many as thirty examples of this were recorded in France in 1954.[10] Some have a hollow on top of the skull, as if intended for libations. Many stone heads have been found in Britain in recent years, but they are very hard to date, and some indeed may be as late as the nineteenth century. Clearly the production of such carved heads is not confined to the Iron Age, but there are some striking examples known to date from that period, such as heads from Roman sites at Corbridge and Gloucester.[11]

While the 'exaltation of the head', as Lambrechts called it, leads on to such questions as the representation of deities and the commemoration of ancestors, there is no doubt that the preservation of *têtes coupées* was an important part of Celtic battle ritual. To gain a head, it was necessary to kill an enemy single-handed, and this is brought out in many vivid stories of encounters and battles in the Irish sagas. Conall's wife in 'Bricriu's Feast', for instance, boasted that her husband returned proudly from battle carrying heads in his hands. Cú Chulainn took an enormous number of heads in his various contests, and in the same tale, when he was guarding the stronghold of Cú Roí, and was threatened by unknown intruders, he beheaded them all: '... Cú Chulainn sprang at them, then, and nine of them fell dead to the ground. He put their heads into his watch seat, but scarcely had he sat down to watch when another nine shouted at him. He killed three nines in all and made a single heap of their heads and goods.'[12] Cú Roí later received the heads and war-gear of twenty-seven men from the hero and put them into the centre of the house, together with the head of a monstrous sea-beast which was also slain in the course of the night. Since Cú Chulainn had collected all these trophies while keeping watch, it was decided that he had earned the champion's portion at the feast. In another tale he was attacked by two young men in chariots, and cut off the heads of both together with those of their drivers; he fitted them on to a fork of wood to carry them away, leaving chariots, horses and blood-stained bodies behind.[13]

This ferocious aspect of head-hunting is summed up in the boastful words of another hero, Fergus, after he had lost his sword:[14] 'If I had my sword today, I would cut them down so that the trunks of men would be piled high on the trunks of men and arms of men piled high on arms of men and the crowns of men's heads piled on the crowns of men's heads and men's heads piled on the edges of shields, and all the limbs of the Ulstermen scattered by me to the east and to the west would be as numberless as hailstones.' It is echoed again in the account of the fearful slaughter wrought by Cú Chulainn to avenge the boy-troop, when it is said of his enemies:[15] 'They fell, sole of foot to sole of foot, and headless neck to headless neck, such was the density of the carnage.'

Such accounts of the furious fighting of the Celts were not without foundation. A heap of bodies was left beside the gate of a hill fort in Gloucestershire, Bredon Hill, thought to have been captured and then deserted by the Romans, which bear the marks of savage conflict and decapitation. When it was excavated in 1935–7, a group of about fifty headless skeletons was found, most of them young adult males.[16] Their heads had been severed, and their legs, arms and hands in many cases hacked off, apparently soon after death. Some of the skulls had been set up on a gate or some similar structure which was afterwards set on fire. The laconic account of the excavators bears out the frenzied descriptions in the *Táin*, and the cleaving off of the head, often by a cut through the jaw, was evidently part of the deliberate and savage mutilation of the vanquished. While the bodies might be abandoned, heads and weapons were usually carried off as booty, and in some cases treated with honour. A head might be brought to the feast celebrating the victory, when food and drink might be offered to it, according to the tales, and sometimes such a severed head placed on a pillar or spike in the hall is said to speak or sing.

When words were uttered by a severed head on the battlefield, these were usually part of a prophetic utterance or a command which men would be bound to heed. A good example is that of the head of Sualtam, the father of the hero Cú Chulainn, after he had failed to persuade the men of Ulster to go to his son's help.[17] He rode away in anger, and then his horse suddenly reared and his head was cut off by his own shield. The horse galloped back to the Ulstermen, and the head then uttered the same words as he had spoken to them before his death. Conchobar thereupon swore a solemn oath to call out the army and to go to the assistance of Cú Chulainn without delay.

The most detailed account of a head singing at a feast is the tale of Donn Bó in the Battle of Allen, from the Yellow Book of Lecan.[18] A battle was fought between Fergal, king of northern Ireland, and King Murchad of Leinster, whose territory Fergal invaded. The Leinstermen were victorious, and Fergal and many of his followers were killed. At the feast held after the victory, the king asked that someone should go to the battlefield and fetch a man's head, for which he would pay a rich reward. A man named Báethgalach went to where King Fergal lay, and as he drew near he could hear a voice commanding the musicians and poets on the battlefield to make music and to sing for their lord. Then came music unsurpassed in sweetness, and the head of Donn Bó began to sing for Fergal. Donn Bó was a youth famed for his skill in story-telling and song, who had been unwilling to sing for the king on the night before the battle but had sworn to make music for him the following night, no matter where they might be. Báethgalach asked if he might take the head of Donn Bó to the hall, and the head consented, if he promised to bring it back afterwards and lay it on his body.

The head of the minstrel was carried to the feast and placed on a pillar in the hall. All recognised Donn Bó, and grieved for the loss of the finest minstrel in Erin. Then the head turned towards the wall where it was dark, and sang a lament, and so sweet was the song that none could refrain from weeping. Aterwards the head was taken back and replaced on Donn Bó's body, and because Columcille had promised the youth's mother that he should return to her unharmed, it was joined to his body again. Later King Fergal's head was also taken and carried to the hall of King Cathal of Munster, who was angry at Fergal's slaying because he had made a truce with him. He treated the head with much honour: 'Then Fergal's head was washed and plaited and combed smooth by Cathal, and a cloth of velvet was put around it, and seven oxen, seven wethers and seven bacon-pigs – all of them cooked – were brought before the head. Then the head blushed in the presence of all the men of Munster, and it opened its eyes to God to render thanks for the respect and great honour that had been shown to it.' Afterwards Cathal took the head back to Fergal's people, and it was buried among them.

Another memory of the setting up of a head to preside over a feast is found in the tale of the death of Bran in the Welsh *Mabinogion*. Bran is thought to have been an early Celtic deity, and he is said in 'Branwen, Daughter of Llyr' to be so huge that no house could contain him. After he had been wounded in battle by a poisoned spear, he told his men to cut off his head and carry it with them, 'and the head will be as pleasant company as ever it was at best when it was on me'. During the years of their travels, the head of Bran presided over their feasts; the eighty years spent at Gwales was known as 'The Assembly of the Wondrous Head', for under its influence they forgot all their sorrows. Finally the head was buried at the White Mount in London with its face turned towards France, guarding the island as long as it remained there.

The motif of the enormous head at a feast suggests the representation of a god, and the head of a slaughtered hero, was said in one tale to be huge enough to hold four men.[19] Beside their connection with feasts, severed heads are associated with wells and springs, and Anne Ross gives a number of examples from Irish heroic and folk tales.[20] Men are said to be beheaded beside wells, and sometimes their heads left behind, while in saints' tales severed heads are again linked with wells which possess healing properties. The link between water and the severed head certainly survives in folk tradition and has long persisted in the British Isles.

It may be noted that the pursuit of enemy heads was not a practice confined in Europe to the Celtic peoples. Strabo in his account of head-hunting (IV, 5) notes that this barbarous custom was to be found among most of the northern tribes. It was evidently established among the Thracians of eastern Europe, and in the fifth century Herodotus (IV, 63f.) describes in unpleasant detail the methods used to preserve and decorate the skulls of enemies, and how to strip off the skin and make it into a kind of cloth which the victor could fasten to his bridle as a trophy. The Thracians also collected scalps and even made cloaks from them, while the skin from the right arms of slain enemies was utilised to make covers for their quivers. A man who possessed no trophies of this kind was much despised and was not permitted to drink with the chief at the annual feast, but those who could show that they had killed many enemies were allowed two cups, and drank from both at the same time. Beheaded warriors have been found in Sarmatian graves as late as the third century AD,[21] and on Trajan's Column human heads are shown mounted on Dacian ramparts.

The setting up of heads as trophies was familiar also in the Germanic world. In Tacitus' detailed account of the visit of Germanicus to the Teutoburg wood where three Roman divisions had been destroyed six years earlier, the bodies were found lying where they fell, while human heads were fastened to tree-trunks (p. 59 above). Pope Gregory the Great in the sixth century referred to holocausts of severed heads among the Alamanni.[22] In the tenth century Leo the Deacon, the Byzantine historian, was present at the Emperor John's campaign against the Rus in Bulgaria in 970, and was shocked when the head of a Greek commander was mounted on a spear and set up in a tower in the besieged town of Dristra.[23] In the Anglo-Saxon poem *Beowulf* the hero fastened the severed arm of Grendel on the wall of the king's hall, and later brought back the monster's head together with a splendid sword, just as Irish warriors took back heads and weapons after a kill. Grendel however was no ordinary fighting man, and in medieval literature the severing and display of a head is often set in the legendary world, used as a method of dealing with monsters or with the over-active dead.

In Norse literature men are frequently beheaded in battle or as an act of vengeance after being taken prisoner. In the famous account of the execution of the Jomsburg Vikings, one man speculates whether he will remain conscious after his head is off.[24] Earlier traditions of speaking heads may have influenced such episodes in the sagas as that of a man being killed while counting silver, whereupon his head utters one more number as it is cut from his neck.[25] The idea of a head demanding vengeance is brought out in the tale of a woman who digs up her husband's body and carries his head to the man whom she hopes will avenge him; she whips the head out from under her cloak at the appropriate moment, and utters the bitter words: 'This head would never have held back from demanding vengeance for you, had it been needful.'[26] In *Svarfdœla Saga* (23) the valiant Klaufi, treacherously killed and walking after death, had his head cut off to stop his activities, but he continued to appear carrying his severed head and even using it as a weapon: 'He struck with his bloodstained head in both hands fiercely and often, and ... men began to run away; it was as if a fox had got among a flock of sheep.'

In a prophecy of fighting to come in *Njáls Saga* (133), a supernatural figure seen in a dream conjures up a picture of severed heads on the battlefield: 'Heads in plenty / will be seen on the earth ...'. On another occasion, a severed head even utters a verse. In *Eyrbyggja Saga* (43) a skull lying on a line of scree called Geirvǫr where a battle was later to take place was heard speaking:

Red is Geirvor
with men's blood.
She will kiss
human skulls.

Both these examples come from sagas which show a particular interest in pre-Christian traditions concerning the supernatural world. A similar image, however, is found in a dream recorded not long after the events described in *Sturlunga Saga*.[27] Among a series of dreams before the Battle of Örlygsstaðir (p. 140 below), there was one dreamed by a woman who saw a man she knew sitting on the wall of a deserted cattle-pen looking at a man's head which was lying on the ground inside; she heard him speak a verse asking her why the head was there.

There is also a vague tradition of Odin consulting the head of Mimir. According to *Ynglinga Saga* (4), Mimir was one of the Æsir who was beheaded by the Vanir when they held him as hostage, and his head was sent back to Odin: 'Odin took the head and smeared it with herbs so that it would not rot, and spoke spells over it and wrought magic so that it spoke with him and told him many hidden matters.' This may be Snorri's own interpretation of the lines in *Vǫluspá* which state briefly that Odin speaks with Mimir's head before Ragnarok. In the poem Mimir is the guardian of the spring into which Odin casts an eye in return for hidden knowledge, and 'Mimir's head' may be an image for the spring itself, taken literally by Snorri.[28] However, as Jacqueline Simpson has pointed out, there is a tradition in both English and Norwegian folktales of a speaking head which rises from a well and can provide gifts and good fortune for those who treat it with reverence.[29] In any case, the brief, almost casual, reference in *Vǫluspá* makes it unlikely that we have a borrowing here from Irish tradition. Snorri may have been drawing on a different use of the head in his account, that of preserving it to use for consultation and magic purposes. Such a use of the head of a dead person – either a drowned man or a child, it is said – is found in an Icelandic folktale recorded by Jón Árnason. Thorleif the wizard had it in a chest, and when his wife looked in she was terrified by the head addressing her and warning her against meddling with her husband's property.[30]

The power of a severed head and its ability to speak after separation from the body is evidently not confined to Celtic tradition, although it has been elaborated in Irish literature to an unusual degree. Among the Germanic peoples the conception of the hanged man as a means of acquiring hidden knowledge seems to have gained more prominence. However there are plenty of carved heads and mask-like faces, some of terrifying force, to be found in Scandinavian art. Heads of men or monsters, some realistic and some fantastic, may be carved on wooden terminals, as on the ninth century Oseberg sledge. Giant heads are depicted on a sword hilt made from an elk antler from Sigtuna and again on a furnace stone from Denmark. Earlier than this we have the so-called 'mantic faces' on early Anglo-Saxon brooches, and stylised masks with staring eyes like that on the pommel of the Coombe sword hilt of the seventh century,[31] while there are faces on the Sutton Hoo whetstone which recall the *têtes coupées* of Celtic tradition (p. ooo below). Earlier still there are fantastic heads on gold bracteates of the Migration Period; these are imitations of the heads of Roman emperors on medallions, but they appear to reflect native tradition in their imaginative power. The importance of the head as a seat of intelligence, together with its use as a battle trophy, bringing luck as well as enhancing the reputation of its possessor, is emphasised in the early traditions connected with warriors and battles among both Celts and Germans, and the conception was sufficiently strong to live on long afterwards in art and legend.

2 Dedicated warriors

The violence of Celtic warriors is echoed in descriptions of the fighting prowess of the Germans. Ammianus Marcellinus (XXXI, 7) refers to the terrible cutting blows of the long swords of the Germans in the Battle of the Willows in AD 176, a favourite stroke being a slicing blow from above which cut through the head of an opponent. The state of men's skeletons in Alamannic cemeteries shows what damage such swords could indeed produce, confirming the grisly descriptions in the literature.[32] An analysis of accounts of battles in Continental sources showed that the strokes most often mentioned were those cutting through the head, the sideways stroke which beheaded a man, and that which cut off an arm or leg.[33] To deal blows of this kind, a warrior had to be in a state of battle frenzy, and this is how the Scandinavians are said to have fought in eastern Europe in the Viking Age; Leo the Deacon describes them dealing sword strokes in a state of madness, howling and roaring like wild beasts, and Arab writers have left a similar picture.[34]

The outstanding example of such ruthless fighting in Scandinavia was that of the berserks. In *Hrafnsmál*, a poem composed about AD 900, they are described as the privileged warriors of Harald Fairhair of Vestfold in Norway, who receive rich gifts from the king because of their fierce fighting qualities. They are also called 'wolf-coats':

> Wolf-coats are they called, those who bear swords
> stained with blood in the battle.
> They redden spears when they come to the slaughter,
> acting together like one.

The name *berserkr* may have originated from the wearing of a bearskin in proof of valour, taking the meaning as 'bear-shirt'. The alternative name 'wolf-coat' could similarly be based on the wearing of some symbol of the wolf such as a wolfskin belt; there was a popular tradition in Norway that 'shape-changers', men who turned into beasts at night, would put on a belt of wolfskin before they left the house.[35] There are several episodes in the sagas where a young man in Norway has to prove his strength and courage by tackling a bear single-handed, just as German youths were said to kill an aurochs in a pit as a proof of manhood (p. 51 above).

The bear and wolf were seen as symbols of valiant warriors, and they are familiar images in heroic poetry and saga as well as providing the basis for many personal names. The bear seems to symbolise the lonely champion, fighting in single combat and leading his men. The wolf can symbolise the outlaw, who preys on society, but also the young warrior hiding in the forest, waiting for the opportunity to carry out a deed of vengeance. When the celebrated hero Sigmund with his son Sinfjǫtli prepared to avenge his dead kinsmen on King Siggeir, the two hid in the forest, put on wolfskins and spoke with the voice of wolves.[36] Such tales seem to reflect the training of young warriors by stern and demanding discipline, until they could live like dangerous creatures of the wild. The identification of wolves with young warriors being trained in fighting and hunting skills is deeply rooted in the tradition of various peoples descended from the Indo-European group and found far beyond the limits of Celts and Germans,[37] but among these two peoples it was certainly well established. The Scandinavian berserks are one example of this; they howled and bayed like wolves and fought in bands, and in battle Odin was said to free them from fear so that they became heedless of the threat of wounds or death in battle. Snorri so describes them in *Ynglinga Saga* (6): 'His men went without their mailcoats and were as mad as hounds or wolves. They bit their shields, and were as strong as bears or bulls. They slew men, but neither fire nor iron had effect on them. This is called "to run berserk" (berserkgangr).'

In the literature there are accounts of bands of dedicated warriors like the legendary Jomsvikings, and sometimes lists of the laws governing such communities are given.[38] One long description of such a group, said to be brothers, on an island in Denmark is given in Book VI of Saxo's *Danish History*, and it may be noted that members of the group have names formed from *biǫrn* (bear). The transformation of men into mad creatures fighting like wild animals comes out in many tales of shape-changing, one well-known example being the tale of Biarki in the saga of Hrolf Kraki, who took on the shape of a huge bear and fought furiously in the battle in which his king was slain, while his body meanwhile remained in a state of sleep or trance. Such traditions may well lie behind the figures of bears and wolves shown beside warriors on helmet plates from Swedish or Alamannic graves; some of these are purely animal figures, but others seem to be men with animal heads. They are sometimes accompanied by a naked warrior holding weapons, who seems to represent the battle god Odin or one of his emissaries (p. 88 below).

An intimidating picture of a dedicated warrior of the berserk type who spent his life in the service of Odin is that of Starkad the Old, whose story is told in a number of separate episodes in the late Icelandic sagas and in Saxo's *History*.[39] He is portrayed as an inhuman creature without pity or affection for human kind, scorning those who enjoy feasting and comfort; he is capable of enduring terrible pain without complaint, and of sitting out all night in a blizzard. When he fought, heaps of corpses piled up around him. He was regarded as an outstanding hero, although under the baleful influence of Odin he caused the deaths of two kings whom he served, which according to heroic rules of conduct was the ultimate act of betrayal. Such figures, while exaggerated, were not wholly fictitious. Many centuries earlier, Tacitus knew of similar men among the Chatti, whose duty, like that of the berserks, was to fight in the vanguard of the army and lead the attack against the enemy, and describes them in *Germania* (31):

> Every battle is begun by these men. They are always in the front rank, where they present a startling sight; for even in peace-time they will not soften the ferocity of their expression. None of them has a home, land or any occupation. To whatever host they choose to go, they get their keep from him, squandering other men's property since they think it beneath them to have any of their own, until old age leaves them without enough blood in their veins for such stern heroism. (Mattingly's translation).

Starkad fits this description well enough, and the berserks in the Icelandic sagas appear to live in a similar way, taking the property and women of other men who cannot defend themselves against them.

The heroes of the Irish tales would have been at home in just such a company. While the hero Cú Chulainn had a wife and sometimes enjoyed himself at feasts, he had much in common with Starkad in his stormy wandering life, his ability to go without food or sleep, and his endurance of a series of appalling wounds. Finn and his *fían* or warrior band lived a life separate from the community, as did the berserks. They fought as mercenaries, like the bands of warriors in the Viking Age. Youths who joined them lived throughout the year by hunting and plunder, and had to undergo rigorous tests in hunting skills as well as in fighting ability before being finally accepted. They might, it is said, have to be buried up to the waist and required to defend themselves with only a shield and hazel stick while javelins were hurled at them, or to slip noiselessly through the forest without stirring a twig or ruffling their braided hair while pursued by armed warriors.[40] They were recognised outsiders like the berserks, with the right to rob householders or seize women. Like the berserks also, they had close connections with the animal world. A link with fierce hounds is particularly marked in the traditions concerning Cú Chulainn, and dog names are frequently found among the Irish heroes.[41] One of Finn mac Cumaill's wives was a doe, while his sister's sons were hounds, and he declared that he preferred them that way: 'If I were their father, then I would prefer that they be as they are rather than that they be humans.'[42] He himself sometimes appeared as a man, a dog or a deer according to how he wore his hood. Sometimes women fought along with men in these bands, like the shield-maids of Scandinavian tradition, and young men formed into groups of nine or twelve, like the berserks and warrior companies.[43] We hear also of *diberga*, brigands who might be pledged to kill, like the Germanic warriors, and who might wear some special sign, the *signa diabolica*, which could not be removed until the deed of killing was accomplished.[44]

The resemblances struck some early scholars as so marked that it was suggested by Zimmer that the Fenian hero tales were derived from memories of the Vikings in Ireland, but as Sjoestedt pointed out, the cycle was already popular in the seventh century before the Vikings established themselves there:[45]

It is not by comparison with the Vikings who invaded Ireland in the ninth century that Fenian mythology can be explained, but by comparison with the myths of the *Einherjar*, the chosen of Odin, or with the savage

81

Berserkir, the 'bearskin warriors'. On both sides we find the same violent
life, on the margin of ordered society, the same fury, the same personalities with animal components and the same type of warlike fraternities.

The difficult and dangerous feats required of young warriors are
remembered in the Irish tales, and Cú Chulainn in particular is pictured
as the ideal dedicated warrior on the heroic scale. We are told much of
his training and youthful deeds. As well as more than holding his own
with his peers in ball-play and wrestling, and keeping off outsiders who
attacked the territory, he won the right to his name, Hound of Culann,
by overcoming the fierce and terrible hound who guarded the cattle and
taking his place. This is the equivalent of the solitary contest with a wild
beast of which we hear elsewhere as a test of manhood. Next he receives
arms, on a day of good omen for such a ceremony, and on another day is
given his chariot, receiving the good wishes of those he meets. After this
he has encounters with hostile warriors, and hunts deer and birds. Then
comes the episode in which his heroic fury is cooled by the warriors
seizing him after he had been halted by a company of women with naked
breasts, and plunging him into water (p. 84 below). This, as McCone
has pointed out, could be viewed as the final rite of initiation, signifying
his return as a fully mature warrior.[46]

3 Feats and skills

Cú Chulainn also possessed a series of skills of which he was master, all
with elaborate names, whose exact meaning has puzzled scholars. A
literal translation of the list given in 'The Feast of Bricriu' is offered by
Henderson: 'Over-breath feat, apple-feat, sprite-feat, screw-feat, cat-
feat, valiant-champion's whirling-feat, barbed spear, quick stroke, mad
roar, heroes' fury, wheel-feat, sword-edge-feat, climbing against spike-
pointed things (or places) and straightening his body on each of them.'[47]
In 'The Wooing of Emer', Cú Chulainn learns various feats from
accomplished teachers, and a similar list is included. Domnall the
Warlike taught him the feat called 'the pierced flagstone', which he had
to perform above the bellows that blew up the smith's fire until his soles
were blackened and discoloured. The most effective and dangerous of
his feats however were learned from Scáthach, the woman warrior who
instructed the greatest champions. These included the use of the *gáe
bulga*, a kind of barbed spear sent through water which rendered him
practically invincible, since there could be no adequate defence against
it. On one occasion Cú Chulainn was said to be so engrossed in
practising his feats as not to realise that he was being attacked: 'No blow
or thrust reached Cú Chulainn in the wild excitement of his feats.'[48]

After this statement, a list of feats is given once more. As the heroic traditions were increasingly distorted by later story-tellers, so the feats of the hero grew more fantastic, so that we find him poised on a spear-point, or making a 'salmon's leap' over an enormous area to come down on his enemies from above.

In Germanic and Norse literature, the main emphasis is placed on the skills of sword-fighting. Technical terms may be used, as in the Anglo-Saxon poem *Waldere*, and there are occasional accounts of sword strokes used in duels in *Beowulf*, as well as in Saxo's *Danish History*. Saxo gives an account of how a king trained his warriors to be expert with the sword (VII, 250, p. 228): 'Some of them became so adroit in this remarkable exercise of duelling that they could graze their opponent's eyebrow with unerring aim. If anyone at the receiving end so much as blinked an eyelid through fear, he was shortly discharged of his duties and dismissed from court.' In another passage he describes the method of duelling, which was to strike blows in rotation (II, 56, p. 54):

> They did not try to exchange a rain of blows but hit at one another in a definite sequence, with a gap between each turn. The strokes were infrequent but savage, with the result that it was their force rather than number which won acclaim. Precedence was given to Agner because of his higher rank, and the account has it that he gave a blow of such might that he clove the front of Biarki's helmet, tore the skin on his scalp and had to let go of the sword which was stuck in the vizor-holes. When Biarki's turn came to strike, he braced his foot against a log to get a better swing to his sword and drove the knife-edged blade straight through Agner's midriff. (Fisher's translation).

Delight in relentless strokes of this kind comes out in quotations from fragments of lost heroic poems from Denmark or Iceland (VII, 252, p. 229): 'Let the first slash break our foe's shoulder-blades, then the steel rip off his two hands . . .'

There are references to other austerities and endurance tests which formed part of a Scandinavian warrior's training. In *Hrólfs Saga kraka* (39) the king and his men are exposed to intense heat in the hall of the Swedish king at Uppsala, and Odin himself underwent a similar torment, according to the prose introduction to the poem *Grímnismál*. This might be compared with Cú Chulainn's performance on hot stones. Warriors might also be forced to endure intense cold; Starkad allowed himself to be almost buried in snow when he sat uncomplaining on a mound in a blizzard, and again there is a resemblance to the toughness of Cú Chulainn who sat naked in the snow.[49] The inference here appears to be that the heat of the hero in his battle fury was

83

sufficient to melt snow and ice. We are told of the Ulstermen who sat outside Ailill's hall in 'The Intoxication of the *Ulaid*' that their heat was such 'that the snow softened and melted for thirty feet on every side'.[50]

The berserks howled when going into battle, and Cú Chulainn was said to scream hideously when he put on his helmet and prepared to go out to kill his enemies: 'Then he put on his head his crested war-helmet of battle and strife and conflict, from which was uttered the shout of a hundred warriors with a long-drawn-out cry from every corner and angle of it.'[51] The rage of battle transformed the hero into something monstrous and inhuman. A kind of spasm is said to overcome him so that his body was twisted and his face distorted, explaining why one of his names was the Distorted One:[52]

> He became horrible, many-shaped, strange and unrecognisable ... He performed a wild feat of contortion with his body inside his skin. His feet and his shins and his knees came to the back; his heels and his calves and his hams came to the front ... His face became a red hollow (?). He sucked one of his eyes into his head so deep so that a wild crane could hardly have reached it to pluck it out from the back of his skull on to his cheek. The other eye sprang out on to his cheek ... The torches of the war-goddess, virulent rain-clouds, sparks of blazing fire were seen in the air above his head with the seething of fierce rage that rose in him.

It was said that 'the hero's light' rose from his forehead, and a straight stream of dark blood went up from his head to dissolve into a dark magical mist, like 'the smoke of a palace when a king comes to be waited on in the evening of a winter's day'. On another occasion Cú Chulainn was said to swell like a bladder blown up, so that he became huge,[53] while the heat from such accesses of rage was so great that he had sometimes to be plunged into a series of vats of cold water to restore him to a normal state, as after his first raid as a young warrior: 'Then the warriors of Emain seized him and cast him into a tub of cold water. That tub burst about him. The second tub into which he was plunged boiled hands high therefrom. The third tub into which he went after that he warmed so that its heat and its cold were properly adjusted for him.'[54] It has been suggested that such warrior fury is reflected in the distorted faces sometimes found in the art of the La Tène period. There is a frowning face from Czechoslovakia of about the second century BC with pursed-up features,[55] and in a completely different style, a harness fitting in metal from northern France showing a series of faces with one large and one tiny eye recalling the description of the hero in his rage (Fig. 7).[56] Distorted faces also appear on Celtic coins.[57] It is possible that the so-called 'leaf-crowns' which surmount the heads of some

84

early stone figures might have suggested the idea of the mysterious 'hero-halo', or been an attempt to represent it.

Welsh heroes in the *Mabinogion* are described as though endowed with fantastic powers and strange and hideous characteristics. Of Arthur's warriors in 'Culhwch and Olwen', one is said to be as ugly as the devil and covered with hair like a stag; another could burn down any obstacle with the intense heat which came from the soles of his feet; and another could drink up the sea on which three hundred ships were sailing and leave a dry shore. Their achievements were like those of gods or giants, and such descriptions, partly humorous, seem to be attempts to express the wild fury and abnormal strength and heat of a warrior in the frenzy of battle. The Welsh Cei had powers of endurance like Starkad and Cú Chulainn; he could breathe under water for nine days and nights or go without sleep for a like period, while the hero of the Anglo-Saxon *Beowulf* could endure for many days and nights in the sea in a great swimming contest (506f.).

Such feats and skills were learned from teachers, who might be of the Other World. Cú Chulainn's teacher, Scáthach, has a name suggesting a link with the realm of the dead, since *Scáth* means 'shadow' or 'phantom.' She was said to be a woman chieftain, behaving much as do the valkyries in Norse literature, training and instructing the young hero, giving him an invincible weapon, the *gáe bulga*, and foretelling his destiny. He was encouraged to take her daughter as a lover. In the Icelandic sagas there is a series of tales about giantesses who help young heroes in the same way, first fostering them and then welcoming them as lovers.[58] They may give them valuable weapons, and after the youths return to the normal world, their giant 'brides' may still come to their help if called upon (p. 96 below). The young hero Sigurd the Volsung in the poem *Sigrdrífumál* is taught battle-spells and runic lore by a valkyrie. One of Saxo's heroes, young Regner, is in Book II of the *History* helped and advised by a figure from the Other World called

7 Distorted faces on metal tube from harness fitting, probably from northern France, third century BC?

Svanhvita; she gives him a sword, battles with monsters on his behalf, and reveals her beauty to him out of clouds and darkness (p. 114 below). The battle god Odin himself presents weapons to his chosen heroes and teaches them spells to use in battle. He gives a wonderful sword to Sigmund and a horse to Sigmund's son Sigurd, and is said in a poem to come aboard Sigurd's ship to teach him runic spells and counsel him how to avenge his father.[59]

The great weapons of the heroic past were said to have supernatural origins. Some famous swords were reputed to have been forged by Weland, the underworld smith, or by skilful dwarves under the earth. Sigmund's sword was plunged by Odin into a tree trunk and only the chosen hero was able to pull it out, just as the sword of Arthur was said to have been pulled from a stone in the churchyard by the destined king. The sword Tyrfing, forged by dwarves, was represented in Hervarar Saga as a sinister weapon which could only be sheathed when it had human blood on it, and was doomed to cause a man's death each time it came from the scabbard. This was a family treasure, recovered from her father's burial mound by the courageous girl Hervor, but doomed to bring destruction upon her descendants. In Germanic and Norse legends swords frequently form a link between generations and are used as symbols of destiny.[60] On the Irish side also supernatural weapons are used by the heroes. The *gáe bulga*, the spear given by Scáthach to Cú Chulainn, may have been based on memories of the barbed spear of the Continental Celts as has been claimed, but in the *Táin* it becomes a weapon of incredible, sinister power used in water, which cannot miss its victim. It was said to enter a man's body and then to open out into thirty barbed points 'and it was not taken from a man's body until the flesh was cut away about it'.[61]

Beside skill in fighting and endurance of hardships, the ideal warrior was possessed of special inspiration and secret knowledge. Sigurd the dragon-slayer attained widom by eating part of the dragon's heart, which gave him understanding of the speech of birds so that they could give him warning of danger. The Irish Finn mac Cumaill gained the ability to compose poetry by tasting the flesh of a salmon from the River Boyne, nourished on nuts from the Otherworld well of wisdom (p. 180 below).[62] The links between the young warrior and the poet are significant.[63] Understanding of the speech of birds could give a hero entry into the world of ravens and valkyries, where defeat and victory were ordained, or in more everyday terms it could mean an ability to interpret calls and movements of birds and thereby receive warning of future events. Such aspects of bird lore are referred to in the *Edda* poems, and in the ninth century *Hrafnsmál* the stanzas form a dialogue between a raven and a valkyrie. She is said to account herself wise because she understood the language of birds, and is herself described as 'the white-throated one with bright eyes', which suggests that she herself was in bird form. Goddesses, as well as Odin himself, travel in the form of birds, and the same is true of the battle-goddesses of Ireland. One bears the name Badb (Crow), while the Morrígan, an ominous figure who encounters Cú Chulainn in various shapes, is called Battle Crow (*an badb catha*). Cú Chulainn once sees her as a crow on a bramble bush and takes this as an ill omen: 'A dangerous enchanted woman you are!', he exclaims.[64] It is as a crow that she settles upon his shoulders at his death, while she perches on a pillar in bird shape to warn the Brown Bull to leave Ulster.[65]

References to bird omens in the literature are not usually detailed, being mostly restricted to vague rules such as that it is a good omen to meet a dark raven on the road, as in the poem *Reginsmál* (20). No doubt they were far more complex in earlier times, but we are limited to a few memories retained in popular tradition. A note in a Middle Irish manuscript in Trinity College, Dublin, lists the various cries of the raven which indicate that visitors are approaching, and attention is paid to the number of calls, the position of the bird, and the direction from which the calls come.[66] Young warriors must have been trained in such skills; in *Rígsþula* the language of birds is among the wisdom taught to a young prince, and when the poem breaks off he is being instructed by a crow as to what his next move shall be. Two birds on a tree warn the young hero Sigurd against the wicked smith, and appear on carvings of the tenth century in the British Isles, considerably earlier than the literary sources of the tale.[67] In a prose note to *Reginsmál* they are called nuthatches, and there seem to be a number of them; in one verse they refer to themselves as 'we sisters', which suggests they are valkyries in bird form. However the earlier tradition of a pair of birds makes it possible that originally they were the ravens of Odin.

Various rituals and techniques must have been employed to rouse the ferocity of warriors before battle. In the eighteenth century the suggestion was made that the berserks made use of the 'magic mushroom', the fly agaric, to stir them to battle fury, and this has been repeated from time to time. However Wasson, after a detailed investigation into its use among various peoples, could find nothing in Old Norse sources to support such a theory, and pointed out that the fungus tends to produce a tranquil state of mind rather than wild rage.[68] Other drugs may have been known, the use of which was a carefully guarded secret, and knowledge of some hallucinogenic substance might account for some of the wilder elements in tales of distortion and shape-changing.

87

Intoxicating drink no doubt played a part, but in any case it would not be difficult to stir up a band of tough and highly-trained youths into a state of murderous rage and fearless confidence. There are indications that warriors deliberately worked themselves into a mood of excitement before battle by wild leaps, shouts and songs. This was claimed to have been the case with both Celtic and Germanic warriors in Roman times, and Livy describes the Celts preparing for battle (XXXVIII, 17) with '... songs as they go into battle and yells and leapings and the dreadful din of arms as they clash shields according to some ancestral custom – all these are deliberately used to terrify their foes.' Similarly Tacitus (*Germania* 3) refers to songs sung by German warriors, and how before a fight they would yell into their shields held up in front of their faces. When two armies met, he observed, those who could produce the more fearsome noise had an initial advantage over their opponents. Mass behaviour of this kind can still be observed among rugby players before a match or youths engaged in gang warfare. When two men met to fight a duel, the exchange of insults was an important preliminary; this is brought out in accounts of battles in the *Táin*, and in meetings between champions in the *Edda* poems and the early books of Saxo's *History*.[69]

The leaping of warriors mentioned by Livy may have been part of a warrior dance before battle, and dances also took place after victory. Ornamental plates from helmets, sword scabbards and belt buckles used by the Anglo-Saxons, Swedes and Alamanni show figures of naked men, clad in only a belt and a horned helmet, who hold in their hands two spears or a spear and sword, and have their feet in a dancing posture.[70] An outstanding example is the naked warrior wearing only a horned helmet and girdle on a seventh century bronze buckle from a grave at Finglesham in Kent; he holds a spear in each hand, and his knees are

8 *left* Dancing warrior on metal plate from Obrigheim, West Germany. *right* Dancing warrior on buckle plate from grave 95, Anglo-Saxon cemetery at Finglesham, Kent, eighth century AD.

bent. A similar figure appears with a wolf-headed man on a die for a helmet plate found at Torslunda in Öland, and others are shown on scabbards from Alamannic cemeteries. Paulsen suggested that they were associated with funerals, when the warrior's weapons were borne to the grave with ritual dances.[71] Such figures seem to be linked with the cult of Odin, and the men might represent his champions from Valhalla, the *einherjar* (outstanding warriors) who welcomed dead heroes and who in the poems are said to decide the outcome of battles like the valkyries. One such figure is shown guiding a warrior's spear on a helmet plate from Sweden.[72] Hauck thought they represented Odin himself,[73] and a symbol of this kind could have more than one meaning, standing both for the dedicated champion and the god who ruled the battlefield.

Somewhat similar figures of naked men with horns holding a sword and shield have been found in northern England and are apparently native British gods equated with the Roman Mars.[74] We hear of warriors fighting naked among both Celts and Germans. The Romans depicted them in statues and carvings, and Polybius (II, 28) describes them in the forefront of the Celtic armies: 'Very terrifying too were the appearance and gestures of the naked warriors in front, all in the prime of life and finely built men,' while one section discarded clothes: '. . . owing to their proud confidence in themselves and stood naked with nothing but their arms'. Similarly Diodorus Siculus declares that the celts 'so far despise death that they descend to do battle unclothed except for a girdle.'[75] Irish warriors much later are said in the *Táin* to answer the summons to battle 'stark naked except for their weapons'.[76] The Germans too had spear-throwers described as 'naked or lightly clad in short cloaks' by Tacitus in *Germania* (6), and he refers also to youths who danced naked, 'jumping and bounding between swords and upturned spears' (24). These, he assures us, received no payment for their skill, and they were presumably dancing in honour of the god of battle. Some of the feats of Cú Chulainn suggest a kind of dance, while there are references to members of the *fian* who were expert at leaping.[77]

4 Odin and Lug as battle gods

Behind the rich tapestry of battle-ritual is the conception of a power or powers controlling the fortunes of war and giving support to heroes or dooming them to destruction. There does not seem to have been one sole god of battle. While many of the main Celtic deities were warriors, none is predominantly a war-god, while although Odin in the Viking Age was closely associated with kings and warriors, he had many other functions also (p. 208 below). The Roman Mars is sometimes identified with a local deity, sometimes with the god Lug, and sometimes with the

Germanic Tîwaz, but Lug and Tîwaz also were much more then war-gods. Odin's predecessor Wodan was identified by the Romans with Mercury, and Odin later may have taken over some of the attributes of Tîwaz, since his huge spear could deal out victory or defeat in battle. His increasing link with war may have been due to the fact that he was closely associated with royal houses, and also was thought to conduct the dead to the Other World.

It would appear that in the Viking Age not all men who died in battle were held to be welcomed into Valhalla, the hall of Odin. He was primarily interested in kings and leaders, and it is indicated in the poems that he needed their support at Ragnarok, the final battle between gods and giants (p. 192 below). On the memorial stones of Gotland erected about the eighth century, dead warriors are shown arriving at Odin's hall and welcomed by a woman with a horn (p. 45 above). Poems like the tenth century *Eiríksmál* describe the scenes when princes arrive from the battlefield, and these were memorial poems, presumably recited at the funeral feasts of distinguished warriors. Such tales and poems must have been compulsory hearing for young fighting men, helping to build up their desire for a fine death in battle.

In Irish tradition the picture of the otherworld 'hostel' (*bruiden*), a banqueting hall haunted by horrific red and black figures and presided over by a supernatural host, has something in common with the Norse Valhalla. Löffler describes such hostels as primarily houses of death to which kings are lured or invited, generally losing their lives as the result of their visit. Feasts are organised there, it would seem, in order to stir up conflict.[78] The nearest parallel to Odin seems to be Lug, the 'Shining One', although he is often represented as a youthful figure, while Odin is more often an old man in a hood or a broad-brimmed hat. Both however were identified with the god Mercury, and were gods of many skills. Julius Caesar (*Gallic War* VI, 17) states that the Celtic Mercury was 'a guide on roads and journeys ... the most powerful help in trading and making money', and similarly Odin could protect both warriors and traders, was known as the 'god of cargoes' and according to Snorri in *Ynglinga Saga* (7) could lead his followers to treasure buried in the earth as well as help them to gain booty in warfare. Both gods carried huge spears, and both had horses to take them over land and sea; Odin had the eight-legged Sleipnir, while we are told of Lug's horse Aenbarr: 'She was as fleet as the naked cold wind of spring, and sea and land were the same to her, and the charm was such that her rider was never killed off her back.'[79]

Both Lug and Odin were associated with the crow and the raven, the birds of the battlefield. Odin's two ravens brought him tidings every day, presumably from the battles of the world, and a pair of birds are often shown in the art of the Migration period. They appear on gold bracteates of the sixth century, and on a helmet plate depicting Odin as a rider,[80] while the motif of a bearded head between two birds was a favourite motif on the chapes of scabbards.[81] Lug also had two ravens, which warned him when the Fomorians were approaching, and indeed his connection with ravens has led some to put forward the theory that he was originally a raven god.[82] The link with the raven in both cases may be due to its image as a source of wisdom and prophetic knowledge as well as its fondness for dead bodies as a bird of prey. Both gods are also associated with the eagle, primarily a symbol of the sky and also of sovereignty because of its association with the Roman emperors. Lug assumed eagle form in his Welsh character of Lleu in the tale of 'Math Son of Mathonwy' in the *Mabinogion*, and Odin takes eagle shape in a number of tales. The popularity of eagle brooches among the Germanic peoples in the Migration period seems likely to be due to the growth of the cult of Wodan.

Both Lug and Wodan had cult places on hills. The festival of Lug on 1 August was celebrated in many parts of Ireland by visits to hill-tops (p. 39 above), while in Anglo-Saxon England the evidence of early placenames indicate that Woden was associated with hills and artificial mounds.[83] Both were remembered as rulers of the Land of the Dead. Odin was lord of Valhalla, while Lug was represented as sitting in state in the Other World, attended by the woman who symbolised the sovereignty of Ireland.[84] Both gods made use of deceiving magic. Both had powers of healing; Lug visited the wounded Cú Chulainn and healed him; while Saxo has a tale of Odin healing the hero Sivard after terrible wounds received in battle, in return for the promise that Sivard would offer those he killed to the god. Odin does not often appear as a healing god, but there are some grounds for thinking that the Germanic Wodan possessed such characteristics.[85] Both Lug and Odin were regarded as the ancestors of kings, and heroes could be represented as their sons.

The differences between the two are as significant as their resemblances. Some of Wodan's characteristics can be seen not in Lug, but in a god called Donn, who seems to be an ancient god connected with death and the underworld, still remembered in Irish folklore (p. 176 below). However the parallels between Lug and Odin are impressive, particularly so because they are by no means neat and logical, and therefore unlikely to result from borrowings in the Viking Age, when Scandinavians and Irish were in contact with one another. Here we have two gods worshipped centuries earlier who in the Roman period were both identified with Mercury and who developed in different ways in literature and folklore, but who still seem to have retained their basic characteristics. Both are closely associated with battle ritual and with the traditions of kings, warriors and heroes, although they cannot be seen as gods of war only. One of the most striking links between them is their association with supernatural women possessing power over the results of battle, and this needs to be discussed in more detail.

5 The battle goddesses

The part played by battle-goddesses, battle-maids or valkyries is of major importance in both Scandinavian and Irish tradition, and can be traced back well before the Viking Age. By the tenth century the valkyrie had become a stock figure in literature and art. She was represented as an attendant on the god Odin, and described as a dignified figure on horseback with shield and sword and helmet, sent to carry out the will of the god in apportioning victory in battle and deciding which warriors must fall. She is also shown welcoming heroes in Valhalla after they have fallen on the battlefield. Her duty was to conduct dead kings and heroes to Odin, and this is the picture of the valkyries in the tenth century poem *Hákonarmál*, a funeral poem composed in praise of the Norwegian king Hakon the Good:

> Then spoke Gondul, leaning on her spearshaft:
> 'Now will the forces of the gods be increased
> since they have summoned Hakon with a great host
> to come to the abode of the Powers.'

> The prince heard the speech of the valkyries,
> noble women, sitting on their steeds;
> they sat helmeted, in deep thought,
> holding their shields before them.

In the early Viking Age the popular representation of a valkyrie in art was that of a woman holding a horn, which she offers to a warrior (Plate 2b). This aspect of the valkyrie is closely associated with battle, and those whom she conducts to Valhalla are kings and leaders.

In the *Edda* poems we find another aspect portrayed. She appears here as the spirit wife of the hero, appearing to announce his future greatness as a leader, to urge him on to heroic deeds, perhaps to present him with his sword, and finally to receive him as husband and lover after he dies in battle. Such a conception is found in the Helgi lays, in the story of Sigurd the Volsung told in the late *Vǫlsunga Saga*, and in a number of heroic poems in the *Poetic Edda*. The hero Sigurd discovers a valkyrie

92

asleep, clad in armour, in a hall ringed by fire, and she gives him counsel and teaching as to how he should behave as a warrior leader, as well as battle spells to use when he needs them. In later versions of the Sigurd cycle she is identified with Brynhild, a proud princess who was won by Sigurd on behalf of his foster-brother, and who later brought about Sigurd's death rather than see him married to another woman. She finally killed herself in order to become his wife in the next world. Saxo knew a number of heroic tales from Danish and Icelandic sources, and he introduced into his *History* a series of valkyries figures of this type, who assist young princes and become their brides.

An earlier aspect of the valkyrie, however, may have been that of a primitive spirit of slaughter, haunting the battlefield and rejoicing in the bloodshed and the deaths of men. In Saxo's Latin version of the *Biarkamál*, a lost heroic poem telling of the last battle of King Hrólf Kraki and his warriors, there is a passage which seems to refer to a terrible battle-spirit of this type (II, 61, p. 58):

Arise too, Ruta, and show your snow-pale head,
come forth from hiding and issue into battle.
The outdoor carnage beckons you; fighting now
shakes the doors; harsh strife batters the gates.

It seems that the Anglo-Saxons remembered spirits of this kind, since in the eighth century the term 'Chooser of the Slain' (*wælcyrge*), equivalent to the Icelandic *valkyrja*, is given as a gloss for one of the names of the Furies, and also for Bellona, Goddess of War, and the Gorgon.[86] An Anglo-Saxon charm, 'Against a Sudden Pain',[87] has a description of a company of mighty women riding over a hill, whose spears are the cause of the trouble. This little poem has strong heroic imagery, and could have been modelled on an earlier battle-spell to protect a warrior from injury or panic in battle (p. 70 above). Another memory of powerful women is found in an early German spell from Merseburg; these are called the *Indisi*, and are described as sitting fastening bonds, holding back the host, and tugging at fetters, presumably to paralyse or to give freedom to men in battle. They are apparently deciding the fortunes of war and the fates of warriors.[88]

The double aspect of the valkyrie in Germanic literature, then, seems to be first that of a relentless battle-goddess, and secondly that of a spirit helper who decides the destiny of a young warrior and gives him help and counsel. Saxo has a group of female spirits who appear to a young hero Hother in the third book of his *History*, and he states that their function is to 'control the fortunes of war by their guidance and blessing'. It is possible that a similar tradition lies behind the tale of the three Weird Sisters who appear in the Scottish *History* of Hector Boethius and were used by Shakespeare in his play *Macbeth*.[89] Like Saxo's spirits, these women appear and disappear at will, foretell the fate of the hero, and encounter him at crucial points in his career. Their deceiving promises which arouse Macbeth's fury resemble the treacherous counsels of Odin, who is frequently berated by doomed heroes in a similar way. Such spirits are also concerned with the bestowal of kingly power and the choosing of a king, as are those in Saxo; in one of Saxo's tales Svanhvita and her sisters appear in a lonely place and reveal themselves to the dispossessed prince Regner, assuring him that he will win the kingdom. When in the first of the Helgi poems in the *Poetic Edda* nine valkyries appear to the young hero and give him his name, this apparently decides his destiny as future king and leader.

The destinies of princes were obviously closely linked with the results of battles, and here the valkyries take a decisive part. The most detailed description is that in the poem *Darraðarljóð*, the Song of the Spear, quoted in *Njáls Saga* (157). This is said to have been chanted in Caithness on the morning before the Battle of Clontarf was fought, the battle which decided the future of the vikings in Dublin. No recognisable names are, however, given in the poem, and it may originally have referred to another battle. Twelve women were seen in a house in Caithness, where they sat weaving on a grisly loom, with severed heads for weights, arrows for shuttles, and entrails for the warp. Their weaving had a background of dark spears with a crimson weft running across it, and they exulted as they worked at the loss of life which would take place in the fighting to come:

> All is sinister now to see,
> a cloud of blood moves over the sky,
> the air is red with the blood of men,
> and the battle-women chant their song.

When their weaving is completed, they depart on horses, presumably to ride through the air to the field of battle. The emphasis throughout the poem is on the spear, and on blood and slaughter; they declare that they can allot victory and change the destiny of kings and peoples, and call themselves valkyries: 'the valkyries have the choosing of the slain'. One is called Hild, a valkyrie name, and two other names, Gunn and Gondul, are referred to as the guardians of one of the princes concerned in the battle.

These women on their horses are far removed from the noble riders of *Hákonarmál*, escorting the king to Valhalla, and have more in common with the giantesses and trollwomen who appear in Old Norse literature. Another parallel is found in descriptions of huge female beings seen in dreams or visions, and represented as portents of battle to come. The death of Harald Hardraði in Yorkshire is presaged in *Heimskringla* by a series of omens,[90] one of which is in a dream reported by a man on the king's ship: 'He thought he was on the king's ship looking towards the island, where a great trollwoman was standing, with a short sword in one hand and a trough in the other. He thought also that when he looked over all their ships he could see a bird perched on every prow, all eagles or ravens.' A trough is associated with sacrifice, presumably because it was used to hold the sacrificial meat, and is mentioned in this connection in pre-Christian poetry.[91] Another man dreamed of a great army awaiting them on their arrival: 'And in front of this land army there rode a huge trollwoman, sitting on a wolf, and the wolf had a man's body in its mouth and there was blood around its jaws. When it had devoured the body, then she threw another into its mouth, and then another and another, and it swallowed them all.' The idea of death as a wolf-like monster is an ancient one, and the Celts in southern France had a huge stone figure, the Monster of Noves (p. 29 above) which is shown devouring men in a similar way to that described above.

The giantesses in the dreams described chanted verses expressing delight in the slaughter of men. 'This is profit for us', declared the first, while the second displayed her red shield as she 'stained the wolf's jaws with blood'. She too is like a monstrous travesty of the valkyries who lean on their shields in *Hákonarmál*. Other huge troll-like women occur in dreams recorded in *Sturlunga Saga*, written in the thirteenth century as a record of recent events.[92] They rock two and fro in a house where blood rains down, or ride at the head of a company of men holding a bloodstained cloth, which they use to jerk off the heads of their victims. A similar pair in *Víga-Glúms Saga* (21) sprinkle blood over the land from a trough, and these are represented in a verse as valkyries: 'The scatterer of neck-rings saw a great troop of divine beings riding above the farms (?). The time has come for the singing of the grey spears, swords will clash in the place where the battle-goddesses, eager for the fray, poured blood over men's bodies.' This particular tradition survived into the Christian period because of the convention by which the battle-goddesses were turned into omens and visions, and in this way the saga-tellers could use them freely. In some cases the descriptive verses on which the prose is based may have been considerably earlier in date. The use of ominous dreams as a sign of violence to come is common in the sagas, and the deliberate choice of valkyrie figures to express this shows that it must have been a familiar image to the early Icelandic poets.

There are also giantesses in the legendary sagas who behave like the valkyries in the *Edda* poems, helping and fostering young heroes (p. 92 above).[93] Sometimes these beings appear in ugly and threatening shapes, like one with a horse's head and tail who throws a sword into the air and challenges the hero to kiss her. When accepted, however, they become fair and alluring. One such figure, in Saxo's *History*, claims to be able to alter her appearance at will, becoming huge to terrify her opponents and shrinking to mortal size when taking a mortal lover.

Such supernatural women may be encountered singly, but are often in groups of two, three or more. They sometimes ride through the air on horses or wolves. An Anglo-Saxon charm for taking a swarm of bees refers to the bees as *sigewíf* (victory women), and this seems likely to have been a name for valkyries,[94] who like the insects moved in troops through the air to accomplish their purpose. The link with birds is also close, since they converse with ravens and give dead bodies to birds waiting for the slaughter, as in the dream of the birds perched on the ships in the poem quoted above. The raven itself is called 'chooser of the slain' in the Old English poem *Exodus* (line 164).

The Scandinavian valkyrie is clearly a complex figure. Valkyries are seen in the poems as attendants on the god Odin and denizens of Valhalla, sent out to do his will and to apportion victory or defeat in battle as he has decreed. They are associated to some extent with swan-maidens, and may have links with the 'spirit wives' of the shamans in northern Eurasia,[95] who help and protect their human husbands and do battle with hostile spirits on their behalf as well as helping them on their journeys to the Other World. Another link is with 'shield-maids', women in the Norse sources who wear armour and fight along with men; another is with seeresses who predict the future destiny of children, and with the Norns, supernatural women who weave the fates of young heroes (p. 164 below). A name given to one of the Norns, *Skuld*, is found in lists of names of valkyries.

There are several lists of valkyrie names,[96] and many stress their association with battle and with the spear, which was Odin's weapon used to determine the results of a battle. *Hildr* and *Gunnr* are poetic words for battle; *Gǫndul* (?Staff-Carrier) may refer to the bearer of a spear, and *Hrist* may mean a spear-brandisher (from *hrista*, to shake). *Geiravǫr* means Spear-goddess, and *Geirahǫð*, Spear of Battle. *Skǫgul* may mean 'high-towering', and if so might be a reference to the gigantic size of these beings. *Herfjǫtur* (war-fetter) would presumably refer to the power of such spirits to lay invisible fetters on warriors to render them helpless in battle (p. 70 above). These names have no individuality, but are descriptive of the nature of the war-goddesses, perhaps creations of

96

the poets. Saxo's supernatural protectors of heroes may also be seen as bearing symbolic names: *Sigrún* could stand for a rune of victory, and *Svanhvita* for a battle spirit in bird form. In the Roman period it seems that descriptive names were given to Germanic goddesses attending on the god of battle. Two inscriptions on altars at Housesteads mention *Baudihillie* and *Friagabi*, names which have been interpreted as 'Ruler of Battle' and 'Giver of Freedom'.[97] These would be in agreement with the ideas of the valkyries deciding the outcome of battle, and freeing their chosen champions from the fetters which might be laid on them to make them helpless. On one stone these goddesses are seen associated with Mars.

In Irish tradition also we find female spirits associated with battle and death. They appear in the tales under the collective name of *Morrígan*, which may be used either of a single goddess or of a group of three. There is a strong erotic element in the Morrígan, as in the Scandinavian valkyries who offer themselves to warriors. The name has been interpreted as Great Queen, or Demon Queen; other names given to the battle goddesses are *Nemain* (Frenzy), *Badb* and *Macha* (both probably meaning Crow). The Morrígan may appear as a lovely girl in a dress of many colours, as when she asks Cú Chulainn to take her as a lover. When he refuses, she threatens to harass him in various forms in the midst of battle: 'It will be worse for you when I go against you as you are fighting your enemies. I shall go in the form of an eel under your feet in the ford so that you shall fall . . . I shall drive the cattle over the ford to you while I am in the form of a grey she-wolf . . . I shall come to you in the guise of a hornless red heifer in front of the castle and they will rush upon you at many fords and pools yet you will not see me in front of you.'[98] The function of the goddess here, it may be noted, is not to attack the hero with weapons but to render him helpless at a crucial point in the battle, like the valkyries who cast 'fetters' upon warriors. The threats made by the Morrígan are carried out, but Cú Chulainn, protected by the god Lug who fathered him, was sufficiently powerful to wound the goddess, and she was forced to come to him in the end to seek healing. She approached him in the guise of an old woman, an ugly creature who offered him milk when he was wounded and exhausted, so that he gave her his blessing three times and she became whole again. 'Had I known it was you', he declared afterwards, 'I should never have healed you.'

Later on, after Cú Chulainn uttered his terrible battle-cry, it is said that the war-goddess Nemain attacked the host, and so fearful was her onslaught that a hundred warriors fell dead with terror. Nemain is referred to in this way three times in the later part of the *Táin* as recorded in the Yellow Book of Lecan, and it appears to be a figurative way of describing the onset of battle fury, which was so violent that some men died before the fighting began.[99] Another name for the war-goddess, Badb, emphasises the link with birds, and Cú Chulainn's hostility towards the Morrígan extends to the Otherworld ravens, which he pursues and destroys; on one occasion he is said to cut off a raven's head and set it on a rock while he covers himself in its blood.[100] Like the valkyries, the war-goddesses call on ravens to enjoy the results of the battle which they have brought about: 'Then the Morrígan spoke in the dusk between the encampments, saying: "Ravens gnaw the necks of men. Blood flows. Battle is fought" ...'[101] An association between goddess and raven existed in Gaul, for Nantosvelta is shown on stones from Speyer and Sarrebourg with a raven, and also holding a small house on a pole which might be a dovecote.[102] Her name means 'Winding River', and she has no obvious connection with battle, but there are links between the battle-goddesses and water; for instance the threats of the Morrígan to Cú Chulainn could only be effective when he was fighting in or beside water.

Birds were sacrificed in the Viking Age both at funerals and as part of the great sacrifice for victory at Uppsala (p. 59 above). There is also the image of birds receiving and rejoicing over sacrificial victims, particularly the raven. A man hanged on the gallows is described in *Beowulf* (2448) as a 'delight to the ravens'. In an early Icelandic poem attributed to Helgi Trausti, who killed his mother's lover, the killing is said to be a sacrifice to Odin, and also to be offered to the ravens: 'I have given the bold son of Asmoth to Odin, and offered to Gaut [i.e. Odin], bold lord of the gallows, his sacrifice; the corpse is offered to the raven.'[103] The dead killed on the battlefield were also viewed as a sacrifice and as a feast for ravens, strengthening the sinister link between valkyries and birds of prey. If ravens can be identified with Irish battle-goddesses, they were seen both as victims and as the powers to whom the sacrifice was offered. Anne Ross suggests that in the grim description of three war-goddesses in 'The Destruction of Da Derga's Hostel', we can see them as sacrificial victims in bird form: 'naked on the ridge-pole of the house; their jets of blood coming through them and the ropes of slaughter on their necks. "Those I know", said he, "three of them of awful boding. These are the three that are slaughtered at every time."'[104] The bird shapes do not seem to be established from the passage as it stands, and these might be naked goddesses, of which Anne Ross herself gives an example from Alauna in Cumberland.[105] However they are described as the beings which are slaughtered, and they have ropes round their necks while blood spurts from their bodies, like the victims sacrificed to Odin. The persistent image of the Raven Banner, on which victory in battle depended, in a series of Norse tales may be seen as another illustration of the strength of the link between the raven and Odin as giver of victory.[106]

The goddesses could appear in other shapes beside those of birds. The Badb on one occasion was seen as a 'big-mouthed black sooty woman, lame and squinting with her eyes, dark as the back of a stag-beetle', while on another occasion she is described with shins long and black as a weaver's beam, a beard reaching to her knees and a mouth on one side of her head.[107] When this creature is asked for her name, she gives a long list of titles, one of which is Badb. She may also appear as a red figure beside a stream, washing the chariot and harness of a king doomed to die.[108] The motif of the Washer at the Ford is found in medieval sources and remembered in later Irish folklore in tales of a woman by a river washing the spoils of battle, the limbs of the slain, or garments taken from the dead. On one occasion Cú Chulainn sees a fair young woman 'moaning and complaining and squeezing and washing purple, hacked, wounded spoils on the bank of the ford', and Cathbad tells him that she is the daughter of the Badb, and that this foretells the young hero's death in battle.[109] 'Horrible are the huge entrails which the Morrígan washes', it is said in the *Reicne Fothaid Canainne*, dated by Meyer to the late ninth century. A hideous hag washing heads and limbs, armour and robes, until the blood from them dyes the river red, appears in two fourteenth century sources, in accounts of a battle fought at Corecomroe Abbey in 1317 and another at Dysert O'Dea the following year. She was seen by the leader of the army which was afterwards defeated. Patricia Lysaght, who has collected the evidence for such appearances, links them with later Irish folk traditions concerning the death messenger. There is an obvious resemblance in such passages to the descriptions of giantesses scattering blood from a trough and bathing men in blood in Norse sources.

Irish tradition also includes the conception of the warrior queen able to instruct and help young heroes, who belongs to the Other World. The outstanding example is Scáthach, who taught Cú Chulainn and other heroes fighting skills and use of weapons.[110] She seems to be an Otherworld being (p. 85 above), and the journey to her abode is a long and dangerous one. She is described as a woman chieftain and an expert warrior, and Cú Chulainn has to threaten her with a sword before she will take him as her pupil and let him be her daughter's lover. He later gave her help against another woman warrior, Aífe, who bore him a son. In one tradition it was Aífe and not Scáthach who gave him his famous weapon, the formidable *gáe bulga*, which rendered him invincible in desperate battles, and by which his own son was slain.

99

The Irish battle-goddesses, like the valkyries, can appear either singly or in groups, and they are so depicted on altars and carved stones from Gaul and Britain. Sometimes they are seen in company with a male figure. Nemain had a consort, Nét, but he seems little more than a personification of battle. They seem to have some links with other supernatural women, such as the goddess representing the sovereignty of Ireland, said to have been seen with Lug (p. 91 above). This territorial goddess had two opposed aspects, and could appear like the Morrígan both as a hideous hag and as a beautiful woman richly adorned.[111] She proffers a cup to a man destined to be king, recalling the figure of the valkyrie with a horn in Norse iconography. Patricia Lysaght came to the conclusion that the Banshee, the death-messenger, is also partly derived from this territorial goddess, and that this could account for the strong association of the Banshee with certain families said to be of ancient origin.[112]

Thus both in Irish and Scandinavian literature we have a conception of female beings associated with battle, both fierce and erotic, who foretell the deaths of young warriors and princes but who also reveal to them at the outset of their careers the glorious future which awaits them. Such a being may be attached to a warrior throughout life, and the conception was sufficiently powerful to leave a deep impression on later poems and tales. Such spirits add to the complexity of the figures of the gods to whom sacrifice was made for victory. Emphasis has been laid on Odin and Lug, because there are striking resemblances between them, and because the valkyries are so closely associated with Odin. Other gods however received offerings for victory, and the various figures of Mars on altars and carved stones in Gaul, Germany and Britain were identified with many local gods of varying character and attributes. The importance of battle in the lives of the Celts and Germans resulted in a rich treasury of battle-lore, and there must have been a great deal which formed part of the training of young men as warriors, kept secret or only faintly remembered, which has resulted in many legends of shape-changing, witchcraft, prophecies, and strange and terrifying omens connected with battles. This is what might be expected of peoples whose life was largely taken up with fighting on land or water, so that it formed an unescapable part of their experience.

The beliefs and mythology associated with battle indicate that Celts, Germans and Vikings had few illusions about its nature. The heroic tales for all their fantasy and exaggeration possess a realism of their own which is expressed through the images of their mythology. The supernatural beings to whom they turned for protection and help were two-faced, with double personalities. Odin was said by Snorri to be fair and generous to his friends but terrible towards his enemies, and the same is true of the battle-goddesses. However glorious the faces of the protective spirits of battle to the young warrior at the height of his powers, they were bound to turn against him in the end, when famous weapons were shattered by the spear of Odin or the war-goddesses declared doom against a hitherto invincible warrior. The supreme importance of luck in battle is emphasised throughout the many beliefs and customs which the literature preserves for us. Battle, moreover, is associated with inspiration and wisdom, and the pursuit of the heads of slaughtered men was not simply an expression of destructive ferocity but a means of attaining supernatural wisdom and knowledge of what was hidden from men. We have seen the lengths to which men were prepared to go in sacrifice, to seek help from friendly powers and to uncover the future as it was to be played out on the battlefields. Those with special skills, like the druids, might be called on to work elaborate magic against the enemy, like the 'druidical fires' which could be driven against their opponents' territory (p. 150 below). Men searched for powerful images to set on weapons and armour, and for battle-spells against their enemies, and hoped to obtain the necessary inspiration when the time of testing came. All this no doubt took up a fair amount of time and energy, but was regarded by fighting men as an essential and important side of their activities.

Tales of the ancient heroes and myths of the fighting gods aiding them in their conflicts, constantly repeated and illustrated in their art, were more than mere entertainment and decoration. They were of serious importance as examples to young warriors, a constant reminder of the uncertainty of life, the need to seize opportunity when it came and to face death in the end without flinching. It is the battle mythology of these peoples which provides us with some of the finest literary material, the heroic poems and sagas remembered and retold long after the campaigns which inspired them were over. The horrors of blood, carnage and hideous wounds, the wasteful slaughter of splendid young men, and the dark side of warfare were never concealed or ignored in the tales, but they are transmuted by the emphasis on fate and the imagery of supernatural guardians and protectors, as well as the insistence on the fame of the outstanding heroes. This side of their religion was no superficial one, but formed part of their conception of the supernatural world and helped to build up their attitude to life and death.

IV Land -spirits and ancestors

The state of the year is good, how good it is!
The state of the year is fair, how fair it is!
I have come down with the Twin Companies of the gods upon the flood;
I am the creator for the Twin Companies
provider of the fields with plenty.

Pyramid Texts 1195f.

Although some of the early settlers were Christians when they arrived in Iceland, it is said in the account of the Settlement that in the next generation such beliefs were forgotten, and their descendants 'raised temples and sacrificed, and the land was fully heathen for well-nigh a hundred years'.[1] As we have seen, there were memories of holy places in Iceland, of feasts and sacrifices to the gods, and of magic skills. There were also beliefs in the spirits of the land (*landvættir*), and these continued in folk tradition long after the Icelanders had officially accepted Christianity.

While luck in battle was essential to success and survival in a violent age, luck and protection in daily life was also needed to make a living in a difficult and infertile land, subject to blizzards, rough seas, landslides and lava flows which might ruin the pastures for good. We do not hear much in the sagas about help from the war-god Odin, although he was well known in Iceland and praised by its poets. We hear more of help given by the sky-god Thor to aid travellers and to establish and uphold the law, and of his protection of men against the forces of chaos. But when it came to the practical needs of every day, the people seem to have turned to a company of local spirits closely linked with the land itself, whose favour could bring them good fortune in farming, hunting and fishing and protect their children and animals.

1 Scandinavian land-spirits

In *Landnámabók* we hear something of dealings with such spirits. There is a reference to a family of brothers who were obliged to move their

102

farm because of a flow of lava on their land, and were left with few animals until one of them had a lucky dream:[2]

> One night Bjorn dreamed that a rock-dweller (*bergbúi*) came to him and offered to enter into partnership with him, and it seemed to him that he agreed. Then a he-goat joined his goats, and his livestock increased so rapidly that he was soon prosperous; after that he was called Goat-Bjorn. People with second sight saw how all the land-spirits followed Goat-Bjorn to the Thing, and followed his brothers Thorstein and Thord when they went hunting and fishing.

Goat-Bjorn was held in considerable respect, and it is noted in the records that many great men of Iceland, bishops and laymen, were among his descendants.

Who or what is this 'rock-dweller'? The word is sometimes translated 'giant', but this is no frost-giant of the kind who oppose the gods of Asgard. The most detailed account of a rock-dweller is to be found in a strange saga, *Barðar Saga Snæfellsáss*, which is included among the 'Family Sagas' because it is set in Iceland and not in remote lands of magic and adventure. However it is filled with supernatural characters, and the hero, Bard, is called 'god of Snæfell'.[3] He was a Norwegian, fathered by a giant, and fostered by another giant, Dofri of Dovrefjeld in Norway. From Dofri Bard learned history and genealogies, feats of arms and knowledge of the future, while the giant's daughter became his wife. Later Bard avenged his father after a killing, and then left for Iceland. Things did not go well for him there, and after a time he disappeared from among men, moving across a glacier and living in a cave in the mountain beyond it. The saga states that he was more of a troll than a man, so people called him the god (*Áss*) of Snæfell. People in that district made vows to him as to a god, and they called on him when they were in trouble. He helped one man in a wrestling match, and another after an attack by a troll-woman, and was always ready to defend men against evil and hostile beings. From time to time he was seen wearing a grey cloak and hood with a belt of walrus hide, carrying a two-pronged stick with a spike for crossing the ice. Like his foster-father Dofri, he acted as fosterer and teacher to promising young men. A twelve-year-old boy called Odd accepted an invitation to visit him in the mountains, and found himself in terrible conditions of storm and cold: 'He stumbled on, not knowing where he was going, and at last became aware that a man was walking through the darkness with a great staff, letting the point rattle on the ice ... Odd recognised Bard, god of Snæfell.' (*Barðar Saga* 10). Odd stayed a winter in Bard's cave studying law, and was later known as one of the wisest of the lawmen. He married one of Bard's daughters, but she died three years later. Bard was said to have nine daughters, and one, Helga, was a strange figure who wandered about the land, 'usually far from men', and made secret visits to farms. She would stay up most of the night playing a harp, but resented intrusion, and a Norwegian who tried to discover who she was had his arm and leg broken to punish his curiosity. Bard associated with various supernatural beings and was respected as the strongest among them. Although he gave protection against evil spirits and trolls, he was hostile to Christianity, and after his son Gest became a Christian he deprived him of his sight.

While this saga is late and confused, it seems to contain traditions about the land-spirits in western Iceland which lived on in local folklore. A similar set of stories was told of the giant Dofri in Norway, who was said to have fostered and taught young men, and had Harald Fairhair, the ninth century king of Vestfold, among his pupils. But the land-spirits were not all mountain dwellers. One Icelandic settler was said to make sacrifices of food to a waterfall near his house, and his sheep increased greatly because he made good decisions as to which should be slaughtered in the autumn and which were worth keeping.[4] Another man made offerings to one of the rare woods in Iceland,[5] while another trusted in a spirit dwelling in a great stone near his house. This being was finally expelled with his family when a Christian bishop dropped holy water on the stone.[6] In one version of this tale the spirit is called ármaðr; ár means harvest or season, and the implication is that the being in the stone could bring about a prosperous harvest. In the second version however he is called spámaðr (seer), the word used for someone with power to foretell the future. These two functions of the land-spirits appear to be linked, for not only did they bring good luck and prosperity to their worshippers, but they also had knowledge of the future and could give advice to those who consulted them. In this case the farmer received counsel by means of dreams: 'He tells me beforehand many things which will happen in the future; he guards my cattle and gives me warnings of what I must do and what I must avoid, and therefore I have faith in him and I have worshipped him for a long time.'

There is no suggestion that these spirits accompanied the settlers to Iceland; the implication is that they were already there, closely bound to the new land. Friendly spirits were distinguished from evil vættir, who were hostile and destructive, like the Norwegian trolls. The land-spirits could be offended by violence, and it was said that for a long time no one dared settle in southern Iceland where Hjorleif, one of the first settlers, was murdered by his Irish thralls; this was not because the place was thought to be haunted, but 'because of the land-spirits'.[7] It was evidently risky to alarm or anger these powers. The early Icelandic laws included a prohibition against ships with dragon-heads on their prows coming into harbour, in case the land-spirits were offended by a threat of hostility.[8] In the nineteenth century an Icelandic clergyman recorded that certain rocks and stones in north-eastern Iceland were called 'Stones of the *Landdísir*' (land-goddesses). It was said to be unwise to make a loud noise near them, and children were forbidden to play there, for bad luck would come if they were not treated with respect.[9]

There is a detailed account in *Egils Saga* (57) of how the poet Egill Skallagrimsson declared enmity against the Norwegian king Erik Blood-axe, and called on the gods to avenge Erik's flouting of the law. Erik had cut the ropes marking the court of law and so cut proceedings short before judgement could be given, when Egill was claiming his right to his wife's lands in Norway, and he then declared Egill to be an outlaw. Egill retaliated by raising a horse's head on a pole and carving runes as a spell against the king, and two verses quoted in the saga are said to have been composed by him on this occasion. These appear to be genuine early material,[10] and are of considerable interest. In one verse Egill appeals for justice, and mentions the gods Odin, Freyr and Njord by name. In the second verse he addresses the Land-Elf, and accuses the king of breaking the laws and of murdering his brothers. He then appeals to 'the land-spirits who dwell in the land', declaring that they shall wander restlessly and never find their way back to their homes until Erik and his queen are driven out of Norway.

The names of the three gods mentioned by Egill are significant. Odin was the god particularly dear to the warrior poet and mentioned frequently in his poems. But he also appeals to two of the Vanir deities, Freyr and Njord, the gods of fertility, when one might have expected Thor to be mentioned as guardian of law. The Vanir, however, are linked with earth and sea, and presumably therefore with the land-spirits, who were likely to resent the king's action in overthrowing the court.

Elves and land-spirits are generally mentioned in the plural, and seem to live in groups and families. This is also true of the Vanir in the myths and poems. At their head is Freyr, with Freyja his sister, and Njord is their father; he is linked with ships, lakes and the sea. In the *Edda* poems the formula 'Æsir and Elves' is used more than once where one would expect 'Æsir and Vanir'.[11] It seems reasonable to equate the Vanir with the elves and land-spirits worshipped by the early settlers, and indeed in the poem *Grímnismál* (5) Freyr is said to rule over Alfheim, land of the elves.

According to the poet Sigvat (p. 40 above), sacrifices to the elves took place in the autumn in Sweden. This was the time when sacrifices were made to the *dísir* or goddesses, on the 'winter-nights', either in the hall or out of doors.[12] The term *dísir* is a wide one, and seems to include the female guardian spirits attached to certain individuals or families. The poet Hallfred, for instance, had such a guardian, who wore a coat of mail like a valkyrie. In *Hallfreðar Saga* (11) she is said to follow his ship over the sea and appear to him just before his death. He told her that their partnership was now ended, but his son, Hallfred the younger, agreed to receive her, and the *fylgjukona* (following woman) then vanished. In *Víga-Glúms Saga* (9) a guardian spirit of a similar kind is described coming from Norway to Iceland after the death of Glum's grandfather, and Glum saw her in a dream approaching his house (p. 122 below) He invited her to stay with him, and when he awoke he interpreted his dream: 'This is a great and remarkable dream, and I would read it thus: Vigfuss my grandfather must be dead, and the woman who was higher than the mountains as she walked must be his *hamingja*,[13] for he was above most men in honour; his *hamingja* must be seeking an abode with me.' Evidently such female guardian spirits are not linked with the land like the Vanir or land-spirits, since they may travel over the sea to reach the men they are protecting. Their link is rather with a particular family, and they seem to symbolise the luck which can be passed on from one generation to another. But in spite of some overlapping and confusion in the later sources, there is no doubt that the conception of a company of supernatural beings associated closely with the natural world can be seen as an important element in the religion of the Viking Age.

2 Guardian spirits

Under Christian influence the *dísir* might be seen as equivalent to guardian angels in a pagan context. The story of the death of Thidrandi, son of Hall of Siða in Iceland, illustrates this.[14] Hall was in favour of the acceptance of Christianity, and when the autumn feast was held at his house it was presumably without sacrifices. On the first night there was a knock on the door when all the folk were in bed, and Thidrandi thought it must be a late guest. He opened the door, in spite of earlier warnings that no one should venture outside that night. There was no one there, so he walked round the house; then he saw nine women in black on black horses approaching from the north and carrying drawn swords in their hands. Nine other women in shining white were riding from the south, but the dark women arrived first and attacked him. He was just able to relate what had happened before he died, and Thorhall, a man of much wisdom, told the family that the dark women were their attendant spirits who knew of their change of faith and had seized Hall's son as a victim before they lost their powers. The white riders were the spirits of the new religion, but they were as yet too far off to be able to intervene.

Here the protective spirits are identified with evil beings hostile to Christianity, but behind this it is possible to see memories of the land-spirits, who protected individuals and families who made them regular offerings, even though in this tale they are pictured like valkyries armed with weapons. It is perhaps significant that in *Njáls Saga* (100) and *Kristni Saga* (7) Hall, when accepting Christianity, asks if he may have St Michael the Archangel as his guardian spirit. The feast of St Michael was at the time of the winter nights, and this seems to have also been the time when sacrifice to the land-spirits took place.

The land-spirits may be represented in human form, but like valkyries and the Vanir they could take on bird or animal shapes. Snorri has a tale of how the Icelanders made insulting verses about King Harald Gormsson of Denmark because he impounded the cargo from one of their ships.[15] The king sent a wizard to Iceland in the form of a whale, but as he drew near he saw a vast number of land-spirits ready to defend the island: 'All the mountains and mounds were filled with land-spirits, some great and some small.' A dragon advanced to meet him with a crowd of snakes and toads, while from the other quarters of the island came a huge bird, a bull and a rock-giant with a staff. It has been suggested that these four creatures are based on the four symbols of the Evangelists,[16] and this might be a typical Icelandic jest, but in any case it is significant that a crowd of spirits, some in bird or animal form, are prepared to defend Iceland from aggression. In the poem Snorri quotes, from which presumably he took the story, there is a reference to the 'mountain powers' driving out the official of the Danish king responsible for the removal of the cargo from the Icelandic ship. The same idea is found in later tales from the Danish island of Bornholm.[17] Thiele recorded a tradition that the 'Underground People' of Bornholm became visible when they defended the island from attack; this was said to happen in 1645 when two Swedish warships attempted a landing. Bødker in a later version tells how a solitary old solder on sentry duty saw the Swedish invaders and knew that there were no troops within call; however he heard whispering voices: 'Load and shoot!', and when he shot at them, scores of little red-capped men became visible and shot at the Swedes and drove them off.

Long before the Viking Age, Celts and Germans evidently pictured local spirits of earth and water resembling the land-spirits. When in the Roman period they depicted their gods in human form, many carved stones and altars showed male and female beings who were not major

107

deities. They often had local names, and were linked with natural features of the landscape. In Gaul the goddesses usually kept their own native names, whereas the male deities were identified with Roman gods such as Apollo and Mars. The goddesses are shown singly, in partnership with a male god, or in groups of two, three or more, often associated with water and healing. Two types of supernatural figures show a particular resemblance to the land-spirits; these are the *Genii Cucullati*, the Hooded Ones, who appear to be male, and the *Matres* or *Matrones*, the Mother Goddesses. It is often difficult to distinguish between native deities and those inspired by classical or foreign cults in the religious art of countries under Roman rule, but in this case both classes of being appear to have preserved their identity and they are accepted as being of native origin.

The hooded figures in Britain are generally in groups of three, and are most frequent in the area around Hadrian's Wall and in the Cotswolds (Plate 3a). Jocelyn Toynbee listed fifteen examples in 1957, most of them depicted on stones.[18] The figures appear to be male, but they wear cloaks which are sometimes drawn close in front and may come down to their feet, so that only the face is visible. Some are young and childlike, others older and bearded, and they tend to be short and stocky, so that some resemble dwarfs or hunchbacks. In two instances they accompany a goddess, and they hold baskets, bunches of grapes, and what may be eggs, all familiar symbols of fruitfulness and plenty. In Gaul the hooded men are mostly found as single figures. The hooded cloak worn by these figures was a popular garment not only in northern Europe, where it probably originated, but also in southern countries where it gave protection from the sun. It was worn by humble folk, by those who worked out-of-doors, and by travellers, as well as by more important people who wished to conceal their identity. However, as Deonna has shown in an important study of hooded men,[19] it also serves as a symbol of the supernatural world, worn by beings normally invisible to men. These depicted in the art of the Roman period appear to be associated with protection and healing, with fertility (they are sometimes shown with a prominent phallus), with sleep, and with death. Deonna points out that some form of hooded cloak was used in later times to mark someone set apart from the normal world, such as a monk, a mourner, or a bride in her veil. It seems possible that these hooded men can be seen as early examples of the brownies of popular belief, including figures such as Robin Goodfellow and his companions. These too appear in folktales as small male beings, who were benevolent when not angered or alarmed, and usually attached to a particular farm or family; they were merry mischievous beings, who brought prosperity to animals and crops, and who helped with the work of the house. The brownies belonged to a much larger circle of supernatural beings in English fairy tradition, and in this also they resemble the land-spirits.

The second group of Mother Goddess figures was widespread in England, Gaul and the Rhineland during the period of Roman rule (Plate 3b). They are clearly linked with plenty and fertility. They carry fruit, horns of plenty, baskets, bunches of grapes, loaves or eggs, and often have babies at their breasts or hold them swaddled in their arms. They may be accompanied by a small dog, or by the prow of a ship which emphasises their connection with water. They wear robes of varying length, and some are young, with flowing hair, while others appear to be matrons, with hair elaborately dressed. They are usually seated, either singly or in groups; three is the favourite number, but a group of four was found in London in 1977.[20] They are often found in the vicinity of rivers, healing springs, or temples, and in Gaul sometimes on house sites. Little goddess figures seated in what may be household shrines are also found.[21] Sometimes the women hold what is thought to be a roll of destiny, along with a sphere or a spindle, attributes of fortune; it is believed therefore that they were thought to foretell men's destinies, and particularly the futures of young children.[22] Dedications to the *Matres* were often set up by women, but there are a number bearing names of men in the lower ranks of the Roman army.

Shrines formerly associated with the Mothers might in later times become sanctuaries of the Virgin Mary. Thevenot gives a striking example in the remote valley of Doron de Belleville north of Lyons,[23] where pilgrimages to the shrine of Notre-Dame-de-la-Vie were still continuing in 1960. He was told that in the period before the war gifts such as cereals, wheat, cheese and butter were brought in large quantities and placed around the altar in the little chapel, while a number of farm animals were brought as gifts and sold by auction. The Virgin of the chapel is a woman in a kind of hood, simply but impressively carved; she could be of considerable age, and Thevenot thinks it possible that she dates back to the Roman period. The figure was previously in a niche in the wall beside a spout through which water flowed from the spring, but has now been removed to a covered gallery beside the chapel. Women pilgrims are said to have brought cloths to soak in the water, which they rubbed over their faces and other parts of the body. The figure holds a rounded object like a muff, which apparently represented the source of the stream, with drops of water carved on it. According to local tradition, the figure was originally that of a pregnant woman, but was mutilated in the last century because this was thought to be improper. The spring at Belleville has long been held to possess healing properties. Mural paintings of the seventeenth and eighteenth centuries represent cures, and there are records of infants believed to be dead who were brought to the spring and revived sufficiently to be given Christian baptism.

The goddesses are frequently associated with running water. One called Coventina had a shrine at Carrawburgh, close to Hadrian's Wall,[24] and is represented on one of the carved stones there in a reclining position, holding a vessel out of which water pours and a leaf of what seems to be a water plant. Many offerings were made at her well, and at another not far away beside the Mithraeum, to which a carving of three nymphs probably belonged.[25] Finds at Coventina's Well included incense burners in bronze, one inscribed with the goddess's name, bronze masks, brooches, glass vessels, shrine bells and perhaps as many as sixteen thousand coins, although a number of these were lost. There were said to be twenty-four stone altars, twenty-two of which survive, some erected by members of the Roman army with grateful thanks for help, in fulfilment of a vow. It is not certain if Coventina was a local spirit, but she seems in course of time to have been accepted as one; the spring was walled in by the army builders, and is thought to have been an enclosed area open to the sky. The other shrine was dedicated to the Nymphs and Genius of the place, and the spring may have been regarded as holy before the coming of the Romans.

Beside many altars and plaques from shrines of the goddesses, a number of small figurines of pipeclay survive from Gaul and the Rhineland, some as early as the first century AD. Some of these represent a goddess in a high-backed chair, and others a naked female with sun-symbols such as wheels and rosettes either on the body or beside it. Miranda Green suggests that this is a native fertility goddess in association with a sun diety.[26] Such goddesses, as well as the seated Mothers, could be viewed as belonging to a company of nature spirits such as we find in Scandinavia in the Viking Age.

The Mother Goddesses were important for both Celts and Germans. De Vries gives a number of Germanic names from dedications, some of these apparently soldiers from Germany quartered in Britain.[27] Inscriptions are frequent in the Lower Rhineland from about the second century AD. Some of these beings have tribal names, such as *Matres Gallaicae*, and others names denoting them as generous givers, such as *Alagabiae* and *Arvagastae*. Later, in the Viking Age, goddesses in the Vanir group had similar names which represented them as Giving Ones, such as Gefn and Gefion.

The Mothers continued to be worshipped by the pagan Anglo-Saxons, since Bede in *De tempora ratione* (13) records that the night before Christmas was known as *Modraniht*, which he translates as 'night of the Mothers'. The long life of such traditions is shown by a wealth of folklore in Germany, Switzerland and Austria concerning female super-natural beings linked with women and children. Waschnitius collected much of this in 1913, and it has been reviewed by Lotte Motz.[28] She interprets it as representing various manifestations of a winter goddess, but it seems more probable that we have here a persistent tradition developing out of earlier beliefs in the Mothers and the Vanir. The supernatural beings have a variety of names, such as Percht, Holda, Stampa, Rupfa, Luzie, Frau Frie, Frau Gode and so on, and were said to bring fertility to the fields and to poultry and cattle, as well as influencing the weather. They were associated with trees, rocks and lakes, and women who wanted children appealed to them for help. They were also said to foster and train children, as the land-spirits sometimes did, and to encourage girls to be good housewives, as the English fairies were thought to do. It is significant that they had a dual aspect, and could appear in both terrifying and attractive forms. Sometimes they took on monstrous shapes, and it has been suggested that the long iron nose characteristic of Percht and Holda is based on memories of the long beak of a bird of prey.

The festivals of these female spirits were in the winter, and food might be left for them on Christmas Eve, as for the elves, or on the eve of Epiphany. Like the Mothers, they were associated with spinning, although they seem to encourage girls to be diligent spinners rather than to be concerned with the spinning of destiny. Folktales like that of 'Habetrot' from the Scottish Border, however, preserve a tradition of old spinning women beneath the ground who instead of punishing a feckless girl, do her spinning for her, and help her to become the laird's wife.[29] As for the connection with winter, it is hardly surprising to find it among land-spirits of northern and mountainous countries. Skadi, the wife of Njord, who travelled on snow-shoes, is one example of this, and Bard in his home beside a glacier is another.

Traces of similar female beings who have lived on in folk tradition have been collected by A. D. Hope in a study of fairy lore in Scotland.[30] He found traditions of local goddesses and female tutelary spirits linked with wells, rocks and mounds, particularly in the old kingdom of the Picts, while in the west and north-western Highlands and the Isles there were many legends of the Cailleach, the Old Woman or Hag. Groups of maidens ranging from three to nine in number were associated with stones, monuments, megalithic circles and natural rocks as well as springs, like the Nine Maidens at the well at Achindoir and at the Nine Wells at Ochils in Perthshire.[31]

III

3 Celtic goddesses

Similar beings are to be found in Irish popular tradition. Áine, for instance, is remembered as a member of the *Síd*, living with her father in a fairy mound at Limerick. The son of the King of Munster is said to have encountered her while he slept outside on the night of Halloween; he forced her to lie with him, and got a badly bitten ear as a result. In the fifteenth century she was said to have been the wife of the Earl of Desmond for some years, after he seized her cloak as she sat beside the river. In the nineteenth century she was reputed to be attached to the O'Corra family, and about 1896 there was a legend that she lived in the hill called Cnoc Áine.[32] On St John's Eve it was customary to carry bunches of burning hay and straw round the hill which were then taken to the fields to bless the cattle, and one year it is said that a group of girls stayed there to watch and lingered until it grew late. Áine then appeared to them and politely asked them to leave, since 'they wanted the hill to themselves'. To explain her words, she let them look through a ring, and they saw that the hill was crowded with folk who had previously been invisible. Here we have a parallel to the picture of the land-spirits thronging round the hills of Iceland given by Snorri some centuries earlier.

Another figure closely related to the land was the Caillech Bherri (Hag of Beare, from *caille*, veil or cloak), a being associated with a peninsula in the south-west of Ireland, but who appears in tales found over a wide area, and also in Scottish tradition. MacCana emphasises her function as a divine ancestress with many descendants, marrying a series of husbands and passing from youth to age more than once.[33] Under the name of Búi she is represented as the wife of the god Lug, and she has special associations with the megalithic burial place at Knowth. The Hag has survived as a lively figure in modern Irish folklore. The idea of such spirits guarding and protecting the land in which they dwell is firmly established in Irish tradition. When the Sons of Míl arrived in Ireland, they were confronted by three goddesses, Badb, Fodla and Ériu, who demanded that the land should be called after them if they allowed the newcomers to settle there. They belonged to the Túatha Dé Danann, and in the end it was agreed that the Sons of Míl should rule the surface of the land, while the Túatha Dé continued to hold the region underground, each of their chiefs ruling a mound. As late as the seventh century the writer of a *Life* of St Patrick could refer to the people of the Síd as 'the gods of the earth'.[34] The idea of the fairies as a former race who remained hidden from men has been explained as memories of an earlier culture displaced by more powerful invaders, but it might also be based on traditions of the land-spirits, who, as in uninhabited Iceland, possessed the land before settlers came to live there.

4 The bright Other World

The hidden community of the Túatha Dé in Ireland resembled that of men, save that they were free from the tyranny of time, living 'without grief, without sorrow, without death, sickness or wasting away, without age, without corruption of the earth'.[35] From time to time heroes in Irish or Welsh literature were drawn away to this realm outside time, lured by fair maidens in strange garb who enticed them into a mound or bore them away to an enchanted land across the sea (p. 181 below) One such woman appeared to Bran son of Febal as he slept and sang to him of Emain, a holy island inhabited by women, where nothing harsh could be found and there was no death and decay. He set out in his boat to find it, and when he finally reached the island the woman of his dreams appeared and threw him a ball of thread, so that the boat could be drawn to shore. After what seemed to him a stay of a year, he returned home only to find that hundreds of years had slipped by and that he was only a dim memory to his people, a figure in ancient tales.[36] Connla too was invited by a beautiful girl to visit her dwelling in the Land of the Living, where death and sin were unknown and he could keep young for ever. He left with her in her boat, in spite of his father's entreaties, and was never seen again.[37]

The hero Cú Chulainn also was once tempted to seek out this land. Two sisters from the Plain of Delight appeared to him in a dream, one in a cloak of crimson and the other in green, and beat him with whips until he was exhausted. When he awoke, he was still languid and weak, and later a messenger arrived to tell him that the woman in green was Fand, who desired to take him to her own land where she would heal him of his sickness and welcome him as her lover.[38] He joined her for a month, but his wife Emer intervened, and he returned to her while Fand went back to her former husband, the god Manannán mac Lir. Manannán shook his cloak between Cú Chulainn and Fand, and they were parted for ever.

Sometimes the way to the enchanted world is not by sea but through a fairy mound, or a cave. In an early tale, 'The Adventures of Nera', the hero makes a grim journey on the eve of Samain with the corpse of a hanged man on his back urging him on, and 'great was the darkness of that night and its horror'.[39] He went through the Cave of Cruachan to join the people of the Síd and married one of them. The mound in which he dwelt was afterwards destroyed by his own people after he had warned them of danger threatening from the Síd. However he returned to join his Otherworld family. Another Irish hero, Lóegaire, once gave

113

E

help to the people of the *Síd* and married one of their women, and he too refused to return to the world of men, although his father, the King of Connacht, offered him the kingdom. His reply was: 'One night of the nights of the *Síd* / I would not give for your kingdom.'[40]

A similar pattern may be discerned behind the tale of 'Pwyll Prince of Dyfed' in the Welsh *Mabinogion*. A strange lady in a golden robe rode past on a white horse while the prince was sitting on a mound. He followed her, but could not overtake her, until finally she stopped, unloosed her mantle and revealed her beauty, like the valkyrie in Saxo's tale (p. 86 above). He was drawn away to her kingdom where time had no meaning, since she was Rhiannon, and when the birds of Rhiannon sang men lost all sense of its passing. This motif of a woman from another world luring away a young hero or holding him captive was further developed in the Arthurian romances, as Lucy Paton has shown in her study of Morgain and the Lady of the Lake. Other echoes of the Celtic supernatural world can be discerned in Middle English poems such as *Sir Orfeo* and Chaucer's *Wife of Bath's Tale*.

The traditions of land-spirits and mother-goddesses and fair women from a world outside time are clearly powerful and long-lived in both Irish and Scandinavian tradition, and they seem to extend back into earlier times among the Celtic and Germanic peoples. Traces can be seen in folktales of a belief in land-protecting spirits who bring prosperity to farmers and hunters, and also play unpleasant tricks on those who fail to treat them with respect. The question must be raised as to how far such spirits were connected with the dead in the earth, helping and sometimes harming the living. The Túatha Dé dwelt in burial mounds, and were often encountered at Samain, the time when the dead were held to be active and could revisit the world of living men. In Germany and Scandinavia it was said that they came back either at Halloween or at Christmas, and there are records of food left out for them on Christmas Eve and the fire made up, while folk went to midnight Mass. Next morning their footprints might be seen on the ashes of the hearth, and in Iceland the elves were said to visit houses in a similar way. A good example of a dead man who guarded the luck of a family comes from Orkney, where Marwick quotes a story told in 1911 of a *hogboy* (howe-dweller, from *haugbúi*) who lived in a mound and was given offerings of milk or wine.[41] When the farmer dug into his mound, however, he appeared in great anger, and caused six cows to die as a punishment. He is described as old and grey-whiskered, dressed in tattered old clothes and with old shoes of horse-hide on his feet.

In early Iceland, however, the dead could hardly be pictured as waiting in their mounds for an opportunity to visit the living. There seems little doubt that the natural world in both Celtic and Germanic areas was held to be peopled with independent spirits dwelling in rocks, waterfalls, springs and mountains. These were prepared to befriend the living and make the land fertile, but violence and bloodshed were offensive to them, in contrast to the battle-spirits. No doubt the dead in their graves might also help the living, and the spirit of a dead king, in particular, might possess such powers. Iceland, however, was without kings or ancestors, and there seems to have been a vigorous belief in a host of supernatural powers in wild places as well as on the farms, and in natural hills and mounds as well as burial places. The spirits driven out when Christianity came were not those of the pre-Christian dead within the earth. There are many stories of spirits forced to leave their ancient abodes, so that on certain nights people kept their beasts indoors to prevent injury from the departing hosts. Some of these dwelt in inaccessible places in the cliffs or far from human habitation. One forced to flee by the prayers of St Olaf in *Olafs Saga helga* (179) in *Heimskringla*, came from a mountain pasture in Norway, and others were expelled by the early Icelandic bishops with prayers and holy water. A tale told of more than one holy man was that he was let down by a rope to bless the cliffs where seabirds nested, and was challenged by a voice calling on him to let those who dwelt there alone: 'Wicked folk must have somewhere to live'. Occasionally a skinny arm and hand holding a knife could be seen about to cut the rope, and the tale ends with mention of a cliff left unblest as a result, and afterwards known as the Cliff of the Heathen.[42]

As time went on, the power of dead ancestors became important in Iceland as it had been in the land from which the Icelanders came. A number of Icelandic families were said to 'die into the hills'. It is not clear exactly what is meant by this. In the account of Helgafell, the holy place of Thorolf and his descendants in western Iceland (p. 13 above), it is said in *Eyrbyggja Saga* (11) that Thorolf's son, Thorstein Codbiter, was thought to have joined his father in the hill after his death at sea. Thorstein was a great fisherman, and when he was twenty-five he went out one night to fish, and he and his crew were drowned. Before the news reached his home, a shepherd going past Helgafell in the darkness thought he saw one end of the hill open, with firelight within: 'Inside the hill he saw great fires and heard much merriment and noise over drinking-horns; when he listened to what was said, he heard that Thorstein Codbiter was being welcomed with his companions, and men were saying that he was to sit in the high-seat opposite his father.' Thorolf, Thorstein's father, had in fact been buried elsewhere according to the saga, in a mound to the west of Helgafell, but local tradition preserved the belief that he dwelt inside the rocky hill which he had chosen for his sacred place. Helgafell is not unlike a large burial mound, and here we may have a transference of beliefs about dead leaders in their great mounds in Scandinavia who brought blessing to the land when they were laid to rest in their graves. Snorri in *Ynglinga Saga* (10) traces such beliefs back to the god Freyr, who once ruled over the Swedes at Uppsala and had his chief temple there. He is said to have brought good seasons and prosperity to the land, and so when he died the Swedes brought great offerings to his mound, and believed that he remained alive and potent in the earth. The connection which seems to exist between Freyr and the elves and land-spirits thus provides an additional reason to associate them with the dead in their graves.

Snorri goes on to trace similar ideas continuing in Sweden and Norway, so that it was of the utmost importance to know where each of the early kings was buried. Those who had been lucky rulers in life and whose reigns were marked by good seasons and plenty could continue to bring blessings to men after their deaths. There is a possibility that such kings bore each in his turn the title of *Freyr* (Lord) in Sweden. It may have been so also in pre-Christian Denmark, since Saxo in his history of the early kings has several who bear the name *Frothi*, and some of these are said to have been carried round the land after death. He translated into Latin a verse which he claims was the work of an early poet, referring to this custom:

> Because they wished to extend Frothi's life, the Danes long carried his remains throughout their countryside.
> This great prince's body, now buried under turf, is covered by bare earth beneath the clear sky.
>
> (VI, 172, Fisher's translation)

The name Frothi corresponds to one of Freyr's titles, and comes from an adjective *froðr*, meaning 'wise fruitful'. Just as these kings were carried round the land after death, so Freyr himself was borne in a sacred wagon in an annual procession round the farms in Sweden to bring good luck and prosperous seasons.

The most detailed account of such a custom is late, in a comic tale attached to the Saga of Olaf Tryggvason in *Flateyjarbók* (I, 277, p. 337f.). This is the story of Gunnar Helming, a fugitive from Norway who had offended King Olaf and fled to Sweden. There he joined the procession of Freyr, who was being taken in a wagon to visit the farms, accompanied by an attractive young priestess known as the god's wife. The wagon was held up by a late snowstorm in the hills, and all the attendants made off, leaving Gunnar and the girl to struggle on alone. Then the god became angry, and came out of his wagon to fight with Gunnar, but after he appealed for help to King Olaf, Gunnar managed to overcome Freyr, and he took his place and impersonated the god. The story-teller paints a humorous picture of the simple-minded Swedes, delighted to find that their god could now eat and drink with them, and to observe after a time that the god's wife was with child. Gunnar refused to accept sacrifices, but took gifts instead, and he brought great renown to Freyr's cult, until at last King Olaf, guessing what had happened, summoned him back to Norway, and he left with his wife and child and much wealth obtained from the credulous Swedes. The idea of a man impersonating a god may have been taken from classical sources, but the main outline of the tale must have been based on what men knew of the cult of the fertility god in Sweden, since otherwise there would be no point in the jest.

Much earlier, in *Germania* (31), Tacitus describes a similar ritual among the Germans in Denmark, when processions formed an essential part of the cult of the goddess Nerthus, who bore the title of Mother Earth (*Terra Mater*). Her wagon was drawn by oxen through the land and welcomed everywhere with delight, and all weapons were set aside while the people gave themselves up to feasting. The idea of a wagon bearing an invisible deity, or possibly a symbol or image of the deity, takes on more reality when we consider two delicately made little wagons from about the time when Tacitus was writing, which were found dismantled in a peat bog at Dejbjorg in Denmark.[43] These had wooden frames and a seat of wood and leather, with openwork sheet bronze to decorate the outer frame, and small human faces on the uprights. Another decorated wagon of wood comes from the Oseberg ship and was buried in the Viking Age, in the late ninth century. It has been thought to be a copy of an earlier one of primitive type, because of the style of the elaborately carved decoration, and is covered with scenes with human and animal figures, difficult to interpret.

It seems reasonable to suppose that such wagons were used for religious ceremonial, and the contents of the Oseberg ship, well-preserved in the peat soil, suggests that this rich burial was associated with the fertility deities. Corn, apples and nuts had been placed in it, the apples in an elaborate container, and the two women in the ship, thought to be a princess and her attendant, may have played some part in the Vanir cult. The ship itself, with its richly carved prow, was unsuitable for the open sea but could have been used for voyages round the coast; it would have been admirably suited to take a priestess of the Vanir from one settlement to another on a course of visits like those made by

Nerthus in Denmark. This is something difficult to prove, but it may be noted that a surprisingly large number of women are buried in ships and boats in Norway and Sweden, and eight rich ship-graves containing women in Tuna in Sweden, in particular, suggest there may have been a cult centre there.

The ship was one of the symbols of the Vanir, and it is found also beside figures of goddesses from the Roman period in Gaul and the Rhineland. The beautiful maids from the Land of Youth in the Irish tales often arrive in boats, and the voyage over the water is remembered in Celtic tradition along with the entry into a burial mound as a route to the Other World. If the Oseberg ship was indeed associated with the Vanir, this helps to explain why the grave was broken into and deliberate damage done to the ship's prow and the great bed included in the contents of the vessel, while one body was removed to leave only a few bones behind. There was more hostility against the Vanir than the other gods among the new Christian church in Scandinavia, and according to Brøgger the entry into the Oseberg mound in the Viking Age was an organised attack on the grave rather than a secret entry by treasure-hunters.[44]

Indeed the association between the spirits of fertility and the ship seems to have been slow to die. A Belgian Chronicle has a reference to a strange occurrence at St Trond in 1135.[45] A boat on wheels was made and pulled by men of the Weavers' Guild first to Aachen and then to other towns. At St Trond the abbot tried to prevent its entry, but the townspeople welcomed it with enthusiasm. In the evening bands of half-naked women ran through the streets and a crowd of about a thousand people gathered to dance round it until midnight. This continued for over a week, after which some urged tht the ship should be destroyed, but in the end it went on to Louvain, where the gates were closed against it. This is a confused account, and it is not explained why the weavers were responsible for the ship. However the outburst of wild merriment sounds like a echo of the celebrations around the wagon of Nerthus centuries before, and of the welcoming of fertility deities into homes and communities in the Viking Age.

It seems established that in Scandinavia certain graves were regarded as sacred places because of association with the Vanir. These are sometimes ship-graves, and an interesting example comes from Kaupang, a trading centre in southern Norway.[46] On a headland near the settlement, a number of graves of men and women were found tightly packed together, and the dead had been placed in boats or portions of boats, sometimes with more than one body interred in a grave. This strongly suggests that the headland was a sacred place

LAND-SPIRITS AND ANCESTORS

where it was desirable to be buried, and may help to account for the
market at Kaupang, since it would attract many visitors.

5 Fertility deities

Unfortunately we know comparatively little about the cult of the fertility
god who bore the title Freyr. He seems to have some association with the
sun, and also with elves. In *Ynglinga Saga* Snorri emphasises the
importance of the royal grave mound in which he was buried and Freyr's
power over the fruitfulness of the earth. Sometimes he appears to be
represented as a young child journeying over the sea, which gives an
additional meaning to the symbol of the ship.[47] In one of the Edda
poems, *Skírnismál*, he is represented as a youth seized with passionate
love for the maiden Gerd, daughter of a giant in the underworld. The
Swedes also associated him with battle (p. 49 above), setting the image
of his boar on weapons and armour; this may have been the result of
adopting him as ancestor and protector of the kings of Uppsala, who
took the name Ynglings from his title of Yngvi-Freyr. The image of the
dead king and of the child coming over the sea from an unknown realm
to bring the land blessing suggests a deity continually dying and being
reborn, like the growing things of earth.

Another significant element in the cult of Freyr as remembered in
Iceland was that of the sacred field. According to *Víga-Glúms Saga* (7), a
certain family in north-east Iceland had the guardianship of a field near
Freyr's temple, which bore the name *Vitazgjafi*,[48] translated as 'Certain
giver' or 'Yielding assured harvest'; this echoes the 'giving' element in
the names of the goddesses (p. 10 above). The field in the saga was said
to be exceptionally fruitful, and those responsible for the temple had the
right to take crops from it. The great crime of Slaying-Glum, the hero
of the saga, was to kill a man in this field, thus defiling it with blood and
arousing Freyr's anger; for this and other offences against the god he
finally lost his land (p. 138 below). Certain Icelandic chiefs bore the title
Freysgoði, Priest of Freyr, and there were a number of places sacred to
the god in Iceland, while placenames in Norway and Sweden indicate
that sacred fields were known there also.[49]

What marks out the cult of the Vanir from those of other major gods is
the large number of supernatural beings, male and female, included in it.
No obvious equivalent to Freyr has been found among Anglo-Saxon
placenames, although some may have been based on the name of a
goddess Frig.[50] There was, however, a god Ing known to the Anglo-
Saxons; the rune NG stood for his name, and there is a verse about him
in a Runic Poem:[51]

Ing at first among the East Danes
was seen of men. Then he went eastwards [*or*: came back]
across the sea. The wagon sped after.
Thus the Heardings have named the hero.

This short verse is full of problems. Did Ing travel to the east (*est*) or return back (*eft*)? Is the wagon a symbol for travel to the Other World? The wagon graves of the Celts in the late Hallstatt and early La Téne periods might indicate the adoption of such a symbol, later replaced in Scandinavia by a ship. The early name of the god Ing among the North Germanic peoples seems to have been *Ingwaz*, and according to Tacitus (*Germania* 3) he founded the race of the Ingaevones.[52] The name has been retained in Freyr's title of *Yngvi*.

Freyr belonged to a family group, with a wife and child, a sister Freyja, and a father Njord, and Njord in turn may have been one of a pair of divine beings, with Nerthus as his female partner. As for the goddesses of the Vanir, it seems that their names were legion. Freyja among the Germans was Frija, mentioned as the wife of Wodan by Paul the Deacon in the eighth century (I, 8); she may also be equated with Frigg, the Scandinavian consort of Odin. Frigg and many other Scandinavian goddesses should probably be seen as variants of Freyja. There was *Mardǫll*, linked with the sea; *Hǫrn*, connected with flax and presumably weaving; *Skialf*, whom Snorri in *Ynglinga Saga* makes into an early queen of Sweden with a wonderful necklace, who killed King Agni. There is also *Gefn* and the Danish *Gefjon*, described in *Ynglinga Saga* (5) as a giantess who turned her sons into oxen and ploughed the

9 Figures (much enlarged) on piece of gold foil, approximately 1.6–1.5 cm, one of set of 16 found at a farm at Hange, Rogaland, Norway.

island of Sjælland away from the mainland of Sweden, and many lesser names. Indeed it seems that all the wives of the gods, many of whom are said to be the daughters of giants, came from the Vanir.

In the Viking Age we have a series of small symbolic pictures which appear to represent the coming together of god and goddess. They were engraved on minute pieces of gold foil, and show two figures either embracing or facing one another with a leafy bough between them (Fig. 9). They were used in Scandinavia from the Migration Period into the early Viking Age, possibly as a kind of amulet, and have been found in sets, sometimes as many as sixteen at a time, chiefly on house sites and not in graves.[53] The figures are clothed and sometimes their knees are bent, and it has been suggested that they are taking part in a dance. They may have been associated with weddings, and seem to be linked with the Vanir deities, representing the conception of the divine marriage as found in the *Edda* poem *Skírnismál*, with the coming together of Freyr and Gerd. Some of these gold pieces are found in the foundation of what is thought to have been a pre-Christian sanctuary at Mære in Norway, presumably placed there to hallow and protect the building, and possibly to evoke for it the protection of the land-spirits (p. 31 above).

Among the Celtic peoples in Gaul there is evidence for the representation of a divine pair, god and goddess, associated with healing. In the Roman period the male figure was identified with Apollo, shown at sacred sites with a goddess who retained her Celtic name. Sometimes he had a title emphasising his link with the sun, such as *Amarcolitanus* (?with piercing glance), *Grannus* (?shining), or *Belenus*, suggesting light and heat.[54] Another symbol of such a union might be seen in the small figurines of a woman with solar symbols on her body (p. 110 above). Not only healing but also wealth was seen as a gift of the fertility deities. Njord, for instance, associated in Scandinavia with ships and the sea, was said in the *Prose Edda* (*Gylfaginning* 22) to be '... so rich and prosperous that he can bestow abundance of land and property as he will, and he must be invoked for this.' Freyja is said to weep tears of gold, and this is a popular image in the poetry of the Viking Age.[55] The horned god in Gaul, generally known as Cernunnos, is not only depicted as Lord of the Animals but also as a dispenser of wealth, holding a neck-ring or a sack from which coins pour out. While the god Odin gave booty to his followers and helped them to find treasure hidden in the earth, the fertility deities dispensed riches of a different kind. Wealth came to their followers largely as a result of the increase in crops and herds, for this was in the power of the land-spirits to grant to those who made contracts with them.

The evidence indicates that worship of the ancestors can probably not be clearly separated from that of the land-spirits. The dead king may have been identified with the fertility god, just as the Pharaoh of ancient Egypt was seen as Osiris after his death. In the ninth century *Life of St Anskar* (26), it is related that Anskar returned to Birka and found tht strange traditions had crept in among the Christians there. A man had dreamed that he was present at a meeting of the gods, and that they had complained that people were neglecting their sacrifices. 'If you desire to have more gods and we do not suffice', they declared, 'we will agree to summon your former King Erik to join us.' So the people began to make offerings to him and set up a shrine in his honour. We hear also of one of the Norwegian kings, Olaf of Geirstad, being worshipped after death, and he bore the significant title of Elf of Geirstad.[56] The followers of St Olaf believed that he was in some way a reincarnation of this earlier Olaf, and when they passed the mound where he was buried they asked the Christian king: 'Tell me, lord, were you buried here?' Olaf vehemently denied any such link with the dead, declaring: 'My soul has never had two bodies; it cannot have them, either now or on the Resurrection Day; there would be no common truth or honesty in me if I spoke otherwise.' St Olaf was said to possess the sword of the earlier king, which had been taken from the grave at the time of his birth and kept for him by his mother. The relationship here may have been like that between Slaying-Glum and his grandfather, whose guardian spirit, in the form of a huge woman in armour, journeyed to Iceland after the older man's death and attached herself to his grandson, bringing with her something of the luck which Vigfuss had enjoyed during his life (p. 106 above).

In this case the idea is personified, and the word *hamingja* used of a huge woman resembling a valkyrie or one of the *dísir*, acting as guardian spirit to the family and as a protector to a chosen one in each generation. But the term *hamingja* sometimes seems to stand for luck and special powers which can be passed on in life from one person to another, and which kings in particular could grant to their followers for a limited period. In a late saga of Harald Fairhair, he sends out his poets on a dangerous quest, and they beg him to grant them his *hamingja* for the journey. Although Harald is angry with them, he consents to do as they ask. St Olaf possessed the same power, promising one of his men on one occasion: 'Be sure that I will grant my *hamingja* to you and to all the party.'[57]

6 Rebirth of the dead

From the Migration Period onwards it was customary to name Germanic kings after their predecessors, sometimes by using only a part of the name again, while in the Viking Age a child would usually be named after someone in the family who had died, frequently a grandparent.[58] This could have developed out of an assumption that the dead might in some way 'return' in his descendant, or that at least the former luck and strength which he had enjoyed might accompany the name. To call this a belief in rebirth would be an oversimplification, but it seems to be a recognition that the gifts and powers of the dead might be passed on to the living in a later generation. Such conceptions seem particularly to be associated with the fertility powers, and there is a strong link between them and the burial mound, while the goddesses are represented as foretelling the destiny of the newly-born or of a youth on the verge of manhood. The Helgi poems in the *Edda*, recounting the achievements of more than one hero called Helgi and of their relationship with a valkyrie first called Sigrun and then Svava, are another example of this emphasis on continuity: 'Of Helgi and Svava it is said that they were born again', runs the prose note at the end of *Helgakviða Hjorvarðssonar*.

A similar emphasis on the link between the generations is found in Irish literature, although there is no close parallel which suggests direct borrowing from one side by the other. Some of the tales of the births of heroes and heroines are strange and illogical. They may come about as the result of an incestuous relationship between father and daughter, although no disgrace comes from this, and it is not represented as the deliberate or accidental violation of a taboo within the family group. Daelgas son of Cairrel, for instance, was kissed by his daughter as he lay dying, whereupon a spark of red fire passed from his mouth to hers, and she became pregnant, to bear a son given her father's name. The boy's first 'feat of youthful folly' was said to be to leap over his own gravestone.[59] One version of the birth of Mes Búachalla (cowherd's fosterchild) makes her the result of a union between Eochaid of Tara and his daughter.[60] He intended that the child should be killed, but she was brought up by a herdsman without his knowledge.

In other tales there is a rebirth in the direct family line, with the same name retained. One elaborate example is the tale of Étáin, daughter of the King of Ulster.[61] She was married to Mider, a ruler of the *Síd*, with the help of the Mac Óc, who was Mider's fosterson. Mider's first wife, Fuamnach, resented this marriage, and since she had magical skills she turned Étáin into a pool of water from which emerged a worm which turned into a scarlet insect. This was a beautiful winged creature whose fragrance and musical humming so satisfied those who saw it that they needed no food, while drops from its wings brought healing. For a while the fly took refuge in the house of the Mac Óc, but Fuamnach sent a strong wind to carry her away, and she continued as an insect for seven years until she fell into a beaker of drink and was swallowed by the wife of Étar of Ulster. She was born anew as Étáin, and became the wife of Eochaid of Tara. Her former husband Mider came to the court, beat Eochaid at a board game, and claimed a kiss from Étáin as his prize. He took her in his arms and they rose together through the smoke hole in the roof and flew off in the form of swans. Eochaid searched everywhere for his wife, digging into the fairy mounds, and at last he recovered her when he was able to choose her out of fifty women who all looked alike. Then Mider told him that Étáin was pregnant when he carried her away and had given birth to a daughter, whom he took as his wife instead of Étáin. In this case the girl is not represented as a supernatural being but as the daughter of a human king, and yet she essentially belongs to the Other World, and her first husband was a king of the *Síd*. After she is born for the second time, she is represented as having no memory of her former existence.

Another example is that of Túan, a survivor of the company of Partholon, an early invader of Ireland. He was changed into a deer, a boar, an eagle and finally a salmon, and then eaten by the wife of King Cairrel and reborn as her son. He however retained all his past experience in his memory:[62] 'I also remember when speech came upon me as it comes to any man, and I knew all that was being done in Ireland, and I was a seer.' Túan knew every history and pedigree in Ireland, because he retained the knowledge of all that had happened in the land since the time of Partholon. Another elaborate example of transformation is that of Gwion Bach in the Welsh tale of Taliesin, a historical poet of the late sixth century. In the *Hanes Taliesin*,[63] the witch Ceridwen pursued Gwion, who turned into various shapes and became a hare, a fish, a bird and finally a grain of wheat. Ceridwen also changed her shape as was needed, and at last became a black hen and gobbled up the wheat grain. Nine months later she gave birth to Gwion, but he was so beautiful that she was unwilling to kill him and instead wrapped him in a bag and threw him into the sea. He was washed ashore on a weir near Aberystwyth and rescued by Elphin, who brought him up as Taliesin.

There are other strange birth tales in the Irish sagas of heroes who are provided with official human fathers, but at the same time are said to be of divine parentage, such as Cú Chulainn and Mongán. The mother of Cú Chulainn was Dechtine, the daughter of King Conchobar, and one day she swallowed a tiny creature in a cup of water. This caused her to be pregnant, and the god Lug visited her in a dream and told her that the boy to be born to her was to be called Sétanta, and was his son. However Dechtine brought about a miscarriage, and later married Sualtam mac Reich; she afterwards had a child who was called Sétanta, but won the name of Cú Chulainn in boyhood. In another version of Cú Chulainn's birth,[64] Dechtine was not the daughter but the sister of Conchobar, and she and her maidens flew away in the form of birds. When Conchobar found his sister again, she was with a man who proved to be the god Lug, and was about to give birth to a child: when a son was born to her, she had him laid in the lap of the king, who brought him up. These tales are muddled and inconclusive, but the pattern is that the hero had a human father, Sualtaim, and also a divine father, Lug; there are also hints of an incestuous birth as in other tales, for Dechtine's father Conchobar was thought to have caused his daughter's first pregnancy and to have slept with her when he was drunk.

Mongán was a historic king who ruled at Mag Line on Lough Neagh in the late sixth or early seventh century.[65] When his father Fíachna Lurga was king, he was asked to give support to a friend in Scotland who was fighting a desperate campaign, and while he was away and engaged in battle, the god Manannán appeared to his wife. He promised that her husband should return unharmed if she would spend one night with him, so that a son might be born to her who would become a glorious hero, and in a later version of the tale the husband also consents to this. In due course Mongán was born, and when he was three days old, Manannán took him away to the Land of Promise and fostered him there. It was said that Mongán lived before as Finn mac Cumaill, but like St Olaf he was unwilling that this should be mentioned: 'Mongán was Finn though he would not let it be told.' Manannán was the ruler of the fair country beyond the sea to which heroes were enticed away, and there is more than one allusion to him begetting a child upon a human mother. He has something in common with the Scandinavian Heimdall, a god about whom not much is known, but who was probably one of the Vanir (p. 211 below). Nora Chadwick suggested that these tales of children who were fathered by supernatural beings on human mothers, including those of several Irish saints 'without a human father', might account for a strange statement by St Augustine that the women of Gaul were visited by '*Sylvani* and Pans', that is, by supernatural beings linked with the countryside.

A frequent element in these birth tales is that the child emerges from the sea or from a spring or river. Taliesin was carried by the sea in a bag of skin. Mongán was immersed in the sea at birth, and the ninth wave which washed over him removed the caul or membrane from his head. Several of the women in the tales conceived children when they swallowed some small creature floating in water. The mother of Cernach drank water from a special well which had a worm in it, while Ness, the mother of Conchobar, brought water from the river to her husband and strained it through her veil, but there were two worms in the cup, and the druid Cathbad forced her to drink it. Ness gave birth to Conchobar sitting on the river bank, and the infant went head over heels into the water, but was seized by Cathbad and named Conchobar after the river.[66] In one of the tales of Finn, the new-born son was thrown into the loch because of a prophecy that the child would cause his grandfather's death, but the baby reappeared with a live salmon in his hand, and his grandmother took him away and brought him up.[67] These traditions are worth noting because of the close link between moving water and the Celtic goddesses of Gaul and Britain in the Roman period, as well as the Scandinavian land-spirits. The idea of a child from the sea bringing the land prosperity and becoming a king was also remembered in Scandinavian tradition, in the account of Scyld of Denmark as told in the Anglo-Saxon *Beowulf* (12f.; 43f.).

Passages in Greek and Roman writers claiming that the Celts had a firm belief in immortality, and were even familiar with the doctrine of the transmigration of souls, have been much discussed.[68] It seems hardly probable that any elaborate philosophical theory was prevalent among them, but the concept of a close link between the living and the dead, imaginatively expressed in the Irish tales of conception and birth of certain men and women, may have given rise to such an impression among outside observers from a more sophisticated world. Posidonius stated that there was a belief among the Celts that the souls of men were immortal and that 'after a definite number of years they live a second life when the soul passes into another body'.[69] 'If we understand your hymns', Lucan declared in *Pharsalia*, addressing the druids, 'death is halfway through a long life' (455f.). Julius Caesar in his *Gallic War* (VI, 14) gave as one of the main points of the teaching of the druids that 'souls do not become extinct but pass after death from one body to another'. It seemed to him that this might be an incentive to perform noble deeds, since man would have less fear of death.

To explain away such statements by the suggestion that the Celts had a primitive belief that life continued in the grave much as on earth is not very satisfactory.[70] Such naive ideas of the continuation of life after burial must have been familiar to classical writers from their knowledge of various peoples, and their own lower classes; all men were not learned philosophers, even in Rome and Athens. The ideas connected with fertility and the natural world concerning a link between the dead and the living can hardly be equated with the theory of the transmigration of souls as taught by Pythagoras, but it seems that the recognition of heroic and intuitive qualities passing on from one generation to another was important in Celtic tradition. It has left its mark on tales and poems concerned with unusual births and special links between young children

126

and their forebears. These are not logical tales, and details of the rebirths vary considerably, but they appear to symbolise ideas about the family which can be compared with those in Norse tradition concerned with goddesses and valkyries. Such tales are usually told of royal births, and as with the Norse conception of Valhalla it is unlikely that they applied to the people as a whole, but rather to their leaders and heroes and to women who made royal marriages and were daughters of kings.

There are indications of a cult of ancestors among both Irish and Scandinavians, but these are difficult to establish clearly. Sacred places were often set up where earlier graves had existed, as at Tara in Ireland, Tynwald Hill in Man and many other sites (pp. 16, 22 above). The son of the Dagda, Oengus the Mac Óc, was said to inhabit the great prehistoric tumulus of New Grange. The holy place of the Swedes at Uppsala was dominated by burial mounds large and small, and the outstanding ones were the graves of kings who reigned long before the Viking Age. Much earlier, at the sanctuary of Entremont in southern France, a line of seated figures was set up along the sacred way, and Benoit argues that these represented the heroes and ancestors of the people.[71] Here, and at other sanctuaries in Gaul, skulls were preserved and displayed (p. 72 above) and this strongly suggests the practice of venerating the heroic dead. One of the seated figures at Entremont has its hand placed on a severed head, in a gentle rather than a menacing pose; this could represent a god welcoming a dead hero, or a new generation of kings being gathered to his dead predecessors. At an earlier period still, the stone figure of a warrior was apparently set up on a burial mound at Hirschlanden, and this gives the impression of a dead leader rather than a god (p. 18 above). Here our judgement, based on chance survivals from an early culture, can only be tentative, but it is evident from the traditions concerning the dead Freyr in his mound in Sweden that the conception of a fertility deity can easily merge with that of a dead king who brought benefit to the community in his lifetime. The two ideas are likely to become merged in the minds of poets and story-tellers.

A possible example of a line of hero ancestors to set beside the stone figures from Entremont is the series of masks on the whetstone 'sceptre' from Sutton Hoo.[72] This was found in what appears to be a royal grave of the seventh century AD in an East Anglian cemetery used for burials over a long period of time before the arrival of the Anglo-Saxons. The object is a whetstone, although never put to practical use, and its large size and ebaborate decoration make it unlikely that this was ever intended. It bears marks of handling, however, and it is thought that it was held by the king on ceremonial occasions, as sceptres are sometimes

127

shown resting on the laps of kings in manuscript illustrations of the Anglo-Saxon period. A small bronze stag also found in the grave is now thought to have been fastened on top of the whetstone, although it seems to have been a later addition, fitted after the sceptre had been in use for some time. A whetstone is a suitable symbol for a king, since part of his duty was to provide his warriors with weapons and to see that these were sharpened and in good condition. It was also a symbol which could be associated with the sky god, probably because it produced sparks when it came in contact with metal, and the Scandinavian Thor was said to have a piece of whetstone in his forehead.[73] The stag however, is not a typical example of Anglo-Saxon workmanship, while other examples of whetstones with faces on them have been found in Celtic areas of the British Isles, and Michael Enright in 1983 put forward persuasive arguments for a British rather then an East Anglian origin for this sceptre.[74]

There are four faces at each end of the whetstone, and each is individual; different hair styles are used, and three faces are bearded while the rest are not. It has even been suggested that some of these might represent women, but if so they must have been grim and aged females. There are no attributes to connect the faces with deities, as in the case of the set of busts on the Gundestrup Cauldron. The faces are set into pear-shaped frames, and analogies can be found for this. One example is on the shield from the Sutton Hoo grave, where a small

10 *right* Whetstone sceptre from Sutton Hoo ship grave, 82 cm long as reconstructed, early seventh century AD. *left* Metal mount, possibly from wooden staff, from bog-find at Vimose, Denmark.

human mask in an elaborate frame is set on the leg-joint of the eagle which decorates it. This suggests a link with the god Woden/Odin, who like Freyr was said to be the ancestor of kings, and Hauck has emphasised the importance of Woden symbols which can be recognised on various pieces of regalia from this burial.[75] Other examples of faces set in pear-shaped frames come from Denmark, and the most impressive is from Vimose on a mount which was thought possibly to have been fitted on a wooden staff.[76] There could be a link between such framed heads and those carved on a stone from the Celtic sanctuary at Entremont, in association with the niches which held human skulls (p. 71 above). These are surrounded with what might be described as pear-shaped frames with a flattened base, and take us back to the 2nd century BC. Enright has also seen a parallel between the whetstone heads and those on the stone pillar from Pfalzfeld in Germany, of about the 4th century BC, which was believed to have had a carved stone head on the top (p. oo above). A link between the heads on the whetstone and the severed heads treasured and represented in art by the Celts would suggest that they represent the heads of dead ancestors. The sceptre was put into the grave along with other splendid treasures bearing pre-Christian symbols, and one reason for abandoning it may have been its religious associations, making it unsuitable for the hands of a Christian king.

The custom of preserving and honouring the heads of kings and respected enemies must surely have been based on the belief that they could bring luck and power to the living, who might inherit their heroic qualities. Enright has pointed out that the whetstone sceptre might be regarded as a phallic symbol, and compares it to the 'stone penis' in the royal centre at Tara (p. 20 above). He quotes a passage from the Irish Annals where after the Battle of Belach Mugna in 908 the followers of Flann brought him the head of the defeated king and bishop, Cormac mac Cuilennáin, and addressed him thus: 'Life and health, O powerful, victorious king! We have the head of Cormac for thee, and, as is customary with kings, raise thy thigh and put this head under it, and press it with thy thigh.'[77] Flann however was angry, and declared that he intended to honour the head of the holy bishop 'instead of crushing it', and he had it restored to the body and buried, after which it was said to perform signs and miracles, The practice of crushing the head under the thigh when a king has been defeated seems clearly linked with the idea of the continued fertility of the royal line and of the acquisition of the strength and powers of a dead leader for the sons of his conqueror. Moreover it provides a possible explanation of the framed head on the thigh of the eagle on the Sutton Hoo shield. Another possible explanation of the heads on the sceptre which has not been suggested is that they may originate in a record of slain leaders, continuing from the custom of preserving the actual skulls of dead enemies in the temple in Gaul. The difference between the bearded and hairless faces might then simply be that between aged and young kings who had fallen in battle. Even if this were so, however, there could still be an obvious link between the slaying of enemies and the continuation of the royal family; fertility is recognised as a gift of the dead king to the living, and the preservation of the head is a one aspect of this.

Another sign of dependance on dead ancestors in Norse tradition is the practice of sitting or sleeping on a burial mound in order to gain help or inspiration. There are tales of this being done by kings, seers, and those destined to become poets. An Icelandic shepherd, according to one story,[78] used to sleep on the mound of a dead poet when he was out with the sheep, and thought he would like to compose a poem in the dead man's honour, but had no skill with words. One night the poet appeared to him in a dream and offered to recite a verse to him, telling him: 'If you learn the verse by heart and can say it when you wake, you will become a great poet.' A Christian version of such an experience is Bede's tale of the poet Caedmon, who received the gift of poetry from an angel who visited him at night when he was lamenting his inability to compose songs. In general however it was kings and princes who sat on burial mounds, as did one king in *Vǫlsunga Saga* (1) when he prayed to the gods to send him a son. The daughter of the giant Hrymnir came to him and dropped an apple into his lap, and after he shared this with his wife a son was born who was named Volsung, father of the famous Sigmund. Here we have a link between the mound and the goddess who determines the fate of princes, and this particular goddess, Hljod, became the protector of the king's son, for Volsung is said to have made her his wife. In the Helgi poems, a young prince sits on a mound and he meets his guardian spirit who gives him his name and presents him with a sword, while she foretells his destiny (p. 94 above). This may be linked with the practice of a king sitting on a mound when he claims his kingdom by right of succession.[79]

Similarly in Irish tales a young king or prince may be sitting on a mound when a visitant from the Other World appears to him. In this way Sin comes to Muircertach and sits on the mound beside him,[80] and a warrior from the Land of Youth appears to Cormac as he sits on Ben Etain.[81] Pwyll in the *Mabinogion* encounters Rhiannon as he sits on a mound (p. 114 above). It is not always clear that a burial mound is indicated in such episodes, but the pattern is well established. The mound which may be the abode of the dead and the home of supernatural beings is the spot where communication may be established with men, and it is linked ith kingship continuing through the generations.

7 Offerings to the fertility powers

Offerings to the fertility powers, although less easy to recognise than those made to the gods who governed battle, evidently formed part of the religious practices of both Celts and Germans. Women are likely to have been much involved in this, although inscriptions to the goddesses from the Roman period, as well as evidence from *Landnámabók*, shows that men also were fully active in such a cult. It seems that both priests and priestesses were engaged in the worship of these deities, and some may have been of high or even royal birth. In the great offering places which have been carefully excavated, such as Skedemosse, and Käringsjön in Sweden, there is evidence not only for the sacrifice of animals and weapons, but also of offerings of a more personal and domestic nature. Gold rings and various ornaments have been found on sites of the late Roman period on Öland and Gotland and elsewhere. These could be offerings to a deity whose symbol was a ring, and various gods, such as Thor, Freyr and Ull, have their names associated with the sacred ring on which oaths were sworn, but it might also be a suitable offering in gold to the gods of peace and plenty. Neck-rings and bags of coins were associated with the Celtic horned god (p. 121 above), and the Vanir also were dispensers of wealth and linked with gold in early skaldic poetry. The throwing of gold objects into bogs or lakes was probably in the hope of acquiring wealth in return for the gift. It may be noted in early Icelandic poetry that gold is frequently described as the fire or flame of the sea, rivers, lakes or wells,[82] and the basis for such imagery may have been the large amount of gold thrown into the water in earlier times. According to Diodorus Siculus (V, 27) the Celts laid down much gold for the gods, and no one dared to touch it, even though, as he observed, 'the Celts are an exceedingly covetous people'. Strabo (IV, 1, 13), quoting Posidonius, states that the Romans later came into possession of lakes into which precious things had been thrown, and sold them to enrich the treasury. Some of the buyers recovered hammered silver millstones from the water, which suggests offerings made for the grain harvest.

Another set of offerings pointing to the cult of the fertility gods is that of wooden farming implements found at Käringsjön and elsewhere.[83] Flax and implements thought to have been used for beating it have been found, and at Hedenstorp in Sweden bundles of flax had been deposited on and in a cairn; it may be recalled that one of the goddess names recorded by Snorri for Freyja is Hǫrn, related to horr, the word for flax.

At one of the great bog-finds at Thorsbjerg in Denmark, there were gold rings, personal possessions, pottery, wooden objects and textiles, suggesting family and community offerings in which women must have taken a considerable part. Gregory of Tours refers to a lake in the territory of the Gabalitani where offerings of this kind were made. He was writing in the sixth century and looks back on them as something in the recent past: 'Into this lake the country people used to throw, at an appointed time, linen cloths and pieces of material used in male attire, as a firstling sacrifice to this lake. Some threw in woollen fleeces and many also pieces of cheese, wax and thread and various spices, which would take too long to numerate, each according to his ability. They also used to come with carts, brought with them food and drink, slaughtered animals for the sacrifice and feasted for three days.'[84]

There were evidently no fixed rules about what could be thrown into the water as a sacrifice, and much local variation, a point stressed by Geisslinger in a study of votive offerings in south Scandinavia and northern Germany.[85] We cannot expect to decide with any degree of certainty to what particular god or cult various objects belong. When however there are finds of ships and boats, as at Nydam and Hjort-spring, apparently left as votive offerings, together with food, farm implements and dairy produce, these all suggest offerings to the fertility deities. Food, woven cloth and ornaments are indications of women's part in such rites. Hagberg has noted placenames formed from *kvinn* (woman) in the neighbourhood of Skedemosse, and thought it possible that women had met at such places, either to share in special occupations or for ritual purposes.[86] Alternatively, such names might indicate places once associated with the goddesses, like those in Scotland and Ireland connected with maidens or hags. In the case of names found near Käringsjön, Arbman suggests that there may be links with the rites of Nerthus, and that *käring* (old woman) stands for a goddess.[87] This is in agreement with the association in the British Isles of such natural landmarks as trees, rocks, springs and lakes with female fertility spirits (p. 111 above).

Evidently the conception of land-spirits linked with the dead within the earth was a persistent one, although it remains vague and unspecified in the literary sources. Belief in the potency of such spirits to help or hinder men and women in their daily lives on the farms, and to unite with the king to bring blessing to the community, was something difficult to eradicate. The evidence of folklore makes it clear that it lived on in local legends long after the coming of Christianity, and it survives in vigorous folktales and rhymes which can still stir our imagination. Long after the adoption of Christianity, gifts and offerings continued to be made in simple spontaneous rites and ceremonies, part of the link with the Other World which was felt to be right and appropriate. The evidence of the great offering places in use in the early centuries AD reminds us that there was another side to sacrifice beside that of presentation of booty to the gods dealing out victory and defeat. Cultivation of the soil, weaving and spinning, and the raising of animals all fell into the province of the nature spirits, and so apparently did the destiny and upbringing of children.

The presentation of gifts to these powers was unlikely to have been highly organised, nor the ritual solemn and dignified. Men threw into the water what seemed right to them, 'each according to his own ability', according to Gregory of Tours, just as an Icelandic settler threw regular offerings of food into a waterfall near his house, as part of the contract made with whatever dwelt there (p. 104 above). In such simple ceremonies individuals, families and the community could all join light-heartedly, and it seems as if they did so with willingness and delight, from brief glimpses which we receive of the welcome accorded to Nerthus, or from the archaeological evidence of feasting round the fires beside the sacred lake into which offerings were thrown. When in *Ynglinga Saga* Snorri stated that Freyja alone of the pagan deities still lived on in his own time, we may sense the meaning behind the statement. Freyja, goddess of the Vanir, stands for the cult of fertility in later times more clearly than the god Freyr, whose association with the king had waned with the establishment of the Christian Church. She was a survival from the world of land-spirits and giving goddesses which were once part of the everyday life of the people, and many of her more shadowy sisters continued to influence folk and fairy beliefs for centuries after the conversion. The land-spirits were not so much renounced as adapted to the new faith, and they were never completely banished from the countryside.

V Foreknowledge and destiny

The word of Yahweh was addressed to me asking, 'Jeremiah, what do you see?' 'I see a branch of the Watchful Tree', I answered. Then Yahweh said, 'Well seen! I too watch over my word to see it fulfilled'.

Jeremiah 1, 11–12 (Jerusalem Bible)

It seems from the available evidence that one of the strongest elements in the approach of both Celtic and Germanic peoples to the supernatural world was the desire to obtain luck in future enterprises and in everyday life. A contract was made with the powerful gods governing battle and the destiny of men, and on a more homely scale with the local spirits of the countryside. Rites and offerings were gifts to the powers, in the hope that they would be repaid; if all went well, a neigbouring tribe would be decimated or a Roman legion destroyed, flocks and herds would increase, and new wealth become available from trade or booty. Kings and leaders solemnised the contract by annual rituals at feasts, or made urgent appeals with offer of sacrifices in time of peril or famine. The common people kept up the relationship in a more casual but enthusiastic way, their rituals varying according to the background of those who took part. The seeking of luck was linked closely with the rites which marked the revolution of the seasons, the gathering of harvest, and the reopening of campaigns in spring. It was associated with the keeping up of holy places, varying from ancient tombs and well-established sanctuaries to spots near lakes and springs where offerings were regularly left for the unseen powers.

These efforts were made in order to obtain the luck, energy and resources without which no enterprise could succeed in a world of unforeseen calamities and unreliable weather. Much depended on chance, and men realised that in many cases the ability to predict chance happenings would determine the outcome. Thus religious ceremonies were constantly linked with revelation of the future. Sacrifice was a means of divination as well as a freewill offering, since the giving up of life was the strongest method known of obtaining a favourable answer or

134

warning of what would come. Certain men and women were held to possess special skills in discovering hidden knowledge through dreams or visions, through established ritual acts, or through observing natural phenomena. It was no easy gift to possess, demanding much of the practitioner and acquired not only through natural gifts but through long and hard training. And always behind the lesser chances which governed events came the implacable decrees of fate, to be averted by neither men nor gods.

1 Consulting the gods

Since this was the case, men were bound to concern themselves with questions of fate and destiny when they thought about the Other World. Many sought hidden knowledge deliberately, and were concerned with discovering the secrets of the past as well as those of the future. When we look again at the settlers in Iceland at the end of the ninth century, we find certain assumptions in the tales about them which are at variance with the Christian ways of thought to which the recorders presumably subscribed. Some of the settlers are said to have thrown their high-seat pillars overboard as their ships approached Iceland, so that they might settle at the spot where the sea carried the wooden pillars ashore. These were probably the central pillars supporting a house or shrine which was abandoned in Norway, and they were associated with the god Thor, whose image in one case is said to be carved on them. Thor, as thunder-god and deity of the sky, was associated with the great oaks of the Scandinavian and German forests; he was also the protector of homes and the community, land boundaries and the law. He is said in the sagas to have given counsel to his worshippers as to what action they should take and where they should settle when they arrived in a new land.

Thorolf of Mostur, who declared Helgafell to be a sacred place (p. 13 above), is one of those said to have sacrificed and enquired of Thor. He asked 'his dear friend' whether he should come to terms with Harald Fairhair of Vestfold or leave Norway, and the reply which he received was that he should move to Iceland. The phrase used in *Eyrbyggja Saga* (4) for making an enquiry of the god, *gekk til fréttar*, occurs again in *Landnámabók* concerning Helgi the Lean.[1] Helgi had Christian relatives, but he himself was mixed in his beliefs, trusting in Christ but depending on Thor for sea voyages and when faced with hard decisions. When his ship drew near Iceland he too consulted Thor, and he was directed to Eyjafjorðr in the north-east and told that when he reached the fiord he must not go either east or west of it but follow it into the land. *Frétt* is evidently a technical term for one type of divination, relating to the Scots dialect word *frete* (various spellings recorded), which in Craigie's *Dictionary of the Older Scottish Tongue* is defined as 'a superstition, belief or observance, especially a belief in omens, anything regarded as an omen or foreboding'. Thor was evidently not regarded as the sole authority on such matters. One man was said to be guided by ravens to his place of settlement in the new land, suggesting reliance on Odin.[2] Freyr was the god who caused Ingimund to leave Norway, according to *Vatnsdœla Saga*, (9), although he was in high favour with Harald Fairhair. An amulet of some kind in the shape of Freyr disappeared from his possession and was afterwards discovered in Iceland in the place where it was intended that he should live. Ingimund had not meant to move from Norway, but, as the saga comments, 'few things are stronger than fate'.

Among the early settlers was Lodmund the Old, a man remembered for his powers of foreknowledge and magic skills; he was 'troll-possessed' (*trollaukinn*), as the Christian writer expressed it.[3] He too was said to throw his high-seat pillars overboard, but in this case did not find them when he reached land, and in due course he settled in north-eastern Iceland and built a house for himself. Three years later he learned that the pillars had been washed ashore in the south of the island, and he took immediate action. He moved all his goods on to his ship and then went on board, hoisted the sail, and forbade anyone to speak his name as he lay down and remained silent. After some time there was a great crash as a landslide came down on his house and destroyed it. Lodmund's ship was some way from the land, and he now uttered a spell or formal curse (*álag*) declaring that no ship which sailed from that landing place in the future should reach its destination. Then he sailed southwards and settled where the pillars had been washed ashore. The explanation of his strange behaviour seems to be that he was transferring away from himself the ill-luck which he knew would come upon him because he had failed to follow the guidance of the high-seat pillars, and so broken the contract with his supernatural helper. The landslide which he brought down on the house, and the curse on all ships sailing from that place thereafter may have been an attempt to transfer the ill-luck to the spot where he had settled, while he escaped it. This little tale is told without comment or explanation, as is usual in *Landnámabók*, but something of the urgency and terror of Lodmund's situation is brought out in the account.

Another story of Lodmund's powers comes from the end of his life, when he had become blind. An unfriendly neighbour, skilled in magic, had his land flooded, and contrived to drive the water on to Lodmund's territory. Lodmund's thrall told him that the sea had come over his land, but Lodmund sent him to collect some of the water in a bowl, and then

declared that this was not sea-water. He stuck his staff into the earth at
the point where the water was rising, held the staff in both hands and bit
the ring on the staff; thereupon the waters began to retreat on to his
neighbour's land. Each man endeavoured to drive the water away, but
finally a compromise was reached, and the water was allowed to flow
down a gully which formed the the boundary between them, and so into
the sea. Thor was the god who protected boundaries, and it may be
presumed that he was the deity favoured by Lodmund, who had brought
his high-seat pillars out to Iceland and entrusted them to the sea for
guidance. Here the knowledge which enabled the blind man to know the
source of the flood is linked with the power to drive it back.

Several early settlers are singled out because they knew what others
did not, and so could decide on the right actions to take. Helgi the Lean
(p. 135 above), faced with a hard winter on first coming to Iceland, noted
that further along the coast there was a patch free from frost, and he took
a boar and sow out there by boat and put them ashore. Three years later
there was a herd of seventy pigs there. Helgi seems to have had some
connection with the Vanir, for all his official Christianity, and the fact
that he was said to call on Thor when making voyages. His son was called
Ingjald, presumably based on Ingi, one of Freyr's names (p. 120 above),
and built a shrine for Freyr.[4] Increase of a herd of pigs was something
characteristic of the land-spirits, and similarly Goat-Bjorn received help
from them with his goats (p. 103 above). Another settler, Thorstein
Rednose, did well with his sheep,[5] and his good fortune was attributed
to the fact that he regularly sacrificed to a waterfall, and was able to know
which animals should be slaughtered in autumn in order to improve the
quality of the flock. Thorstein finally foresaw his own death, and after he
died the sheep plunged into the waterfall and perished; the implication
of this story is that this was a final offering to the powers which had
helped him now that their association had come to an end.

2 Interpretation of dreams

These attempts to seek help and knowledge give no indication of any
organised divination rituals. They are represented as the attempts of
individuals to establish a relationship with the Other World, whether
through the worship of Thor or Freyr in Scandinavia or through a link
with the local land-spirits in the new island. Communication is sometimes by means of dreams, and in a few instances a supernatural figure
appears to the dreamer. Goat-Bjorn made his contact with a rock-
dweller by means of a dream, while the man who relied on a spirit
dwelling in a great stone near his house used to receive warnings and
counsel in the same way, and the spirit appeared to him in a dream

several times to protest about the harsh treatment he had received from the bishop (p. 104 above). In *Víga-Glúms Saga* (26) the hero has a significant dream when he sees the god Freyr in company with dead members of his family. Freyr was sitting in a chair beside the river which ran through Glum's land, and there was a crowd of people around him: 'He seemed to see many men on the gravel bank beside the river while Freyr was sitting on a chair. He thought that he asked who these people were who had come there, and the reply was: "They are your departed kinsmen, and we are entreating Freyr that you should not be driven out of the land round Thwer River, but it is of no avail; Freyr answers shortly and angrily and now calls to mind the gift of an ox from Thorkell the Lean."'

Freyr, it seems, had already made a contract with Thorkell, not through a dream but by giving him a favourable sign when the ox was offered to him, so that it bellowed and fell down dead. It may be noted that here we have another indication of a connection between the Vanir and the dead in the earth, together with the assumption that the dead can help the living by their appeals to the god, although here the entreaties of the ancestors were unsuccessful. The persistent emphasis on the relationship between Slaying-Glum and Freyr is significant, since Glum was a direct descendant of Helgi the Lean, and through him of Eyvind of Sweden and King Frothi, while his grandfather was said to have built a temple for Freyr in Iceland. It seems from the saga that Glum deserts the cult of Freyr which had been long kept up by his family for the cult of Odin, through the influence of his other Norwegian grandfather.[6]

Thor too occasionally appears in dreams, and Thorgils in *Flóamanna Saga* (20–1) has a series of dreams in which he is confronted by the angry god because he has accepted Christianity. 'God will help me', Thorgils replied on one occasion, 'and I am glad that our partnership is at an end.' Although this tale is told from a Christian viewpoint, it reflects a traditional memory of how messages were thought to be received from a god. Again an offering is involved, as Thor accused Thorgils of keeping his property, and Thorgils then realised that he had an ox which he had given to Thor when it was a calf. He at once threw it overboard, declaring that it was not surprising that they had bad luck when they had Thor's beast on the ship.

This story might be compared with an account of an unusual dream in *Laxdœla Saga* (31) apparently introduced to foretell the slaying of Kjartan. Kjartan's father, Olaf the Peacock, had a splendid ox called Harri, very large and grey in colour, with four horns; it used one of the horns to break the ice and scrape through snow to get at the grass in winter. Like the pigs of Helgi the Lean, this ox went to a distant

138

pastureground one very severe winter, taking sixteen cattle with him, and found grazing for them so that they all survived. When he was eighteen years old, his horn used for breaking the ice fell off, and that year Olaf had him slaughtered. Next night he dreamed that a huge woman came to him, looking very angry, and asked if he were asleep:

> He said he was awake. The woman said: 'You are asleep, but it makes no difference. You have had my son slain and he has come to me in wretched condition, and because of this you shall see your own son covered in blood by my contrivance, and I shall choose the son whom I know you would least want to lose.' Then she went away, and Olaf awoke and thought he caught a glimpse of the woman. Olaf took the dream greatly to heart and told his friends about it, but he was not satisfied by any interpretation offered him. He was best pleased by those who declared that what he had experienced was a simple case of imagination (*draumskrok*).

This is a significant episode, as it emphasises the link between certain animals on the farm and the land-spirits, to which company the huge woman seems to belong. As in many Irish and Scandinavian tales, cattle are linked with the people of the Other World. It also shows how an interpretation of a dream was sought if it was felt to be an important one. Although in this saga deliberate use is made of dreams as a literary device, the particular form which this one takes appears to be traditional, and fits in with various passages from *Landnámabók*.

There are times when the dead are represented as appearing in dreams. They may be benevolent to the sleepers, like the dead poet who enabled a shepherd to compose poetry (p. 130 above) or may complain that they are disturbed in their graves, like the dead seeress buried under · the church in *Laxdœla Saga* (76). In the *Edda* poem *Atlamál*, Gudrun recounts a series of dreams to her husband, King Atli, and in the last of these, 'dead women' appear to summon him to their hall, a sign of approaching death.[7] These seem to be akin to valkyries however rather than to dead members of his family, and the queen remarks that his *dísir*, the protective spirits, are now parted from him. This kind of dream, described by Ursula Dronke in her commentary[8] as 'not an omen but a visitation' differs from the other dreams described, for these are symbolic ones, of the type encouraged by the reading of foreign dream-books in Iceland,[9] with lists of logical and easily recognisable symbols, some of which, like lions and snakes, were out of place in an Icelandic context. The dream of the summoning women also differs from the kind of dream which shows a future event before it happens.

Belief in foreknowledge through dreams has always been strong in Iceland, and after the sudden eruption in the Westman Islands in 1975 there were many letters in the newspapers claiming that the writers had had warning of it beforehand in dreams. An interesting series of warning dreams is given in *Sturlunga Saga*,[10] and it is claimed that other 'important' ones were reported from both the north and south of the island. A number of these were said to take place before the Battle of Örlygsstaðir in 1238, when Sturla Sighvatsson was killed. They are not of the symbolic type, with the exception of one where Sturla sees a huge rock coming down to crush his company, but most of them are in the form of visits from sinister figures of both men and women, who tend to be dark and threatening and speak brief verses prophesying calamity. One, a woman dark clothes on a grey horse, gives her name as Gudrun daughter of Gjuki, wife of Sigurd the Volsung and the queen in *Atlamál*, and seems to have come from Hel; she appears several times to a girl of sixteen. These figures seem to belong to a tradition independent of the dream books, and based on earlier beliefs; the beliefs were no longer admissable for Christian people, but they could legitimately be relegated to dream imagery.

There is a reference to 'foreseeking *dísir*' summoning him to death in an early skaldic poem by Bjorn of Hitdale, who also mentions a woman in a helmet who calls him home in every dream.[11] The most elaborate example of dreams of this type, however, is in *Gísla Saga* (22f.). They are described in prose, and also in verses which are not usually accepted as the work of Gisli, but as twelfth-century additions.[12] However, the image of a dream woman welcoming the dead hero as a lover is hardly in keeping with Christian teaching, and it seems probable that we have here a literary elaboration of an earlier traditional motif. Gisli had a series of dreams while he was an outlaw pursued by enemies, over a period of seven years. These came to him in the long nights of winter, and in the dreams he encountered two women, one hostile and one welcoming and compassionate. In the first dream he entered a hall where he recognised friends and kinsmen sitting drinking beside a line of seven fires, some of which burned brightly while others were low. The prose narrative explains that these represented the seven years that he had left to live, and they presumably showed what his fortunes in these years would be. The friendly woman gave him pious counsel and warning to refrain from evil deeds, in words that seem based on Christian sources.[13] Next autumn his dreams began again, and now he saw the sinister dream woman frequently; she threatened him and washed him in blood, and he was filled with fear. The dreams then ceased until two years before his death, when he dreamed again of the hostile woman, but one night the other woman returned, riding on a grey horse, and took him to a hall richly adorned. She promised him that this was where he should come when he died, and that he should possess riches and have her as his companion. In one verse she is referred to as the Fulla of Odin, and Fulla is mentioned in *Gylfaginning* (34) as one of the goddesses. After this however his dreams grew worse, and the threatening dream woman declared that he should enjoy no happiness; she again washed him in blood and put a blood-stained covering on his head. Then followed some straight-forward dreams of attack by enemies and of being wounded, presaging his slaying. The last recorded dream is of his benevolent dream woman bending over him and binding up his wounds.

It seems to be assumed in the sagas that disaster and death are frequently revealed beforehand in dreams, and that this knowledge is brought either by some supernatural power from the Other World or by the dead. The threat received during sleep may not be recognised as such at the time, as in *Laxdœla Saga* (74) where Thorkell misinterprets a dream of death by drowning. Again the dreamer may reject a particular dream as not significant, as Olaf the Peacock did in the case of his dream of the ox Harri. There were acknowledged experts who could be consulted about dreams; Gudrun in *Laxdœla Saga* (33) went to Gest Oddleifsson about the dream which foretold her future marriages. Gest could foretell the future, and is described in *Njáls Saga* (103) as 'a very wise man, able to foresee the destinies of others'. The early Norwegian kings had their favourite seers, and Halfdan the Black is said to have consulted Thorleif the Wise when he wanted to induce dreams foretelling the future of his descendants.[14] Thorlief advised the king to sleep in a pigsty, saying that this is what he himself did when he wanted to have a meaningful dream. Nora Chadwick suggested that this was a figurative expression for a burial mound, the abode of Freyr whose symbol was a boar, and that Thorleif was advising the king to sleep on a mound as seers used to do.[15]

Halfdan followed Thorleif's advice, and dreamed that his hair grew long and fell in locks of different lengths and colours, one lock being much fairer than the rest. Thorleif interpreted this as meaning that he would have one outstanding descendant among many, and this would be St Olaf. Although Halfdan seldom dreamed, it seems that his wife Ragnhild did, and her dreams are said to be 'great ones', presumably because they were related to the future of the kingdom. One was of a great tree with rich fruit whose branches spread beyond the land of Norway, which grew from a thorn which she plucked from her gown. Prophetic dreams of this kind are frequently concerned with the future of a reigning king and his descendants, although in the Icelandic family sagas such dreams are connected with less important people, and used to build up an atmosphere of fateful and tragic intensity.

In Welsh and Irish literature there is a similar interest in prophetic dreams, which may be interpreted by a druid or a seer. Becc mac Dé, for instance, described as the best seer of his time, interpreted a dream of King Dermot foretelling the death of a prince.[16] He foretold the death of Suibne at the hands of his cousin Aed, who was then unborn: 'The son that the woman carries, he it is shall slay yonder stripling.' He also foretells the future of the kingdom, and Columcille acknowledges his power, saying: 'It is a marvellous prophecy; from God comes the great knowledge which is vouchsafed thee.' Druids are also called on to interpret symbolic dreams, like one that came to King Cathair:[17] he dreamed of a fair woman bearing a son beside a hill on which stood a rich fruit tree whose branches reached to the sky. This was said to represent a river from which a new lake would be formed, while the tree symbolised his prosperous reign. Another king, Muircertach, dreamed of his own death, and awoke screaming, because it was a dream of fire.[18] The woman Sin who was luring him to his death promised to watch over him while he slept, and his next dream was of a shipwreck, when a griffin carried him away to her nest and he and the nest were burned. He asked Dub Da Rinn, the son of a druid, to interpret this, and the interpretation sent to him was that the ship stood for his reign, which was about to end, while the griffin was the woman who would cause him to be burned to death and would then die herself. However the message did not reach him in time, for that night he was indeed trapped in a fire, and drowned in a cask of wine in which he took refuge. In the earliest form we have of the Macbeth story, the prophecy that Macbeth was to gain the kingdom of Scotland came to him in a dream;[19] his later vision of the future rulers of the land is another example of 'great dreams' concerned with the future of the kingdom.

Not only kings but the gods themselves might be perplexed by dreams. In the tenth century poem *Eiríksmál*, the funeral poem which was composed to commemorate the death of Erik Bloodaxe, Odin dreams that a great host is approaching Valhalla and that he is preparing for their reception; this dream is explained when Erik and the kings killed with him are heard outside. In *Baldrs Draumar* the gods meet to discuss the ominous dreams of Balder, and Odin rides down into the underworld to find an interpretation.[20] Similarly on the Irish side there is the dream of Óengus, son of the Dagda, who has a series of dreams of a beautiful girl and is overcome by desire for her which makes him ill.[21] Fergne, a skilled physician and also a seer, declared the cause of his sufferings to be 'love in absence'. With the help of his brother, Óengus finally discovered and won his bride.

There is a close parallel here to the tale of the love of the god Freyr for

Gerd, a giant's daugher in the underworld, as told in the *Edda* poem *Skírnismál*. Freyr sees the girl while he is sitting in the seat of Odin, but this might be interpreted as a dream-vision.[22] It seems that in both Norse and Irish tradition the dream is associated with great happenings in the Other World, pointing to a divine marriage, the deaths of heroes, and the slaying of Balder which ushers in Ragnarok. The gods themselves require additional knowledge, gained, it seems, from the underworld, to interpret great and significant dreams which indicate the destiny of gods, kings and heroes.

There were recognised methods of inducing a dream which would reveal the future. One is mentioned in the *Mabinogion* in the tale of the 'Dream of Rhonabwy', where the hero sleeps on a yellow calfskin and dreams of a fair youth in green and gold; this is the beginning of an elaborate dream sequence lasting three days and nights. Keating mentions the use of a bull's hide by druids, who would spread out the hide of a sacrificed animal on wattles of mountain ash, raw side uppermost, in order to win knowledge from demons.[23] In Armstrong's *Gaelic Dictionary*, it is said under *taghairm* that this was a rite performed by a diviner, who was wrapped in the 'warm smoking hide of a newly-slain ox, and laid at full length in the wildest recesses of some lonely waterfall'. The purpose of the rite was to discover the future, presumably by dreams. Another reference to this custom occurs in a Scottish book on the Western Islands published in 1703:[24] a man wrapped in a cow's hide and left in a lonely place overnight is said to learn from 'invisible friends' what he desires to know. The *tairbfeis* in Irish tales is associated with the choosing of a king; in 'The Destruction of Da Derga's Hostel' a man had a dream of the king who was to come after he ate the flesh of a bull and drank the broth, while an 'incantation of truth' was chanted over him. He saw in his dream a naked man coming along the road with a sling in his hand, and this was fulfilled next day with the arrival of Conaire.

The idea of sitting or lying on a hide occurs also in Icelandic tradition, although here the sources are late. In the thirteenth century *Maríu Saga*, a man is directed to sit on a 'freshly flayed ox-hide' with squares drawn round it until the devil reveals the future. Jón Árnason refers to those who 'sit out' to gain knowledge from the dead being wrapped in a sheepskin or the hide of a bull or a walrus and left to lie at the cross roads.[25]

3 Seeking hidden knowledge

It is not possible to distinguish in these accounts between an induced sleep and a trance, a dream or a vision, since we are dealing with vague memories of earlier practices and fragments of tradition. In the twelfth century Giraldus Cambrensis in his *Description of Wales* (I, 16) gives a detailed account of Welsh seers called *awenyddion*, although he does not state if these were men or women. Their method of obtaining knowledge of hidden matters resembles that indicated in the evidence from Scotland:

> Among the Welsh there are certain individuals called *awenyddion*, who behave as if they are possessed by devils. You will not find them anywhere else. When you consult them about some problem, they immediately go into a trance and lose control of their senses, as if they are possessed. They do not answer the question put to them in any logical way. Words stream from their mouths, incoherently and apparently meaningless, and without any sense at all, but all the same well expressed; and if you listen carefully to what they say you will receive the solution to your problem. When it is all over, they will recover from their trance, as if they were ordinary people waking from a heavy sleep, but you have to give them a good shake before they regain control of themselves. There are two odd things about all this: when they have give their answer, they do not recover from their paroxysm unless they are shaken violently and forced to come round again; and when they do return to their senses they can remember nothing of what they have said in the interval. If by chance they are questioned a second or a third time on the same matter, they give completely different answers ... They seem to receive this gift of divination through visions which they see in their dreams ... (trans. Lewis Thorpe, 1978)

The word *awen* in *awenyddion* seems to have a meaning close to poetic inspiration.

The utterance of a poetic prophecy in language hard to understand is well illustrated both from Norse and Irish sources. Sometimes in the Irish tales a brief statement is made followed by a poetic lay, as in the case of the prophetess encountered by Queen Medb, who asked her what the result of the campaign then beginning would be.[26] Medb had already consulted a druid, but she only received a statement from him that she would return alive, no matter what happened to the rest of her people. The situation for her armies appeared favourable, yet his words clearly left her uneasy. Then she met a beautiful girl in a green spotted cloak, walking along the road and weaving a fringe as she went. Medb asked what she was doing, and the reply was: 'Promoting your interest and your prosperity, gathering and mustering the four great provinces of Ireland with you to go into Ulster for the Táin bó Cúailnge.' Medb then asked who she was, and was told that she was a prophetess from the *Sid*. In reply to the repeated question: 'Feidelm Prophetess, how do you see our army?' she gave each time the brief reply: 'I see red upon them, I see crimson.' Medb was unwilling to accept this ominous statement, and then Feidelm chanted a lay telling how Cú Chulainn would defeat her army: 'He will lay low your entire army and he will slaughter you in dense crowds. Ye shall leave with him all your heads. The prophetess Feidelm conceals it not. Blood will flow from heroes' bodies. Lond will it be remembered.'

In the account of this episode in the Yellow Book of Lecan[27] there is a reference to Feidelm claiming knowledge of the practice known as *imbas forosnai*. This term is found in Cormac's *Glossary*, described as a divination ritual used by the *filid* (seer-poets) to gain hidden knowledge. Kuno Meyer's translation runs as follows:[28]

> The *Imbas Forosnai* sets forth whatever seems good to the *fili* and what he desires to make known. It is done thus. The seer chews a piece of the red flesh of a pig, or a dog, or a cat, and then places it on a flagstone behind the door. He sings an incantation over it, offers it to the false gods, and then calls them to him. And he leaves them not on the next day, and chants then on his two hands and again calls his false gods to him, lest they should disturb his sleep. And he puts his two hands over his two cheeks till he falls asleep. And they watch by him lest no one overturn him and disturb him till everything he wants to know is revealed to him.

There has been much argument over points of detail in this passage,[29] but the essential outline of the rite is in agreement with other sources. It may be that Cormac is describing something about which he had only vague knowledge, but it is unlikely that he invented the whole account. It was evidently essential that an animal be killed, and the seer has to chew a piece of its flesh which is uncooked. The eating of raw meat is associated with the people of the *síd*; in the tale of 'Finn and the Phantoms',[30] Finn refuses to partake of such food and so escapes without harm. Sacrificial blood is known to be of importance for divination (p. 58 above). The chewing of the flesh might be connected with the practice of Finn biting his thumb with his 'tooth of knowledge', used as a means of interpreting a dream or solving a problem. Again the reference to chanting on the hands may be compared with other passages where the seer chants 'on his fingers' or 'on the ends of his bones' (see below). The purpose of this rite was evidently to discover what was hidden, and in the ancient Irish Laws it is stated that the *imbas forosnai* was later abolished by St Patrick, together with the *tenm laída*, because these were heathen rites which could not be performed without a heathen offering.[31] Another method, *dichetal di chennaib*, which has been translated as 'extemporary incantation', could however be used without making any offering. There are two accounts of Finn receiving

F

enlightenment through *imbas forosnai*. In the tale of 'Finn and the Man in the Tree',[32] Finn followed Culdub, a man from the *síd*, who had been stealing food from him and his men, and caught hold of him just as Culdub was entering the *síd* mound. At that moment Finn came into contact with a woman carrying a vessel of liquor, and she pushed back the door and jammed Finn's finger against it; he put it into his mouth, and was immediately inspired and began to chant. After this he had only to put his thumb into his mouth to acquire knowledge, and in this way was able to recognise Culdub. In the tale of 'The Death of Mac Con',[33] an old warrior of the Fían, named Ferchess, was sent by Ailill to kill Mac Con, and Finn saw him following them: 'Tis then that Finn said, using the incantation called *imbas forosna*: "A man on the track", said he. "Warriors will be the more delighted at the number", said Mac Con. "A man on the track", said Finn. "One man is always good sport", said Mac Con.' Ferchess then sang a spell over his spear and hurled it at Mac Con, who received a fatal wound, while Finn recited a short poem through the power of *imbas forosnai*.

This last example follows the pattern of Feidelm's prophecy; one sentence is repeated more than once, and states what has been visible to the speaker, so that we have 'I see red', and 'A man on the track'. Then follows a lay, apparently a comment and extension of the orginal revelation. Some commentators have been perplexed because there is no reference to Finn making elaborate preparations such as are descibed in Cormac's *Glossary*, but this is not really surprising. It is hardly to be expected that Finn, a legendary figure and master of supernatural lore, would need to go through the same procedures as those followed by an ordinary seer, while Feidelm was a supernatural figure, an inhabitant of the *síd*. The term *imbas forosnai* appears to be associated with the revelation of knowledge (*fius(s)*), and is probably derived from **imb-fiuss/*imb-fess*; Cormac's derivation from *bas*, the palm of the hand, is judged to be incorrect. The term must refer to the act of divination and utterance of prophecy, probably linked with mantic poetry, since, as Nora Chadwick pointed out, prophecies were usually expressed in poetic form.[34] The writer of the passage in the *Glossary* may have had no more than a vague idea of rites used by seers in the past to obtain the knowledge necessary for prophecy or the solution of a problem. When supernatural beings such as Feidelm uttered revelations concerning the future, it would be natural to make use of the term without using it in an exact technical sense. It may be noted that she was weaving as she walked, so that we have a parallel, all the more striking because the imagery and presentation is widely different, with the weaving valkyries prophesying slaughter to come (p. 94 above).

Other terms connected with divination are mentioned in the *Glossary* and the *Laws*. The expression *tenm laida* is one of them, and is used in the tale of the 'Death of Lomna'.[35] Lomna was Finn's fool, and the *fianna* came upon his headless body and demanded to know whose it was: 'A body here without a head! Let it be known to us.' Finn then put his thumb in his mouth and sang a lay 'through *tenm laida*', in which he disclosed that it was Lomna who lay dead. First however he uttered a number of negative statements which suggest replies to probing questions:

He has not been killed by people;
he has not been killed by the people of Luighne;
he has not been killed by a wild boar;
he had not been killed by a fall;
he has not died on his bed: O Lomna!

O'Curry assumed from this that the term *tenm laida* was a method used to identify dead persons; he refers to another tale in the *Glossary* where it is used to discover the identity of a dog's skull, pronounced to be that of the first small dog ever brought to Ireland.[36] But it is unwise to make rigid distinctions of this kind when discussing methods of divination. In the type of literature in which such traditions are preserved, the evidence is not of the kind which makes accurate definitions possible, and in any case any seer worth his salt would surely be prepared to vary his techniques according to the nature of the problems confronting him.

Other methods of obtaining hidden knowledge are indicated. Finn several times sets his thumb on his 'tooth of knowledge', as when he learns of his own approaching death: 'He came upon a well, out of which he took a drink. Under his 'knowledge-tooth' he put his thumb then, and worked the incantation of *tenm laida*, whereby it was revealed to him that the end of his term and of his life had come.'[37] This must be linked with the tradition of the young hero putting his thumb in his mouth when cooking a special meal, and thus obtaining wisdom (p. oo above). Sigurd the Volsung is shown in this posture on a large number of carvings of the Viking Age and later, and at least one Irish cross thought by some to be of eighth century date shows two figures with their thumbs in their mouths, possibly indicating seers or even Finn himself.[38] The staff of the seer seems also to be used in such endeavours. In the *Senchas Mor* the *fili* is said to place his staff on the body or head of a person whose name he wishes to know, or to gain other information.[39] An Icelandic parallel can be found in the tale of the seer Lodmund, who placed his staff on the ground and then bit the ring on it, when he wanted to drive back flood waters from his land (p. 137 above). Ogam characters and runes might be used in the same way.[40]

There were clearly many recognised techniques for obtaining knowledge, and these seem often to be associated with the chanting of the appropriate lay or spell. In the Icelandic *Hávamál* (144) a list of separate practices associated with the use of runes is worth noting:

> Do you know how to cut (*rista*)? Do you know how to interpret (*raða*)?
> Do you know how to paint (*fá*)? Do you know how to test (*freista*)?
> Do you know how to enquire (*biða*)? Do you know how to sacrifice (*blóta*)?
> Do you know how to send forth (*senda*)? Do you know how to make offerings (*sóa*)?

While some of these terms can only be translated tentatively, they clearly refer to practices connected with divination. Runes were both cut and painted, the painting perhaps referring to the smearing with blood. The right questions had to be put, and the reply provided by the runes interpreted. Sacrifices might be made. The meaning of 'sending forth' might mean using the runes to affect others, or gaining contact with supernatural powers. Certainly divination was a complex art, although we only obtain brief glimpses of the techniques involved in the literature.

Divination might be employed to discover hidden matters in the past as well as in the future. The gifted seer-poet in Ireland was expected to provide information about the past, as can be seen from the tale of young Mongán, son of Fíachna of Ulster.[41] The chief poet of Ireland, Eochu, feared that Mongán would challenge him, but Fíachna promised that his son would not attack him openly. One day four novice clerics asked Eochu in the king's presence to declare who it was who had set up six great pillar stones:

> 'We are here in quest of knowledge and information: God has brought to us the King poet of Ireland, to wit Eochu, to make clear to us who planted these stones and in what manner he set them in array.' 'Well', says Eochu, 'I have no recollection of that. Methinks twas the Clanna Dedad that raised them for the building of the castle of Cú Roí.' 'Good, Eochu', said one of them, 'the novice clerics declare that thou art gone astray.'

They then told him the true origin of the stones, which were raised to commemorate the men slain by young Illand, son of Fergus, assisted by Conall Cernach, 'for it was the custom of the men of Ulster that, whenever they should perform their prentice deed of valour, they raised pillar stones to the number of the men they slew'. This information had of course been given by Mongán, and Eochu was shamed a second time when he could not give the origin of two great earthworks. It is indicated that the seer could either remember or discover such information, and those said to have lived previously, such as Tuán and Gwion, are said to know all that had been done in the past (p. 124 above).

In Scandinavia also divination might be used to discover how a man died, or to unravel the forgotten past. In the Saga of the Faroe Islanders, Thrand, a man skilled in magic arts, set out to find how a man met his death.[42] He made elaborate preparations, setting up four enclosures in the hall and a figure of nine squares on the floor. Thrand sat on a stool outside the enclosure and told all to keep silence. After a time three dead men entered one at a time; two were soaking wet, and the third, the subject of the enquiry, carried his head in his hands. Each came up to the fire, stood there for a while, and went out again. Thrand then drew his breath heavily (usually a sign of awakening from deep sleep or a trance) and said: 'Now you may see how this man met his death.'

Such investigations might be undertaken by the gods themselves. When Olaf Tryggvason wanted to learn about an ancient king buried in a mound near his hall, the Devil 'in the form of Odin' came to him one night and talked to him about the past.[43] Odin might seek out hidden knowledge, as when he visited the wise giant Vafthruthnir for a contest in knowledge; the giant questioned him about the future and Odin questioned the giant about the past. He finally won the contest by asking a question which no one but he could answer; what had he whispered into the ear of the dead Balder? In the poem which gives the dialogue between the two sages, *Vafþrúðnismál*, this contest in the mythical world may be seen as a parallel to that between the learned poets in the story of Mongán.

4 Divination and war

Observation of birds and animals might form part of the process of divination. Bird lore has already been mentioned (p. 86 above). According to Dio Cassius (X, 62), Boudicca loosed a hare before her revolt in the first century AD in Britain, and watched which way it ran. Its movements were taken by the people as a good omen, and Boudicca thanked the goddess Adraste for giving them a favourable sign. Julius Caesar (*Gallic War* V, 12) stated that the Britons looked on the hare, the cock and the goose as creatures which were unlawful to eat; nevertheless they bred them, and it seems likely that this was for the purpose of divination. The Germanic peoples at about the same period placed much reliance on their sacred horses, kept by the priests in sacred groves. Tacitus in *Germania* (10) declares that whereas priests and nobles were the servants of the gods, the horses were in their confidence and could reveal the divine will to men. The method of consultation was to yoke the horses to a special chariot and observe their movements. Much later the Slav peoples south of the Baltic were also using horses for divination, but their method was to lay spears on the ground and then observe in what way the animals stepped over them, and it is uncertain whether they took this type of divination from the Germans or not.[44] Almgren has pointed out that the image of the empty wagon, the riderless horse and the unmanned ship, all of which could be seen as guided by invisible hands, was a powerful one among the peoples of northern Europe.[45]

Another method of divination was through observation of the natural world. In the Irish tale of 'The Siege of Druim Damgaire', which contains a good deal of material about practices of druids in warfare,[46] a druid goes out to observe the sky on more than one occasion. This might mean nothing more than study of weather conditions before battle, but there are a number of references to clouds used as omens. In the 'Colloquy of the Ancients' a wise man among Finn's followers drew omens 'from the firmament's clouds' in Finn's presence.[47] Finn declared that he saw 'three clouds of woe', one clear as crystal, one grey foreboding grief and one of crimson foretelling slaughter. We have more information about the use of druidical fires, when part of the countryside was set alight and the druids fanned the flames in the desired direction away from their own territory, just as the two Icelandic magicians drove floodwater against one another's land (p. 127 above). In the tale of the Siege of Druim Damgaire, King Cormac of Ulster attacked Munster, and at first had it all his own way. He was helped by a group of druids, including three women, but when things seemed hopeless for the Munster men they appealed to a famous blind druid, Mog Ruith, to help them, and the position then changed. Cormac in turn was threatened with defeat, and when he called on his druid Cithruad to give him counsel, the reply was: 'Nothing can help you, except to make a druidical fire.' The army was then told to collect ashwood faggots, and to watch to see if their opponents were doing the same; if so, then they must watch which way the flames were turning when the fires were lit, and if they came northwards this meant defeat. Sure enough, the men of Munster were also preparing a huge bonfire, and Mog Ruith gave them detailed instructions as to how to make it, although these are unfortunately obscure. By the time the fires were ready to be lit, all were seized with fear. Mog Ruith directed the men of Ulster to provide shavings of wood from their spear-shafts, probably made of ash, and with these he lit the fire, chanting a verse as he did so. Then he seated himself in his chariot, and sent a 'druidical breath' up into the sky, which became a dark cloud from which came a rain of blood. The cloud moved over Cormac's camp and then over Tara.

Mog Ruith demanded three times: 'How is it with the fires?', and was told that they were sweeping westwards and northwards away from Munster, travelling one behind the other while woods and pastures burned before them. He then took his bull's hide, put on a bird headdress, and rose into the air to drive the fires northwards against Ulster, chanting as he went. Cithruad opposed him, but his power was less than that of Mog Ruith; the men of Ulster were unable to drive back their enemies, and Munster was victorious. This is a long and impressive account of battle magic, and for all the fantastic elements in the tale, the account of the building and lighting of the fires could be based on actual divination ritual.

The rain of blood which formed part of the omen of defeat for Munster is also found in Scandinavian accounts as a omen of disaster,[48] associated also with visions of valkyries and giant women scattering blood before battle (p. 95 above). This may have been partly based on a natural phenomenon, the reddening of the sky by the Northern Lights.[49] Other reference to fires as a means of gaining knowledge and power are found in the Irish tales. The druids were said to be alarmed by the lighting of the New Fire at Easter by St Patrick, and wanted it quenched before it spread over their territory.[50] The druid Lugaid lit a fire which spread in five separate directions, so that his sons could find land for themselves;[51] this might be compared with the practice of going round newly acquired land with fire to establish ownership, as was said to be done by Icelandic settlers (*Eyrbyggja Saga* 4). It was also said in *Ynglinga Saga* (9) that when the bodies of the followers of Odin were burnt, the direction of the smoke from the cremation fire and the height to which it rose in the air was a sign of how the dead had been received by Odin. This idea of the funeral fire as a sign of the fate of the dead is borne out by words reported by Ibn Fadlan, when he watched the funeral of a Scandinavian chief on the Volga in 921, and was told: 'Out of love of him his Lord has sent his wind to take him away' as the funeral fire burnt up and the ship and its contents were swiftly consumed (p. 18 above).[52]

Another means of gaining knowledge was by consultation of the waves, referred to in both Norse and Irish sources. In the Book of Lismore there is a tale of a gifted young seer, Nede, son of the poet Adnae of Connacht, who was sent to Scotland to be trained in prophecy and divination. He used to go down to the sea when he sought inspiration:[53]

> One day the boy walked at the edge of the sea, for the edge of the water was a place of revelation of knowledge for poets, and he heard a sound from the waves which seemed to him strange. Then he made an incantation on the waves, and it was thereupon revealed to him that the wave was lamenting for his father, for the robe of the dead had been given to the *fili* Ferchertne and the distinction of *ollam* accorded to him in place of Nede's father Adnae.

Such a tradition may lie behind a strange episode in *Ljósvetninga Saga* (11) perhaps due to Irish influence. The Icelandic chief Gudmund the Mighty had made many enemies, and one day consulted a wise woman as to whether vengeance would be taken on him for a killing. She met him on the seashore, dressed as a man and wearing a helmet, with an axe in her hand. To obtain an answer for him, she waded into the sea and thrust with her axe at the waves, but nothing happened, and she told Gudmund that he need have no anxiety. He then asked her whether vengeance might be taken on his sons. Again she waded into the sea and brought down the axe, and this time there was a loud crash and the water seemed stained with blood. She told him one of his sons would have a narrow escape, and then declared that she would answer no further questions, since this had caused her much pain and effort. There is often emphasis in the sagas on the strain involved in discovering the secrets of the future, but otherwise the episode stands alone, and may show a mixture of motifs. The use of axe and helmet suggests the imagery of the valkyries, and the earlier form of the tale may have been an account of a revelation received in a dream. The association with the sea, however, the noise from the waves, and the staining of the water with blood could have been derived from Irish tradition. The tales of the 'Washer at the Ford', when the war-goddess is seen washing clothes or chariot, and the water is turned red as a sign of impending slaughter, is familiar in Irish sources (p. 99 above). The idea of a message brought by the waves is found also in stories of the Irish saints, and the practice of praying at the edge of the sea seems to have continued in Christian tradition. One example can be found in Bede's *Life of St Cuthbert* (10), when Cuthbert goes at night to the edge of the sea and prays in the water until dawn.

Methods of discovering the future and exploring the past were clearly many and varied, and could depend on the observation of dream images, visions, omens or messages. Sometimes the significant sign was only obtained after considerable effort by those seeking it; sometimes elaborate ritual might be used, possibly to impress the recipient and possibly to provide the necessary conditions for receiving inspiration. Sometimes some happening in the natural world was accepted as a portent, and the skill of the seer lay in interpretation. Among the Germanic peoples and the Scandinavians the most popular organised divination ritual seems to have been the casting of lots. This was sufficiently well known in the first century for Tacitus to record it in detail in *Germania* 10:

> Their procedure in casting lots is always the same. They cut off a branch of a nut-bearing (i.e. fruitful) tree and slice it into strips; these they mark with different signs and throw them completely at random on to a white cloth. Then the priest of the state, if the consultation is a public one, or the father of the family if it is private, offers a prayer to the gods, and looking up at the sky picks up three strips, one at a time, and reads their meaning from the signs previously scored on them. If the lots forbid an enterprise, there is no deliberation that day on the matter in question; if they allow it, confirmation by the taking of auspices is required. (Mattingly's translation)

This account gives the impression that the lots were used when a definite decision one way or the other was required. The signs on the slips of wood could well have been similar to the runic symbols used by the Germans at least as early as the third century AD, and continuing to be employed both in inscriptions and for messages in Anglo-Saxon England and Scandinavia long after conversion to Christianity.[54] Runic letters could be employed for simple statements on wood, stone or metal, and also for magical purposes, and they were well suited for the kind of divination described by Tacitus, since each sign had its own name and signified a definite object: the rune U stood for the aurochs, the rune R for a journey (*rád*) and the rune M for man, as stated in the Anglo-Saxon Runic Poem. Some runes represented supernatural beings, NG standing for the god Ing, T for the god Tiw, and the rune þ (th) for *þurs*, giant. If as described by Tacitus, three signs were taken up, the interpreter could then decide on their significance and bearing on the question asked. The choice of three symbols is in accord with the division of the runic 'alphabet' into three rows, retained in Germany, Scandinavia and England even though the total number of signs differed from one period to another.

One decision which seems to have been determined by lot was the number of prisoners to be sacrificed. A young Roman officer in Gaul escaped immediate death by burning because the lots went against this (p. 61 above). Willibrod in the seventh century had a similar escape in

Frisia (p. 64 above). A similar method was used when a decision had to be made as to whether to attack the enemy, and according to Julius Caesar this might be organised by women (p. 157 below). An account of such a consultation in the Viking Age is given on two occasions by Rimbert in his *Life of St Anskar*, written in the ninth century not long after the events described.[55] The Swedes, when fighting the Danes for the possession of certain towns in the Baltic region, found themselves losing the struggle and cast lots to discover 'any god who was willing to aid them', but the result was a negative one. They then decided on the advice of some merchants to turn to the Christain god and gained the victory. The second account is more detailed. An exiled Swedish prince, Anund, made an attack on the market town of Birka in east Sweden, supported by Danish vikings. The undefended town lay at their mercy, and the citizens paid a ransom, but even after this the Danes wanted to plunder the town. Anund then proposed that they should cast lots to see if it was the will of the gods to do this:

> As his words were in accord with their custom they could not refuse to adopt the suggestion. Accordingly they sought to discover the will of the gods by casting lots, and they ascertained that it would be impossible to accomplish their purpose without endangering their own welfare and that God would not permit this place to be ravaged by them. They asked further where they should go in order to obtain money for themselves so that they might not have to return home without having gained that for which they had hoped. They ascertained by the casting of the lot that they ought to go to a certain town which was situated at a distance on the borders of the lands belonging to the Slavonians. The Danes then, believing that this order had come to them direct from heaven, retired from this place and hastened to go by a direct route to this town.

Rimbert naturally believed that this happy escape for Birka was due to the intervention of the Christian God, but he is hardly likely to have invented the consultation of the lots, which he states was a method much used by the Danes and accepted without question. It seems that on this occasion a fairly detailed answer was obtained, since the Danes were told where to go next, but it would be possible to use the method as described by Tacitus with someone acting as interpreter. The Danes are said to believe that the reply came from the gods.

The casting of lots may have been known among the Celts in some form, and the expression *crannchur* (throw the wood) indicates some such method.[56] Lots were said to be used in a form of ordeal, with the names of the king and the accused man inscribed on them to decide the guilt or innocence of the man under trial.[57]

5 Seers and druids

The poet-seer, the *fili*, is represented in Irish literature as carrying out various rituals to obtain knowledge, and both he and the druid were regarded as repositories of ancient wisdom. In Old Norse literature the *þulr* is able to discover what is hidden. The word is linked with the verb *þylja* (chant or murmur). It is used of the wise giant with whom Odin had a contest in knowledge in the poem *Vafþrúðnismál*, and of Regin the Smith in *Fáfnismál*, who is again a supernatural figure. It is apparently used of Odin himself in *Hávamál* (142), although the passage is a cryptic one and the identity of the Mighty Thul not wholly clear. This is the section of the poem which refers to the various skills needed to make use of runes as a source of wisdom (p. 148 above). It is clear that the High Powers were believed to determine the message of the runes. The Thul and the one who utters, possibly the interpreter, mentioned in the poem might be seen as the equivalent of the seer and the poet in Irish tradition. In stanza 111 of *Hávamál* there is a reference to chanting from the seat of the Thul beside the Well of Urd, who appears to represent Fate or Destiny: 'It is time to chant from the seat of the Thul, at the Well of Urd. I beheld and was silent; I beheld and pondered; I listened to the speeches of men. I heard deliberations concerning runes, nor were they silent as to their meaning in the hall of the High One.'

Again the Thul who speaks may be Odin himself, said in *Vǫluspá* to gain knowledge from the Well of Urd, and who has his special seat from which he is able to see into all worlds. But in passages concerning prophecy in the literature, both Norse and Irish, there is a constant element of ambiguity, so that it is hard to tell whether the various supernatural figures mentioned are thought to be themselves responsible for the events which they foretell, or whether they are merely mouthpieces for a higher power. It is the High Powers and not Odin who are said to create the runes, and in the passage where he hangs on the tree it seems that he is seeking to obtain wisdom which is not in his possession.

The office of Thul is not necessarily confined to the Other World; it appears to have been one held in royal halls, like that of the *fili* at Irish courts. In the Anglo-Saxon *Beowulf* (499f.), the man Unferth at the court of the king of the Danes bears the title of *þyle*, the equivalent of *þulr*, interpreted as 'orator' in an Old English gloss. Unferth sits near the king, and interviews the hero Beowulf on his arrival, showing that he has information which apparently the others do not possess concerning Beowulf's origin and past achievements. No special powers of clairvoyance are indicated here, but there is a parallel with the need for the Irish poets to produce information when challenged about the heroic past, and the achievements of heroes living or dead (p. 148 above). Beowulf counters Unferth's challenge, and shows that he too has information about the past of Unferth, outdoing him in knowledge as Mongán outdid Eochu. In the mythological poems of the *Edda*, such contests in knowledge are raised from a human setting to a cosmic level, as gods and giants compete and the loser is destroyed. A link with the interpretation of runes is suggested in *Beowulf* when Unferth is said to 'unbind runes of hostility' (501).

Those with the power to obtain and reveal hidden knowledge play an important part in the literature of both Iceland and Ireland. In earlier times, accounts of Celts and Germans emphasise the importance of priests, druids and seeresses. As far as druids are concerned, there has been vigorous controversy concerning their function in society. Two groups of Greek and Latin writers left descriptions of the druids of Gaul and Britain in the Roman period. One consists of Posidonius and those who used his writings in the last two centuries BC, and the other is made up of later writers of the Alexandrian school, who had no direct knowledge of the druids and appear to have idealised them as philosophers and repositories of ancient knowledge.[58] Posidonius was a Syrian Greek who lived from about 135 to 50 BC, and among those who used his descriptions of life among the Celts in Gaul was Julius Caesar, although he also made additions of his own.[59] As to the reliability of these accounts there is considerable disagreement. It is generally agreed that the druids represented the priestly class among the Celts as opposed to that of the warrior, but the position is more complex than this, as other groups of diviners (*vates*) and bards are also named. In later Irish sources three classes emerge, those of druids, diviners and *filid* (poet/seers). Caesar however seems to use 'druid' for the whole priestly class as distinct from he *equites* or warrior aristocracy, possibly because he was not interested in sub-divisions within it. As to the origin of the word 'druid', Piggott claimed in 1968 that in spite of much argument current opinion supported Pliny's derviation from *drus* (oak).[60] The last part of the word is presumably derived from Indo-European *wid* (to know). The association of druids with forest sanctuaries and the choice of these by the Celts as centres of teaching makes the link between the druid and the oak appear a reasonable one.

It can never have been easy to make an exact distinction between priests and diviners, poets, seers and visionaries, since their functions must have overlapped. In later literature the druids were to an increasing degree represented as expert magicians. In Gaul and Britain they appear in pre-Christian times to have organised sacrifices, acted as judges, and been responsible for the preservation and handing on of learning and traditional lore, which was largely oral. Special skills such as the compilation of calendars, medical knowledge and Ogam writing also fell within their province, and their responsibilities included the teaching of young chiefs and warriors, so that they had considerable political influence. The fact that they influenced and advised rulers made them important in Caesar's eyes. The emphasis on the secret wisdom of the druids has tended to be emphasised from the Roman period onwards, so that they became romantic and impressive figures in the minds of poets and scholars in seventeenth century England and Wales, and it is difficult to take a objective view of them. The controversy still continues, and the one point which we can be fairly sure about is that the position was never as fixed and clear cut as many scholars have tried to make it.

Much less is known about the Germanic and Scandinavian priesthood, which seems never to have been as efficiently organised as were the druids. Julius Caesar (VI, 13) emphasises this difference, and indicated that the priests and seers among the Germans had less political influence. There are references to priests and priestesses however who could punish criminals and sentence them to death (p. 61 above), and who organised sacrifices in the sacred groves, as well as presiding over the casting of lots and other divination rituals. According to Tacitus it was the priests who called the people to silence when the leader addressed the assembly, and he mentions them together with the nobles as 'servants of the gods' as well as referring to them as organisers of the procession of Nerthus in Denmark.[61] According to Bede, a chief priest (*primus pontificium*) named Coifi took an active part in the assembly called by Edwin of Northumbria to decide whether Christianity should be accepted (p. 31 above). He was responsible for the shrine of the gods, and himself destroyed it by fire after the decision was taken to support the new faith. How far Bede was here inventing appropriate scenes and suitable speeches, in the manner of Latin historians, is difficult to determine, but his representation of the priest as the guardian of the local shrine is in keeping with what we would expect at this period.

Priests did not have the monopoly of divination ceremonies, since Tacitus refers to those carried out privately by the heads of households, and Julius Caesar (*Gallic War* 1, 50) mentions the *matrones* who consulted omens before battle: 'It was a custom among the Germans that their matrons should declare by lots and divinations whether it was expedient or not to engage [in battle]'. In Iceland the chiefs undertook certain priestly duties, organising the religious feasts and sometimes taking responsibility for shrines of the gods, although these might be under the guardianship of particular families. The term *goði* used for a chief in Iceland who represented his district at the Thing seems likely originally to have been a priestly title; it is found in runic inscriptions in Denmark, but its exact significance is unknown.[62] There are references to wise men who might be described as seers rather than priests, like Thorleif the Wise in Norway (p. 141 above), and a later Thorleif the Wise who was said to be among the victims of Olaf Tryggvason, who sent his follower Hallfred to blind him. Whereas in Bede's account of the conversion of Northumbria the king allowed the assembly to decide on whether the kingdom should become Christian, and was supported by the priest, the matter was managed differently in Iceland. The decision here was left to the Law-Speaker Thorgeir, one of the 'wise men' of the community, the greatest authority on law and the man responsible, like the druids, for preserving it in his memory. He arrived at this in the traditional manner, according to Ari's account in *Íslendingabók*, and although Thorgeir himself was still a heathen, such was his reputation for wisdom that he was accepted by all. When the men had gone back to their booths, Thorgeir lay down, spread his cloak over himself and stayed motionless without speaking for the rest of that day and the night following.[63] Next morning he stood up, summoned the Assembly, and announced his ruling. There could only be one law in Iceland, he declared, to avoid endless strife and dissension. All should therefore accept the Christian faith and the law that went with it, and all should be baptised. However they might continue the old practices in private and sacrifice if they wished, and there would be no prohibition against the exposure of children and the eating of horseflesh. In this way, as Ari heard on what seems good authority, Christianity was accepted as the official Icelandic religion without conflict or the making of martyrs on either side. The answer to the problem came to Thorgeir, according to this account, when he kept silence and opened his mind to receive wisdom, following traditional practice.

Men like Thorgeir and his predecessors were actively concerned with the maintenance of learning and law in Iceland, with the genealogies of families and traditions about the past, like the druids in Ireland and Gaul. Like them, they taught young men, and pupils grew up in their houses, like Ari and Snorri Sturluson who were taught by older scholars before any university was founded in Iceland. While there is little evidence in Germany or Scandinavia for the existence of a closely-knit priestly class practising divination and amassing learning, this does not mean that traditions and practices were fundamentally different from those among the Celts in Gaul. There may have been more individualism among the Germans, but it has to be borne in mind that most of our information comes from a late period, and that the organised priesthood could hardly have survived in strength in Iceland. In any case, divination and prophecy are unlikely to be wholly confined to a priestly class. However among the Germans there is evidence for one important class of women, the seeresses, who took on the duty of interpreting omens and making enquiries on behalf of the people. They seem to have possessed considerable political influence which can be compared with that of the druids, and for this reason were of interest to the Roman historians.

6 Seeresses

Tacitus insists on the importance of these women. One famous seeress was Veleda of the Bructeri in the Rhineland, whose name is derived from *veles* (seer) and was therefore presumably a professional title. According to Tacitus (*Histories* IV, 61). Veleda 'enjoyed extensive authority according to the ancient Germanic custom which regards many women as endowed with prophetic powers, and, as the superstition grows, attributes divinity to them'. He refers again to such women in *Germania* (8): 'They believe that there resides in women an element of holiness and a gift of prophecy; and so they do not scorn to ask their advice, or lightly disregard their replies. In the reign of the Emperor Vespasian we saw Veleda long honoured by many Germans as a divinity; and even earlier they showed a similar reverence for Aurinia and a number of others.' Veleda had much influence, and was one of the arbiters when an agreement was made between the Romans and the people of Cologne. She did not meet the Roman representatives directly, but is said to have remained in a high tower while one of her relatives carried questions to her and brought back answers, 'as if he were the messenger of a god' remarks Tacitus (*Histories* IV, 65). When a flagship of the Roman navy was captured, it was taken up the river to be presented to Veleda (*ibid.*, V, 22). She was renowned for her prophecies, and was said to have foretold correctly the destruction of the Roman legions in AD 69. The Roman general Cerialis was thought to have carried on secret communications with her, and to have urged her to cease encouraging the Germans to revolt. In 78 BC she was brought to Rome, and Statius (*Silvae* IV, 89) refers to her as a captive, but the circumstances which made her leave Germany are unknown.[64] Veleda was a well-known figure with considerable influence outside her own tribe, but we know little of how she practised her calling as a seeress, and whether the relatives mentioned by Tacitus were really part of her family or members of a religious community to which she belonged. Other seeresses besides Veleda to whom reference is made in Latin sources are Aurinia or Albruna, also mentioned by Tacitus, Ganna, a priestess of the Semnones who was honoured by Domitian,[65] and an unnamed wise woman of the Chatti.[66]

In Icelandic literature the seeress still occupied an important position. One name used for her is *spákona* (from *spá*, prophecy or to prophesy), the equivalent *spámaðr* being used of a man. The more usual term is *vǫlva*, with no masculine form. In the sagas the *vǫlva* is represented as visiting houses and making predictions, particularly concerning the future destinies of children or young persons, and being visited by those wishing to consult her. She might conduct a divination ceremony in a house if invited to do so and answer questions about the future of the community, as well as individual questions from those present concerning their problems. The amount of material which survives from literature of the thirteenth century onwards gives the impression that consultation of the seeress was an important and widely known practice in pre-Christian Scandinavia. Certain poems are also presented as the revelations of a seeress, unveiling the remote past or the future of gods and men.

The special rite used to obtain hidden knowledge and revelation of what was to come was known as *seiðr*,[67] and the seeress was sometimes called a *seiðkona*. The word is thought to be connected with song or singing, and there is occasionally reference to a small choir which assisted the seeress by singing appropriate songs and spells. Although the accounts do not always agree, the important feature appears to be the provision of a high seat for the seeress, which may be referred to as a platform (*hjallr*), and it is while she is seated high above the audience that she is able to 'see' what is not revealed to men. She seems to have obtained her knowledge while in a state of trance, although this is implied rather than definitely stated: she is said to sigh or breathe deeply before beginning her revelations. In the most detailed account of the divination ceremony in *Eiríks Saga rauða* (4), she first gives an answer to the question which had been the reason for the ceremony, assuring the people that the famine afflicting them would soon end. Then she prophesies the future destinies of individuals present, and similarly in other accounts of *seiðr* members of the audience go up in turn to consult the seeress. The seeress can also reveal secrets of the present time, as in a story in Saxo's *History* (VII, 217–18). Here a woman with second sight was paid by the wicked King Frothi to discover the whereabouts of his nephews, whom he intended to kill. The boys had been hidden by a man skilled in magic, and the seeress revealed that they were being brought up in secret and called by the names of dogs so that their identity was not known. The boys themselves were in the hall in disguise, and realised that the seeress might reveal this to the king:

The power of her incantations was such that she could apparently
summon to her hands something in the distance visible to her alone, even
when it was up tied tightly with knots ... When the youths perceived that
they were being drawn out of their recess by the weird potency of the
enchantress's spells and pulled under her very gaze, in an effort not to be
betrayed by such strong, horrifying compulsion they dashed into her lap a
shower of gold which they had had from their protectors. As soon as she
had received the bribe, pretending to fall ill suddenly she collapsed like
one lifeless. (Fisher's translation)

This account is from the late twelfth century, and in a later version of
the tale in the Icelandic saga of Hrólf *Kraki* (3), one of the legendary
sagas, the revelations of the seeress are given in the form of short, cryptic
verses, and here the terms *vǫlva* and *seiðr* are used. The woman is said to
leap down from her seat when given a gold ring by the mother of the
boys as a bribe not to betray them. The account of 'knots' which conceal
the youths is an allusion to spells which had hitherto prevented their
discovery, but the seeress's powers are such that she is able to pierce the
mist and darkness in which they were concealed.

The accounts of *seiðr* given in the sagas have awakened much interest
because of their close resemblances to accounts of shamanistic ceremonies recorded in later times in northern Europe and Asis.[68] The 'little
seeress', as she is called in *Eiríks Saga* (4), was invited by an Icelander in
Greenland to hold her ceremony because of the anxiety over shortage of
food. She demanded that a special spell be sung so that she can obtain
power, and this is a song called *Varðlok(k)ur*, a name linked by
Strömbäck with the Scots dialect word 'warlock' (wizard), the meaning
of which is connected with the idea of shutting or enclosing.[69] The only
person who knew the spell and could sing it was a girl on a visit from
Iceland, who had learned it from her fostermother, although she was
herself a Christian. At first she was unwilling, but finally consented to
help: 'The *spákona* thanked her for the song, and said that many spirits
had come there and thought the song fair to hear, "those which before
would have turned away from us and given us no hearing; but now there
are many matters open to my sight which before were hidden from me
and also from others." '

The seeress here claims to have received help from spirits, as in the
practice of shamanism, when the shaman is thought to be assisted by
friendly spirits when his body lies in a trance so that his spirit can
journey to the Other World. He has his own special spirit protectors,
who are ready to help him against hostile forces and ensure his safe
return. Before the ceremony, the Greenland seeress was given a meal
composed of the hearts of all living creatures procurable, which

indicates a sacrifice. She sat on a special platform, and afterwards was able to reveal many matters to her audience, and to name the illustrious descendants to be born into the family of the girl who had helped her. The seeress wore a special costume, described in detail: a cloak with ornamental stones on the skirt, a lambskin hood lined with catskin, catskin gloves and calfskin boots; she had a pouch to hold her charms, and a staff with stones on the end, bound with brass. It is even noted that her knife had an ivory handle and a broken point.

The account gives the impression that it was originally based on an eye-witness report of such a ceremony, but it is hard to believe that this ever took place in Greenland, or even in Iceland at so late a date. It has been suggested that the description came from northern Norway, although the two elements characteristic of Lapp shamans, dancing and the use of the drum, are lacking. A tale of the thirteenth century in the *Chronicon Norwegiae*[70] is much closer to what is known of shamanism among the Lapps; here two men called 'diviners' are summoned to restore a woman to life, and they drum and dance and are then said to make a journey in animal form to the Other World to rescue her spirit. In spite of the resemblances between *seiðr* and shamanic practices, two important characteristics found in saga accounts, the raised seat of the seeress and her ability to 'see' what is hidden, seem likely to be Germanic in origin. There is no clear connection between the seeress and healing, which forms a fundamental part of shamanistic ceremonies. *Seiðr* in the literature is said to be linked both with Odin and with the goddesses, and Odin shows some characteristics of the shaman. In *Ynglinga Saga* (4, 7) Snorri states that the goddess Freyja was a priestess and taught *seiðr* to the gods, and also that Odin was an authority on *seiðr* but, since certain aspects of it were felt to be unmanly, it was taught to the priestesses.

The connection between such divination ceremonies and the goddesses is in keeping with their association with fate. Like the early mother goddesses, the seeress declares the destiny of the young. She also forecasts the coming season, as was done at the main religious feasts. Odin himself consulted a seeress when he desired to know his own fate and the coming of Ragnarok, and in the *Poetic Edda* the poem *Vǫluspá* is represented as the revelation of a *vǫlva*. This poem is thought to have been composed about AD 1000, although there is no clear evidence for dating. It gives a brief but impressive account of the creation of the world from chaos, the bright beginning of the kingdom of the gods, and the strife and treachery which brought about disaster, until gods and men alike were destroyed in a cosmic catastrophe. Only the World Tree survived, but at the end of the poem the world arose again from the sea, cleansed and fertile, to issue in a new age. The attitude of the unknown poet to Christianity is ambiguous. Some have believed that he clings to the old religion in spite of its defects and laments its end as Christianity banishes the gods. Others claim that he was a Christian poet influenced by Christian apocryphal literature, and that at the close of the poem he is welcoming the kingdom of Christ. In any case, this is no work of crude propaganda, for the treatment is objective and shows great imaginative power. According to Boyer, its essential message is that 'fate is the supreme power, responsible for everything, towards which all things aim, and according to which everything is ordered.'[71] Such a summing-up may help us to appreciate the importance of divination as a key to the world-picture of the Celtic and Germanic peoples.

The seeress begins by addressing both gods and men, but at certain points she seems to be responding to questions put by Odin, like the seeress in *Baldrs Draumar*, and like her appears reluctant to answer. She describes the creation, when the gods ascended their thrones, *rokstólar*, which might be interpreted as seats of power or of destiny.[72] A refrain occurs three times in the early part of the poem:[73]

> Then went all the gods
> to seats of destiny,
> the gods most holy
> took counsel together.

Among the activities of the gods is the playing of a board game, perhaps a game of chance in which dice would be used.[74] Then comes a sinister intervention, when three giant maidens enter, described as *ámáttigr*, which might be translated as powerful or fearsome. There is a later reference to three maidens of great wisdom who come from the Well of Urd; their function is to determine the destinis of men:

> They established laws,
> they meted out life
> to the sons of men,
> and declared their destinies.

There must be a deliberate parallel intended here, and it may be that we have the two contradictory aspects of the goddesses of destiny, first hostile and destructive and secondly protective and benevolent, as we see them portrayed in the literature. They are called giantesses on the first occasion, but both goddesses and valkyries may be represented as huge, menacing and hideous.

The names of the wise maidens or Norns are *Urðr*, *Verðandi* and *Skuld*, and it has been suggested that this is an imitation of the three Fates of classical mythology. However *Urðr* is the word used elsewhere for Fate; *Verðandi* is the present participle of the verb *verða* (be, become) and could refer to the goddess governing the present moment; *Skuld* has the meaning of something owed, a debt, and could therefore refer to the time appointed for death; in *Njáls Saga* (119) there is reference to death as 'a debt that all must pay'. The Norns are said to 'cut on wood' (*skáru á skíðu*), and this could refer to the cutting of runes. Anne Holtsmark, however, has pointed out that the word *skíð* indicates a large piece of wood such as a plank, and that it was customary in Norway as late as the nineteenth century to record dates and numbers of days or years by notches cut in wood, often in the plank above a window in the the farmhouse.[75] This suggests that the Norns cut a record of the life-span of each individual, and would be a familiar native image instead of the classical one of the spinning Fates. The Norns however were also pictured as weaving, like the women in the Lay of the Spear, determining the course of battle (p. 94 above), and in one of the heroic poems of the *Edda* they are said to weave the web of fate for the young hero Helgi at his birth, making the golden threads fast in the hall of the moon.[76]

A seeress working *seiðr* is also mentioned, and there is a reference to valkyries riding to battle, since they too are concerned with the workings of destincy. The board game of the gods is recalled at the end of the poem, when their golden playing pieces are found in the grass when the earth has been renewed, a symbol of its destiny in the dawning age. There is also a link between a gaming board and fate in Irish sources; the game of *fidchell* is said to be an invention of the god Lug, and Finn, an expert at gaining hidden knowledge, is as gifted at this game as at hunting. Interference with play has an effect on the fate of the players in life; men from the *Síd* steal pieces from the board when Art plays with his wicked stepmother Becuma, and he loses the game and is banished from the Kingdom.[77] In the 'Dream of Rhondabwy' in the *Mabinogion* a board game between Arthur and Owein is accompanied by a desperate battle between men and ravens, and when Arthur realises that his forces are losing, he crushes the gold playing pieces in his hands so that the game ends. One of the chief treasures of Ireland was said to be the Board of Crimthan, brought from the depths of the sea,[78] and this is mentioned along with two other treasures which were royal crowns. There is clearly a link between the board game, in which a king is usually one of the pieces, and the fate of an earthly king. In Welsh tradition the board *Gwenddoleu* is mentioned as one of the Thirteen Royal Jewels of Britain, and the pieces on it are said to move of their own volition; memories of similar magic boards are found in the legendary Icelandic sagas, in the possession of giants or giantesses.[79] Van Hamel saw a link between such boards and the power of a king, and claims that the board of gold used by the gods in *Voluspá* symbolises peace and plenty.[80] His suggestion that the giant women steal the pieces is not borne out by the poem, but they seem to interrupt the game in some way and thus bring evil into the world of the gods. The playing boards and pieces found in some of the finest burials of the early Anglo-Saxon period, including that at Sutton Hoo, may represent something more than entertainment in a king's hall; they could be symbolic objects associated with the rule and prosperity of a kingdom. The fact that dice were used in a number of board games emphasises the element of chance, of such importance in divination.

The poem *Voluspá* has a series of images evoking the power of destiny over gods and men. The seeress by the spring beneath the World Tree seems to be one of these, standing for Fate which has ruled the world from the beginning, powerful enough to unseat the very gods themselves. Once more we are faced with the problem of how far the figure foretelling the future holds control of it. Another symbol is that of the World Tree, which precedes the gods and outlasts their rule; this again must have links with the centre and the destiny of kings (p. 24 above). The name *Urðr*, linked with the well or spring to which Odin came to discover what the future held, is found again in Anglo-Saxon literature as *Wyrd*. It appears to stand for man's allotted destiny, and in a Christian context for the providence of God. Neumann claimed that it was derived from *wurði*, a feminine word for Necessity.[81] It seems that in both Germanic and Celtic tradition fate has been associated with a feminine figure, represented as goddess or giantess. Another world used for fate is *ørlog*, given to the first man and woman in *Voluspá*, when the gods bring them to life. This is apparently the force which decides the luck and destiny of men, a powerful concept in Icelandic literature. Neumann himself differentiates between fate and necessity, as represented by the powers of the Æsir and the Vanir; he thought that the Æsir were the powers that force and restrain, and could bind monsters and men, while the Vanir were those whose force is that of the natural world, resulting in creative life and growth. Behind both concepts however there seems to be a group of figures representing ultimate fate, and the divine women who are found symbolising this are not necessarily due to influence from classical sources, since the image seems to have existed early among both Celts and Germans.

The idea of implacable Fate is opposed to that of Chance, which is something which can be governed by supernatural powers. Chance was clearly emphasised in the religion of the Viking Age, in the dependence of kings and heroes on omens, the casting of lots, and pleas to gods and supernatural protectors. Lots were seen as a revelation of the will of the divine powers, based on their knowledge of the future rather than any moral judgement, but the implication is that this knowledge was by no means complete, since they themselves went in search of additional knowledge, and could not avert catastrophe determined by Fate. Yet there was also a belief in the value of luck, by which a man could be in tune with the supernatural world and receive help during his sojourn on earth. The importance of luck was recognised as keenly by a king as by a new settler struggling to establish himself in inhospitable Iceland, since on a ruler's possession of it the prosperity of his land would depend. In a violent and warlike society, men were constantly aware of the narrow edge on which all stood, where some unexpected chance or accident could bring disaster upon them. Heroes might be doomed, for all their courage and fine qualities, and many splendid royal halls, we are reminded in Irish and Scandinavian tales, went up in flames.

The poets recognised this threat. It lent a sombre quality to their poetry, and yet did not result in negation or despair. 'Wyrd is wholly inexorable' declared the poet of the Anglo-Saxon *Wanderer*. 'Evil is the decree of the Norns', agrees the poet of the *Battle of the Goths and Huns*, quoted in *Hervarar Saga*. *Vǫluspá* seems to show fate as closely linked with the passing of time; the setting of the sun and moon on their appointed paths and the granting of activity to mankind usher in the maids of destiny. A favourite symbol of the period before the Viking Age in the north was a great whirling wheel, sometimes in the form of a swastika, which appears to be associated with the journey of the sun and therefore with the movement of the year, as well as with the power of Fate: 'The whirligig of Time brings in his revenges', as Shakespeare expressed it. There is a link here also with the movement round a fixed centre, which for the northern peoples was represented by the World Tree. Because it was in the centre of the turning world, it was independent of the moves of Fate, and Fate as a goddess sat beneath its branches. The use of this powerful symbol may now be considered further, in the wider outline of the cosmology and the picture of human and supernatural worlds in early mythology.

VI The Other World

Grasp with thy hand the guiding vine
By which the god Tane ascended to the highest heaven,
That thou mayest be welcomed by the Celestial Maids
Assembled on the courtyard of Te Rauroha
And so enter within the palace of Rangiatea.
Then and only then shall all desire for this world cease,
Ah, little maid of mine.
Lament for a favourite grandchild of a Maori chief (translated Peter Buck)

The tales and poetry of both Iceland and Ireland show a constant
awareness of worlds beyond the everyday life of men. In earlier times,
contacts with these worlds were by means of sacrifices and religious
feasts and access to holy places. Their inhabitants might come among
living men of their own volition and bring good luck to those who turned
to them for counsel and exchange of gifts. In mapping the realms
making up the Other World, we must leave the realistic background of
Landnámabók for more fantastic accounts of poets and story-tellers, the
framework of myth and legend. This is difficult to analyse because it is in
the main a literary creation, open to outside influences once it was
presented to new audiences in Christian times. Familiar and ancient
motifs like the hammer of the gods or the gaming board which
determined the course of events lived on to enrich new tales of marvels,
losing the religious awe which may once have invested them. Not that
the myths and symbols were necessarily treated with reverence and
solemnity in the period when the gods were still accepted as the ruling
powers; what we know of early religion lead us to suppose that the
element of humour and entertainment was there from the beginning.
Men could laugh heartily at the discomfiture of Thor or the Dagda or
the cunning wiles of Loki without rejecting the gods as mighty powers.
But to laugh at the boisterous humour of the myths or even to enact
them as comic entertainment[1] was something different from the
rejection of the gods by mocking at their absurdities. Probably more

167

destructive of the ancient world picture was to turn the once powerful myths into realistic or moral tales, cutting them down to size for a sophisticated audience.

In Iceland in the twelfth century men were still familiar with fragmented traditions concerning the cosmology of the Other World. The position here and in Christian Ireland was like that in the islands of Polynesia after the coming of the Christian missonaries to the Pacific, as described by Frank Buck in *Vikings of the Pacific*: 'Priests and scholars who had accepted the new teaching refused to pass on the concepts and the legends of the their old cult. Thus the continuity of oral transmission was broken. When questions were asked in after years, only scattered, dislocated fragments could be recalled.'[2] Further back still among the continental Germans and Celts, we have to rely on the evidence of outsiders, with all the possibilities of misunderstanding and corruption of tradition which this involves, along with iconography and funeral rites, never easy to interpret. This is little enough from which to reconstruct an ancient cosmology. In the thirteenth century, Snorri Sturluson in the *Prose Edda* and *Ynglinga Saga* relied chiefly on old poems and the traditional imagery of poets of pre-Christian times, along with scraps of folklore of his own day. Fortunately we still have most of the poems which he drew on, and we know that he turned to *Vǫluspá* and other peoms of the *Poetic Edda* for much information, especially on the creation and the worlds of gods and giants.

1 The Scandinvian cosmos

In the literature the cosmos is represented as a round area of land, with the World Tree at its centre, surrounded by ocean. 'The fair shining plain which the water encompasses' serves as a description in a song of creation sung in the hall of Heorot in the poem *Beowulf* (93f.). Beneath the central tree was the spring of Fate. Many beings dwelt under the roots of the tree, while other creatures lived on the branches or fed upon them. A great serpent, *Miðgarðsormr* (World Serpent), lay curled in the ocean round the circular disk of the world. Such a conception could hardly have evolved in treeless Iceland, but it is a widespread image; the central tree is found in northern Eurasia, the Pacific, Mesopotamia and India, so that one can hardly theorise as to its origin. But the cosmology of a people must be based to some extent on the features of the natural world around them, and the World Tree in northern mythology may have come from memories of forest sanctuaries. The tree does not often appear in recognisable form in Viking Art, but there is one impressive memorial stone of an earlier period from Sanda in the island of Gotland, dated to about AD 500, found beneath a church floor (Plate 1c).[3] This shows a tree in association with other symbols in such a way as to suggest a picture of the cosmos not unlike that in the literature.

In the upper part of the stone is a great whirling disk, a motif found on other Gotland stones of this period. It may have been derived from monuments in southern Europe, since it appears on Roman tombstones and mosaic pavements.[4] Below are two smaller disks, each encircled by a serpent, which could represent day and night, corresponding to the round faces of sun and moon on Roman memorial stones. This disk could be a symbol of the cosmos, based partly on the conception of the turning circle through which the sun and moon pass, and thus, as was suggested earlier, an image of time's passing and therefore of the power of fate. Such a conception could also be represented by the wheel and the swastika, found on many ornaments of the period, and later associated with Thor, the sky god. The idea of the turning heavens as an expression of time is found in one of the *Edda* poems, *Vafþruðnismál* (23), where the father of Moon and Sun is called *Mundilferi*, a strange name which has been interpreted as 'Turner of Time':

He is called Mundilferi who fathered the Moon
    and likewise the Sun.
They must revolve round the heavens each day
    to mark the years for men.

Below the disks is a tree in the centre of the stone, faint but unmistakable, and below this again a dragon-like creature, which could represent the serpent in the depths. Then comes a ship, which could represent the surrounding ocean. The ship remained a favourite motif on Gotland stones throughout the Viking Age, long after the whirling disk had been given up as a memorial symbol, and was evidently associated with the journey of the dead to the Other World. It is an ancient image in the North, for in the Bronze Age in Scandinavia, ships appear in designs on metalwork and on numerous rock-carvings; it has been suggested that the sun's journey across the heavens by day was then represented by a wagon while the ship symbolised its voyage through the underworld by night.[5] Certainly the ship continued to be associated with funerals, since in Norway and Sweden from about the seventh century onwards some hundreds of men and women were buried and cremated in ships and boats, or the outline of a ship might be made round the grave.[6] While the design on the Sanda stone is not an exact diagram of the cosmos as a modern man might draw it, based on the mythology of the poems, it seems to correspond in essence to the literary picture. Attempts to interpret the descriptions in the poems literally and produce a plan of the worlds round the central tree have never wholly succeeded, because the impression the poems give is not of a planned and rational world, but rather a series of vivid images which build up a vague but powerful world-picture.

2 The central tree

The position of the tree in the centre as a source of luck and protection for gods and men is confirmed by the custom in Germany and Scandinavia, continuing as late as the nineteenth century, of having a guardian or lucky tree beside a house. Symbolic offerings might be made to it, and ale poured over its roots at festivals, as in the case of a huge birch standing on a mound beside a farm in western Norway, which fell in 1874.[7] The gods used to meet beneath the World Tree to hold their assembly, and it might also be equated with the pillar in the holy place which symbolised the centre of the world (p. 22 above). It would be difficult to say whether tree or pillar came first, and this would probably depend on whether the holy place was in a thickly wooded area. There is no mention of a special tree at Thingvellir, but there may well have been one at Uppsala, the holy centre of the Swedes. Adam of Bremen, writing about 1075 (IV, scol. 138) stated that a huge tree stood beside the temple there, remaining green summer and winter, but that no one knew what kind of tree it was. Whether his informant actually saw the tree is uncertain, but the existence of sacred trees in Germany in the pre-Christian period is borne out by reference to their destruction by early Christian missionaries like St Boniface.

The World Tree has various names in the poems, but the one most used is *Yggdrasil*. *Yggr* was one of the many names of Odin, and the usual interpretation is 'Horse of Yggr', since Odin in a sense rode the tree when he hung upon it.[8] The tree is repeatedly called 'the ash Yggdrasil', and a possible reason for the choice of an ash might be the bunches of 'keys' which hang from the branches like bodies of tiny men, recalling the practice of hanging sacrificial victims from trees (p. oo above). The ash has also peculiarly wide-spreading roots, and in descriptions of the tree its roots are said to extend to various regions of the underworld. Other trees of symbolic importance in North-Western Europe were the oak, the forest tree associated with the god of the sky, the evergreen yew which lives to a great age, and the apple tree, the favourite fruit-bearing tree of the people of the North.

The World Tree was a provider of nourishment and a source of healing; dews from it enriched the valleys of earth and drops from its leaves brought benefit to men. It was also the source of the world's rivers, for they flowed from the horns of the hart which fed upon its foliage, while from the horns of the goat which did likewise came the mead which supplied the warriors in the hall of Odin. The tree was constantly eroded by these creatures and by the serpents which gnawed at its roots, yet it remained ever green and living and apparently survived the fires of Ragnarok. In this it seems to symbolise life on earth, the continual destruction and recreation of the race of men and of the kingdoms of the world. This may be one inspiration behind the restless patterns of Viking Age art, as for instance on the carved panels from the stave church at Urnes in western Norway, where creatures are seen biting at foliage and at one another in a flowing pattern full of aggression and enormous energy.

The roots of Yggdrasil are said to extend into different realms. According to the poem *Grímnismál* (31), Hel, the abode of the dead, lay under one of them, Jotunheim, land of giants, beneath another, and the world of men under a third, implying that these realms lay side by side, while that of the gods was above, in the sky. Snorri placed this also under one of the roots, but then suggested that the root itself was in the sky. He also refers to three separate springs under the Tree, but in the poems there seems to be one, the Well of Urd. He evidently found it hard, as we do, to comprehend the geography of the *Edda*, and more problems are encountered in seeing where the bridge *Bifrǫst* (quivering road) should be placed. This is the rainbow bridge which burns with fire, and is guarded against the giants by Heimdall; De Vries suggests it was originally the Milky Way.[9]

There have no doubt been changes in the course of time in the conception of the supernatural worlds. The seeress in *Vǫluspá* declares: 'Nine worlds I remember, / nine in the Tree ...' This could mean that the worlds surround the Tree, or that they were set one above the other, while the Tree formed the centre, as in descriptions of the shaman's journey up to heaven in the oral literature of Eurasia.[10] The idea of symbolic levels of this kind was not unfamiliar in the Viking Age; Tynwald Hill on the Isle of Man, where the assembly met, was built in a series of steps (p. 19 above), while the stave churches in Norway represent rising levels by their series of roofs rising to a central point (p. 34 above). In one early manuscript of Snorri's *Prose Edda*, King Gylfi consults three mysterious powers who tell him of the world of the gods, and they are shown sitting on three thrones, one above the other.[11]

Certainly the myths give no impression of a neat, circumscribed universe. Tales and poems suggest vast spaces and long, lonely journeys through cold and darkness, over rushing rivers and high mountains, an echo of the experience of Viking adventurers in northern and eastern Europe. Hel lay to the north, it was said, the direction where one would expect frozen wastes and long periods of darkness. The messenger seeking Balder in Hel in Snorri's tale[12] took nine nights to reach it after leaving Asgard. He passed through deep valleys and over a great bridge resounding under the marching feet of the dead, and finally descended downwards and northwards to the mighty gate which shut in the walled region of Hel, kingdom of death. The road to Jotunheim, the underworld of the giants, was represented by Snorri as running eastwards; travellers first crossed the sea and then traversed mighty forests like those Thor and his companions journeyed through in their search for Utgard-Loki.[13]

Whatever the spatial relationship between the worlds, there is general agreement that a number of these existed, inhabited by different races of beings, and there are usually said to be nine. A possible clue as to what these might be is given in the poem *Alvíssmál*, one of the 'wisdom' poems of the *Edda*, in the form of questions and answers. Here the names for various aspects of the natural world, sun, wind, the sea and so on, are listed, and different terms are said to be used by the dwellers in the various worlds. In reply to the question: 'What is Wind, greatest of travellers, called in each of the worlds?', the reply is as follows:

> It is Wind among men, Waverer to the gods,
>   Neighing One to the Mighty Powers;
> Shrieker to the giants, Whistler to the elves,
>   while in Hel they say Breath of Storm.

The lists of worlds overlap in the different stanzas. The three occurring most frequently are the worlds of Men, Gods and Giants; there are references to those of the Vanir, Elves, Dwarves and Dwellers in Hel, and those of the Mighty Powers, the Holy Ones and the Sons of the Gods are mentioned once only. It would be easy to list seven of the worlds: (1) mankind; (2/3) gods (Æsir and Vanir); (4) giants; (5) elves; (6) dwarves; (7) The dead in Hel. The remaining two could be the most powerful group of gods, called the Holy or Mighty Ones, and the heroes dwelling in Valhalla, called the Sons of the Gods, (or alternatively this might mean the younger gods who survive Ragnarok).

It would be unwise however to insist on a exact ruling. It would not have been thought necessary or desirable to provide a logical plan of the supernatural world, plotting out the various realms with dogmatic insistence on agreement. The names must have emerged out of the general lore of the poets and from men of wisdom who preserved the ancient traditions of the race. The Æsir and Vanir were evidently regarded as two separate groups, although they dwelt together in

Asgard, since there are allusions to a separate realm called Vanaheim. The Elves may originally have been the same as the Vanir (p. 116 above), and later a distinction was made between Light and Dark Elves, perhaps as a result of Christian teaching about Angels. The world of the dead might be pictured as a land far away, a realm of decay and dismal shades, or equated with the burial mounds close at hand. There is additional mention in the poems of Niflheim or Niflhel, a place of mist and darkness below Hel, which seems to have been the realm of utter stagnation and sterility. But it is hopeless to expect this to fit into a precise and orderly plan, as the Swedish Rydberg hoped to prove in the last century. If in our strong desire for the rational we try to create a logical scheme out of such scattered ideas and images, we are doing violence to the traditions of poets and seers who left us clues as to the nature of the Other World.

3 Myths of the beginning

The poems dealing with the Other World are usually concerned with the creation of the universe and its ultimate destruction. In the beginning, order emerged out of chaos. Formlessness before creation was not represented by water, as in some mythologies, but by a great abyss, *Ginnungagap*, which might be translated Gulf of Deceiving, because its deceiving emptiness was in reality pregnant with potential energy and life.[14] Ice formed in the gap, and embers of fire came into it from the realm of Muspell, the region of burning heat, and from these extremes a mighty giant was created. He was both male and female, and his name Ymir seems to mean Two-fold Being. Tacitus records *Tvisto* as the first ancestor of the Germans, and this name appears to have a similar meaning.[15] A race of giants emerged from Ymir's body, and he was nourished on the milk of a primeval cow, which licked the ice-blocks to release a new set of beings, three brothers called the Sons of Bor. These slew Ymir, and then formed the earth from his body and the sea from his blood; the sky was raised aloft by four dwarves, creatures which bred in Ymir's body, and then sun and moon were set in place and time began. Three creator gods, perhaps the same as the Sons of Bor, walked on the seashore, which we have seen represented as the place of creative inspiration (p. 152 above). There they found two trees, driftwood washed ashore, breathed vitality and spirit into them, and gave them movement, so that the first man and woman came to life.

Here the gods are seen as the creators of the world of men, and of mankind, but the giants preceded them. In the poems the giants are seen as the possessors of ancient wisdom, since only they can remember the far-off beginnings, and even Odin turned to them when he wished to increase his knowledge. We cannot be sure who these creator gods were. In *Vǫluspá* they are said to be Odin with Lodur and Hœnir, two gods of whom little is known. Lodur has been identified by some with Loki, who is often the companion of Odin and in some ways might be seen as a shadow creative figure, giving birth to Odin's horse Sleipnir, to monsters and to Hel, goddess of death. Another god associated with creation is Heimdall, called 'father of created beings', who in the poem *Rígsþula* appears as the god who begets the three classes of men, noblemen, farmers and slaves. He is said to have existed 'in the beginning', and has characteristics in common with the Irish Manannán. It has been suggested that the concept of a creator god is found on brooches of the early Anglo-Saxon period, showing a face with an open mouth, from which issues a kind of cloud which encloses a fragmented animal form.[16] But if this is really one of the Germanic gods, he has not yet been satisfactorily identified.

Myths of the beginning were represented on memorial stones of the Viking Age. One from Heysham in Lancashire shows four little figures supporting a central arch, as the dwarves were said to hold up the sky. On either side is a monster, and there are animal figures below. A stone from Sockburn in north Yorkshire shows a figure with his hand in the jaws of a beast, and this must surely depict Tyr binding the wolf but losing his hand in his endeavour to save the gods.[17] The binding of the forces of evil in the early days of the world was clearly a powerful concept in Scandinavian mythology. The wolf was bound by Tyr; the

11 Faces on bronze brooches from early Anglo-Saxon graves at Baginton and Warwick.

serpent was cast down into the sea and prevented by Thor from breaking loose; Loki was bound by the gods and left under a rock until he emerged at Ragnarok to join the other monsters. There are some Viking Age carvings showing a bound giant, but it is difficult to tell whether this represents Loki or the bound Satan of Christian tradition.[18]

The tradition of the treasures of the gods is remembered among the myths of the beginning. In Scandinavian poetry one of these was Odin's mightly spear *Gungnir*, hurled through the air to begin a conflict. Another was his gold ring *Draupnir*, from which eight more rings dropped every ninth night, so that it was an unending source of wealth. A third was Thor's hammer *Mjǫllnir*, on which the gods relied for defence against the giants. A fourth was the golden boar of the Vanir deities (p. 50 above), and a fifth their magic ship *Skiðblaðnir* (wooden-bladed), which could bear them over the sea at their will. Snorri tells in *Skáldskaparmál* (33) of the forging of these treasures by the dwarves, urged on by Loki, although he afterwards took a perverse pleasure in trying to spoil their work. The treasures were coveted by the frost giants, who once stole Thor's hammer, so that it was only recovered with Loki's help (p. 205 below). Another precious possession of the gods once stolen from them was the stock of golden apples guarded by the goddess Idun, who may be the same as Freyja. These preserved the gods' eternal youth, and once they were gone they found themselves beoming old and wrinkled, but again Loki intervened and by his cunning brought back the goddess and her fruit from the giant's stronghold. It has been suggested that these may be a late addition to the treasures of the gods, imitated from the golden apples of the Hesperides, and indeed in the earliest source of the tale of Idun in the poem *Haustlǫng* of the ninth or early tenth century, no apples are mentioned, and we are only told that the goddess possessed the secret of immortal youth.[19] However golden apples are among the gifts offered by Freyr to Gerd in the poem *Skírnismál*, and refusal to take them was to mean sterility and decay. Apples were a known symbol of fertility, together with nuts (p. 181 below) and both are brought into the tale of Idun, since Loki is said to have changed the goddess into a nut so that he could bring her back to Asgard when he escaped in the form of a hawk.

Finally the gods possessed the divine mead which brought inspiration to gods and men, said to have been brewed by the Æsir and Vanir after the war between them ended (p. 44 above). This was one of the treasures coveted by the giants, but Odin recovered it for the gods with the help of the daughter of the giant who had hidden it within a mountain. He crawled through the rock in the form of a serpent, and after drinking the mead changed into eagle form and flew back to Asgard. There he vomited it out into vessels which the gods had made ready, and this myth was depicted in stone, and survives on a memorial set up about the eighth century in Gotland.[20] The mead was often referred to in early poetry, representing as it did the gift of poetic inspiration and skill in words which Odin could grant to his followers.

In Irish literature we have no detailed account of the creation to put beside that in the *Edda* poems, for the Irish monastic writers fitted tales of the arrival of the gods into a framework of Biblical history. We are told by Julius Caesar that the Celts believed that they were descended from Dis Pater, the Roman god of the dead, which could indicate a tradition of a giant ancestor of the race. Memories of such a belief might be seen in the traditions of the mysterious dark god Donn, which long persisted as folklore in Ireland, although he plays little part in literary sources.[21] Donn had his home on a small rocky island off the Kelly coast known as *Tech Duinn* (House of Donn), and it was said that the dead journeyed there and received a welcome. In more recent times he was said to receive athletes and sportsmen, such as footballers and hurlers who died young. Donn is described as a gloomy lord of the dead, and as the ruler of the storm, riding through the air, and tales were told of fishermen seeing the dead crossing to the Skellig Rocks on their way to the Other World. There were other reputed entrances to his kingdom, such as a cleft at Knockfierna, where a cairn of stones was raised to him, and gifts and offerings might be left at such places.

In the literature Donn appears in the *De Gabálaib Érenn* (*Lebor Gabála Érenn*) as the leader of the Sons of Míl, the company which twice invaded Ireland and who on their first arrival defeated the Túatha Dé.[22] Donn offended their queen, Ériu, and afterwards died when his ship was wrecked. His dying words are quoted: 'To me, to my house, you shall all come after you die', which may go back to an early tradition. On one of the Skellig islands there was an early monastery, and those who made a pilgrimage there had to ascend a pinnacle called the Eagle's Nest, rising about 215 m above the sea, and lean over to kiss a cross carved on the overhanging rock face. It has been suggested that this demanding ritual could have developed out of an earlier belief in the perilous journey of the dead across these rocky islands.[23]

The tale of the invasion of the Sons of Míl has features which suggest memories of a creation legend. Donn arrived with his brother Amairgen the seer, and a poem is quoted in which he identifies himself with various aspects of the natural world:[24]

I am Wind on Sea,
I am Ocean-Wave,

I am Roar of Sea,
I am Bull of Seven Fights,
I am Vulture over Cliff,
I am Dewdrop,
I am Fairest of Flowers,
I am Boar for Boldness,
I am Salmon in Pool,
I am Lake on Plain ...

MacCulloch explained away such passages as a mere string of shape-changing boasts. Nora Chadwick pointed out, however, that similar phrases are found in early Irish and Welsh mantic poems, while the Rees brothers compare them with passages concerning creation in the *Bhagavadgita*.[25] Amairgen also blessed Ireland, promising fruitfulness to wood and river and to the well of Tara at its centre. The origins of various natural features are listed, such as lakes which came into existence with the digging of a grave, while there is an account of the sharing out of land and naming of places. The listing of skills and crafts established in Ireland may be compared with the skills introduced by the gods at the beginning in the poem *Vǫluspá*. Another confused account which may contain memories of the creation is the *Second Battle of Mag Tuired*, where various 'first acts', such as curing by herbs, wailing for the dead, and the custom of ploughing on Tuesdays are given.[26]

These battles between supernatural beings may be compared with the conflict between the Æsir and Vanir, (p. 44 above) although the framework is quite different. In the case of the Scandinavian material, we are told nothing of the actual battle, only that hostages were exchanged and that finally a truce was made, and the result of this was the preparation of the mead of inspiration. In the Irish accounts, the Túatha Dé were victorious in their first battle, but after a time they refused to continue with Bres as their king because of his meanness and tyranny, and so he left Ireland and gathered together an army of the Fomorians, a demonic people who had earlier destroyed Partholan and his followers in one of the first invasions of Ireland. Against this enemy the Túatha Dé employed all their skills and magic powers, taking Lug the Many-skilled as their new leader. They had with them four treasures, which may be compared with those of the Scandinavian gods. There was the Stone of Fál, which gave a sign when the right king was chosen (p. 20 above), the spear of Lug which like Odin's spear ensured victory, the sword of Núadu from which none could escape once it was out of the scabbard, and the cauldron of the Dagda, from which none went away unsatisfied (p. 45 above). Elizabeth Gray has pointed out

177

G

the strong emphasis on the duties of kingship in the choice of these possessions, and the importance of this theme in the tale.[27]

There is much debate as to the possible form of the myth behind the confusing accounts of the First and Second Battles of Mag Tuired. Some scholars have argued for one battle only, seeing the account of the first as a late addition which did not exist before the eleventh century.[28] Mag Tuired is usually identified with Moytirra near Lough Arrow in Sligo. O'Rahilly thought the basis of the legend was the duel between Lug and Balor,[29] but this is not now generally accepted (p. 196 below). Theories that it was dependent on vague memories of attacks by invaders in the remote past of Ireland seem unconvincing, although some of the names which have found their way into the story may have been suggested by those of earlier tribes and peoples, such as *Gáiléoin* (?Gauls), *Fir Domnann* (?Dumnoni) and *Fir Bolg* (?Belgae). Sjoestedt is probably right in her summing up of the situation: 'Witnesses of a relatively recent past have come to be introduced between the fanciful Fomorians and the divine "People of Dana"; supernatural and human are blended into the crucible of the myth.'[30]

Dumézil's approach is to see the battles as based on a very ancient myth concerned with the maintenance of sovereignty, when the gods of the first function, representing kings and priests, joined with the god of warriors against the gods of the third function, those concerned with herding and agriculture, and the conflict ends in an agrement between them.[31] There are difficulties in making the Irish tales fit neatly into this pattern, but after the struggle in which Núadu loses his hand there is a compromise between the two sides: 'The Túatha Dé took counsel, and their decision was to offer Sreng his choice of the provinces of Ireland, while a compact of peace, goodwill and friendship should be made between the two peoples. And so they made peace, and Sreng chose the province of Connaught.'[32] While it seems hardly possible to disentangle early myths concerning the beginnings of society and the creative work of the gods from the pseudo-history built up around it, Dumézil's theory has a least, as MacCana points out,[33] 'the not inconsiderable merit of recovering order and purpose from apparent chaos', offering as it does the possibility of tracing a coherent system of gods inherited from the Indo-European past.

4 The sacred tree in Ireland

The series of separate supernatural worlds is less clear in Irish sources than in Norse literature, since the tales are mostly set in Ireland, and the gods who appear in them are not acknowledged openly as such. However the Túatha Dé are represented as the people from the fairy mounds,

178

although they are constantly in touch with mortals. They are the People
of Danu, probably the same as the goddess Anu, called by Cormac the
mother of the Irish gods. Both goddesses have general characteristics of
the Great Mother, partly identified with the earth itself, as suggested by
the name of the two rounded hills in Kerry known as the Paps of Anu.
The conception of a great divine mother who nourished and protected
the gods themselves can be dimly seen behind these names.

As in Norse myths the gods dwell in separate halls, so the people of
the *Síd* inhabit a number of separate mounds, with a different king
ruling each one.[34] Some appear to dwell on islands and others beyond
the sea or beneath the waves, where the kingdom of Manannán is to be
found. The people of the Other World come and go between these
different realms, visiting the haunts of men and perhaps taking individuals back with them for a season or for ever. There are traces also of
the image of a central tree, which joins the world of men to the other
worlds. Five special trees are mentioned in the *Rennes Dindsenchas* as
sacred trees now said to have fallen: 'The Tree of Ross and the Tree of
Mugna and the Ancient Tree of Datha and the branching Tree of
Uisnech and the Ancient Tree of Tortu.'[35] Three of these trees are ash
trees, while the Tree of Ross was a yew, and the Tree of Mugna an oak,
although no ordinary one, since it bore three crops of different fruit each
year: 'apples, goodly, marvellous, and nuts, round, blood-red, and
acorns, brown, ridgy.' Moreover, it was evergreen: 'Its leaves were
upon it always', like the Tree at Uppsala as described in the *Edda* and
by Adam of Bremen (p. 24 above).

Alden Watson claims that these trees were closely associated with
poetry and with kingship, and regarded as sources of ancient wisdom.[36]
They figure in legends of legendary or historical kings, and many of the
epithets used to describe them in the poems have to do with kingship;
indeed at times the tree is addressed as if it were a king. The epithets
resemble those used by Amairgen in his poem, and again there seems to
be a link between these trees and the account of the creation. They are
said to have grown from a branch brought by an Otherworld being,
bearing nuts, apples and acorns, and the most ancient man in Ireland,
the wise Fintan mac Bóchra, remembered his coming and how he
received the berries from the branch from which the trees were grown.[37]
The visitor also left them a description of each of the provinces, and the
trees are therefore represented as witnesses to the past history of Ireland,
just as in *Vǫluspá* the seeress remembers the past 'in the Tree' (p. 171
above).

The sacred trees appear to symbolise the four quarters of the island
and its centre, which was at Uisnech, where *Craeb Uisnig*, the ash tree,

would have stood, together with the Stone of Division which marked the centre (p. 20 above). The idea of the great central tree going up into the sky like Yggdrasil would explain the epithet *dor nime* (door(?) of heaven) used in one of the poems.[38] When it fell the tree at Uisnech was said to cover a distance of something like twenty miles. Another of the trees, *Eo Mugna*, was said to shelter thousands of warriors – presumably the whole population of the tribe. The lack of agreement as to what type of tree was chosen to represent the centre is similar to that in Germanic tradition (p. 170 above). It appears that any great tree of the forest might qualify as a *bile* or sacred tree.[39]

Memories of a tree of the Other World seem to have been preserved in traditions concerning Lough Cair, a lake which was said to dry up every seven years. A tale recorded from an old woman in 1879[40] tells how when this happened the tree could be seen covered by a green cloth, the *Brat Úaine*, beneath which a woman sat knitting. Once a man riding by snatched away the cloth, whereupon she called on the waters to rise, and he was caught by the torrent as he rode away and his horse cut in two. This lake is about two miles from Cnoc Áine, the abode of the local goddess (p. 112 above), and the woman knitting beneath the tree recalls the figure of the spinning or weaving goddess of fate beside the spring at the foot of Yggdrasil. It seems likely that the link between a flood and the spring or well of fate is very old, since it was found by Carney in an early poem,[41] a version of the Bran legend. The spring in the Other World known as the Well of Connla, from which the rivers of Ireland are derived, was also linked with a tree or trees, as hazel nuts dropped into the water and were eaten by the salmon who swam down the rivers, so that those who ate the fish received the gift of poetic inspiration. (p. oo above).

One of the fruits mentioned on the tree of the Other World is the apple. When one of the people of the *Síd* came to invite a human hero to visit the Land of Youth (p. 113 above) he might carry a branch of an apple tree with him, described as silver with white blossom or golden apples upon it, and leaves that made tinkling music which could lull men to sleep or banish pain. Such a tree is described in the *Rennes Dindsenchas*: 'A shining tree like gold stood upon the hill; because of its height it would reach to the clouds. In its leaves was every melody and its fruits, when the wind touched it, specked the ground.'[42] Lúag describes such a tree when he returns to tell Cú Chulann of his visit to the Other World:[43]

A tree at the doorway to the court,
fair its harmony;

a tree of silver before the setting sun,
its brightness like that of gold.

This tree, it seems, formed part of an orchard. We hear also of a silver branch bearing three golden apples brought to King Cormac,[44] and of a branch given to Bran from 'the apple-tree from Emain which produced sweet music'.[45] It was at Emain Ablach (Emain of the Apples) that Manannán was said to dwell, which was presumably regarded as the centre of the Other World, as Emain on earth was the centre of Ulster.

A girl from the Other World who came to summon Connla brought with her not a branch but an apple, on which he lived for a month without any other food.[46] The apple is a symbol of fertility, and in *Vǫlsunga Saga*, one of the Icelandic late legendary sagas which uses some earlier material, an apple was dropped by a goddess into the lap of a king who had prayed for a son (p. 130 above). The son who was afterwards born to him had a great apple tree in the centre of his royal hall, and this appears to symbolise the continuation of the family.[47] This episode in the saga is sufficiently different from those in the Irish tales to make direct borrowing unlikely, but the symbolism is basically the same. It was golden apples which brought everlasting youth to the Scandinavian gods, and in Irish tradition those in the realm of Manannán were said to remain young and vigorous because they partook of the ale brewed by Goibniu the smith, called 'Goibniu's Banquet', which apparently was made from the fruits of the Other World Tree.[48]

5 Visits to the Other World

The land where the wondrous trees grew has various names:[49] *Mag Mell*, Plain of Delight or perhaps Plain of Sports; *Tír Tairngiri*, Land of Promise, which came to be used in a Christian context for the Promised Land or Heaven but may originally have referred to the pre-Christian Other Word; *Tír na mBec*, Land of the Living Ones, also used in a Christian sense but likely to be of pagan origin; and *Tír na mBan*, land of Women, as well as *Tír na n-Og*, Land of the Young or Pure. The tales known as *Echtrai* (?outings) and the poems included in them, thought to go back in some cases to the seventh century, build up a picture which is vivid and consistent. The realm described is a place of happiness and beauty where sickness, death and decay are unknown; trees there bear rich fruit, while their leaves make music and birds sing in their branches; there is abundance of gleaming gold and silver, and everywhere lovely women, the welcoming goddesses of the *Síd*. It is they who lure human heroes and the sons of kings to this fair land, where time no longer passes as on earth. The men who visit there may return after a short while to find that on earth centuries have slipped away, or, as in 'The Adventures of Nera', come back after three days and nights to find the meat still uncooked and those left by the fire unaware that any time has passed.

There is also a series of tales known as the *Immrama*, accounts of voyages to strange and fantastic islands. Most of these have obviously been influenced by Christian teaching and antiquarian speculation; as David Dumville points out, they are 'frame tales'[50] and it was easy to fill the frame with ingenious fantasies and marvels. However the best-known tale, 'The Voyage of Bran', goes back to the tenth century in its present somewhat confused form, and is thought by most scholars to be considerably earliers.[51] This has many of the characteristics of the *echtrae* and deals with a voyage to the Other World. Bran is visited by a woman with a silver branch in her hand, who tells him of wonderful islands he may visit. He sets off with three foster-brothers and a number of followers, and on the sea they meet Manannán in his chariot who tells them of the marvels of his kingdom under the waves:

> Though you see but one chariot-rider
> in Mag Mell of the many flowers,
> there are many steeds on its surface
> though you do not see them.

> Along the top of a wood
> your coracle has sailed, over ridges
> there is a wood of beautiful fruit
> under the prow of your little skiff.

After visiting the Island of Joy where everyone laughs without cause, a somewhat bizarre episode in the prose narrative, but not in the poem, they arrive at the Island of Women, to be welcomed by fair maidens. They spend what they think is a year there, but find when they return home that centuries have passed. Other accounts of visits to islands, some conerning people set adrift in a boat as a punishment for crime,[52] are fantastic in the extreme. Some may have been suggested by romances, and others taken from learned Christian sources, while others may simply be exercises in ingenuity in finding new combinations of marvels. Thus on one island a cat leaps round four pillars in a house filled with treasures, and when one of the voyagers takes a necklace the cat leaps through him and he is burned to ashes. Other islands are inhabited by giant ants, by people continually lamenting, or by a smith in a huge forge, while one holds an arch of water in which salmon are swimming. The Rees brothers suggested[53] that they represent the 'tattered remnants of an oral celtic "Book" of the Dead', proclaiming the

182

mysteries of the world beyond death. However although there is a tradition of the dead journeying to islands off the Irish coast (p. 176 above), the marvels in the *Immrama* can scarcely be accepted as reliable pictures of an early mythological world. In these poems we are faced with the usual difficulties of distinguishing between Christian and learned elements and those from an earlier pre-Christian tradition. The idea of Paradise and the joys of heaven certainly helped to popularise these Otherworld themes and, as MacCana puts it,[54] the *Voyage of Bran* can be seen as an attempt 'to create an aesthetic rapport between the pagan concept of the Otherworld and the Christian concept of Paradise'. Nevertheless certain features in the description, and particularly the theme of the Island of Women, seem likely to go back to an early date.

Medieval Welsh literature also contains some indication of a traditional land of the dead which can be visited by travellers; it is known as Annwn, the 'not-world', a term later identified with Hell. In the tale of 'Pwyll Prince of Dyfed' in the *Mabinogion*, the hero goes there for a while to help its king to defeat an enemy, just as kings in Ireland are said occasionally to go to the help of the people of the *Síd*. A beautiful woman dressed in green, like those from the Land of the Living in the Irish tales, comes from Annwn, followed by a pack of Otherworld hounds. A poem called 'The Spoils of Annwn' refers to an expedition made by Arthur into this land, in which many of his men were lost.[55] Mention of his ship Prydwen suggests that it was over the sea, and suggestive names are used for the places reached by Arthur, such as *Caer Siddi* (probably a borrowing from the Irish *síd*), *Caer Feddwid* (Court of Intoxication), and *Caer Wydyr* (?Court of Glass). Evidently this was a place of brightness and feasting, and there is mention of a cauldron carried off from Annwn which was warmed by the breath of nine maidens, linking this tale with others dealing with magic cauldrons from an Otherworld kingdom. Glass is a characteristic material used for buildings in this supernatural realm.[56]

In Old Norse sources the journey to the land of the dead receives much emphasis. It is strengthened by the funeral symbolism of the Viking Age, when ships or boats were placed in large numbers of graves, suggesting an early tradition of a journey over the sea to the land of the dead; the ship is also an established symbol on memorial stones set up in Gotland from the fifth century onwards (p. 169 above). Wagons are also occasionally found, as in the Oseberg ship-grave, just as at one time they were included in the rich graves of the Celtic people (p. 4 above). In the poetry, those journeying to the land of death are sometimes said to ride and sometimes to go in wagons, as Brynhild did in the poem *Helreið Brynhildar*. In the account of the death of Balder in the *Prose Edda*

(*Gylfaginning* 48) Hermod made a long journey on horseback from Asgard to Hel, through dark valleys, over mountains and across rivers, until he reached the high wall which encircled the realm of death. Echoes of such a tradition can be found in the only contemporary account of a Viking Age funeral ceremony which we possess, that of the Arab traveller Ibn Fadlan who witnessed a ship-funeral on the River Volga in the year 921 (p. 18 above). He describes how a slave-girl was put to death at her master's funeral, and how before she died she was raised up in front of something resembling a door or gate; she sang a lay in which she declared she saw her dead kinsfolk and her husband, the dead chief, in a land 'green and fair', and asked to be sent to join them. Other references can be found in the poetry to *Helgrind* and *Valgrind*, gates which shut in the dead; and it is said in *Grímnismál* (22), of Valgrind: 'Ancient is that gate, and few can tell / how that latch can be made fast.'

Another account of a visit to the land of the dead is found in the *History* of Saxo Grammaticus (I, 31), when the hero Hading was taken by a giantess to visit a land 'where fresh herbs grow in winter', and this, he was told, was the region to which he must go when he died. The woman who came for him did not carry an apple branch, but she had a stalk of hemlock in her hand. She led him down a path 'worn by long ages of travellers', where there were strange rivers, one filled with weapons like the stream flowing with knives and swords in the poem *Vǫluspá* (36), and they watched two armies battling together, said to be men who had died in warfare. Finally they reached a high wall, and the woman then wrung the neck of a cock and flung it over, whereupon it was heard crowing on the other side. Once more there is an echo of this symbolism in Ibn Fadlan's description of the tenth century funeral, for there the slave girl who was held up to look over the 'door' cut off the head of a cock and threw it down, presumably on the other side of the barrier, while its body was put in the ship with other animals sacrificed. There are what sound like Christian elements in Saxo's tale, such as people dressed in white who could come from some source such as the *Dialogues* of Pope Gregory, but otherwise this picture of the Other World is markedly unlike anything derived from the Bible or from Virgil, while there are a number of points in agreement with the representation of the world of the dead in the poems.

The same hero, Hading, was also carried over land and sea by an old man on horseback, who wrapped him in his cloak, and who appears to be Odin. He took Hading to his house and allowed him to be refreshed by a draught of ale before being brought back to earth. Hading has never been satisfactorily identified and may be an invention of Saxo,[57] but these supernatural journeys could well be based on incidents in poems and tales which he had read or heard told by Icelandic friends. Further indirect indications of the long and dangerous journey to the Other World are found in a late poem *Svipdagsmál*, where the hero consults his dead mother, and she teaches him spells from her grave mound which will be of use to him on the expedition. These have allusions to mighty rivers and a raging sea, as well as to intense cold in the mountains, to enemies and 'dead Christian women' lying in wait, and to binding with fetters. The final spell is to enable him to find the right answers when confronted by a terrible giant at the end of his journey. There is a complex mixture of material in this poem, some of which Annelise Talbot believed to be influenced by Celtic traditions,[58] but it certainly seems to preserve memories of a journey to the underworld realm of the dead, and may be compared with the perils encountered by Skirnir in an earlier poem in the *Edda*, *Skírnismál*, in his ride to find the giantess Gerd.[59]

There is also a group of Icelandic tales known to Saxo in the twelfth century which are set in eastern Europe but show marked resemblances to the accounts of the Irish Other World, and may have been influenced by Irish sources. The country to which the travellers make their way is called the 'Field of the Not-Dead' (*Ódáinsakr*), and also Glasisvellir (Glittering/Glassy Plains). In a poem quoted by Snorri, now lost, Glasir is the name of a bright tree resembling those in the Land of Youth (*Skáldskaparmál* 32): 'Glasir stands with golden leaves / before the halls of Sigtýr (Odin)' and Snorri assumes this to be part of an orchard. The realm of Glasisvellir is said in *Hervarar Saga* (1) to be ruled by a king called Gudmund: 'His house was called Grund (green field/plain) in the district called Glasisvellir; he was wise and powerful. He and his men lived out many men's lifetimes, and because of this heathen men believe that in his kingdom is the Field of the Not-Dead, and that everyone who came there turned his back on sickness and age and would not die. After the death of Gudmund his men worshipped him and called him a god.' Those who entered Gudmund's realm were welcomed by his daughters as lovers, so that his land might well be described as the Land of Women. In one of the legendary sagas in *Flateyjarbók* (I, p. 359f.), a man called Helgi Thorisson lost his way in a forest in Finnmark, and then met 'twelve beautiful maidens dressed in red mounted on horses splendidly adorned', King Gudmund's daughters. He spent three nights with one of them, and was then sent home with rich gifts of gold and silver. Next Yule he was carried off in a storm, and returned a year later with two companions called Grim, bringing two splended gold drinking-horns for King Olaf Tryggvason from Gudmund of Glasisvellir

(p. 43 above), But when the bishops blessed the drink in the horns, the Grims became angry and vanished, taking Helgi away. Next Yule he returned once again, but now he was blind; he told the king that Gudmund's daughter had put out his eyes because she was angered by Olaf's prayers.

An earlier account of a visit to Gudmund's kingdom is in Book VIII of Saxo's *History*, in the account of the voyage of Gorm, who set out to visit the giant Geruth's abode. This was close to Gudmund's realm, and the travellers met his twelve beautiful daughters.[60] Gudmund is described as a fair giant, with a kingdom full of rich treasures, and an orchard of fruit-trees beside his palace. The men are warned by their wise guide Thorkill not to partake of food or receive gifts during their stay, while the king must resist the lures of Gudmund's daughters. He also forbade them to set foot on the golden bridge leading from Gudmund's realm, as no mortal was permitted to cross it. After this they went on to the neighbouring kingdom of Geruth, a dark and gloomy land with severed heads on the battlements and fierce dogs guarding the entrance. It was full of foul smells and evil phantoms, giving the impression of a rock tomb. Geruth and his three daughters lay on the rocks which had been smashed by the hammer of Thor, who left them dead after his visit, as recorded in the *Prose Edda*. Around them were rich gold ornaments, wine jars, a great aurochs horn and other treasures, but when some of the party laid hands on these objects, these changed their form and caused instant death. Even the wise Thorkill was tempted by a rich mantle, and when he touched it the apparently dead forms leapt up and attacked them so that many lost their lives. One man, who was tempted by one of the king's daughters to stay behind, went mad and drowned, and the rest of the party left for home.

Saxo evidently knew the story of the killing of the giant Geirrod and his daughters, as told by Snorri in *Skáldskaparmál* (18) and also in an early poem, *Þórsdrápa*. In Snorri's tale Thor went into the realm of the giants, but was nearly drowned in a flooded river, turned into a raging torrent by one of the giantesses urinating into it. Thor was saved by clinging to a rowan tree, which has since been known as 'Thor's deliverance'. This introduces another means of entry into the Other World, a descent through a whirlpool beneath the waves. it occurs again in an account given by Adam of Bremen in the eleventh century of some Frisian merchants who sailed to the north of Norway and were caught in a whirlpool in the sea.[61] They finally escaped and reached an island where giants lay concealed, surrounded by rich treasures hidden in caverns in the rocks. When they tried to carry off some of these, they were pursued by huge dogs, and one man was torn to pieces. This is told as a realistic tale, but bears a close resemblance to some of the Otherworld stories, particularly to Saxo's account of Gorm's visit to Geruth's realm.

It seems as if the entrance by way of a descent into the sea is an early tradition which has been vaguely remembered and used in a number of tales. Rydberg worked out a theory of a great World Mill grinding out the sands of the sea as part of the picture of the world, quoting the legend of the magic mill worked by two giantesses which turned the sea salt.[62] Carney argued that there was an early tradition about the overflowing of the central well or spring under the tree and that this preceded the tales of a voyage over the sea to wonderful islands.[63] There are traces also of two separate and contrasted realms in the Other World. On the one hand we have the visit to the land of Youth or to Glasisvellir, a bright realm with abundance of gold and a bevy of beautiful welcoming women, ruled by Manannán or Gudmund. This is either beyond or beneath the sea, and the travellers commonly set off in a ship to reach it. Another possible echo might be seen in the kingdom of Ægir under the sea in the *Edda* poems, where the gods meet to feast (p. 210 below). As a contrast to this bright kingdom there is a dismal rocky region where dead giants lie in rocks and caves, springing up to attack interlopers who lay hands on their treasures, found in the Scandinavian sources. In the Gudmund tales the two realms are said to lie side by side with a river between, and in the poem *Vafþruðnismál* (15–16) this is named as the river Ilfing, dividing the land of the gods from the giants: 'It shall flow freely for ˄vermore, / no ice shall bind that river.' Another contrast of the same kind is given in *Vǫluspá* by the hall Gimli, bright with gold and with a gleaming roof, and the sinister hall on the Strand of Corpses (*Nástrond*), whose doors face the north and whose roof is formed of serpents dripping poison. This evidently represents the horrors of death and decay in contrast to the Land of the Living or the Not-Dead.[64]

Although one might suspect Christian influence here, the contrasting realms have no obvious resemblance to the Christian Heaven and Hell, nor to the dark kingdom beside the abode of the blessed in classical and oriental accounts of Otherworld journeys. The introduction of Thor into these tales may be significant, and it has been shown that some of the late Gudmund tales appear to have been composed as a deliberate parody of Thor's adventures among the giants.[65] Memories of a land of brightness, fertile green, and golden treasures seem to be preserved in the names of the halls of the gods in the *Edda* poems. In *Grímnismál* there is a list of these, and we may note *Glitnir* (Shining), *Glaðsheimr* (Bright Abode), *Himinbjorg* (Hill of Heaven) and *Søkkvabekkr* (?Sunken Hall). These stand near Valgrind, the gate into the land of the dead, just as in Saxo's account a bridge leads from Gudmund's realm into the land which no mortal may enter.

Certainly there seems to be no ground for the assumption that there was ever one belief in a universal land of the dead to which all travel after death. Contrasts between the realms of the supernatural world are continually made, and we have gods and giants, fair giants and frost giants, Túatha Dé and Fomorians. If such varied realms formed a basic part of the mythology, this might explain the puzzling lines in Lucan's *Pharsalia* (I, 454): 'They do not believe that souls live on in Erebus ... but the same spirit rules in another world.' The outstanding characteristic of the dark realm is that the dead forms are hostile towards the living and bitterly resent any attempt to rob them of their treasures. Set against this however is the conception of ancestors who are ready to greet the newly dead in a mound or hill, as well as the image of a shining realm of fruit trees within an encircling wall or a distant island. Such contrasting pictures may be fragmentary and confused, but they may also be of considerable age. One important factor which determined the fate of men after death was their rank on earth. A realm to which a privileged few and in particular those of royal birth could find entry during their lifetime seems to have been a conception familiar to both Irish and Norse writers. Those visiting the Land of Promise were usually members of royal families and celebrated heroes, while Odin's hall of Valhalla was no general abode for the dead but reserved for mighty kings and valiant champions. Since poets and artists attached to local kings were likely to keep up this tradition, representing the triumphant entry of a dead king into the next world in poetry and on memorial stones, it was likely to remain a familiar theme in the Viking Age.

6 The world's ending

However, these kingdoms were not seen as eternal ones, and the idea of a tremendous catastrophe bringing destruction both to gods and men was apparently known to both Celts and Germans from early times. Strabo (IV, 4, 4) stated that according to the teaching of the druids: 'Men's souls and the universe are indestructable, although at times fire and water prevail', and he may have taken this from Posidonius. Various inferences have been drawn concerning what the druids taught, but the statement is simple and direct, and in agreement with the Norse tradition of Ragnarok, when fire and water bring about the world's destruction for a time. Strabo also reports the reply of certain Celts on the Adriatic coast to Alexander the Great, when asked what they feared most. The expected reply was that they went in fear of the power of

Alexander, but they declared that they feared nothing except that the heavens might fall on them.[66] This has a suggestion of heroic rhetoric, and similarly in the *Táin* the men of Conchobar declare before a battle: 'We shall hold the spot where we now stand, but unless the ground quakes beneath us or the heavens fall down on us, we shall not flee from here.'[67] The suggestion that the end of all things is at hand may be made at some crucial moment in a heroic narrative, as when Sualtam hears that his son Cú Chulainn is in desperate straits, and exclaims: 'Is it the sky that cracks, or the sea that overflows its boundaries, or the earth that splits, or is it the loud cry of my son fighting against odds?'[68] A similar comparison is made in Saxo's *History*, when he is describing a terrible battle in Sweden in his eighth book (262): 'You might well have imagined that the heavens were suddenly rushing down at the earth, woods and fields subsiding, that the whole of creation was in turmoil and had returned to ancient chaos, all things human and divine convulsed by a raging tempest and everything tumbling simultaneously into destruction.' Even when this is given a Christian slant in a reference to Doomsday, as in the account of the Second Battle of Mag Tuired, when the terrible cry of 'furies and monsters and hags of doom' is likened to that 'on the last dreadful day when the human race will part from all this world', it seems likely that the comparison is based on an earlier tradition, from the heroic past.

The idea of the world's destruction may also be used in oaths, when an agreement is sworn to endure until the world's end, or in rhetorical praise, when someone is described as without an equal as long as the world lasts. A tenth century Icelandic poet, Kormak Ogmundarson, made this claim for Steingerd, the girl he loved: 'Rocks will seem to float as easily as corn on water and the land to sink ... The great and glorious mountains will find themselves in the depths of ocean before so fair a tree of riches as Steingerd will be born.'[69] In a poem of Arnor Jarlaskáld, composed in the eleventh century in praise of Thorfinn of Orkney, he refers to the sinking of the earth and the collapse of the sky in imagery very close to that of *Vǫluspá*: 'The bright sky will become black, earth sink into the dark sea, the sky, load of dwarves, will shatter, and the whole ocean thunder over the mountains, before a finer chief than Thorfinn is born in the Isles.'[70] Such examples seem to indicate familiarity with the imagery of the destruction of earth, sky and sea and return to chaos. While there may be verbal echoes from one poet in the work of another, the image itself appears to be a basic one, going back to pre-Christian tradition.

In the tenth century *Hákonarmál*, the imagery of the end of the world is used again in a praise poem on a king, but this time it is the breaking loose of the monsters which is chosen: 'Fenriswolf free from bonds will move against the dwellings of men before good a ruler as he as shall succeed to the vacant seat.' The escape of the bound monsters, when the wolf breaks loose from his chain, the serpent emerges from the depths where Thor placed it, and Loki escapes from his fetters laid on him by the gods, is given a prominent place in *Vǫluspá*. A number of Scandinavian myths carry the implicit threat of the monsters freed from the domination of the ruling powers, such as Thor fishing for the World Serpent, or Tyr chaining the wolf, and these were chosen as subjects on memorial stones in Scandinavia, northern England and the Isle of Man in the early Christian period.[71] They were sometimes deliberately contrasted with Christ's victory over Satan, but certain stones are thought to have been erected before the Christian period, like the one at Sockburn showing Tyr and the wolf.

Thus the end of the world may be seen as the time when the chained monsters break loose to destroy the gods, or when the forces of nature are unloosed against men and the inhabited earth ceases to exist. In 1902 the Danish scholar Axel Olrik set out to analyse the various themes which were included in the conception of Ragnarok in Norse literature.[72] He showed that destruction by the land sinking beneath the sea was a familiar theme in Danish folklore, and known farther afield in Frisia and parts of Germany; it was particularly strong in folk tradition along the coast Jutland, exposed to the force of North Sea gales. There are many local traditions foretelling the world's end, when the sea will rise as high as the church tower, and a red ox or some other creature will be able to swim through the openings in the tower walls. There were prophecies in seventeenth century Iceland about the world sinking into the sea by a certain date, and a fresh outburst of such predictions were inspired by the great earthquake of 1896. For the Icelanders, however, a more potent threat was offered by volcanic activity and overflow of burning lava, since Hekla erupts on an average every thirty-five years, and minor outbursts occur persistently. The account of the destruction of the world in *Vǫluspá* shows striking resemblances to detailed reports of a particularly severe eruption of Skaptar Yokull in 1793, beginning with tremors in the mountains, followed by clouds of smoke and ashes darkening the sun, together with blazing flames, smoke and steam as the ice melted in the intense heat.[73] Now that we have detailed films of more recent volcanic activity, such as the eruption under the sea in 1963 which produced the new island of Surtsey, the eruption of Hekla in 1970, and the awesome volcanic upheaval in the Westman Islands in 1973, which produced a second mountain peak and destroyed much of Heimaey, the influence of impressive natural phenomena on the imagery of the poem should be increasingly apparent.

One more element in Ragnarok, not mentioned in *Voluspá* but found in another poem, *Vafþruðnismál*, is that of the Great Winter (*Fimbulvetr*). Snorri puts this before the destruction of the world by fire and water, and precedes it again by three years of strife, when men forsake all the loyalties by which they are bound. The winter is to continue for three years, with no summer between, and Olrik links this with the practice of the Scandinavians recorded by Procopius, who describes the great joy with which the sun is welcomed after the winter darkness, since each year they fear it may be gone for ever (p. 40 above). Such a basic fear, resulting in various popular practices to ensure the return of the sun, is likely to go back to very early times. The logical cause of the great winter was the swallowing of the sun by the wolf on the one hand, and the overthrow of the gods who brought the assurance of repeated harvests to men on the other. It is a chastening thought that the old fear of the Great Winter has returned, linked now with the consequences of the use of the atomic bomb on a large scale.

The idea of the wolf swallowing the sun continued in popular tradition, and has been found in various parts of the world as an imaginative description of the sun's eclipse. In the poem *Grímnismál* two monsters are mentioned:

A wolf called *Skǫll* pursues the goddess,
the shining one, to the sheltering wood.
A second wolf, *Hati*, son of Fenrir,
runs before the bride of heaven.

The line 'Now goth sunne under wod' is found in one of the most haunting English medieval lyrics, where it is used to symbolise the death of Christ on the cross.[74] Olrik found that the expression to 'go into the wood' was still used of the sun's setting in both Iceland and the Faroes. He noted also that terms such as 'sun-dogs' and 'moon-dogs' are found in England used of natural phenomena such as mock suns or clouds round the moon. The picture of Ragnarok built up in *Vǫluspá* and afterwards brilliantly elaborated in prose by Snorri clearly contains a number of diverse elements, as Olrik claimed, but there seems no reason to doubt that the basic picture is a pre-Christian one, possibly given new impetus by the Christian teaching concerning Judgement Day in the tenth century. The picture in *Vǫluspá* links the threats of the natural world with the mythological theme of the death of Odin and the ruling gods, while it also serves as a requiem for the old religion and a replacement of the ancient gods by Christ and his angels. Surt, the fire-giant who sets the world ablaze, can be seen as a figure from the company of beings dwelling in and under the earth, since in a volcanic island like Iceland this region included areas of fire from which the blazing lava emerged at frequent intervals to overwhelm the homes of men. A similar figure is introduced into *Brennu-Njáls Saga* (125), a work which contains many echoes of the imagery of Ragnarok and the fate of Odin. A man in a dream before the burning took place heard a tremendous crash which shook earth and sky, and then saw a man black as pitch, riding furiously on a grey horse and holding a blazing firebrand, while around him was a ring of fire: 'It seemed to him that he hurled the brand eastwards towards the fells, and that a great fire blazed up with such fury that the fells were blotted out. He thought that the man rode eastwards to the fells and vanished.' When he told this dream, the response was: 'You have seen the *gandreið*, and this always means that momentous things will happen.' The exact definition of *gandreið* (later used for witch-riding) is uncertain, but the term is used for a company of sinister supernatural beings riding through the air, and in later folklore is echoed by accounts of the Wild Hunt and the Riding of the fairies. Ragnarok in fact seems to be ushered in by the sound of furious riding. Men rode down to Hel from the stricken earth; the sons of Muspell, a mysterious region associated with fire, apparently of Saxon origin,[75] ride over the rainbow bridge and shatter it with their weight; the gods ride out from Valhalla with forces of warriors from Odin's company. In one of the Edda poems, *Helgakviða Hundingsbana* (II, 39) a girl asks the question: 'Is this Ragnarok, when dead men ride?', when the dead hero Helgi and his men ride to the burial mound after death in battle.

The great battle at the end of the world was something long awaited, and is consistently given as the reason why Odin collected the great champions in his hall of Valhalla (p. 90 above). 'The grey wolf watches the abodes of the gods' is the reply given in *Eiríksmál* to the question of why the god has condemned Erik to defeat and death on the field of battle. Various names for the battlefield are given in the poems, indicating different traditions concerning its location and nature.[76] In *Vǫluspá*, however, little interest is shown in the battle, and instead we have a series of separate contests between the gods and the monsters. There are parallels to the battle in the Iranian account of the world's destruction, which have led to the suggestion that this is an ancient Indo-European myth which has left traces in different literatures. Here too we find a terrible winter, deterioration of life on earth, and abandonment of all ties of loyalty and kinship. A demon breaks loose from his bonds, a fettered serpent escapes and lays waste a third of the earth until a hero smites off its head. Certain chosen people are sheltered from the horrors of destruction and enabled to survive to a new age. It is possible that some of these traditions reached Scandinavia in the Viking Age, when many men from the North visited south-eastern Europe and came into contact with people from further east.[77] But the complexity of beliefs and traditions concerning the world's ending in eschatological literature makes it very difficult to trace influences of Iranian themes on the medieval literature of the north-west. Such themes may also have had influence on the accounts of the two battles of Mag Tuired, but here again the position is very complex, and difficult to analyse.

Olrik drew attention to resemblances between the Ragnarok tradition and the account of the Second Battle in the Irish account (p. 190 above). The gods Lug and the Dagda took an active part, the Dagda laying about him with his club as Thor does with his hammer. Núadu who lost his hand in the earlier battle, takes part, as does Tyr, who lost his binding the wolf, at Ragnarok. Bres forsook the gods for the Fomorians, just as Loki brought back an army of giants against Asgard. At the end of the account the Badb prophecies a time of treachery and famine like that in *Vǫluspá*:[78]

> I shall not see a world that will be dear to me.
> Summer without flowers,
> Kine will be without milk,
> Women without modesty,
> Men without valour ...
> Son will enter his father's bed,
> Father will enter his son's bed ...
> An evil time.

Prophecies of evil before the world comes to an end are found in the religious literatures of the world, and Biblical prophecies like that in Matthew 24 may have been a favourite theme of preachers in the tenth and eleventh centuries.[79] Once Christian learning reached the North, all kinds of eschatological ideas and images are likely to find a way into the literary sources. Nevertheless the fact that in both Norse and Irish literature there are accounts of battles in which the gods take part associated with the last days of the world is worth noting. There is little surface resemblance between the two accounts such as might indicate direct borrowing by one from the other. In the Irish version, Lug emerges as the triumphant leader in spite of considerable losses, while in the Norse, Odin is devoured by the wolf and the gods go down fighting against the monsters. Bres has little in common with Loki the Trickster, and the Badb's gloomy forecast is presented as an afterthought at the very moment of victory. However the desperate struggle of the gods against their opponents, to be succeeded by a new age, is the basis of both accounts, and the parallels with Iranian traditions of a fearful battle make it possible that here we have remnants of an ancient myth.

Neither account ends in ultimate destruction. In *Vǫluspá* the earth rises renewed from the sea, a new sun circles the heavens, and the sons of the gods take up the ruling of the world and men's destinies. There is even a hint that the Vanir deities survived when the leaders of the Æsir perished. In *Vafþruðnismál* there is a section concerned with the new age of the world, and here there is a reference to the 'wise maidens who travel over the sea'. They are said to arrive in three companies 'over the villages', '... the only guardian spirits on earth / although of giant kindred.' If these companies are those of the goddesses, known as *dísir*, land-spirits or valkyries, it may indicate that these come from the sea depths to take up their tasks anew on earth. This could fit into the pattern of the coming of the three maidens at the beginning of the world as described in *Vǫluspá* (p. 163 above). Njord also is said to return to the wise Vanir at Ragnarok, presumably when the Æsir with whom he had remained since the first battle, when he was sent as a hostage, were destroyed. Thus for some of the gods, as for Lug and the Dagda in the Irish tradition, life begins afresh after the catastrophe in which so may perished. In *Njáls Saga*, where many parallels can be seen to the Ragnarok myth, the same final pattern unfolds; after Njall and his sons perished, their friend and avenger Kari survived and in the last chapter was reconciled with Flosi, the leader of those who burnt Njall in his hall.

The conception which preceded the myths of creation, destruction and renewal as they have come down to us is not easy to make out. The old themes may grow in richness as time passes, as they are used symbolically by gifted poets and story-tellers, who may be deliberately seeking as in the 'Voyage of Bran' 'to create an aesthetic rapport' between pagan and Christian concepts (p. 183 above). At least some hint of the original pattern survives, and the bringing together of Norse and Irish material makes this more apparent. There are glimpses of various worlds making up the cosmos, sufficiently vigorous to live on in later literature and in poetic imagery, and to give out echoes in local folklore in our own time. Again it seems unlikely that a rational and detailed framework of the beginning and the end of the world was ever set up and taught to men. What we have are memories of a rich and varied world, peopled with supernatural beings among which men feel themselves to be one company out of many. The inhabited worlds are ranged round a central point, and extend under the earth and beneath the sea, and against such a background the gods and goddesses of the myths move to and fro. It remains now to see how consistent a picture of the main characters of these myths has been left in the literature and art which has survived.

VII The ruling powers

Zeus, whoever he is, if this
be a name acceptable,
by this name I will call him.

Aeschylus, Agamamnon 160–62

1 Interpretation of myth

Gods and godesses appear in popular mythologies in a fossilised and
static form. From the way in which they behave in various tales, often
simplified in their turn, they are assumed to be deities of certain fixed
types. As to which these types are, this depends on the prevailing
theories about early religion. At one time the main god was assumed to
be a solar deity, and indeed since the sun is essential for the continuation
of life on earth, it is bound to play some part in the symbolism associated
with the most powerful gods. O'Rahilly claimed that the one-eyed Balor,
slain by Lug, was a sun god, on account of his single eye (p. 178 above).
This presents obvious difficulties, since Balor is a destructive figure,
whose glance like that of the Gorgon brought death wherever it fell, and
his eye was said never to be opened except on the field of battle.
O'Rahilly attempted to explain this by making the sun god the guardian
of the lightning. He also takes Mac Cécht, a heroic figure who plays a
part in 'The Destruction of Da Derga's Hostel', to be a sun god on
account of his huge spear and the fact that he journeyed over the whole
of Ireland 'before morning', carrying a great golden cup, and found that
all the rivers and lakes were dried up.

The weakness in this kind of mythological thinking is shown by
O'Rahilly's note on the phrase 'before morning'. It was clearly inappro-
priate for the golden cup of the sun to be carried across the land during
the night, and so he declared confidently: 'Originally, of course, this was
"before evening" '. Even if he were correct in this assumption, the
analogy of this cup with the sun is not satisfactory, since it belonged to
King Conaire and not to Mac Cécht, and the purpose of the journey was
to find water for the wounded king, while the rivers were dry before Mac

196

Cécht reached them. Eleanor Hull and Sir John Rhys had assumed Lug to have been a sun god, on rather better evidence, since his face was described as shining brilliantly, but O'Rahilly refused to hear of this, since he was determined that Lug must be the youthful hero who attacked the sun god and overcame him.

This is the method of the jigsaw puzzle, starting with a preconception of what the picture is going to be and selecting all the pieces which seem to support it, while ignoring those which do not fit and declaring that they cannot be part of the same puzzle. The picture is never completed, and some pieces have to be roughly forced into place, but in spite of large gaps and possible alternatives the scholar is ready to attack anyone with a different solution with the utmost ferocity. Another approach is the fundamentalist one, illustrated by the nineteenth century scholar Rydberg. He accepted every detail in Old Norse mythological literature as reliable, and showed much ingenuity in building up a complex mythological scheme to include it all, smoothing over apparent contradictions. Such approaches arise from an assumption that the mythology was once complete and rational, so that it would prove satisfactory to a modern observer. It was felt to be something which could be decoded, once one discovered the meaning of the different symbols which formed part of it. However we are dealing here with many different levels of belief, and also with confused traditions, which may have been worked on by earlier antiquarians long before modern scholars began their reconstructions. Tales and poems about the gods may also have been influenced by outside traditions and suffered considerable changes by the time they came to be recorded.

We cannot hope to get evidence at first hand, and even if we could, it is all too likely that we would find it confused and contradictory. Men are capable of holding concepts about the supernatural world which, from our modern viewpoint, seem to be opposed to one another, but which nevertheless worked reasonably satisfactorily for them. Hastrup has shown how this could happen in the case of the measurement of time.[2] As long as traditions were passed on orally, those which no longer fitted could be given up while those which could develop along with changing ways of life were retained. Once recorded, however, new confusions were created as it became essential to make a choice between the old and the new. Yet while all this must be borne in mind, it hardly justifies a refusal to search for an overall picture of the gods of Celtic and Germanic tradition from such evidence as is available. There is, after all, a considerable amount of information, complex and uneven although it may be, while the iconographical material, ignored by earlier scholars like O'Rahilly and Rydberg, may help to correct the picture. There is no

197

doubt that ideas about the gods were constantly fluid and changing. Traditions and customs are remoulded along with changing ways of life, as is abundantly clear from the study of folklore, where recent work has highlighted the difficulties encountered in defining popular beliefs and drawing conclusions about them from oral tradition. Folklorists no longer hope to find fixed and definite origins in very early times for groups of tales or ballads, popular customs and beliefs. Instead it is necessary to trace back the development of each particular example as far back as records allow, without assuming that it must conform to a general pattern. The mythologist similarly must be prepared to consider various types of beliefs and symbols with an open mind and be prepared for great variety.

The Celtic and Germanic peoples worshipped a number of gods through the centuries. There were many changes in their way of life, and much movement of peoples over a wide area of Europe, so that their religion could hardly be expected to remain static. Although there were priests and teachers to pass on the old traditions, there were no sacred books to establish a main outline of myths which might be used as a final court of appeal. They had come into contact with many cultures before they finally accepted the teaching of the Christian church and abandoned their early religious practices, and one powerful influence was the sophisticated culture of the Roman Empire which in the end they helped to overthrow. Much of our knowledge of their gods comes from altars and inscriptions to native deities which have been identified with Roman gods, given Roman names, and depicted in anthropomorphic form in accordance with Roman custom and style. While Roman religion in its turn was not static, there was a strong tendency to organise and rationalise supernatural figures, fitting them into an elaborate scheme in which each was responsible for some special department of life.[3] Our familiarity with this way of viewing the gods has led to the assumption that Germanic and Celtic deities must be specialised ones also. As Marie Sjoestedt pointed out: 'When we are tackling a strange mythology, we seek instinctively an Olympus where the gods abide, an Erebus, kingdom of the dead, a hierarchy of gods, specialised as patrons of war, of the arts or of love. And, seeking them, we do not fail to find them.'[4]

She goes on to point out the lack of definite functions to differentiate the Celtic gods. The most powerful deities were characteristic tribal ones, presiding over many aspects of life such as fertility, craftsmanship, battle, law and magic. She felt that it is not possible to find a 'Common Celtic' period in mythology, with clearly defined central deities: 'What we know of the decentralized character of society among the Celts and of the local and anarchical character of their mythology excludes that

198

hypothesis.' This has to be borne in mind when approaching the myths, and no doubt much of the same can be said of the gods of the Germanic peoples. Odin, Thor and Freyr were many-sided gods. Odin may have reigned supreme on the battlefield, but also possessed special skills such as poetry, oratory, divination and the secret of gaining wealth, while he was an expert in magic arts and had entry into the underworld realm of the dead. Thor was the god bearing the thunderbolt, defender of the Æsir and of mankind, yet also had power over the fertility of the earth, while he assisted travellers and protected the homes, laws and boundaries of men. Freyr was one of the fertility gods, yet seems to have been regarded as a war-god by the Swedes, who placed his symbols on armour and weapons. No one of the three possessed sole dominion over the sky, the earth or the underworld. Odin rode through the sky as well as under the earth; Freyr was associated with the sun but also was a power within the burial mound; Thor had dominion over storms and winds, but his hammer could protect his worshippers in the grave. However the character of each god is recognisable, and the choice of one as divine protector was likely to depend on the kind of life a man led. Kings and warriors turned to Odin; those holding land and responsibility in the community were likely to select Thor as their friend; those who wished for luck in hunting, rearing of beasts, cultivation of land and the bringing up of healthy children would seek help from the Vanir.

Another important point made by Marie Sjoestedt in her *Gods and Heroes of the Celts* is the importance of taking seriously the traditional picture of the supernatural world which is to be found in medieval Irish literature. 'If we must ask the Celts themselves for the key to their mythology, it is proper to believe the evidence they have left us, unless there is proof to the contrary.' She reminds us that the tellers of tales were dealing with matters to which they were closer than we can ever be, and therefore their testimony should not be lightly disregarded. As far as she is concerned, 'in the belief that there is a greater risk of error in too much scepticism than in too little, I have decided to follow the native tradition.' This is a more positive approach than that of the German scholar Eugen Mogk, who repudiated the information about northern gods and myths in the thirteenth-century *Prose Edda*. He argued that Snorri Sturluson had probably less knowledge of Germanic mythology than a modern scholar, and that he could have invented much of the material which cannot be traced to surviving poetry, or else taken it from later folklore. This negative attitude to source material which poses problems is as dangerous as dogmatic adherence to one dominating theory, and likely to prove even less fruitful when investigating the mythology.

Georges Dumézil made a new approach to the myths in an attempt to trace the original pattern of the religion of the Indo-European people from which both Celts and Germans are descended. In his book *Mythes et dieux des Germains* which appeared in 1939 (revised in 1958),[5] he claimed to find evidence in the Scandinavian myths for a tripartite system of society, the same as that which survived in the ancient Indo-Iranian caste system. He believed that the same pattern could be recognised in the Roman system of gods, reflected in tales of the early Roman heroes. As his work progressed, he formulated the theory of the 'ideology of the three functions', claiming that the three divisions of society among the Indo-Europeans consisted of a priestly ruling class, maintaining cosmic and judicial order, and skilled in magic arts; a warrior class, ruling by physical force; and the people living as herdsmen and farmers, cultivating the land and promoting the wellbeing of the community. These three classes he saw reflected in the main gods worshipped by the community. The priestly ruling class in Scandinavia, he claimed, were represented by Odin and Tyr, Odin being the ruler of the cosmic order while Tyr was the law-giver among men. The warrior class was reflected in Thor, the god whose prime function was the exercise of physical force. The third class, herdsmen and cultivators of the land, were represented by the gods known as the Vanir, with Njord and Freyr and the goddess Freyja at their head.

For Dumézil such an analysis offered an explanation of the persistent patterns found in the mythologies of peoples descended from the Indo-Europeans. One example is that of the battle between two forces of supernatural beings, which he interpreted as the gods of the first two functions uniting against those of the third and being finally reconciled with them (p. 178 above). Thus confused accounts in one set of myths may be understood by searching for parallels elsewhere, and seeing them as memories of once widespread beliefs. His approach offers a welcome escape from the assumption that mythology is something which needs to be decoded in order to reveal a system of simple fixed beliefs. He sees mythology as something which has developed out of the structure of early society, adapting itself as society changed, but leaving indelible impressions in tales and poems. The difficulty in applying Dumézil's theories to Scandinavian evidence, however, is that the Norse deities refuse to fit satisfactorily into the niches which he has provided for them, and the same is true of the Celtic gods. The most difficult problem is that of the god of warriors; the Roman god Mars was certainly at times identified with the Germanic Tîwaz and not Thor, while the god of warriors both in the Viking Age and in the period preceding it was certainly Odin/Wodan. The Germanic Donar and later Thor were primarily sky deities, in the same class as Jupiter and Zeus, wielders of the thunderbolt. It is difficult to see Thor linked with the warrior class, while as a patron of law he seems to be one of the ruling gods of the first function.

Dumézil would argue for changes in the course of time which have altered the emphasis. It is possible also that both Icelandic and Irish sources have stressed the warlike and chieftain-like qualities of the gods at the expense of their magico-religious powers, which would in any case tend to be suppressed in Christian times.[6] But the problems remain, and are found also on the Celtic side. On the other hand, the dichotomy between the ruling and war gods on one hand and those associated with fertility and the land on the other appears to be an essential part of the structure, and helps to explain the distinction between the two groups of Scandinavian deities, Æsir and Vanir.

2 The community of the gods

The gods as represented in surviving literatures form a group, and there are no indications of an earlier concept of one supreme deity. The Germans and Scandinavians worshipped the gods as a company at their regular feasts, although a toast might be drunk or a sacrifice offered to one particular deity. Two or three are mentioned together in such oath formulae or curses as have come down to us. In Eddic and Skaldic poetry two or three gods have adventures together, while they are pictured in larger companies feasting together or meeting to decide on judgements at the Thing. *Voluspá*, admittedly composed somewhat late in the pre-Christian period, gives a confident picture of the gods as a group at the beginning of time, establishing order, making objects of fine workmanship and setting up buildings. As we have been reminded, it would be foolish to reject such testimony out of hand, and the creation of a pantheon in Asgard cannot be due to Snorri, although he may have added a few details to regularise the vague and confused relationships between various deities, as when he makes Odin the descendant of Thor. The gods are seen also as established in families, with sons who play a small but significant part in the myths, and are married to goddesses who appear to come from the Vanir, and said to be the daughters of giants.

The account of Balder's funeral as described by Snorri in the *Prose Edda* is significant, because of the procession of gods and goddesses which he describes as coming to mourn Odin's son.[7] Odin himself organised the burning of the body on Balder's ship, which was launched by a powerful giantess riding on a wolf. Thor stood beside the pyre to hallow it with his hammer, and when a dwarf ran in front of him he kicked him into the fire. The mourners were led by Odin and his consort Frigg, accompanied by his valkyries and ravens. Freyr came in a chariot pulled by his golden boar, and Freyja in one drawn by cats. Heimdall rode on horseback, and there was a concourse of giants, which could represent the fertility gods and land-spirits known as the Vanir. We do not know if Snorri took this strange account from a lost poem, but its very irrationality makes it improbable that he invented it. It gives a strong impression of a visual source, and it may be noted that the tapestries recovered and restored from the Oseberg ship from ninth century Norway, which deal with supernatural figures and may possibly have been used in some sanctuary, are largely taken up with processions of mysterious figures on horseback, riding in wagons or walking, while some of these are in partial animal form.[8] Those who, like Mogk, claim that Snorri in the thirteenth century had no real knowledge of early myths apart from a few poems should bear in mind that woodcarvings and tapestries dealing with mythological subjects must certainly have survived into his lifetime, and he could have seen them in both Iceland and Norway.

The idea of a company of gods is supported by the language of the poems. *Regin* is used of the gods in general, although it may have referred originally to the chief gods, those in particular who possessed power over the fates of men. A similar Gothic term *ragin* is used to mean 'counsel' or 'decision', and the word is found in the German *Heliand* with the meaning of divine power.[9] In the *Hákonarmál*, composed in the tenth century, the dead king Hakon is welcomed to Valhalla by 'all the council and the powers' (*rad oll ok regin*). Other terms used for the gods in general are *hopt* and *bǫnd*, that is, fetters, or something which binds. When Odin recovers the divine mead, as related in the poem *Hávamál*, the giants enquire whether he has returned to the *bǫnd*, which must mean the group of gods to whom he belongs, those with power to bind. It is to the *bǫnd* also that Egill appeals when he speaks a spell to drive out Erik Bloodaxe from Norway (p. 105 above), apparently addressing his appeal both to Odin and to the Vanir deities. The binding power of the gods might refer to the basic laws which they have created, or to the power of fate from which there is no escape. In battle it is 'fetters' laid upon warriors by Odin and his valkyries which doom them to defeat and death (p. 70 above). Dumézil compares the binding power of Odin with the lines and knots of the Indian Varuna, and indeed the emphasis on twisting knots and net-like patterns in the decoration of Germanic weapons has been pointed out.[10] Possibly of relevance also is the account which Tacitus gives of the religious ritual of the Semnones in Denmark (p. 24 above), by which a man entering the sacred grove had to be bound with a cord, and might not raise himself to his feet once he fell. The binding of the monsters to render them helpless and prevent the return of chaos is another example of the idea of bonds associated with the ruling gods, which appears to be an image of great antiquity.

The conception of a divine company of gods seems to have been well established among the Germans by the time of Tacitus. In his *Germania* he mentions Mercury and Mars, the 'supreme god' of the Semnones who may have been Tîwaz, twin gods known as the *Alcis*, the divine ancestor Tvisto, and the goddesses Isis and Nerthus. He refers to the gods in the plural, reporting that men believed they should not be confined within walls or portrayed in human likeness, and that they could communicate by means of sacred horses and other methods. Similarly Julius Caesar insists on a plurality of deities among the Celts in the last century BC. He mentions Mercury as the god to whom most worship was given, together with Apollo, Mars, Jupiter, the goddess Minerva and the god Dis, the common ancestor of the Celts. In the Irish tales, there is the assumption that a company of divine beings exists, the Tuátha Dé Danann, the people or tribes of the goddess Dana (p. 179 above). In the fairy mounds dwell kings and heroes and fair women known as the people of the *Síd*; the male leaders like the Germanic gods take goddesses of battle or the rivers as wives and lovers. No clear distinction is drawn between earthly heroes and the men of the *Síd*. Lug, the Dagda, Cú Roí, Núadu and possibly Mac Cécht and the champion Ogmios are thought to be earlier Celtic gods who were more than local deities. Lug is said to be accepted as leader of this company and he stands out as the most prominent of the Celtic gods whom we recognise, but there is no indication that any supreme deity was worshipped by either Celts or Germans in early times. It appears that in both Scandinavia and Ireland one god could be known under a multiplicity of names and titles, and this is confirmed by early inscriptions from the Continent.

There are impressive monuments from Celtic areas dating back to the period before Christ which might represent either gods or ancestors, and we have a series of great seated male figures in the temples of southern France (p. 28 above). In any case the legends of gods and heroes are likely to be blended in popular tradition as time goes by, and the exploits of ancestors become linked with the myths. Continental inscriptions indicate that there were a number of gods whose cults were known over a wide area, while the male and female busts set around the Gundestrup bowl give us seven possible deities, four male and three female. Among the recognised gods on the Continent Lug is clearly identified with Mercury. As we have seen, he has a great deal in common with Odin in the Viking Age, both being associated with kings and warriors, and the world of battle (p. 90 above), and Odin's predecessor, Wodan, was also identified with Mercury. There is more than one figure which might be identified with Jupiter. Celtic gods identified with Apollo are Grannus, known as a healing deity, and Belenus, whose name may be remembered in the Irish name for the festival held on the first of May, Beltene. A Celtic Apollo was associated in Gaul with thermal springs to which men came for healing, and vague references to sun-worship among the Irish could be based on his cult.

3 Thor and the Dagda

In Irish tradition one god who seems to have some associations with the sky is the Dagda, who has much in common with the Scandinavian Thor. A significant attribute is his mighty club, since the sky god is expected to possess the thunderbolt, a fearsome weapon. Thor's great axe-hammer which split rocks clearly stood for the lightning. The Dagda's club took eight men to carry it, and it was moved on wheels on account of its weight. With one end he slew his enemies and with the other restored them to life, just as Thor used his hammer to restore his goats after they were slain and eaten (p. 46 above). The club of the Dagda was more than a lightning symbol, however; it was said to leave a mark like a boundary ditch between provinces, and such a ditch could be called the 'mark of the Dagda's Club'. Similarly the hammer of Thor was associated with boundaries, since he protected law and order in the community, and it might be marked on boundary stones as a warning that failure to respect them would arouse the god's wrath. Thor was guardian of the law as well as a fierce wielder of his hammer, and the Dagda, rough and primitive although he appears, had the title Ruad Rofessa, 'Lord of Perfect Knowledge', since 'it is he that had the perfection of the heathen science and it is he that had the multiform triads'.[11] Both then were associated with the preservation and continuation of traditional knowledge, and were not limited to the exercise of brute force.

The Dagda, like Lug, had many different activities at which he excelled, and so he bore the title 'Good God' (Dagda), which means potent and gifted rather than benevolent. 'All that you promise to do I shall do myself alone', he declared to those who promised help in The Second Battle of Mag Tuired, and so he was given his name Dagda, 'and so he was called thereafter'. He was not represented as a youthful figure or as a dignified old man, but as a huge and primitive male, ugly and pot-bellied, in shabby, ill-cut clothes such as labouring men wore, and indeed he worked as a labourer under the rule of Bres. Thor also possessed a variety of powers, blessing the land and men's dwellings, guarding travellers, warding off disasters from the community, ruling over the winds and weather, hallowing the assembly where laws were proclaimed, and guarding the dead in the grave, so that his hammer might be carved on memorial stones. He also was a somewhat crude figure, for all his enormous power, and in *Harbarðsljóð* (24) he is mocked by Odin because he was concerned with thralls rather than with kings. He was pictured in the sagas as huge and red-bearded, with fiery eyes beneath enormous brows; he was said to walk to the Assembly while other gods rode, or to drive in a creaking wagon pulled by goats. He sometimes cuts a ridiculous figure in the tales, but there is never any doubt of his power or of the terror which he inspired in both men and giants, and in the end he triumphs.

Both gods had voracious appetites. The Dagda proved this when he partook of a huge meal prepared for him by the Fomorians in a hole in the ground.[12]

> Porridge is made for him by the Fomorians and this was to mock him, for great was his love of porridge. They fill for him the king's cauldron, five fists deep, into which went four-score gallons of new milk and the like quantity of meal and fat. Goats and sheep and swine are put into it, and they are boiled together with the porridge. They are spilt for him into a hole in the ground, and Indech told him that he would be put to death unless he consumed it all; he should eat his fill so that he might not reproach the Fomorians. Then the Dagda took his ladle, and it was big enough for a man and a woman to lie on the middle of it. Those then are the bits that were in it, halves of salted swine and a quarter of lard.

After his gigantic meal, his belly was 'bigger than a house-cauldron', and the Fomorians laughed at it. Unperturbed however, he succeeded in spite of this in making love to Indech's daughter, as described in a passage which Whitley Stokes felt he could not translate because of its indecency.

In the poem which tells of how Thor recovered his hammer from the giants, *þrymskviða*, he too eats a meal in the enemy camp, although the circumstances are quite different, and reveals his abilities as a trencherman. The cunning Loki had disguised him as Freyja, the fair goddess, by wrapping him in a bridal veil, and brought him into the giants' hall as a bride for Thrym, who had stolen his hammer. The giants were a little disturbed by the huge appetite of the bride at the wedding feast, and also by a glimpse of burning eyes beneath the veil, and Thrym himself was amazed by the capacity shown by his bride for eating and drinking:

Thor ate an ox and eight salmon,
together with the dainties prepared for the women;
Sif's husband drank off three cups of mead.

Then spoke Thrym, lord of the giants,
'Did you ever see a bride eat more ravenously?
I never saw a bride swallow such mouthfuls,
nor a maiden drink such abundance of mead.'

Loki however was there to reassure them by remarking that Freyja had fasted and gone without sleep for eight nights in her eagerness for the wedding, and so Thor went undetected until he got his hands on his own hammer again and swiftly disposed of the wedding party. This is splendid comedy, but it makes the same point of emphasising the physical strength and immense vigour of the god as does the tale of Thor's drinking feats and capacity as a wrestler in the hall of Utgard-Loki. Both Thor and Dagda, indeed, possess something of the untamed forces of the natural world.

The Dagda was also renowned for his sexual prowess. He mated with river goddesses, and was married to the goddess of the Boyne. His union with the dread Morrígan was on a mighty bed extending far over the land, and by this means he gained her favour and help in the battle with the Fomorians. He also lay with the daughter of the chief of the Fomorians who had tried to humiliate him. Thor too was constantly encountering giantesses, although we hear more of his prowess in breaking their backs and shattering their skulls than of love passages with them. His encounter with Geirrod's daughter urinating into the river resembles incidents in tales of the Dagda, who similarly met the Morrígan bestriding a river: '...washing, with one of her two feet in Allod Echae to the south of the water and the other at Loscuinn to the north of the water.' The Dagda was the father of young Óengus, the Mac Óc, and is seen on the whole as a paternal figure, bearing the title of Great Father (*Eochaid Ollathir*). His home was at New Grange, one of the great burial mounds in County Meath within a bend of the River Boyne, dating back to the Neolithic period; this was said to have been taken from him by his son, who cheated him over the agreement. The Dagda possessed the cauldron whose contents never gave out (p. 45 above), and was the dispenser of unfailing hospitality. Thor too was associated with cauldrons; not only did he kill his own goats and cook them in a cauldron before restoring the bones to life again, but he is also represented in the poem *Hymiskviða* as going to the land of the giants in order to obtain a cauldron for the feast of the gods. Thus while Odin entertained dead heroes in Valhalla, Thor was the provider of the feast of the gods when they met together.

While the Germans had a thunder god Donar, identified sometimes with Jupiter, sometimes with Hercules, the Continental Celts depicted a god wielding a thunder weapon when they set up stones and altars in the period of Roman occupation. Sometimes he had thunderbolts and was identified with Jupiter, sometimes a wheel and sometimes a mallet. He might be named *Taranis* (Thunderer), possibly one of his titles. We know that the Celtic Jupiter guarded local communities, and that he was associated with the sun's journey through the heavens (p. 22 above). He is often shown dominating a monster or giant on the 'Jupiter pillars' set up in France and in the Rhineland, and this may represent a struggle between the god and the monster of chaos, like Thor with the World Serpent. However as Lambrechts pointed out,[13] some of the groups do not suggest a struggle, but rather a power from the earth supporting the god. There was also a god with a mallet, sometimes named *Sucellos* (Good Striker), bearded and amiable in appearance and occasionally accompanied by a dog. Sucellos may be found with a river goddess, *Nantosvelta*, and it has been suggested that this pair may be linked with two sinister supernatural figures, one male and one female, who appear in the Irish tales. In the *Táin*, Cú Chulainn meets a woman in red accompanying a man with a fork of hazel wood; she rides in a chariot with a one-legged horse, the chariot pole passing through its body as if it were a sacrificial offering.[14] A similar nightmare pair is encountered in the tale of 'The Destruction of Da Derga's Hostel'; this time the man has one arm, one leg and one eye, and he carries a fork with a roasted pig, still squealing, on his back. A monstrous misshapen woman accompanies him, and when asked her name she recites a long list which includes the names of the war goddesses. The same pair seems recognisable in the tale of 'Branwen Daughter of Llyr' in the Welsh *Mabinogion*; this time they emerge from a lake, and the man carries a cauldron, later used to restore slain men to life (p. 46 above), while the woman is about to give birth to an armed warrior. Once more we have a link with feasting in the symbols of pig and cauldron. It may be noted also that the Dagda's club is sometimes called a fork, associating it with the meat of the sacrifice. In such terrifying and apparently irrelevant episodes where monstrous figures appear, something of the terror and power of the ancient deities is preserved, just as in comic tales about Thor we are suddenly reminded of his blazing eyes and the panic caused by his wrath among gods and men.

4 The grouping of the gods

Thus in Irish tradition we find two gods of great potency, Lug and the Dagda, and two balancing them in Scandinavian tradition, Odin and Thor. In both cases these gods can be traced back to deities worshipped by Celts and Germans in Gaul and Germany, from the evidence of placenames and inscriptions of the Roman period. Each god possesses many and varied powers and is associated both with the sky and the earth. In spite of their versatility however, each of the pair possesses a definite character, so that they cannot be regarded as indistinguishable 'chieftain' gods and nothing more. The evidence from Roman times and the names of the Germanic days of the week indicates that for the Germans there was a third member of a trio, and that one god was identified with the Roman Mars. He seems to have been Tîwaz, remembered as Tyr in Scandinavia and Tîw among the Anglo-Saxons, who gave his name to Tuesday. He was armed with a spear, and associated with the sky and with the rule of law.[15] His great achievement was the binding of the wolf Fenrir in order to save the gods from the monster, and this was how he lost his hand. Odin may have inherited his spear, while Thor became the god concerned with the maintenance of law. There is no obvious counterpart among Celtic deities to Tîwaz. He has something in common with Nodens, a god to whom dedications were found in the Romano-British temple at Lydney Park in Gloucestershire. He was remembered in Ireland as Núadu, said to have been king of the *Túatha Dé* until his hand was cut off in battle and replaced by a hand of silver. His invincible sword was one of the treasures of the gods (p. 177 above), while the loss of a hand suggests a possible link with Tyr. A small bronze hand was recovered from the Lydney site, and the Welsh figure known as *Lludd Llawereint* (Silver Hand) might be a memory of the same deity.

In Ireland a third god might be Donn (p. 176 above), who has been seen as a later form of Dis Pater, the god who welcomed the dead and was said to have been worshipped as one of the main gods in Gaul. He has a good deal in common with the Germanic Wodan, god of the realm of death, equated with Mercury. As Odin in Scandinavia he took on additional attributes and was much more than a death god, until in the Viking Age he was, according to Snorri, ruler of Asgard. There are memories of another huge god with a spear, Mac Cécht, said to be married to one of the three goddesses representing Ireland. He plays a part in the tale of the 'Destruction of Da Derga's Hostel',[16] where he is a champion of huge size, whose eyes resemble two lakes with his nose as a mountain between them. His spear is dark and dripping with blood, and is as large as a pillar of a royal house, while his great sword gleams like a stream of water. He can slay six hundred men in one onslaught, so that heads, cloven skulls and heaps of entrails are as numerous as hailstones, blades of grass or stars in the sky. The connection between this fearsome, destructive figure, who here possesses the characteristics of a war god, and Dían Cécht, the healer among the Túatha Dé, is far from clear.

The third group of gods in Dumézil's scheme, those concerned with farming and herding and closely linked with the goddesses, is easier to recognise, although here there are many different names and elusive memories in tales and folk traditions. A number of impressive figures can be seen as belonging to this group, but our knowledge of possible cults attached to them is limited. One is the horned deity known as *Cernunnos* (Horned or Peaked One), because the incomplete name ... *ernunnos* has been made out on a stone altar from Paris on which the horned deity appears. His horns resemble those of a stag, and he may have been the guardian of the forest animals. He may be the same as the bearded god on the Gundestrup Cauldron, although the latter is without horns, who is shown holding up a stag in either hand. The god with horns is also shown on one of the main panels of the same cauldron, sitting cross-legged with a huge stag beside him, whose horns are a close match to his own; this deity holds a serpent in one hand and a neck-ring in the other, presumably symbolising healing and wealth. He is shown again on a stone from Rheims with a sack of coins, indicating that he could grant prosperity, but can be distinguished from Mercury, who here appears at his side. A link between a horned deity and serpents at a much earlier date has been often pointed out in the huge antlered figure with serpents in a carving of about the fourth century BC at Val Camonica in Italy. How far we can assume that a horned deity is one particular god, however, is uncertain, since horns were a recognised symbol of power and a link with the wild creatures of the natural world.

The literary sources in Ireland give tantalising glimpses of figures which might be memories of deities. In the tale of 'Finn and the Man in the Tree'[17] Finn encounters a figure associated with a blackbird, a trout and a stag; he shares apples with his companions, while they drink water from the bronze vessel in which the trout is swimming. He is described as a leaping man in a cloak. Another deity remembered in the Irish tales is Cú Roí, a somewhat uncouth figure resembling the Dagda, but possessed of great power. He buries the hero Cú Chulainn up to his armpits in the earth and shaves off his hair; he also tests his courage in the Beheading Game, an episode later introduced by an English poet of the fourteenth century into the poem 'Sir Gawain and the Green Knight'. He was also called 'the man in the grey mantle', and held responsible for the death of men: 'Every head that was brought out of the fort, "Who slew that man?" said Conchobar. "I and the man in the grey mantle", each answered in turn.'[18] Cú Roí is called a *bachlach*, a word used for a churl or herdsman. One of his symbols is a fish, since a salmon in a well has to be killed before he can die.

Another god who plays a major part in tales of kings and heroes is Mannannán mac Lir, who rules over the Land of the Living. His name means 'Son of the Sea', and is related to the name for the Isle of Man, *Manau*. He is said to ride in his chariot over or under the waves, and his kingdom lies beneath them. His Welsh equivalent is Manawydan Son of Llyr, who appears in the *Mabinogion*, but no details are given there about his connection with the sea.[19] It may be noted that Manawydan, like other gods, is gifted at many skills and crafts, and that his wife is Rhiannon, a goddess of the Other World; he also causes the land to be fruitful. He is represented as the brother of Bran, who may have been an early deity (p. 75 above). Manannán is concerned with the begetting and birth of kings and heroes, and these births are often associated with the world of water (p. 125 above). In one of the Irish *Glossaries* he is described as a trader living on the Isle of Man, but here his former association with the sea and divine status is mentioned.[20] 'He was the best pilot in the west of Europe. Through acquaintance with the sky he knew the quarter in which would be fair weather and foul weather, and when each of the two seasons would change. Hence the Scots and Britons call him a god of the sea and hence they say he was "Son of the Sea".'[20] To define Manannán simply as a sea god, however, would be to oversimplify matters. The fertility powers often have connections with the depths under the sea as well as those under the earth, and with moving water, while fish formed an essential part of the year's harvest. There are traces of other minor supernatural figures linked with the sea, such as Tethra, one of the Fomorians, of whom it is said that the fish were his cattle, and Nechtan, husband of the river goddess of the Boyne.

In Scandinavia also various names are connected with the sea. Ægir, also called *Hlér*, and his wife Ran seem little more than symbolic figures in poetry and legend, although like Manannán they were famed for hospitality. The gods met to feast in their hall under the waves,[21] and sometimes they are said to welcome drowned sailors, although this may be a touch of sardonic humour rather than serious myth. The poet Egill Skallagrimsson takes Ran as a personification of the devouring sea in his poem *Sonatorrek*, the elegy on his sons, but does not develop the image, whereas allusions to Odin in the same poem are vigorous and detailed, based on various myths. Ran was said to catch sailors in her net, an image which detracts somewhat from the picture of her as a good hostess, and it was this net which Loki used to trap the dwarf Andvari who lived in a river. Njord, one of the main Vanir deities, was associated with the sea, and with ships, lakes and rivers; places named after him are usually on islands or beside water. There are also sea-giants; Ægir is sometimes identified with *Hlér*, a giant whose name was given to an island *Hlésey* in Denmark (now Læsso), and Hymir and Gymir are mentioned in the poems. The Germanic Weland and his father Wade possibly belong to the same company.

The god who has most in common with Manannán, however, is the Scandinavian Heimdall. He is associated with waves of the sea, who are called his daughters, while he is called the son of nine mothers, the daughters of Ægir, who again may be waves; these suggest memories of goddesses under the sea. Like Manannán, he is linked with the begetting of children. In the poem *Rígsþula* the figure of the divine visitor who comes to the house of a thrall, a farmer and a jarl in turn, and brings about the birth of a son with all the characteristics of his particular class, is usually taken to be Heimdall, in accordance with the prose introduction to the poem.[22] The descriptions of Heimdall in the poetry are difficult to reconcile with each other. He has persistent connections with the ram, and yet fights with Loki in the sea in the form of a seal; he is also the watchman of the gods, protecting Asgard from invasion, and possessor of the horn which is to be used to announce the final attack at Ragnarok. The links between him and Manannán, suggestive and yet difficult to define or clarify, are characteristic of the shifting resemblances between Norse and Irish tradition, where memories of divine figures have developed in different ways and gradually grown apart in the separate literatures. Dumézil saw Heimdall as a 'god of beginnings', a 'first god', like the Roman Janus, but later came to reconsider this approach,[23] while De Vries places him in the warrior class. The strong link with the sea and the birth of children, however, makes it probable that Heimdall belonged to the Vanir rather than the Æsir. Of particular interest are the verses inserted into the poem *Hyndluljóð*, sometimes known as the *Little Vǫluspá*. Here there is a reference to one born of nine giant women 'at the earth's edge', that is, at the edge of the sea, 'in ancient days' or 'in the beginning' (*í árdaga*), suggesting a link with other wise giants able to remember the first days of the world and consulted by Odin. The strength of this being came from the earth and the ice-cold sea, and he must surely be Heimdall, who according to the early poets was born of the waves, while the waves are also called his daughters. Dumézil saw a parallel in Welsh folklore in a tradition about the sea-woman Gwenhidwy;[24] of her it was said that the breaking waves were her ewes and the ninth wave a ram, and such an image might reconcile the two aspects of Heimdall, one of a ram and one as a god of the waves.

Other figures to be included among the fertility deities are the young and radiant sons of the greater gods. Freyr, son of Njord, sometimes appears in this guise, particularly in the story of the wooing of Gerd in the *Edda* poem *Skírnismál*. Óengus, son of the Dagda, is the hero of a similar wooing and long search for an elusive bride in the tale of the 'Dream of Óengus'. Balder, whose death takes place in spite of Odin's attempts to prevent it, seems halfway between god and hero, but the mourning for him over the natural world at the coming of winter seems to suggest that he possessed some aspects of a fertility god.[25] In Norse tradition the sons of the gods take the place of their fathers after Ragnarok and avenge themselves on their fathers' slayers; Vidar in particular was begotten for this purpose, and slew the wolf after it had devoured Odin. It is these sons who in *Vǫluspá* take over the bright new world which emerges from the sea and begin a new era for gods and men.

Finally there are divine beings with specialist powers, but these are minor figures, and there is no evidence for cults associated with them; they belong to the world of literature rather than of religion. Goibniu is the smith of the gods in the Irish tales, and represented as a master craftsman. His Welsh equivalent is Gwydion, who made a magic horse, ships and shoes, and perhaps also Arthur's hall. O'Rahilly identifies Goibniu with Gobban *Saer* (craftsman) said to have built churches for the early Irish saints. In a poem from a ninth-century manuscript attributed to Suibne *Geilt*, a woodland oratory overgrown with ivy is said to be his work, while God was its thatcher.[26] Gobban presumably set up the stone or rock while the growing things which made it like a bright garden were the gift of the Creator. The Germanic equivalent was the smith Weland, usually described as a giant, said to have forged the finest weapons of the legendary past and set up great works in stone surviving as impressive ruins from the Roman period. Dian Cécht was the god of healing, who gave Núadu his arm of silver, and sang incantations over the wounded to restore them to health. He seems to have no obvious equivalent on the Germanic side. Both Irish and Scandinavians however have the tradition of a trickster in the divine community, in the figures of Bricriu and Loki.

The position is complicated by the fact that Loki does not appear as a god, but rather as a companion of gods, or sometimes as a giant. He accompanies Odin and an unknown god Hœnir, who is little more than a name, in some of the earliest pre-Christian poems about the gods' adventures in Skaldic poetry of the tenth century. He is also represented as a giant bound by the gods until finally he broke loose at Ragnarok and brought a host of other giants against Asgard. More often however he appears in poems and tales as a nimble trickster, able to change sex and shape, and causing much mirth as well as considerable trouble to his companions. In his female form he could even give birth to monsters, the serpent in the deep, the wolf which finally devours Odin, and Hel, the giantess who rules the realm of death. Yet his creations were not wholly evil, and when he turned himself into a mare to lead away the horse of the giant who was building Asgard, he gave birth to the eight-legged horse of Odin which was one of the treasures of the gods. It was he also who encouraged the dwarves to undertake a contest which resulted in the forging of the other treasures, such as Thor's hammer and Odin's spear, although with his usual contrariness Loki did his best to spoil the hammer in the making. Loki is above all an arch-thief, sometimes attempting to steal or to help others to steal the gods' treasures, and then helping the gods to recover them by his cunning and shape-changing skills. He wins back Thor's stolen hammer and the golden apples of Idun which preserved the gods' youth. He has undoubtedly many of the characteristics of the Trickster figure as described by Radin;[27] he gets himself into awkward and embarrassing situations and breaks the normal rules of loyalty and decency. In the poem *Lokasenna* the gods try to keep him out of the hall of Ægir when they gather there for a feast, but he enters in spite of them and abuses all the gods and goddesses in turn, betraying shameful secrets and accusing the gods of cowardice and the goddesses of infidelity, until Thor returns bearing his hammer and forces him to be silent. Dumézil declares Loki to be 'a truly demotic element' among the Æsir, and finds a parallel to his part in bringing about Balder's death in the myths of the Ossetes in southern Russia in which Sozryko is killed through the cunning malice of Syrdon.[28] If he is right, then Loki the arch-thief and stirrer-up of strife may have formed part of the divine group from early times, although no cult appears to have existed for his worship, and the part he plays seems to be limited to that of a catalyst, affecting the fortunes and behaviour of the other gods without existing as a divine figure in his own right.

The Celtic equivalent of Loki may be seen in the Irish Bricriu, whose nickname *Nemthenga* (Poison-Tongue) would fit Loki admirably. Like Loki he exulted in strife and seized on a feast as an excellent opportunity for this. In the story of the 'Feast of Bricriu' he built a splendid hall in which to hold a banquet to which the heroes of Ulster were invited. They were unwilling to accept, but he threatened them with dire consequences if they refused:[29]

'I will incite the kings and the chiefs and the warriors and the young warriors', said Bricriu, 'so that you will all kill one another unless you come to drink at my feast... I will set son against father and incite them to kill each other...I will set daughter against mother. And if that is not enough, I will incite the two breasts of every Ulaid woman to beat against each other and become foul and putrid.' 'In that case, it would be better to go', said Fergus.

One could hardly find a better image of destruction through useless quarrelling than this, and this emphasis on hostility between kinsmen might be set alongside the picture of the breakdown of loyalties and responsibilities associated with Ragnarok, and included in the passage at the end of the tale of the Second Battle of Mag Tuired' (p. 193 above). It is as though with the final breaking in of chaos and downfall of the world the spiteful desires of Loki and Bricriu for recrimination and strife come to final fruition. The tale of Bricriu's feast illustrates the effects of his scheming on a smaller scale among the Ulstermen. Like the gods in the hall of Ægir, they try to keep the mischief-maker out of the feast, even though he is the host, but he manages none the less to set the champions against one another by inciting each in turn to claim the champion's portion. Then he sets to work on their wives, and there is a wild, undignified rush between them to determine who shall claim precedence over the rest by being first in the hall. Here we have excellent comedy and satire, and Bricriu himself does not come out of it too well; he ends with his hall severely damaged and himself covered with grime, a typical example of the trickster whose clever schemes often fail to benefit the schemer. By the wisdom of the peacemakers and the final intervention of Cú Roí, the contest is decided and Cú Chulainn declared the undoubted champion of them all. O'Rahilly argued that the building of the splendid palace should be the work not of Bricriu but the smith of the gods, but it may be noted that Loki also was a skilled craftsman and artificer. When pursued by the gods, after Balder's death, he is said to have built a house from which he could look out in every direction, and it seems that creative skills form an essential part of the trickster character.

Thus on both the Celtic and Germanic sides it seems possible to distinguish two deities who stand out as ruling powers. Lug and the Dagda, Odin and Thor, survive as vigorous characters in Irish and Norse literature, and can be traced back to what is known of gods worshipped in western Europe in the Roman period. There is also a group of deities associated with the fertility of the natural world and closely linked with the earth and sea. There appears to have been a third great power among the Germans, since they worshipped three deities whose names were given to three days of the week, Donar, the Germanic predecessor of Thor, Wodan and Tîwaz. Here however we encounter difficulties, since if Tîwaz was originally identified with Mars and also

214

associated with law-giving, Odin and Thor seem to have taken over his powers and divided them between them. In the Viking Age they were the dominating figures in the community of gods and goddesses, with Tyr only dimly perceived in the background. The gap left was partly filled by Freyr, who in Sweden at least became a powerful god connected with battle and with the families of kings. It is these three male figures which, according to Adam of Bremen, were to be seen in the main temple at Uppsala.

Similarly in Irish tradition it is difficult to find a third deity, although Donn, the Dis Pater of earlier times, god of darkness and the dead, might be seen as filling the gap, possibly resembling in many ways the Germanic Wodan. Over the centuries it is as though the leading deities shifted positions and changed partners as in a dance. The gods and goddesses of Dumézil's third group, those connected with the cultivation of the earth, herding and hunting, are much easier to recognise. They seem to have protected the animals of the wild as well as those on the farms, and they gave counsel and help to men and women, while they also played an essential part in the birth of children and their destinies. They possessed great powers and were the custodians of ancient knowledge, and even the ruling gods turned to them frequently for counsel and inspiration.

Sjoestedt calls the ruling deities the Chieftain Gods, and we see the Æsir acting as chieftains, organising the building of halls, the creation of fine ornaments and weapons, and the dispensing of justice from their Assembly beneath the World Tree. There are many minor specialised figures who have no definite cults connected with them. Some may be the creation of poets and storytellers, while others may be local gods whose names have come to be included in the pantheon, or titles of the main gods which have assumed some kind of life in the tales and poems. It was to the ruling powers that men turned in times of need, and these were supported by regular sacrifices at the feasts in which all took part. They welcomed men in various ways at death, and were closely linked with the ancestors. Finally, the figures of the goddesses cannot be forgotten. They formed a large and powerful group, important on the local level among simple folk and also playing a prominent part in the working of destiny. The ruling goddess, whatever her name might be, has a place with the great gods, even if we do not hear of her image at Uppsala, and the group of three female beings, balancing those of the three main gods, appears at all periods as the major arbiters of fate and chance.

Undoubtedly the gods and goddesses surviving in mythological traditions, tales and legends are shifting, uncertain figures. As time passes, the distinction between gods, giants and heroes becomes increasingly blurred and elusive. Ancient giant figures like Cú Roí and the all-knowing Vafthruthnir may be shadows of former deities, and the Germanic Weland may appear as a hero, a giant or a supernatural smith and remain a shadowy power in folklore for centuries. When we seek for information about the gods, we are dealing largely in popular traditions, and what gifted story-tellers and poets have created out of the old traditions. The images and symbols of pre-Christian times can strengthen the picture a little, but give us no firm lines of definition. It is all the more impressive that in spite of the confusion in the records, and the complex treatment of the earlier gods in literature of later centuries, certain divine figures still retain clarity and vigour. These outstanding figures from the myths of peoples who grew apart from one another but must once have been closely linked have remained recognisable, and still reflect something of the force which they must once have possessed in the minds of men.

Conclusion

We shall not cease from exploration
And the end of all our exploring
Will be to arrive where we started
And know the place for the first time.

T. S. Eliot, *Little Gidding*

The aim of this book has been to discover what can be learned from the records of the pre-Christian religion in Iceland and Scandinavia, and how far it is possible to trace it back to the past. This includes religious practices, communal and individual, general assumptions about the supernatural world, and the place of religion in the lives of the people, set against the world-picture indicated by surviving myths and legends. The problems encountered in dealing with late, confused sources have been borne in mind, in the belief that, tentative and difficult although such an exploration may be, it is worth making.

It is clear that parallels exist between German and Scandinavian material on the one hand and what is known of the pre-Christian religion of the Celtic peoples on the other. The comparable body of evidence to set against that from Iceland comes from Ireland, where a rich collection of tales and legends preserves memories of religious cults and traditions concerning contacts with the supernatural world. 'There has never been a country in which the sense of tradition was more intense than in medieval Ireland', Robin Flower claimed.[1] Both Ireland and Iceland possessed a lively oral tradition and took pride in their early memories; they were prepared to preserve them in spite of some opposition from the Christian church. The resemblances between the pictures of the Other World which they present are striking, and there is agreement in basic concepts, in spite of wide differences in treatment and presentation. Scholars like MacCulloch and Jan de Vries were well aware of this, but the parallels have tended to be forgotten or ignored because most recent work on early religion has been firmly restricted to one side or the other. There has been a general reluctance to face up to the problems presented by these similarities and to use them for a better understanding of the nature of early religion. The claim made here is that such a comparison throws light on obscure material, offers a new line of approach, and gives us more possibility of estimating the age and significance of certain traditions and motifs.

It might be argued that such parallels are simply due to a similar way of life, a constant background of warrior activity continuing alongside farming and herding at home, so that heroic traditions and close links with the natural world influenced the rites and imagery of religion. But much of the resemblance seems to go deeper than this; it indicates an accepted framework, with emphasis on certain symbols and motifs which may be traced beyond Ireland and Iceland to what we know of the religion of the Celtic and Germanic peoples in earlier times. Another tendency has to been to explain the similarities by assuming borrowings from one people by another at the time when they were in close contact during the Viking Age. It was for instance suggested that tales of Finn and his warrior bands were inspired by memories of Viking activities in Ireland, and that the tradition of Odin consulting the head of Mimir was due to direct Irish influence. In each case it is essential to examine the age and distribution of each separate tradition and avoid dogmatic generalisation. It seems that the Finn tales were current in Ireland well before the Vikings were established there, and that the motif of the speaking head rising from a well is found in various forms in folk tradition in England and Norway, pointing to a wide distribution outside Ireland. Certainly borrowing must have taken place in some cases. One particular series of Scandinavian tales, those relating to Gudmund of Glasisvellir, appear to have been based on Irish tales of journeys to the Land of Youth, as suggested in Chapter VI. The Norse stories are set in the opposite direction and placed in north-eastern Europe, that realm of adventures and marvels for the Scandinavians, but their plots and the description of Glasisvellir have a familiar ring if compared with accounts of Irish journeys and there is no indication of earlier Germanic material to account for them. Even here, however, traditions in the Norse poems of a bright hospitable realm of the gods may have made the Gudmund tales readily acceptable in Iceland.

The resemblances which have been noted here are not in general of this kind. We are not dealing with neat repetition of recognisable plots or the transportation of a foreign tale into a Scandinavian setting – something at which Icelandic story-tellers were adept – but rather of odd episodes which seem out of place, and elusive cryptic references which apparently puzzled the recorder as well as the modern reader, as well as basic images which seem to have developed differently in their separate environments. It is accepted that Celts and Germans were once closely associated, hard to distinguish from one another in the Roman period except by their differences in language, and at an earlier period still having one language in common. The idea of their common ancestry is strengthened by the type of parallels found in their religious symbols and practices, and by the emphasis on certain concepts in their imaginative representation of the supernatural world in later literature and art.

The picture which emerges is one of a rich and vigorous supernatural world with which contact may readily, although not always easily, be made by those who desire it. It is ruled by a plurality of supernatural powers, figures which have been developed and enriched by poets, storytellers and antiquarians through the ages until they have become a vast company of divine beings of varying powers and ideosyncrasies. As we know it, the world of Norse gods and goddesses has become to a large extent a literary one, although behind it lies the evidence of known cults and the witness of early placenames. It consists also of a body of wisdom lore about supernatural beings, as in the *Edda* poems of the question and answer type, contrasted with lively narratives like the account of the recovery of Thor's hammer or Loki's fantastic adventures in the realm of the giants. In the Irish sources, the gods are not openly acknowledged as such; they are portrayed as kings and heroes belonging to an heroic world, or else as dwellers in the fairy mounds. Both literatures have many lighter tales from later periods, dealing with enchantment and marvels, concerning giants or wizards or little people of the countryside and house-spirits who can bring luck or cause annoyance to country folk. It must always be remembered when dealing with this rich body of material that entertainers, poets and scholars may have used the old myths for their own purposes, and also that traditions may have made their way in from outside. Once the Christian church with its body of learning was established, there was a constant influx of Biblical lore; sermons and homilies and tales of the saints could reach the minds even of those who could not read, while literary works ranging from learned commentaries to the masterpieces of Latin poets were available for scholars who studied in the monastic libraries.

It must also be borne in mind that in dealing with the history of past religions we must always be largely at the mercy of chance. What survives by a lucky accident may mislead us as to what was really important in the hierophanies of an earlier age, man's view of the sacred, as Mircea Eliade was careful to point out:[2] 'The religious historian must trace not only the *history* of a given hierophany, but must first of all understand and explain the modality of the sacred that hierophany discloses. It would be difficult enough to interpret the meaning of an hierophany in any case, but the heterogeneous and chancy nature of the evidence makes it far, far worse.' He reminds us also that the religious lives and concepts of the most apparently 'primitive' people are in fact varying and complex, and their notion of the world cannot be reduced to one neat scheme such as 'animism', 'totemism' or 'sun-worship'. The choice of a hierophany as a satisfactory expression of religious experience must vary greatly among the individual members of a community. Mystical experience can be fostered by encouragement and training, but it cannot be supplied by this, nor can it be easily defined in different individuals. What for one may be a profound and satisfying symbol of supernatural power may for another be no more than a pleasing design or an amulet vaguely felt to be lucky.

It might indeed be expected that the old gods and their company would vanish utterly in the ensuring confusion of religious practices and beliefs, and the mingling of diverse traditions, ancient tales and new learning. However some of them at least possessed the secret of survival. They had after all come into being from a baffling mixture of local traditions, study of earlier lore as passed down by the wise in the community, and outside influence from other cultures, such as the imagery associated with Roman deities, shamanistic practices of the Finno-Ugrian peoples, and the horse cults of the nomads from the Steppe. In their wanderings and shifting fortunes and alliances the Celts and Germans had little opportunity to build up established centres of learning, protected by powerful priests and kings. In so far as such centres existed, they provoked the hostility first of the Roman Empire and then of the Christian church. Yet the gods continued to hold men's allegiance, based on shifting foundations though they might seem to be, and men faithfully and instinctively maintained such images of the supernatural world as harmonised with their way of life and concept of the world.

It would clearly be unreasonable to expect a foursquare, established mythological system such as some of the earlier scholars longed to find, and indeed believed at times that they had found, if only their colleagues would have the humility to agree with them. But there is a recognisable body of religious symbolism and myth to be found in the fragmentary evidence which has come down to us from the early religion of the Celts and Germans. The ancient powers which they pictured as ruling the supernatural world and shaping the destinies of men have retained sufficient of their character in later literature and art to enable us to reconstruct something at least of the world-picture on which they are based. In accordance with Dumézil's basic approach, we can recognise a group of two or three powerful deities ruling the worlds, whose help and protection were regularly sought at religious festivals, and with whom contact was kept up by means of sacrifice, communal feasting, and an unceasing endeavour by certain people in the community to ascertain their will and retain their favour. By supporting them, men helped to maintain the existing order, and so ensure the continuing survival of themselves and their descendants in a precarious world, enjoying the regular progression of the seasons and renewal of the earth each year on which their lives depended. They were very much alive to the threats constantly menacing them, and aware that the order of the world and the prosperity of the community would not endure for ever. This is something which comes out very strongly in the literature, and helps to explain the emphasis on the keeping up of regular rites to support the gods on which the maintenance of established order as opposed to chaos must depend. The history of these peoples helps us to understand their awareness of possible destruction; it was something deeply engraved into the framework of their religion.

The gods themselves were divided into two main groups, the ruling gods associated with earthly power, battle, and the guardianship of heaven and earth on the one hand, and the many beings more closely associated with the natural world on the other. The ruling gods set up the machinery by which men's lives were regulated and preserved from falling into chaos. They ordained the movements of sun and moon on which the calendar depended, and the measurement of time in nights, days and seasons. They taught men crafts and skills, as well as inspiring them to search for wisdom and learning, and invented the symbols of runes and letters. They presided over law and the preservation of genealogies, essential for the establishment of a lasting society; they took a hand in the selection of rulers among the people, supporting and assisting the powerful families whose activities on earth mirrored those of the gods in their own realm. They took ruthless vengeance not on the cruel and wicked, but on oath-breaking and sacrilege.

The gods can be seen as a group, but were recognisable as individuals within it. Here complications enter in, for names varied over the long period of time in which they were recognised and worshipped, and functions overlapped. As Dumézil pointed out, there is a close link between the ruling gods and the authority of priests, magicians and kings in the community. The gods were closely associated with the waging of war, the training of warriors, and the maintenance of the families which supplied the warrior leaders. Their will as expressed in the choice of the right king is something which emerges as a main theme in the literature, particularly that concerned with the Norse Odin and the Irish Lug. But apart from these gods ruling the community, there was also a widespread and deep-rooted belief in separate and individual supernatural protectors and guardians. These were worshipped, often with devotion, by particular family groups, and their shrines were family possessions. One of the main ruling gods might be singled out in this way, but it was more often some local spirit associated with a particular place on earth.

Communal worship included the beings concerned with fertility and linked with the natural world. As there were many small local communities and isolated families in Scandinavia, there was bound to be a plurality of tiny gods and goddesses, associated with rocks, mounds natural or artificial, springs or lakes or caverns in the earth. Reliance on such beings was something of paramount importance, and worship, on a communal scale, was always linked with sacrifice and the giving of gifts. It was characterised also by a desire to learn the future in order to prepare more adequately for what was to come. This was an essential part of the religion of both Germanic and Celtic peoples. Here the goddesses, members of Dumézil's third group of supernatural beings, came into their own. There are traditions of a supreme goddess, sometimes viewed as the queen of heaven, sometimes as Freyja, the universal lover, closely linked with the powerful ruling deities. But there was also a host of lesser goddesses, wives of the gods and protecting spirits of various localities, pictured as fair maidens, ancient hags or spirits of the battlefield. These have lived on in the world of imagination and folktales as sinister witches, fairy godmothers, or lamenting spirits wailing for the dead.

Thus we find a fairly consistent picture of the supernatural powers, and Dumézil has helped us to see them in perspective, even if some of his theories do not fit the Scandinavian and Irish material in detail. The value of this approach is that it does not insist on the existence of a well-defined pre-Christian religion clearly established in the beginning and continuing over the centuries on established and recognisable lines where the divinities remain static. All we can hope to do is to make out the main governing concepts which have resulted in the myths and lore which has come down to us. These were kept up as long as they fitted the background of men's lives and the nature of the lands in which they struggled and fought for survival. We can trace a framework going back to ancient times into which the traditions of the Germanic and Celtic peoples fitted, in spite of all the shifting local variations and mixture of traditions over a long period of time.

There seems little doubt that one of the strong prevailing influences in this conception of the supernatural was a deeply-rooted belief in the desirability of luck, and the part played by luck in men's lives. In a dangerous and uncertain world, luck was essential if one was to survive, and this is something constantly emphasised both in the myths and legends and the way in which the gods were worshipped. In battle, hunting, exploration, settling or cultivating a new land, and in the leadership of men, the lucky man was the one who fitted into the natural world in which he found himself, and who therefore possessed the protection of the powers which governed it. Favoured by the land-spirits, he would prosper as a farmer and avail himself of the potential riches of land and sea. Supported by the gods and battle-goddesses, he would win fame in the demanding world of warfare, where reputation was brittle indeed and time soon ran out. If he was helped by the powers who brought men inspiration, he might succeed in a fiercely competitive environment because he could find the right words when needed and influence others, or because his wit and imagination gained him influence as a poet or teller of tales. Success in various walks of life is largely a matter of the instinctive right reaction in a moment of crisis. Men exposed to physical danger and sudden hazards, such as airmen in war, racing drivers or those who go to sea in small ships, are very much alive to the need for good luck, and many rely on mascots, prized amulets and little protective rituals to bolster up their confidence, since confidence is essential when calamity threatens and an instant decision is needed. Life for the warrior peoples of north-western Europe was very much an existence of this kind, and the sword-warrior, the raider or the settler in a new land were alike influenced in their religious rituals by an acute consciousness of the need for luck and protection.

It was realised that skills and outstanding gifts were not sufficient to protect a man if he was 'unlucky-looking', as the Icelandic sagas expressed it. Grettir the Strong, with all the resources of a successful warrior, is none the less a vivid illustration of a fatal inability to be in tune with the powers ruling men's lives. A rebel against the establishment, his inner world was as threatening as the dark beings against which he struggled in the folktales remembered about him, brilliantly used by the Icelandic author of *Grettis Saga* to build up an unforgettable picture of a man dogged by ill-luck.[3] There are allusions in the sagas to pre-Christian heroes boasting that they preferred to trust in their own strength and might than in Thor and Odin, but this seems likely to be due to a romanticisation of the independent Viking hero, something inspired by Christian concepts of unbelievers. In the pre-Christian religion there was no obligation to accept a definite creed or even openly to acknowledge the power of the gods in one's own life. One could abandon a particular cult if one's luck failed, as Slaying-Glum deserted the god Freyr in favour of Odin. Many no doubt accepted the worship of Christ because it gave hopes of better luck than they had known with the old gods, and this is in fact the argument put forward by the priest of the old religion in Bede's account of the conversion of Northumbria: 'If the gods had any power', he declared, 'they would surely have favoured me, since I have been more zealous in their service.'[4] Nevertheless there was a general acknowledgement of higher powers outside the familiar world; this was part of the background of life, not something restricted to earnest believers. The gods were honoured at the feasts in which every family took part, and evoked as a matter of course at such turning-points in life as birth and death, marriage, or the opening of the annual Assembly. The maintenance of the existing order depended on the support of the higher powers, and in particular it was the duty of the ruler to keep up the contact with the Other World; when in Iceland there was no king to perform this function, it became the duty of the *goði*, the leading man in each district.

Contact, then, with the supernatural world was essential for the community, and in the continual emphasis on methods of divination to discover what was unknown and what the future held, much of the strength of the old religion lay. Another of its strengths was the efficacy of holy places where prayer and sacrifice might be kept up over many centuries. These formed the centres of local communities, symbolising the centre of the world and the inner core of life itself. Others were more secret places to which the family or the individual might turn for reassurance, counsel and the acquisition of skill or wisdom. Such places reflected the wider unity of the divine world of whose powers men might, cautiously and with trepidation, avail themselves. The sacred place was a way of entry into that world, by a descent into the earth, an ascent into the sky, or a journey beneath the water. The most powerful symbol, lasting over a great space of time, seems to be that of a great tree or pillar linking the worlds above and below. Just as a desire for luck was one of the strong motives for seeking contact with the supernatural world, so an awareness of a way of entry into the mysterious world beyond by means of natural features of the landscape was a mainspring of religious belief.

Of major importance also was the emphasis on the divine power as manifested in the living creatures of the world, both birds and animals. In their strength, ruthlessness and cunning men saw a reflection of the divine, and held that the power of the gods could be manifested in and through them. By sacrificing living creatures, as in the offering up of human victims, there was a release of divine power, and this was one way of gaining knowledge of what was hidden. There is no doubt that the

224

desire to acquire knowledge was another of the strong instincts which kept the religion alive. The bounty of the gods was not confined to gifts of good harvests or victories in battle, but included the giving of knowledge of past and future, as well as inspiration. We hear something among these peoples of an organised priesthood, but more of individual seers, both men and woman, as well as healers and interpreters of dreams. The poets also were among the tradition-bearers who passed on tales of the gods and the lore of the supernatural world, accounts of the beginning and predictions of the end of all things. Kings and warriors needed to possess something of this knowledge, because of the share which they were required to take in religious rituals. There must have been a wealth of spells and chants suppressed in Christian times, of which only fragments remain, but much of this is likely to have been specialised knowledge, not available to all. The words of power spoken by the gods could be uttered, to a lesser degree, by the lips of men who were in possession of the necessary skills and learning.

For all this, it is not suggested that men as a whole led devout lives, or even lives full of superstitious observances, with their minds set on the gods and the powers of the divine world. Many pursued their own activities in a practical way, using force or special skills to their best advantage, as in all periods of human history. But the assumption that behind what we now regard as the secular world lay the powers and threats of the arbiters of destiny seems to have been shared by the community as a whole. It was taken for granted that law and order in the community as in the universe was maintained by supernatural powers, and to be on their side ensured continuance of luck and survival among dangers. There was no moral obligation to seek help and protection other than the necessity to keep faith and fulfil one's side of the contract. The binding nature of oaths, promises and solemn undertakings is something continually emphasised in the literature. The gods themselves are in danger if they break an agreement, although trickster figures like Odin and Loki may find a way through by a subterfuge or ingenious use of words. Heroes in Icelandic and Irish sagas go to their deaths because they are forced by circumstances to break an obligation or infringe a taboo. It was recognised however that cunning and ingenuity may find a way out of an awkward situation for men as for the gods, and Odin encouraged his followers to use such skills. Trickster tales are always popular, and numerous folktales show humble little men outwitting ghosts or devils, and getting the better of a hard bargain. Both Odin and Loki are amoral and ruthless in the methods they employ, using crooked means for their own protection; the adversaries of the gods are often defeated by double-dealing rather than superior

225

strength, as the wolf was defeated when Tyr bound him. Tyr himself did not cheat, since he gave up the hand he had offered as a pledge, but the gods had deceived the wolf in their assurances about the chain which fastened him until Ragnarok.

The importance of the trickster is recognised here as in other mythologies, and he is an essential element in the divine community. He is associated with creation and innovation. In an introduction to a collection of Hindu myths,[5] Wendy O'Flaherty defines the pattern found in them as that of 'the resolution of chaos into order and its dissolution back into chaos', words which might be taken as the *leitmotif* of the poem *Vǫluspá*. The major gods are represented as creating, arranging, separating and controlling the universe, but progress can only come through conflict. When the powers of darkness and death threaten, then new steps forward are made; a wall is built round Asgard, the divine mead is prepared, the treasures of the gods are forged. The trickster figure plays an essential part, acting as a catalyst to bring about creative innovations and strengthening the communities of gods and men. In particular, the imposing of bonds on threatening monsters, the unbridled forces impinging on the realm of the gods, is a central symbol in Germanic myths. In the Irish tales monsters play a less obvious part, but they are encountered by heroes in the form of giants and hags, while the hideous world of the destructive battle-goddesses and their companions conjures up a threat as sinister as that offered by Loki's offspring, the wolf, the serpent and the goddess of decay and death.

While the ruling gods are warrior leaders, ruling a male world, there is nevertheless a strong female element in the mythology as it has come down to us. The goddesses are figures of tremendous vitality both in generous giving and destruction, and seem to represent ultimate destiny, before whom the gods themselves must go down fighting. The image of spinning, weaving women deities overshadows those of human heroes and ruling gods. The women are present in the myths; they stalk across the newly created world in the opening section of *Vǫluspá*, and survive in humble folktales of later times, punishing the arrogant and cruel and helping the young and innocent to win good fortune. Some understanding of the impressive body of female supernatural beings to be found in Scandinavian and Irish literature is essential if we are to understand the religious outlook aright. They are a varied company, appearing as protectors in battle, as choosers of the slain and gruesome giantesses delighting in blood, daunting figures foretelling destiny, seeresses and priestesses interpreting omens from sacrificial victims, guardian spirits of families, welcoming or hostile women encountered in dreams, and fair daughters of giants luring men to their embraces.

These figures are continually associated with the world of the dead, seen in its contrasting aspects of a fair, hospitable land outside time and a dark realm of horror and decay. Both aspects are associated with the burial mound, a recurring symbol of the dwelling place of the dead, and both are linked with the concept of the ancestors, who welcome their descendants into the earth or the green realm of the gods. There is constant awareness of the link between past and present in the strong sense of the continuity of the family and the importance of inherited characteristics, and gods like Heimdall and Manannán help to bridge the generations. The realm of the dead is not seen merely as a static place, for the emphasis is on the journey to and from it rather than on the state of the occupants. Although the horrors of physical death are frankly recognised, even the lifeless corpse continues to be active in Icelandic tales of the *draugar*, the walking dead, or Irish tales like that of 'Nera and the Dead Man'. The importance placed on the heads of dead heroes and warriors as a source of power and inspiration reveals a different concept of the dead's continued activity. Besides the threat which they display towards the living, an extremely ancient conception of the dead, there is also a strong sense of communication between dead and living and continuing interchange between the two worlds.

This is particularly the case with kings and heroes, for it is on their world that the emphasis in the literature is placed. It is the leaders of the people who have the acknowledged right to enter the divine realm after death, and even during their lifetime, and our evidence is undoubtedly influenced by the survival of memorial stones and funeral elegies in honour of great men, which have affected later mythology. On another level however we have the insistence on contact between simpler country people and the local spirits of the countryside, reflected in sagas and legends and folktales and borne out by the evidence of archaeology. The rich body of fairy lore current in north-western Europe has blended with the more sophisticated traditions concerning kings, and we have to accept both if we are to obtain a balanced picture, since both no doubt existed side by side from early times. The aristocratic influence on the literary sources has tended to emphasise the glory of the fearless warrior and to place much importance on genealogies and the burial places of kings. But although the cult of the gods was organised by aristocratic leaders, the regular feasts were shared by all and welcomed as festivities breaking the sequence of the year and cheering them in the dangerous times of divisions between the seasons and in the winter dark. The lore of poets and wise men was inevitably linked with the fortunes of kings, but to discover more about what religion meant for the people, we must make use of folk traditions in conjunction with mythology. Indeed it is hard to be sure where the exact distinction between the two lies, since one blends imperceptibly into the other.

The intention here has been to sketch out general outlines, not to follow up separate themes in complex detail. Many aspects of the available material, such as the cult of the human head, the use of omens in dreams, the place of animal symbolism in the worship of the gods, or the emphasis on the central tree or pillar, would clearly repay further investigation. Dumézil in a preface raised the question of who was responsible for the preservation of early material about early kings of Rome, pointing out how little we know:[6] 'We are still at the stage of simply recording the results of operations whose mechanism we cannot describe and whose agents we cannot name.'[6] We need to know much more concerning the tradition-bearers to whom we owe our knowledge. When the scholarly writers came on to the scene and began to record, discuss and edit, some with political or theological axes to grind, others anxious to hand on a good story, they were often dealing with material already confusing and complex, consisting of popular traditions and remembered tales. The written words need to be set beside the imagery of religious art, whose motifs and symbols are drawn from a time when the beliefs and legends were still accepted as a living tradition, although the study of sacral art itself is beset with difficulties.[7] Words by themselves can be misleading, if we allow ourselves to be too much bound by them, and Dumézil laid emphasis on the necessity to perceive the spirit and pattern in a story and not simply to dissect it word by word. While there are great problems, there are great riches also in the traditions left by the warrior peoples of north-western Europe, our predecessors and ancestors, which deserve something more than pedantic analysis. We should not be content to wrangle over minute fragments isolated from the whole, but need to search for what can be discovered of a world-picture which endured over a long period of time for many men and women, to perceive where its strengths lay. In this way we may come to understand more clearly the strengths and weaknesses in our own picture of the world.

References

Introduction

1 Elston (1934) pp. 3f. For theories of the relationship between Celts and Germans, Evans (1982) pp. 233f. I owe this reference to Patrick Sims-Williams.
2 For a general account of the site, Ross (1970) pp. 16f. A description of the Hallstatt finds is given by von Sacken (1868).
3 Ross (1970) pp. 23f.; for a detailed account, Vouga (1923).
4 Evans (1982) pp. 247–8.
5 Powell (1958) p. 168.
6 Evans (1982) p. 238.
7 Mattlingly (1970), preface to translation of *Germania*, p. 24.
8 Tierney (1960) pp. 189f.
9 Frankfort (1946) p. 4.

I Holy places

1 Mabire (1971) pp. 20f. for the date of the saga. For the monastery, Jóhannesson (1974) p. 196.
2 MacCulloch (1930) p. 310. The verb *líta* in Old Icelandic is used of a deliberate serious regard rather than a casual glance: e.g. Dives beheld (*leit*) Lazarus in Abraham's bosom in the tale of Dives and Lazarus in the New Testament.
3 Jóhannesson (1974) pp. 38f.
4 *Sturlunga Saga* (Reykjavik 1946) I, pp. 57, 540 (note). There has been considerable argument as to whether this actually took place, since the river has formed several ox-bow lakes in course of time and the change in course might be a natural one.
5 Thevenot (1968) p. 200.
6 Megaw (1970) p. 165, pl. 281.
7 Hauck (1954a) p. 165.
8 Jankuhn (1957) p. 50, taf. 59; Megaw (1970) p. 165.
9 Piggott (1968) p. 84f.
10 Megaw (1970) p. 164, pl. 280.
11 Smyser (1965) p. 97. The complete *Risāla* has been translated into German

with a detailed commentary by Ahmed Zeki Validi Tógan (*Ahhand Kunde Morgenlandes* 24, 3, Leipzig 1939).

12 Megaw (1970) p. 47, pl. 12.

13 *ibid.* p. 48, pl. 14.

14 Lindqvist (1941) pp. 34–5.

15 Megaw (1970) p. 97, pl. 129; for examples from Brittany, Kruta (1985), pp. 111f.

16 First version of the *Topography of Ireland*, trans. J. J. O'Meara, Dundalk, 1951, p. 80.

17 Byrne, F. J. (1974) p. 58.

18 Keating, *History of Ireland* (*Ir Text Soc* IV, 1901) I, pp. 101, 207.

19 *De Síl Chonairi Móir*, ed. L. Gwynn, *Ériu* 6 (1912) pp. 27, 63f.

20 Hartland (1903) p. 28f.; Byrne, F. J. (1974) pp. 27, 63f.

21 Davidson (1980) II, p. 26; Schmidt (1932) pp. 34f.

22 Rees (1961) p. 154, quoting from *The Bardic Poems of Tadhg O'hUiginn* (trans. E. Knott, 1926).

23 O'Riórdáin (1957) pp. 18f.

24 Müller (1961) p. 93f.

25 Chadwick, H. M. (1924) p. 213. Relevant sources are given by De Pierrefeu (1955), who claims that the site of the pillar was the Externsteine in Westphalia in a thickly forested area. For the name Irmin, De Vries (1952) pp. 18f.

26 Hope-Taylor (1977) pp. 158f.

27 Thevenot (1968) pp. 28f.; Benoit (1970) p. 87f.; Green (1986) pp. 61f.

28 Cook (1906) pp. 172f.

29 Davidson (1960) pp. 3f.

30 Thevenot (1968) p. 220.

31 Piggott (1968) pp. 71f.

32 Gelling, M. (1961) p. 15.

33 Marstrander (1915) pp. 246–7.

34 Watson (1981) p. 170.

35 Davidson (1965a) pp. 1f.

36 O'Rahilly, T. F. (1976) p. 322.

37 Leslie (1932) p. 141; from an account in *The Tablet* in 1910.

38 Ross (1979–80) pp. 260f.

39 Green (1986) p. 135.

40 Powell (1958) pp. 142f.

41 Filip (1970) pp. 63f.; Ross (1970) p. 182f.

42 Ellison (1980) pp. 305f.

43 Thevenot (1968) pp. 224f.; Rodwell (1980) pp. 213f.

44 Dillon and Chadwick (1967) pp. 294f.; Benoit (1955) pp. 36f.; (1975) pp. 227f.

45 Thevenot (1968) pp. 113–14.

46 Martin, R. (1965) pp. 247f.; Green (1986) pp. 150–1.

47 Green (1986) pp. 151, 159.

48 Cunliffe (1971) pp. 24f.

49 Wilson (1980) p. 5.
50 Ellison (1980); Rodwell (1980) pp. 213f.; Piggott (1968) pp. 58f.
51 Thevenot (1968) pp. 227f.
52 Hope-Taylor (1977) pp. 97f., 158f., 258f.
53 Olsen (1965) pp. 236f.; (1970) pp. 274f.
54 Lidén (1969) pp. 3f.
55 Grieg (1954) pp. 162f.; Davidson (1967) pp. 95f.
56 Olsen (1965) pp. 143f. (1970) pp. 265f.
57 Blindheim, M. (1965) pp. 3f.; Lindholm (1969) pp. 28f.
58 Blindheim, M. (1965) pp. 16, 36f.
59 Lindholm (1969) p. 18.

II Feasting and sacrifice

1 *De Administrando Imperio* by the Emperor Constantine Porphyrogenitus, ed. and trans. G. Moravcsik and R. J. H. Jenkins (Budapest 1949) p. 61.
2 Ibrahim b. Ya'qub at Tartushi, a Spanish Jew of the Tenth century whose writings are known only in translation: Birkeland (1951) pp. 103f. 159.
3 MacNeill, E. (1926–8) pp. 1f.; Duval (1962–5).
4 Nilsson (1920) pp. 94f.; (1938) p. 44.
5 Hastrup (1985) p. 27.
6 For interpretations, Guyonvarc'h (1961) p. 474f.; Le Roux (1961) pp. 485f.
7 Hamp (1979) pp. 106f.
8 Danaher (1972) pp. 13f.
9 Danaher (1982) pp. 220f.
10 Grimm (1966) II, 720.
11 *History of the Wars* (Loeb trans.) VI, 15, 5f., p. 418.
12 Tierney (1960) p. 248: from Athenæus IV, 3, 7.
13 *Heimskringla, Óláfs Saga helga* 91.
14 De Vries (1932–3) pp. 171f.
15 De Navarro (1928) p. 435.
16 Cunliffe (1979) p. 36; Joffroy (1962) pp. 73f.
17 Megaw (1970) pp. 74f. pl. 72.
18 *ibid.* pp. 68–9, pl. 60–1.
19 Biel (1981) pp. 17f.
20 *Silva Gadelica*, trans. S. H. O'Grady, II (1892) II, p. 104; Cross and Slover (1936) p. 460.
21 *Heimskringla, Óláfs Saga kyrra* 3.
22 Brøndsted (1954); Oxenstierna (1956).
23 Bruce-Mitford (1983) III, pp. 324f. The first reconstruction as one huge horn holding 6 quarts of liquid was found to be incorrect.
24 Grønbech (1931) II, pp. 146f.
25 *Beowulf* 619: *He on lust geþeah/symbel ond seleful* (said of Beowulf when he receives the cup from the queen).
26 *Heimskringla, Óláfs Saga Tryggvasonar* 35.
27 *ibid., Hákonar saga góða* 14.

28 *Flateyjabók* (1860–8) I, p. 361.

29 *Þorsteins Saga bœjarmagns* (*Fornmanna Sögur* 1825–35, III, pp. 175f.) trans. Simpson (1965) pp. 180f.

30 *Hálfs Saga ok Hálfsrekka* (*Fornaldarsögur Norðurlanda*, Reykjavik 1943–4).

31 *Prose Edda, Skáldskaparmál* 1.

32 Campbell (1968) p. 221; Davidson (1978) pp. 102f.

33 *Vita Columbani* (ed. B. Krusch, Leipzig 1905) p. 213.

34 *Mon Germ Hist Scrip Merov* (Hanover 1896) III, p. 410.

35 *Serglige Con Culainn* (The Wasting Sickness of Cú Chulainn) ed. M. Dillon 1953, trans. Gantz (1981) p. 168.

36 'The Adventures of Art son of Conn', ed. Best *Ériu* 3 (1907); Cross and Slover (1936) p. 498.

37 Jackson (1971) pp. 284, 323 (note).

38 Davidson (1976) pp. 301f.; Lang (1972) pp. 241f.

39 Ross (1967) p. 318, where other examples are given.

40 O'Rahilly, T. F. (1976) p. 122.

41 For importance of cooking Nagy (1985) pp. 133, 168; for a good example of firedogs, Longworth and Cherry (1986) pp. 68–9.

42 Brøndsted (1966) III, pp. 131f.

43 *Lebor Gabála Erenn* IV (ed. Macalister, *Ir Texts Soc* 41, 1941) p. 137.

44 MacNeill, M. (1982) pp. 393, 460f.

45 *Prose Edda, Gylfaginning* 43.

46 *Mabinogion*, trans. Jones, 1949) pp. 29f.; for Irish influence, Mac Cana (1958).

47 Chathain (1979–80) pp. 200f.

48 Tierney (1960) p. 247; from Athenæus IV, 40.

49 *Fled Bricrend* (Bricriu's Feast), ed. Henderson, *Ir Texts Soc* 1899; trans. Gantz (1981) pp. 225f.; *Scéla mucce Maicc Da Thó* (Mac Da Thó's Pig) ed. Thurneysen 1935, trans. Gantz (1981) p. 186.

50 O'Sullivan (1968) pp. 119f.; Dobbs (1913) pp. 130f.

51 Megaw (1970) has a number of examples: e.g. 224, 238.

52 Ross (1967) p. 319; cf. *Dunaire Finn, Ir Texts Soc* 1908, pp. 140f.

53 Bromich (1961) 26, pp. 45f. Carey (1981–2) emphasises the importance of such supernatural pigs as sources of Otherworld energy (pp. 171f.).

54 Powell (1958) p. 147.

55 Megaw (1970) pp. 139–40, pl. 226.

56 *Prehist Zeit* 17 (1926) p. 134; discovered in 1774 and now lost.

57 Bruce-Mitford (1974) pp. 236f.; (1978) II, pl. 23.

58 Davidson (1962) p. 49.

59 Davidson (1980) p. 36.

60 *Heimskringla, Ynglinga Saga* 18; cf. OE *sunor*, herd of swine.

61 Green (1986) p. 181.

62 Nilsson (1938) p. 44.

63 Hodgkin (1949) p. 62.

64 Hone (1859) II, p. 1619; Hole (1976) 'Boarshead Ceremony', pp. 39f.

65 As on the Brå and Rynkeby cauldrons from Denmark: Megaw (1970) p. 109, p. 162; p. 138, pl. 222; of C. F. C. Hawkes (1951) pp. 191f.

66 Ross (1967) pp. 303f.; Green (1986) pp. 177, 190f.

67 Gelling and Davidson (1969) pp. 163–4.

68 *Book of Leinster*, ed. Windische, *Ir Texte* (series 3) I, 243–7.

69 *Danmarks Folkesagn*, ed. J. Thiele (1843) II, 257. I am grateful to Jacqueline Simpson for this reference.

70 Copley (1958) p. 162; for Harrow, M. Gelling (1961) p. 9.

71 Owen (1981) p. 45; Green (1986) p. 178.

72 Piggott (1962) pp. 110f.; Hammarstadt (1919) pp. 114f.

73 Jóhannesson (1974) p. 56.

74 Ross (1967) p. 322f.

75 Woolmer (1967) pp. 90f.

76 Fox (1946) p. 97.

77 *Topography of Ireland* (first version), trans. J. J. O'Meara, Dundalk 1951, pp. 93f.; cf. Keating, *History of Ireland* (*Ir Texts Soc* I, 1901) p. 23.

78 *Rgveda* (trans. R. T. H. Griffiths 1963) II, no. 162.

79 Hagberg (1967) II, pp. 79f.

80 *Hákonarmál* 18: 'It was made known that the king had dealt reverently with the holy places' (*vel um þrymt véum*).

81 Owen (1981) p. 47.

82 Green (1986) pp. 192f.

83 Cunliffe (1979) p. 77.

84 Green (1986) pp. 171, 175–6; for Nehalennia, Höndius-Crone (1955); Kooijmans (1971).

85 Green (1986) pp. 159f.

86 Struve (1967) pp. 58f.

87 Roesdahl (1982) pp. 165, 243 (note 39); Davidson (1967) pp. 114f.

88 McCone (1987) pp. 101f.

89 Davidson (1976) pp. 301f.

90 'The Tragic Death of Cú Rói mac Dairi', ed. Best, *Ériu* 2 (1905) pp. 20f.; Cross and Slover (1936) p. 329.

91 Hallowell (1926) pp. 101, 104; A. V. Ström (1966) p. 336.

92 Another reference is in a poem by Hallfred: Strömbäck (1975) pp. 74, 78.

93 *Merseburg Epis Chron* (ed. Holzmann 1935) p. 000.

94 Tierney (1960) p. 251; from Diodorus Siculus V, 31.

95 Aylett Sammes' engraving in *Britannia Antiqua Illustrata* (1676) has appeared in many books on druids.

96 Castleton (1983) pp. 77f.

97 *Folklore* 12 (1901) pp. 315f. I am grateful to Hilary Belcher for this reference.

98 Frazer (1913) pp. 38f.

99 *Heimskringla, Óláfs Saga Tryggvasonar* 67.

100 Ström, F. (1942) p. 144. Difficulties in the classification of sacrifice are indicated by Beck (1970) pp. 240f.

101 Amira (1922).

102 Struve (1967) pp. 47f.

103 Anderson (1951) pp. 9f.

104 Ørsnes (1970) pp. 178f.

105 Fox (1946) pp. 69f.

106 *Letters* (trans. O. Dalton, Oxford 1915) VIII, 6, p. 149.

107 Smyser (1965) pp. 98f.

108 Bersu and Wilson (1966) pp. 6, 47, 91; Davidson (1976) p. 307; a possible example from Ireland, Hall (1978) p. 74; for a literary reference, *Landnámabók* (Reykjavik 1968) S 72, H 60, pp. 102f.

109 O'Duigtennáin (1940) pp. 297f.

110 'Death of Muircertach mac Erca' (ed. W. Stokes, *Rev Celt* 23 (1902) pp. 395ff.; Cross and Slover (1936) pp. 518f.

111 Ward puts forward arguments for this which I do not find convincing (Ward 1970, pp. 124f.).

112 Radner (1983) pp. 180f. I am grateful to Jacqueline Simpson for this reference.

113 Davidson (1980) pp. 160f. Claims that this was an established custom in the Viking Age do not seem justified by the literary evidence.

114 Saxo, *Danish History* VI and the longer *Gautreks Saga*; cf. Davidson (1980) II, p. 100, notes 37f.

III The rites of battle

1 Tierney (1960) p. 250 (from Diodorus Siculus V, 29).

2 Tierney translates 'paean' but I have substituted Reinach's suggestion (1913, p. 39): 'triumphal march'.

3 Reinach (1913) p. 56.

4 Strabo, *Geography* 4. On the Roman reaction to such practices, see Last (1949).

5 Lambrechts (1954) pp. 42f.; Benoit (1975) pp. 245f.

6 Tierney (1960) p. 250 (from Diodorus Siculus V, 29).

7 Sprockhoff (1955) pp. 270f.

8 Megaw (1970) pp. 77–8, pl. 75.

9 Lambrechts (1954) pp. 17f.

10 *Ibid.* pp. 83f. for examples from France; cf. heads from Denmark and Ireland, Megaw (1970) p. 167, pl. 288.

11 *Ibid.* p. 165, pl. 283; p. 145, pl. 243.

12 *Fled Bricrend* (Bricriu's Feast), ed. G. Henderson, Dublin 1899, pp. 25, 107; Gantz (1981) p. 248.

13 *Táin, Book of Leinster* (ed. C. O'Rahilly, 1984) pp. 153f.

14 *Ibid.* p. 266.

15 *Táin*, Recension 1 (ed. C. O'Rahilly, 1976) p. 188.

16 Hencken (1935) pp. 21f.

17 *Táin, Book of Leinster* (ed. C. O'Rahilly, 1984) pp. 246f.

18 *Cath Almaine*, ed. W. Stokes, *Rev Celt* 24 (1903) pp. 44f.

19 *The Cherishing of Conall Cernach*, ed. K. Meyer, *Zeit Celt Phil* I (1897) p. 109.

20 Ross (1967) pp. 108f.

21 Phillips (1965) p. 104.

22 Reinach (1913) p. 44.

23 Davidson (1976) p. 114.

24 Heimskringla, *Óláfs Saga Tryggvasonar* 41.

25 *Laxdœla Saga* 67; *Brennu-Njáls Saga* 158.

26 *Eyrbyggja Saga* 27.

27 *Sturlunga Saga* (trans. J. H. McGrew, 1970) I, 134, p. 327.

28 Nordal (1978) p. 91.

29 Simpson (1962), pp. 43f.

30 Jón Árnason, *Íslenzkar Þjoðsögur og Aevintýri* I (1862) p. 523.

31 Vierck (1967) pp. 104f.; Davidson and Webster (1967) p. 25f.

32 Davidson (1962) pp. 196f.

33 Gessler (1908) pp. 144f.

34 Davidson (1976) pp. 113f.

35 Davidson (1978a) p. 133.

36 *Vǫlsunga Saga* 8; for possible memories of initiation rites, Danielli (1945).

37 McCone (1987) p. 101f.

38 As in *Jómsvikínga Saga* 16, *Hálfs Saga ok Hálfsrekka* 10, *Orvar-Odds Saga* 9.

39 Saxo, *Danish History*, books VI. VII and VIII; longer version of *Gautreks Saga*; *Hervarar Saga*.

40 Silva Gadelica (1892) trans. S. H. O'Grady, II, p. 100.

41 McCone (1985) pp. 13f.; (1987) p. 105

42 *Feis Tighe Chonáin* (ed. M. Joynt, *Med Mod Ir Ser* 7); Nagy (1985) p. 244.

43 McCone (1987) p. 109

44 Sharpe (1979) pp. 86f.

45 Sjoestedt (1982) p. 106.

46 McCone (1987) p. 113

47 *Fled Bricrend* (Bricriu's Feast), ed. G. Henderson, Dublin 1899, p. 37.

48 *Táin*, Recension 1 (ed. C. O'Rahilly 1976) p. 173.

49 Saxo, *Danish History* VI, 196; *Táin, Book of Leinster* (ed. C. O'Rahilly 1967) p. 179.

50 *Mesca Ulad* (Intoxication of the Ulaid) ed. J. C. Watson, 1941, trans. Gantz (1981) p. 203.

51 *Táin, Book of Leinster* (ed. C. O'Rahilly 1967) p. 201; cf. Recension 1 (1976) pp. 182–3.

52 *Táin*, Recension 1 (ed. C. O'Rahilly 1976) p. 187.

53 *Táin, Book of Leinster* (1967) p. 228.

54 *Táin*, Recension 1 (ed. C. O'Rahilly 1976) p. 148.

55 Head from Msecke Zehrovice, Megaw (1970) p. 113, pl. 171.

56 Sandars (1968) p. 243.

57 Sjoestedt (1982) instances the head of Ogmios on coins from Armorica (p. 79).

58 Ellis (1941) pp. 70f.

59 *Reginsmál* in the *Poetic Edda*, where Odin appears as Hnikar.

60 Davidson (1962) pp. 171f.; (1960) pp. 11f.

61 *Táin, Book of Leinster* (ed. C. O'Rahilly 1967) pp. 228–9.

62 In both cases the youth puts his thumb into his mouth after burning it, and in this way obtains wisdom from the special food. The subject is a complex one, and I hope to discuss it in detail in a forthcoming paper, 'The Seer's Thumb'. The tale of Taliesin has some features in common with these episodes: Scott (1930) and Wood (1982).

63 T. F. O'Rahilly (1976) pp. 322, 326f.; Nagy (1985) pp. 19f.

64 'The Cattle-Raid of Regamna', ed. E. Windisch, *Ir Texte*, ser. 2, II, 1887; trans. Cross and Slover (1936) p. 213.

65 'The Great Route of Muirthemne', trans. W. Stokes, *Rev Celt* 3 (1876–8) p. 182. Cross and Slover (1936) p. 338.

66 Best (1916) pp. 120f.

67 Ellis (1942) pp. 216f.; Bailey (1980) pp. 116f.

68 Wasson (1974) pp. 176f.

69 Davidson (1983) p. 26f.

70 Hawkes and Davidson (1965) pp. 17f.

71 Paulsen (1967) pp. 142f.

72 On a helmet plate from Valsgärde, Sweden: Davidson (1972) pp. 13f.

73 Hauck (1954b) p. 46f.

74 Ross (1967) pp. 156f.; pl. 49. 50.

75 Tierney (1960) p. 197.

76 *Táin, Book of Leinster* (ed. C. O'Rahilly 1967) p. 264.

77 Nagy (1985) p. 279, note 24.

78 Löffler (1983) pp. 114f. I am grateful to David Dumville for this reference.

79 'The Fate of the Children of Tuirenn' (ed. O'Curry, *Gaelic Journ* 2, 1884); trans. Cross and Slover (1936) p. 51.

80 Davidson (1965b) p. 24. In this case the two birds are different in form and seem to be a raven and an eagle.

81 Leeds and Harden (1936) pp. 59f.

82 Ross (1967) p. 250.

83 Gelling, M. (1961) pp. 10f.

84 MacCana (1955) pp. 76f.

85 Hauck (1970) pp. 402f.

86 T. Wright, *Anglo-Saxon and Old English Vocabularies* (2nd edition, ed. R. P. Wülcker, 2 vols, 1884) I, 360, 3; 417, 12; 527, 17; 533, 26; cf. 347, 32; 189, 11; O. Cockayne, *Narratiunculae Anglice conscriptae* (1861) p. 34, 6.

87 Sweet's *Anglo-Saxon Reader* (revised D. Whitelock, 1967) pp. 100–1.

88 *Althochdeutsches Lesebuch*, ed. W. Braune and E. A. Ebbinghaus (Tübingen 1962) xxxi.

89 Chadwick, N. K. (1949) pp. 201f.

90 *Heimskringla, Haralds Saga Sigurðarsonar* 80, 81.

91 Strömbäck (1975) pp. 78f.

92 *Sturlunga Saga*, trans. J. H. McGrew, *Amer Scand Found* (New York, 1970) I, 4, p. 142.

93 Davidson (1969) p. 220; (1980) pp. 29f.

94 Sweet's *Anglo-Saxon Reader* (revised D. Whitelock, 1967) p. 100.

95 Sternberg (1925) pp. 487f.; Davidson (1976) p. 296f.

96 Golther (1890) pp. 417f.; Nordal (1978) 30, p. 63.

97 *Journ Rom Stud* 11 (1921) p. 236; Bosanquet (1922) pp. 185f.

98 *Táin*, Recension 1 (ed. C. O'Rahilly, 1976) pp. 177f.

99 *Ibid.* p. 245, note 210.

100 'The tragic death of Cú Rói mac Dairi', *Yellow Book of Lecan*, ed. Best, *Ériu* 2 (1905) pp. 20f.; Cross and Slover (1936) p. 329.

101 *Táin*, Recension 1 (ed. C. O'Rahilly, 1976) pp. 229–30.

102 Ross (1967) p. 248.

103 Turville-Petre (1964) p. 258.

104 Ross (1967) p. 248.

105 *Ibid.* p. 214.

106 Chadwick, N. K. (1953) pp. 16f.

107 'Destruction of Da Choca's Hostel', ed. Stokes, *Rev Celt* 21 (1900) p. 315; 'Destruction of Da Derga's Hostel' ed. Stokes, *Rev Celt* 22 (1901–2) pp. 13f., 165f., 282f., 390f.; Cross and Slover (1936) p. 107.

108 'Destruction of Da Choca's Hostel' (see above) p. 157.

109 Lysaght (1986) pp. 198f.

110 'The Wooding of Emer', ed. Meyer, 1893; Cross and Slover (1936) pp. 163f.

111 MacCana (1955) pp. 76f.; (1970) p. 94.

112 Lysaght (1986) pp. 205f.

IV Land-spirits and ancestors

1 *Landnámabók* (1968) S 399, H 356, p. 396.

2 *Ibid.* S 329, p. 330 (cf. H 284).

3 Ellis (1941) pp. 75f.

4 *Landnámabók* (1968) S 355, H 313, p. 358.

5 *Ibid.* S 237, H 202, pp. 270–1.

6 *Kristnis Saga* 2, *Þáttr Þorvalds ens viðfǫrla* 2.

7 *Landnámabók* (1968) S 330, p. 333.

8 *Ibid.* H. 268, p. 313.

9 Turville-Petre (1963) pp. 196f.

10 Almqvist (1965) pp. 196f.

11 A company of Æsir and Vanir is referred to three times in *Lokasenna* as 'Æsir and Elves'; cf. *Þrymskviða* 6 and *Vǫluspá* 48, where the formula 'How is it with the Æsir? How is it with the Elves?' occurs.

12 Official sacrifice to the *dísir* at Uppsala may have been held in the royal hall: Turville-Petre (1964) pp. 225f.

13 For the use of the term *hamingja*, Davidson (1978a) p. 126.

14 *Flateyjarbók* (1860–8) I, 418–21; *Fornmanna Sogur* (1825–37) II, 192–7.
15 *Heimskringla, Óláfs Saga Tryggvasonar* 33; cf. Almqvist (1965) pp. 119f.; Jóhannesson (1974) pp. 224f.
16 Turville-Petre (1964) p. 233, quoting Matthías Þorðarson (1914).
17 *Danmarks Folkesagn* (1843) II, p. 194, recorded J. M. Theile; *Danske Folkesagn* (1958) pp. 118–9, recorded L. Bødker; I owe these references to Jacqueline Simpson.
18 Toynbee (1957) pp. 456f.
19 Deonna (1955) pp. 7f.
20 *Antiq Journ* 57 (1977) p. 63, pl. xiv.
21 Wightmann (1970) p. 226.
22 Thevenot (1968) p. 174.
23. *Ibid.* pp. 191f.
24 Allason-Jones and McKay (1985) give a detailed account of the finds based on the excavation records. These throw doubt on some statements repeatedly made about the shrine; for instance only two pins were recorded, and the figure of a dog is not mentioned.
25 Smith (1962) pp. 59f.
26 Green (1984) p. 25.
27 De Vries (1957) II, pp. 290f.
28 Motz (1984) p. 151f.
29 Henderson (1866) p. 221. Briggs (1969) compares this with 'The Three Spinners' in Grimm's collection, and 'The Idle Girl with Three Aunts' in Yeats' collection of Irish tales.
30 Hope (1970) pp. 28f.
31 *Ibid.* pp. 37f.
32 Fitzgerald (1879–80) pp. 189f. For a list of such supernatural beings, Löffler (1983) pp. 82f.
33 MacCana (1970) p. 94.
34 *Ibid.* p. 65.
35 *Voyage of Bran, Son of Febal*, ed. K. Meyer (1895) I, pp. 5f.; verses 10, 18.
36 *Ibid.* I, 2–41.
37 'The Adventures of Connla the Fair', ed. Pokorny, *Zeit Celt Phil* 17 (1927) p. 195; trans. Cross and Slover (1936) pp. 488f.
38 *Serglige Con Culaind* ('The wasting Sickness of Cú Chulainn'), ed. M. Dillon, 1953; trans. Gantz (1981) pp. 157f.
39 Delargy (1940) pp. 522f. The early part of this tale remained popular up to recent times, and thirty-nine variants were collected from Irish speakers by the Irish Folklore Commission.
40 Jackson (1942) pp. 380f.
41 Marwick (1975) p. 41. I owe this reference to Jacqueline Simpson.
42 Simpson (1972) pp. 64f.
43 Brøndsted (1966) III, pp. 68f.
44 Brøgger (1945) pp. 1f.
45 *Gesta abbatum Trudonsensium*, quoted O. Almgren (1927) p. 60.
46 Blindheim, C. (1960) pp. 91f.

47 Davidson (1964) p. 107.

48 Holtsmark (1933) pp. 111f.

49 De Vries (1957) II, pp. 188f., 195. *Freysakr*, Field of Freyr, is found in both Norway and Sweden.

50 Ekwall, *Conc Oxf. Dict Engl Place-names* (4th ed. 1960) p. xxx; see also M. Gelling *et alia*, *Anglo-Saxon England* 13 (1984) pp. 150–51.

51 Page (1973) pp. 72, 83–4.

52 De Vries (1957) II, p. 165.

53 Grieg (1954); Holmqvist (1960) p. 101f.

54 Thevenot (1968) pp. 99f.

55 Meissner (1921) p. 227.

56 *Flateyjarbók* (1860–8), II, pp. 6f.

57 *Fornmanna Sögur* (1825–37) III, *Saga Skálda Haralds* 2, p. 69; *Heimskringla, Óláfs Saga helga* 69.

58 Ellis (1943) pp. 142f.

59 *Ossianic Soc Trans* (1955) 2, p. 135.

60 *Togail Bruidne Dá Derga* (Destruction of Dá Derga's Hostel) ed. W. Stokes *Rev Celt* 22 (1901–2) pp. 13f.

61 *Tochmarc Étáine* (Wooing of Étáin) ed. O. Berg and R. D. Best, *Ériu* 12 (1937) pp. 137–96; trans. Gantz (1981) pp. 37f.

62 Nutt (1897) II, pp. 76f.; 285f.

63 Trans. P. Ford, *Mabinogi and other Medieval Welsh Tales* (Univ. of California 1977).

64 For the two versions, Thurneysen (1921) pp. 268f.; 271f.

65 Nutt (1897) II, p. 6; N. K. Chadwick (1958) pp. 82f.; 109f.

66 *Ir Texte* (series 3, 1897) 2, pp. 392f.; Nutt (1897) II, 72f.

67 Gruffydd (1928) p. 126; cf. Wood (1982) p. 621.

68 Chadwick, N. K. (1966) p. 11f.; Piggott (1968) pp. 120f.

69 Tierney (1960) p. 250: from Diodorus Siculus, V, 28.

70 E. g. Piggott (1968) pp. 88, 122. For a different approach, Löffler (1983) pp. 112f.

71 Benoit (1975) pp. 244f.

72 Bruce-Mitford (1975–83) II, p. 312.

73 Davidson (1964) pp. 78f.; Simpson (1979) pp. 97f.

74 Enright (1983) pp. 119f. For other whetstones with heads carved on them, Evison (1975) pp. 79f.

75 Hauck (1954b) pp. 9f.

76 Bruce-Mitford (1975–83) II, p. 359.

77 *Three fragments of Irish Annals* (trans. O'Donavan, Dublin 1960) p. 40.

78 *Flateyjarbók* (1860–8) I, 174, p. 214.

79 Ellis (1943) pp. 107f.

80 'Death of Muircertach mac Erca, ed. W. Stokes, *Rev Celt* 23 (1902) pp. 395f. Cross and Slover (1936) p. 518.

81 'The Adventures of Art', ed. R. D. Best, *Ériu* 3 (1907) pp. 150f.; Cross and Slover (1936) p. 493.

82 Meissner (1921) pp. 234f.

83 Arbmann (1945) pp. 86f. The deposit at Käringsjon is dated to the fourth century.
84 Hagberg (1967) II, p. 67, quoting from *Liber in gloria confess, Mon Germ Scrip* I, 1, p. 749.
85 Geisslinger (1967) p. 87f.
86 Hagberg (1967) II, p. 69.
87 Arbmann (1945) p. 15 (note).

V Foreknowledge and destiny

1 *Landnámabók* (1968) S 218, H 184, pp. 250f.
2 *Ibid.* S 5, H 37, pp. 36f. It has been suggested that releasing birds from a ship was a practical aid to navigation (Lange, 1968, pp. 354f.). However the choice of ravens, to which in one version Floki is said to have made sacrifices, suggests that he was thought to have appealed to Odin for guidance.
3 *Landnámabók* (1968) S 289, H 250, pp. 302f.
4 Turville-Petre (1964) pp. 166f.
5 *Landnámabók* (1968) S 355, H 313, p. 358.
6 Holtsmark (1933) pp. 111f.
7 *Atlamál in Grœnlenzko* 25. There are two different readings, 'ill-arrayed' and 'not ill-arrayed'. Gering in his edition of the *Edda* preferred the first, suggesting that they wore dark clothing like the women who killed Thidrandi, which seems reasonable.
8 Dronke (1969) p. 112.
9 Turville-Petre (1966) pp. 348f.
10 *Sturlunga Saga* (trans. J. H. MacGrew, 1970), *Íslendinga Saga* I, 65, p. 218; 122, p. 307; 130, p. 322; 131, p. 323; 134, p. 326f.; *Hrafns Saga Sveinbjarnarsonar* II, 12, p. 213f.
11 Turville-Petre (1976) p. 90.
12 Foote (1963) pp. 119f.
13 Turville-Petre (1966) pp. 346f.
14 *Heimskringla, Hálfdanar Saga svarta* 7.
15 Chadwick, N. K. (1968) p. 41.
16 *Silva Gadelica* (1892) II, pp. 79f.
17 *Rev Celt* 15 (1894) pp. 430–1; Meyer and Nutt (1895) I, p. 216.
18 'Death of Muircertach mac Erca', *Rev Celt* 23 (1902) pp. 395f.; Cross and Slover (1937) p. 529f.
19 N. K. Chadwick (1949) pp. 203f.
20 He calls up the seeress from her grave in the Underworld, but this is afterwards declared to be an illusion, so that the position is complicated: Davidson (1964) pp. 185f.
21 *Aislinge Óengusso* (Dream of Óengus), *Rev. Celt* 3 (1882) pp. 344f.; trans. Gantz (1981) pp. 108f.
22 Talbot (1982) p. 43.
23 Keating, *History of Ireland* (1905) II, 45, pp. 349f.
24 Martin, M. (1703) p. 173.
25 Simpson (1972) pp. 176f.

26 *Táin, Book of Leinster* (ed. C. O'Rahilly, 1967) pp. 143f.

27 *Táin* (ed. J. Strachan and J. G. O'Keefe, 1912) p. 4.

28 *Sanas Cormaic, An Old-Irish Glossary: Anecdota from Irish Manuscripts* 4 (ed. O. Bergin *et al.*, Halle 1912) paragraph 756.

29 See N. K. Chadwick (1935b) pp. 98f.; T. F. O'Rahilly (1976) pp. 336f.; Nagy (1985) pp. 25f.

30 Ed. L. Stern, *Rev Celt* 13 (1892) p. 12f.

31 N. K. Chadwick (1935b) pp. 128f.

32 'Finn and the Man in the Tree', ed. K. Meyer, *Rev Celt* 25 (1904) pp. 344f.

33 *Fiarnaigecht*, trans. Meyer, RIA Todd Lecture Series 16, Dublin 1910, pp. 29f.

34 Chadwick, N. K. (1935b) p. 110; Nagy (1985) pp. 26f.

35 *Three Irish Glossaries*, ed. W. Stokes (1862) p. xlvi.

36 *Ibid.*, xlviii; O'Curry (1873) II, pp. 209f.

37 *Silva Gadelica* (trans. O'Grady, 1892) II, p. 98; Nagy (1985) pp. 21f. for other examples.

38 Bailey (1980) p. 116f.; for the Irish example from Drumhallagh, Harbison (1986) p. 63; Henry (1965) pp. 109f.

39 N. K. Chadwick (1935b) p. 129.

40 Le Roux (1968) I, pp. 245f.; *Egils Saga* for the testing of a drink by runes to see if it contained poison.

41 *Yellow Book of Lecan* ed. E. Knott, *Ériu* 8 (1916) pp. 156f.; trans. Flower (1947) pp. 2f.

42 *Færeyinga Saga* 40; Foote (1984) pp. 209f.

43 Oddr Snorrason, *Saga Olafs Tryggvasonar af Oddr Snorrason*, ed. F. Jonsson, Copenhagen, 1932).

44 Davidson (1981a) pp. 122f.; Vyncke (1968) pp. 312f.

45 Almgren, B. (1962) pp. 63f.

46 Ed. M. Sjoestedt, *Rev Celt* 43 (1926) pp. 1f.

47 *Silva Gadelica* (trans. O'Grady, 1892) II, p. 161.

48 Davidson (1981b) pp. 157f.

49 Schove (1950) pp. 35f.

50 *The Tripartite Life of Patrick*, ed. W. Stokes, (1887) I, pp. 40f.

51 O'Curry (1873) II, p. 220.

52 Smyser (1965) p. 101.

53 *Colloquy of the Two Sages*, ed. W. Stokes, *Rev Celt* 26 (1905) p. 8.

54 Eliott (1963) pp. 45f.

55 *Vita Anskarii* (trans. C. H. Robinson, 1921) pp. 97f.; 65f.

56 Le Roux (1968) p. 246.

57 *Ir Texte* (series 3, 1891) 23, pp. 192, 209.

58 Chadwick, N. K. (1966) pp. 55f.; Piggott (1968) pp. 120f.

59 Other writers using Posidonius are Athenæus, Strabo and Diodorus Siculus (Tierney, 1960, pp. 201f.).

60 Piggott (1968), pp. 105f.; N. K. Chadwick (1966) p. 12f.; Le Roux (1967) pp. 303f.

61 *Germania* 11, 10, 40.

62 Two inscriptions from Fyn, Denmark: Wimmer, *De dansle Runemindesmærker* (1893–1908) II, pp. 346, 352, 369; Jóhannesson (1974) pp. 53f.; Roesdahl (1982) pp. 26, 163.

63 Jón Aðalsteinsson (1978) p. 103 gives other references to men in the sagas said to cover their heads when they want to obtain hidden knowledge.

64 Paulys, *Reallencycl class Alter*, under *Veleda* (ser 2, VIII, pp. 618f.)

65 Cassio Dio, *History of Rome* 67, 5.

66 Suetonius, *Vita Vitelli*, 14, 5.

67 Strömbäck (1935)pp. 124f.

68 Davidson (1976) pp. 283f.

69 Strömbäck (1935) p. 124f.

70 P. A. Munch, *Symbol hist rerum norweg* (Kristiana, 1850) pp. 4f.

71 Boyer (1983) p. 119.

72 Nordal (1978) takes *rǫk* as 'fate'.

73 Four times in Nordal's edition.

74 Nordal (1978) p. 23.

75 Holtsmark (1951) pp. 81f.; cf. Nordal (1978) p. 40.

76 Opening stanzas of *Helgakviða Huntingsbana* I.

77 'The Adventures of Art' (ed. R. Best, *Ériu* 3, 1916) p. 107; trans. Cross and Glover (1936) p. 493.

78 *Lebor Gabála Érenn* (ed. Macalister 1938–56) IV, p. 128.

79 For instance the board of the giant Dofri, *Kjalnesinga Saga* 12, 13.

80 Van Hamel (1934) pp. 218f.

81 Neumann (1955) p. 24.

VI The Other World

1 Davidson (1979) p. 8; cf. Buck (1959) pp. 55f., 83f. for examples of myths as popular drama in Polynesia.

2 *Ibid.* pp. 169–70.

3 *Gotl Ark* 34 (1962) pp. 4f.

4 Davidson (1975) p. 175.

5 Sprockhoff (1954) pp. 28f.

6 Davidson (1967) pp. 44f., 113f.

7 MacCulloch (1930) pl. xl: painting of a sacred birch-tree on a mound near a farm at Slinde, Sogn in Norway.

8 Sauvé (1970) p. 188; compares the self-sacrifice of Odin to that of the god Prajapati in Indic tradition, who thus was identified with the sacrificial horse, and suggests that the meaning of Yggdrasil is therefore 'Ygg, Horse'. This however would mean that the name belonged to Odin rather than the tree, and it is used many times of the World Tree in the poetry without reference to the god.

9 Dr Vries (1935) pp. 77f.; (1957) II, p. 379.

10 Siikala (1978) pp. 143f., 274f.; Chadwick and Zhirmunsky (1969) pp. 176f.

11 Davidson (1982) p. 126.

12 *Prose Edda, Gylfaginning* 48.

13 *Ibid.* 44.
14 De Vries (1930) pp. 41f.; (1957) II, p. 360.
15 *Ibid.* II, p. 363.
16 Vierck (1967) pp. 104f.
17 Lang (1972) pp. 236f.
18 Bailey (1980) pp. 138f.
19 Holtsmark (1949) pp. 64f.
20 Stone from Lärbro Stora Hammars (3) in Gotland, Lindqvist (1941) I, taf. 30, fig. 85; (1942) II, pp. 83f.
21 Müller-Lisowski (1948) pp. 142f.
22 *Lebor Gabála Érenn* (ed. Macalister, 1938–56) V, 88: 'The Sons of Míl'.
23 Mould (1955) p. 113; Rees (1961) p. 98.
24 *Lebor Gabála Érenn* (ed. Macalister 1956) V, p. 111.
25 MacCulloch (1918) 3 p. 43; N. K. Chadwick (1935a) pp. 10f.
26 *Cath Maige Turedh* (Battle of Mag Tuired) ed. W. Stokes, *Rev Celt* 12 (1891) pp. 69, 95f., 107.
27 Gray (1980), pp. 190f.
28 *Ibid.* pp. 196f.
29 T. F. O'Rahilly (1976) p. 313f.
30 Sjoestedt (1982) p. 17.
31 MacCana (1970) pp. 60f. For difficulties, Gray (1980) pp. 199f.
32 'The First Battle of Moytura', ed. J. Fraser, *Ériu* 8 (1916) pp. 57f.
33 MacCana (1970) pp. 60f.
34 Löffler (1983) pp. 83f.
35 'The Prose Tales in the Rennes Dindsenchas', ed. W. Stokes, *Rev Celt* 15 (1894) p. 420; 16 (1895) pp. 278–9.
36 Watson (1981) pp. 167f.
37 'The Settling of the Manor of Tara', ed. R. I. Best, *Ériu* 4 (1910) p. 135.
38 Watson (1981) p. 171f.
39 Lucas (1963) p. 42.
40 Fitzgerald (1879–80) pp. 185f.
41 Dumville (1976) pp. 86f.
42 *Rennes Dindsenchas*, ed. W. Stokes, *Rev Celt* 15 (1894) p. 430.
43 *Serglige Con Culaind* (The Wasting Sickness of Cú Chulainn) ed. M. Dillon (1973); trans. Gantz (1981) p. 168.
44 'Cormac's Adventures in the Land of Promise', (ed. W. Stokes, *Ir Texte*, ser. 3, 1891), Cross and Slover (1936), p. 503.
45 Meyer (1895) I, p. 4.
46 'The Adventures of Connla the Fair', (ed. Pokorny, *Zeit Celt Phil* 17 (1927) pp. 195f.; Cross and Slover (1936) p. 489.
47 Davidson (1960) p. 3f.
48 *Silva Gadelica*, 'Colloquy with the Ancients' II, p. 243; Hull (1901) p. 437.
49 Dumville (1976) pp. 79f.
50 *Ibid.* p. 75. A detailed account of these tales is given by Löffler (1983) pp. 121f.
51 Dumville (1986) p. 84f. For the poem, Meyer I (1895).

52 Byrne, M. E. (1930) pp. 100f.

53 Rees (1961) p. 325.

54 MacCana (1976) p. 95.

55 MacCana (1970) pp. 128–9.

56 Donn's house is described as a Tower of Glass (T. F. O'Rahilly (1976) p. 493); cf. the kingdom of Glasisvellir in Norse sources.

57 Davidson and Fisher (1979) I, pp. 12f.

58 Talbot (1982) p. 38f.

59 Ellis (1943) pp. 178f.

60 Twelve sons are also mentioned but play no part in the tale and are probably an addition by Saxo.

61 Adam of Bremen, *Hist Archb Hamburg Bremen* (trans. F. J. Tschan, 1955) IV, 40, pp. 220f.

62 Rydberg (1889), p. 385f.

63 Carey (1982) pp. 37f.

64 For the association between serpents and graves, Nordland (1949) pp. 94f.

65 Simpson (1966) pp. 8f.

66 Tierney (1960) p. 196.

67 *Táin*, Recension 1 (ed. C. O'Rahilly 1976) p. 234; cf. *Táin, Book of Leinster* (ed. C. O'Rahilly 1967) p. 247.

68 *Ibid.* p. 247.

69 *Norsk-Isl Skjald* A 87; Turville-Petre (1976) p. 49.

70 *Ibid.* A 348; Turville-Petre (1976) p. 96.

71 Davidson (1982) pp. 121f.; Bailey (1980) pp. 127f.

72 Olriks's work was published in two parts: *Aarb nord Oldkynd* 1902, and *Dan Stud* 1913; also as a complete work in German, *Ragnarok, die Sagen vom Weltuntergang* (Leipzig 1922).

73 Davidson (1964) pp. 208f.

74 *Medieval English Lyrics*, ed. R. T. Davies (London 1963) p. 54. This comparison was pointed out to me by Gale Owen Crocker.

75 Krogmann (1953). Snorri makes Muspell the kingdom of fire from which Surt comes to burn the world.

76 *Vígríðr* (Field of Battle), *Vafþruðismál* 18; the island *Óskópnir* (unformed?) in *Fáfnismál* 15.

77 Davidson (1976) pp. 313f.

78 'Second Battle of Moytura', ed. W. Stokes, *Rev Celt* 12 (1891) p. 111.

79 On the theme of Doomsday in art, Selma Jónsdóttir (1959) p. 83.

VII The ruling powers

1 T. F. O'Rahilly, (1976) pp. 66f.

2 Hastrup (1985) p. 44.

3 Ogilvie (1969) pp. 10f.

4 Sjoestedt (1982) p. 2.

5 Dumézil (1958); for a summary of his theories, Scott Littleton in his introduction to *Gods of the Ancient Norsemen*, ed. E. Haugen, 1973.

6 A suggestion made to me by Jacqueline Simpson.

7 *Prose Edda, Gylfaginning* 48.

8 Hougen (1940); Krafft (1956).

9 De Vries (1957) II, pp. 1f.

10 Paulsen (1967) pp. 118f.

11 *Coir Anmann, Ir Texte* ser. 3 (i) (1891) p. 357.

12 Second Battle of Moytura, ed. W. Stokes, *Rev Celt* 12 (1891) pp. 85f.

13 Lambrechts (1942) pp. 77, 91.

14 *Táin bó Regamna* (The Cattle Raid of Regamna) ed. W. Stokes and E. Windisch, *Ir Texte*, ser. 2 (ii) (1887); Cross and Slover (1936) pp. 211f.

15 Davidson (1964) pp. 57f.; De Vries (1957) II, pp. 10f.

16 *Togail Bruidne Dá Derga* (Destruction of Dá Derga's Hostel) ed. W. Stokes, *Rev Celt* 22 (1901), 23 (1902); trans. Cross and Slover (1936) pp. 114–15.

17 Ed. K. Meyer, *Rev Celt* 25 (1904) pp. 347f.; cf. Nagy (1985) pp. 136f.

18 *Aided Conrói Maic Dáiri* (Tragic Death of Cú Rói Mac Dairi), ed. R. I. Best, *Éiru* 2 (1905); trans. Cross and Slover (1936) p. 329. For additional references to Cú Rói, Baudis (1914), p. 201.

19 'Manawydan Son of Llyr' and in a list of characters invoked by the hero in 'Culhwych and Olwen'.

20 *Three Irish Glossaries*, trans. W. Stokes (1862) p. 31.

21 *Lokasenna* and *Hymskviða* in the *Poetic Edda*.

22 Haugen (1983) assumes this to be Odin, following some earlier scholars, but gives no evidence for this. (pp. 12–13).

23 Dumézil (1959).

24 Dumézil (1973) pp. 136f.

25 Davidson (1964) pp. 182f.

26 R. Thurneysen, *Old Irish Reader* (1981) p. 39, iii.

27 Radin (1956); cf. Davidson (1979) pp. 3f.

28 Dumézil (1973) pp. 64–5.

29 *Fled Bricrend* (Bricriu's Feast), ed. G. Henderson (*Ir Texte Soc* 1899), trans. Gantz (1981) p. 222.

Conclusion

1 Flower (1947) p. 147.

2 Eliade (1958) p. 5.

3 Davidson (1978c) pp. 33f.

4 Bede, *Eccl Hist* II, 13.

5 W. D. O'Flaherty, *Hindu Myths* (Harmondsworth 1975) p. 12.

6 Dumézil, p. viii of preface to *From Myth to Fiction* (trans. D. Coltman, Univ of Chicago (1973).

7 Green (1986) pp. 200f.

Bibliography

Allason-Jones, L. and McKay, B. (1985) *Coventina's Well*, Chesters Museum.

Almgren, B. (1962) 'Den Osynliga Godomen', *Proxima Thule (Sven Arkeol Samf)*, Stockholm, pp. 53–71.

Almgren, O. (1934) *Nordische Felzeichnungen als religiöse Urkunden* (trans. S. Vrancken), Frankfort.

Almqvist, B. (1965) *Norrön Niddiktning* I (*Nord texter och Undersökningar* 21), Uppsala.

Amira, K. von (1922) *Die germanischen Todesstrafen* (*Abhand bayer Akad Wiss: phil/hist Kl* 31, 3), Munich.

Andersen, A. (1951) 'Det femte store Mosefund', *Kuml* I, pp. 9–22.

Arbman, H. (1945) *Käringsjön: Studier i halländsk järnålder (Kungl Vitt Hist Antik Akad*, 59), Stockholm.

Aðalsteinsson, Jón (1978) *Under the Cloak (Stud Ethnol Upsal* 4), Uppsala.

Bailey, R. N. (1980) *Viking Age Sculpture in Northern England*, London.

Baudis, J. (1914) 'Cúrói and Cúchulinn', *Ériu* 7, pp. 200–9.

Beck, H. (1970) 'Germanische Menschenopfer in der literarischen Überlieferung', *Vorgeschichtliche Heiligtümer und Opferplätze in Mittel-und Nordeuropa*, ed. H. Jankuhn (*Abhand Akad Wiss Göttingen*, 74), pp. 240–58.

Benoit, F. (1955) *L'Art primitif méditerranéen de la vallée du Rhône (Annal Fac Lett*, new ser. 9), Aix-en-Province.

—(1970) 'Le symbolisme dans les sanctuaires de la Gaule', *Coll Latomus* 105, Brussels.

—(1975) 'The Celtic oppidum of Entremont, Provence', *Recent Archaeological Excavations in Europe*, ed. R. L. S. Bruce-Mitford, London, pp. 227–59.

Bersu, G. and Wilson D. (1966) 'Three Viking Graves in the Isle of Man', (*Soc Med Archaeol Molographs*, ser. 1), London.

Best, R. I. (1916) 'Prognostications from the Raven and the Wren', *Ériu* 8, pp. 120–6.

Biel, J. (1981) 'The late Hallstatt chieftain's grave at Hochdorf), *Antiquity* 55, pp. 16–18.

Birkeland, H. (1954) *Nordens historie i middelalderen etter arabiske kilder (Norske Vid Akad i Oslo: histfilos Kl* 1954 (ii)), Oslo.

Blindheim, C. (1960) 'The Market Place at Skiringssal', *Acta Arch* 31, pp. 83–9.

Blindheim, M. (1965) *Norwegian Romanesque Decorative Sculpture* 1909–1210 (trans. A. Polak), London.

Bosanquet, R. C. (1922) 'On an Altar dedicated to the Alaisiagae', *Arch Ael* (ser. 3) 19, pp. 185–97.

Boyer, R. (1983) 'On the Composition of *Voluspá*', *Edda*, ed. H. Bessason and R. J. Glendinning (*Univ Manitoba Icel Stud*, 4), pp. 117–33.

Briggs, K. M. (1969) *The Personnel of Fairyland*, Oxford.

Bromwich, R. (1961) ed. *Trioedd Ynys Prydein: The Welsh Triads*, Cardiff.

Brøgger, A. W. (1945) 'Oseberggraven Haugbrottet', *Viking* 9, pp. 1–44, Oslo.

Brøndsted, J. (1954) *Guldhornene*, Copenhagen.

—(1966) *Danmarks Oldtid* III (Jernalderen), rev. ed., Copenhagen.

Bruce-Mitford, R. L. S. (1974) *Aspects of Anglo-Saxon Archaeology: Sutton Hoo and other discoveries*, London.

—1975 ed. *Recent Archaeological Excavations in Europe*, London.

—(1975–83) *The Sutton Hoo Ship Burial* (4 vols), British Museum, London.

Buck, P. H. (1959) *Vikings of the Pacific*, Chicago.

Byrne, F. J. (1973) *Irish Kings and High-Kings*, London.

Byrne, M. E. (1930) 'On the punishment of sending adrift', *Ériu* 11, pp. 97–102.

Campbell, L. A. (1968) *Mithraic Iconography and Ideology*, Leiden.

Carey, J. (1981) 'The name Tuatha Dé Danann', *Éigse* 18 (ii), pp. 291–4.

—(1981–2) 'Coll son of Collfrewy', *Stud Celt* 16–17 (ii), pp. 168–74.

—(1982) 'The Otherworld in Irish Tradition', *Éigse* 19 (i) pp. 36–43.

Castleton, R. (1983) *The Wilmington Giant*, Wellingborough.

Chadwick, H. M. (1924) *The Origin of the English Nation* (*Camb Archaeol Ethnol Ser*), Cambridge Univ Press.

Chadwick, N. K. (1935a) 'Gusfland Ferge', *Scot Gael Stud* 4, pp. 6–17.

—(1935b) 'Imbas Forosnai', *Scot Gael Stud* 4, pp. 97–135.

—(1949) 'The Story of Macbeth', *Scot Gael Stud* 6, pp. 189–211.

—(1953) *Ibid.* continued, 7, pp. 1–25.

(1958) 'Pictish and Celtic Marriage in Early Literary Tradition', *Scot Gael Stud* 8, pp. 56–115.

—1966 *The Druids*, Cardiff/Connecticut.

(1968) 'Dreams in Early European Literature', *Celtic Studies: Essays in memory of Angus Matheson*, ed. J. Carney and D. Greene, London, pp. 33–50.

Chadwick, N. K. and Zhirmunsky, V. (1969) *Oral Epics of Central Asia*, Cambridge Univ Press.

Chatháin, P. N. (1979–80) 'Swineherds, Seers and Druids', *Stud Celt* 14–15, pp. 200–11.

Cook, A. B. (1906) 'The European Sky God (v)', *Folklore* 17, pp. 140–73.

Copley, G. (1958) *An Archaeology of South-East England*, London.

Cross, T. P. and Slover, C. H. (1936) *Ancient Irish Tales*, London.

Cunliffe, B. (1971) *Roman Bath Discovered*, London.

—(1979) *The Celtic World*, London.

Danaher, K. (1972) *The Year in Ireland*, Cork/Dublin.

—(1982) 'Irish Folk Tradition and the Celtic Calendar', *The Celtic Consciousness*, ed. R. O'Driscoll, New York, pp. 217–42.

Danielli, M. (1945) 'Initiation Ceremonial from Norse Literature', *Folklore* 56, pp. 229–45.

Davidson, H. R. E. (1958) 'Weland the Smith', *Folklore* 69, pp. 145–59.

—(1960) 'The Sword at the Wedding', *Folklore* 71, pp. 1–18.

—(1962) *The Sword in Anglo-Saxon England: its archaeology and literature*, Oxford.

—(1964) *Gods and Myths of Northern Europe*, Harmondsworth.

—(1965a) 'Thor's Hammer', *Folklore* 76, pp. 1–15.

—(1965b) 'The Significance of the Man in the Horned Helmet', *Antiquity* 39, pp. 23–7.

—(1967) *Pagan Scandinavia* (*Ancient Peoples and Places*, 58), London.

—(1969) 'The Smith and the Goddess', *Frühmitt Stud*, Univ of Münster, 3, pp. 216–26.

—(1972) 'The Battle God of the Vikings' (*Med Monograph Ser.*, Univ of York, 1).

—(1975) 'Scandinavian Cosmology', *Ancient Cosmologies*, ed. C. Blacker and M. Loewe, London, pp. 172–97.

—(1976) *The Viking Road to Byzantium*, London.

—(1978a) 'Shape-changing in the Old Norse Sagas', *Animals in Folklore*, ed. J. R. Porter and W. M. S. Russell (*Mistletoe Books*, 8, Folkore Soc.), Ipswich.

—(1978b) 'Mithras and Wodan', *Études Mithriaques* (*Act Iran* 4), pp. 99–110.

—(1978c) *Patterns of Folklore*, Ipswich.

—(1979) 'Loki and Saxo's Hamlet', *The Fool and the Trickster*, ed. P. Williams, Ipswich.

—(1980) Commentary on Saxo Grammaticus, *History of the Danes* I–IX, vol. 2, Ipswich.

—(1981a) 'The Germanic World', *Divination and Oracles*, ed. M. Loewe and C. Blacker, London, pp. 115–41.

—(1981b) 'The Restless Dead: an Icelandic Ghost Story', *The Folklore of Ghosts* (*Mistletoe Books*, 15, Folklore Soc.), Ipswich.

—(1982) *Scandinavian Mythology* (2nd ed.), London.

—(1983) 'Insults and Riddles in the *Edda* poems', *Edda* ed. H. Bessason and R. J. Glendinning, (*Univ Manitoba Icel Stud*, 4), pp. 25–46.

—(1984) 'The Hero as a Fool: the Northern Hamlet', *The Hero in Tradition and Folklore*, ed. H. R. E. Davidson (*Mistletoe Books*, 19, Folklore Soc.), London, pp. 30–45.

Davidson, H. R. E. and Fisher, P. *Saxo Grammaticus* I (1979), Ipswich.

Davidson, H. R. E. and Webster, L. (1967) 'The Anglo-Saxon burial at Coombe (Woodnesborough), Kent', *Med Arch* 11, pp. 1–36.

Delargy (Ó Duilearga), S. (1940) 'Nera and the Dead Man', *Essays and Studies presented to Professor Eoin MacNeill*, ed. J. Ryan, pp. 522–34.

Deonna, W. (1955) 'De Télespore au "moine bourru": Dieux, genies et démons encapuchonnés', *Coll Latonus* 21, Brussels.

Dietrichson, L. and Munthe, H. (1893) *Die Holzbaukunst Norwegens*, Berlin.

Dillon, M. and Chadwick, N. K. (1967) *The Celtic Realms*, New York.

Dobbs, M. E. (1913) 'A Burial Custom of the Iron Age', *Journ Roy Soc Antiq Ireland* 43, pp. 129–32.

Dronke, U. (1969) ed. *The Poetic Edda*, I, *Heroic Poems*, Oxford.

Dumézil, G. (1948) *Mitra-Varuna* (2nd ed.), Paris.

—(1958) 'L'idéologie tripartie des Indo-Européens', *Coll Latonus* 31, Brussels.

—(1959) *Les dieux des Germains* (*Mythes et religions* 38), Paris.

—(1973) *Gods of the Ancient Northmen*, ed. E. Haugen (*UCLA Cent Comp Folklore and Mythology*, 3) Univ of California, Berkeley.

Dumville, D. (1976) '*Echtrae* and *Immram*: some problems of definition', *Ériu* 27, pp. 73–94.

Duval, P. (1964–5) 'Observations sur le calendrier de Coligny', *Étud Celt* 10, pp. 18–42, 374–412; 11, pp. 7–45, 269–313.

Ekwall, E. (1935) 'Some notes on English place-names containing names of heathen deities', *Engl Stud* 70, pp. 55–9.

Eliade, M. (1958) *Patterns in Comparative Religion*, London/New York.

Elliott, R. W. V. (1963)*Runes: an introduction*, Manchester.

Ellis, H. R. (1941) 'Fostering by giants in Old Norse sagas', *Med Aev* 10, pp. 70–85.

—(1942) 'Sigurd in the Art of the Viking Age', *Antiquity* pp. 216–36.

—(1943) *The Road to Hel: a study of the conception of the dead in Old Norse literature*, Cambridge.

Ellison, A. (1980) 'Natives, Romans and Christians on West Hill, Uley', *Temples, Churches and Religions: recent research in Roman Britain*, ed. W. Rodwell, BAR (Brit. ser.), 77 (i), pp. 305–28.

Elston, C. S. (1934) *The Earliest Relations between Celts and Germans*, London.

Enright, M. J. (1983) 'The Sutton Hoo Whetstone Sceptre', *Angl Sax Engl* 11, pp. 119–54.

Evans, D. E. (1982) 'Celts and Germans', *Bull Board Celt Stud* 29 (ii) pp. 230–55.

Evison, V. (1975) 'Pagan Saxon Whetstones', *Antiq Journ* 55, pp. 70–85.

Filip, J. (1970) 'Keltische Kultplätze und Heiligtümer in Böhmen', *Vorgeschichtliche Heiligtümer und Opferplätze in Mittel-und Nordeuropa*, ed. H. Jankuhn (*Abhand Akad Wiss Göttingen*, 74), pp. 55–77.

Fitzgerald, D. (1879–80) 'Popular Tales of Ireland', *Rev Celt* 4, pp. 171–200.

Flom, G. T. (1917) 'Alliteration and Variation in Old Germanic Name-Giving', *Mod Lang Notes* 22, pp. 7–17.

Flower, R. (1947) *The Irish Tradition*, Oxford.

Foote, P. G. (1963) 'An Essay on the Saga of Gisli', *The Saga of Gisli*, trans. G. Johnston, London, pp. 93–134.

—(1984) 'Faereyinga Saga, chapter forty', *Aurvandilstá: Norse Studies* (Viking Coll, II), Odense Univ. Press, pp. 209–21.

Ford, P. K. (1977) *The Mabinogi and other Medieval Welsh Tales* (trans.), Berkeley, California.

Fox, C. (1946) *A Find of the Early Iron Age from Llyn Cerrig Bach, Anglesey* (*Nat. Mus Wales*), Cardiff.

France-Lanord, A. (1949) 'La fabrication des epées damasées aux epoques merovingienne et carolingienne', *Pays Gaumais* 10, pp. 1–27.
Frankfort, H. *et al.* (1946) *The Intellectual Adventure of Ancient Man*, Chicago (reprinted as *Before Philosopy*, Harmondsworth, 1949).
Frazer, Sir J. G. (1913) *The Golden Bough* (3rd ed.) pt. VII, vol. 2 (*Balder the Beautiful*), London.

Gantz, J. (1981) *Early Irish Myths and Sagas* (trans.), Harmondsworth.
Geisslinger, H. (1967) *Horte als Geschichtsquelle* (*Offa Bücher*, 19), Neumünster.
Gelling, M. (1961) 'Place-Names and Anglo-Saxon Paganism', *Univ Birm Hist Journ* 8, pp. 7–25.
—(1973) 'Further Thoughts on Pagan Place-Names' *Otium et Negotium, Studies presented to Olof von Feilitzen*, Stockholm, pp. 157–209.
Gelling, P. and Davidson, H. R. E. (1969) *The Chariot of the Sun and other rites and Symbols of the Northern Bronze Age*, London.
Gessler, E. A. (1908) *Die Trutzwaffen der Karolingerzeit*, Basel.
Golther, W. (1890) 'Studien zur germ. Sagengeschichte: 1. Der Valkyrjenmythus' (*Abhand bayer Akad: philos/philol Kl* 18) pp. 401–38.
Gray, E. A. (1981) 'Cath Maige Tuired: Myth and Structure', *Éigse* 18 (ii) pp. 183–209.
Green, M. J. (1984) 'Mother and Sun in Romano-Celtic Religion', *Antiq Journ* 64, pp. 25–33.
—(1986) *The Gods of the Celts*, Gloucester.
Grieg, S. (1954) 'Amuletter og Guldbilder', *Viking* 18, pp. 157–209.
Grimm, J. (1966) *Teutonic Mythology*, 4 vols (trans. J. S. Stallybrass, New York), originally published London, 1883–8.
Grønbech, V. (1931) *The Culture of the Teutons*, 2 vols (trans. W. Worster), London/Copenhagen.
Gruffydd, W. J. (1928) *Math mab Mathonway*, Cardiff.
Guyonvarc'h, C. J. (1961) 'Notes d'etymologie et de lexicographie Gauloises et Celtiques', *Ogam* 13, pp. 471–80.

Hagberg, U. E. (1967) *The Archaeology of Skedemosse*, II (*Roy Swed Akad Lett Hist Antiq*), Stockholm.
Hall, R. A. (1978) 'A Viking-Age grave at Donnybrook', *Med Arch* 22, pp. 64–83.
Hallowell, A. I. (1926) 'Bear Ceremonialism in the Northern Hemisphere', *Amer Anthrop* 28, pp. 1–175.
Hamel, A. G. van (1934) 'The Game of the Gods', *Ark Norsk Filol* 50 (ser. 3, 6), pp. 218–42.
Hammarstadt, N. E. (1919) 'Hudar och Skinn säsom Offer', *Fataburen* (*Nord Mus Skansens Aarb*), pp. 1–175.
Hamp, E. P. (1979) 'Imbolc, óimelc', *Stud Celt* 14 (i), pp. 106–13.
Harbison, P. (1986) 'A group of Early Christian Carved Stone Monuments, *Early Medieval Sculpture in Britain and Ireland*', ed. J. Higgitt, BAR (Brit. ser.) 152, pp. 49–85.

Hartland, E. S. (1903) 'The Voice of the Stone of Destiny', *Folklore* 14, pp. 28–60.

Hastrup, K. (1985) *Culture and History in Medieval Iceland*, Oxford.

Hauck, K. (1954a) 'Halsring und Ahnenstab als herrscherliche Würdezeichen', *Herrschaftszeichen und Staatssymbolik* I, ed. P. Schramm, Stuttgart, pp. 145–212.

—(1954b) 'Herrschaftszeichen eines Wodanistischen Königtums', *Jahr frank Landesforsch* 14, pp. 9–59.

—(1970) *Goldbrakteaten aus Sievern* (*Münst Mittelalt Schrift* I), Munich.

Haugen, E. (1983) 'The Edda as Ritual, *Edda* ed. H. Bessason and R. J. Glendinning, (*Univ of Manitoba Icel Stud*, 4), pp. 117–33.

Hawkes, C. F. C. (1951) 'Bronze-workers, cauldrons and bucket-animals in Iron Age and Roman Britain', *Aspects of Archaeology* (presented to O. G. S. Crawford), ed. W. F. Grimes, London, pp. 172–99.

Hawkes, S. and C. and Davidson, H. R. E. (1965) 'The Finglesham Man', *Antiquity* 39, pp. 17–32.

Hencken, T. C. (1938) 'The Excavation of the Iron Age Camp on Bredon Hill, Glos.', *Arch Journ* 95, pp. 1–111.

Henderson, W. (1866) *Folklore of the Northern Counties of England and the Borders*, Folklore Soc., London.

Henry, F. (1965) *Irish Art in the Early Christian Period* (rev. ed.), London.

Hodgkin, R. H. (1949) *Six Centuries of an Oxford College: a history of the Queen's College, 1340–1940*, Oxford.

Hole, C. (1976) *A Dictionary of British Folk Customs*, London.

Holmqvist, W. (1960) 'The Dancing Gods', *Acta Archaeol* 31, pp. 101–27, Copenhagen.

Holtsmark, A. (1933) 'Vitazgjafi', *Maal og Minne*, pp. 111–33.

—(1949) 'Myten om *Idun* og *Tjatse* i Tjodolvs *Haustlǫng*', *Ark nord Fil* 64, pp. 1–73.

—(1951) 'Skáro á skídi', *Maal og Minne*, pp. 81–9.

Hondius-Crone, A. (1955) *The Temple of Nehalennia at Domburg*, Amsterdam.

Hone, W. (1859) *The Everyday-Book* (2 vols) I, London, pp. 1618f.

Hope, A. D. (1970) *A Midsummer Eve's Dream: variations on a theme by William Dunbar*, Canberra.

Hope-Taylor, B. (1977) *Yeavering* (*Dept Envir Archaeol Reports*, 7), HMSO, London.

Hougen, B. (1940) 'Osebergfunnets Billedvev', *Viking* 4, pp. 85–124.

Hull, E. (1901) 'The Silver Branch in Irish Legend', *Folklore* 12, pp. 431–45.

Jackson, K. H. (1940) 'The Motive of the Threefold Death in the Story of Suibhne Geilt', *Essays and Studies presented to Professor Eoin MacNeill*, ed. J. Ryan, Dublin, pp. 535–50.

—(1942) 'The Adventure of Laeghaire Mac Crimhthainn', *Speculum* 17, pp. 377–89.

—(1971) *A Celtic Miscellany* (trans.), Harmondsworth.

Jankuhn, H. (1957) *Denkmäler der Vorzeit zwischen Nord- und Ostsee*, Schleswig.

Jaskanis, J. (1966) 'Human burials with horses in Prussia and Sudovia,' *Act Balt Slav* 4, pp. 29–65.

Joffroy, R. (1962) *Le Trésor de Vix*, Paris.

Jóhannesson, Jón (1974) *A History of the Old Icelandic Commonwealth*, trans. H. Bessason (*Univ Manitoba Icel Stud*, 2).

Jones G. (1968) *A History of the Vikings*, Oxford.

Jónsdottir, Selma (1959) *An 11th Century Byzantine Last Judgement in Iceland*, Reykjavik.

Keil, M. (1931) *Altisländische Namenwahl* (*Palaestra*, 176), Leipzig.

Kooijmans, L. P. L. (1971) *De Nehalennia-Tempel te Colijnsplaat*, Rijksmus Oudheden, Leiden.

Krafft, S. (1956) *Pictorial Weavings from the Viking Age* (trans. R. I. Christopherson), Oslo.

Krogmann, W. (1953) 'Muspill und Muspellsheim', *Zeit Relig Geist* 5, pp. 97–118.

Kruta, W. (1985) with W. Forman, *The Celts of the West*, London.

Lambrechts, P. (1942) 'Contributions a l'étude des divinités celtiques' (*Rijksuniv Gent Fac Wijs Lett* 93), Bruges.

—(1954) 'L'exaltation de la tête dans la pensée et dans l'art des Celtes' (*Diss archaeol Gandenses*, 2), Bruges.

Lang, J. T. (1972) 'Illustrative Carving of the Viking Period at Sockburn-on-Tees', *Arch Ael* (ser. 4), 50, pp. 235–48.

Lange, W. (1968) 'Flokis Raben', *Festschrift H. Jankuhns*, ed. M Claus et al., Neumünster, pp. 354–8.

Last, H. (1949) 'Rome and the Druids', *Journ Rom Stud* 39, pp. 1–5.

Leeds, E. and Harden, D. (1936) *The Anglo-Saxon Cemetery at Abingdon, Berkshire*, Ashmolean Museum, Oxford.

Le Roux, F. (1961) 'Études sur le festiare celtique', *Ogam* 19, pp. 481–506.

—(1967) 'Introduction generale à l'étude de la tradition celtique', I, *Ogam* 19, pp. 270–347.

—(1968) 'La Divination chez les Celtes', *La Divination*, ed. A. Caquot and M. Leibovici, I, pp. 233–56.

Leslie, S. (1932) *Saint Patrick's Purgatory*, London.

Lidén, H. (1969) 'From Pagan Sanctuary to Christian Church: the excavation of Maere Church in Trøndelag', *Norw Arch Rev* 2, pp. 3–32.

Lindholm, D. (1969) *Stave Churches in Norway* (trans. S. and A. Bittleston), London.

Lindqvist, S. (1941–2) *Gotlands Bildsteine* (2 vols), *Kungl Vitt Hist Antik Akad*, Stockholm.

Löffler, C. M. (1983) *The Voyage to the Otherworld Island in Early Irish Literature* (2 vols), (*Salzburg Stud Engl Lit Eliz/Renais* 103) Salzburg.

Longworth, I. and Cherry, J. (1986) ed. *Archaeology in Britain since 1945*, British Museum, London.

Lucas, A. T. (1963) 'The Sacred Trees of Ireland', *Journ Cork Hist Arch Soc* 68, pp. 16–54.

Lysaght, P. (1986) *The Banshee: the Irish Supernatural Death Messenger*, Dublin.

Mabire, J. (1971) *La composition de la Eyrbyggja Saga*, Caen.

MacCana, P. (1955) 'Aspects of the Theme-of King and Goddess in Irish Literature', *Étud Celt* 8, pp. 76–114.

—(1958) *Branwen, Daughter of Llyr*, Cardiff.

—(1970) *Celtic Mythology*, London.

—(1975) 'On the Prehistory of *Immram Brain*', *Ériu* 26, pp. 33–52.

—(1976) 'The Sinless Otherworld of *Immram Brain*', *Ériu* 27, pp. 95–115.

McCone, K. (1985) *Varia* II, *Ériu* 36, pp. 169–76.

—(1987) 'Hund, Wolf und Krieger bei den Indogermanen', *Studien zum indogermanischen Wortschatz, Innsb Beit Sprachwiss*, Innsbruck.

MacCulloch, J. A. (1918/1930) *The Mythology of All Races*, vols 2 and 3 (*Eddie/Celtic*), Boston, Mass.

MacNeill, E. (1926–8) 'On the Notation and Chronology of the Calendar of Coligny', *Ériu* 10, p. 1–67.

MacNeill, M. (1982) *The Festival of Lughnasa* (2 vols), (*Folklore Stud*, 2) Univ Coll, Dublin.

Marstrander, C. J. S. (1915) 'Thor en Irlande', *Rev Celt* 36, pp. 241–53.

Martin, M. (1934) *A Description of the Western Islands of Scotland circa 1695* (pub. 1703), ed. D. J. Macleod, Stirling.

Martin, R. (1965) 'Wooden Figures from the Source of the Seine', *Antiquity* 39, pp. 247–52.

Mattlingly, H. (1970) *Agricola and the Germania* (trans. S. A. Handford, revised), Harmondsworth.

Marwick, E. W. (1975) *The Folklore of Orkney and Shetland*, London.

Megaw, J. V. S. (1970) *Art of the European Iron Age*, Bath.

Meissner, R. (1921) *Die Kenningar der Skalden (Rhein Beitr Hulfsb germ Philol Volksk*, I), Bonn/Leipzig.

Meyer, K. (1895) *The Voyage of Bran, Son of Febal*, I (*The Happy Otherworld*), London.

Mogk, E. (1923) *Novellistische Darstellung mythologischer Stoffe Snorris, FFComm* 51, Helsinki.

Motz, L. (1984) 'The Winter Goddess: Percht, Holda and related figures', *Folklore* 95, pp. 151–66.

Mould, D. D. C. P. (1955) *Irish Pilgrimage*, Dublin.

Müller, W. (1961) *Die heilige Stadt*, Stuttgart.

Müller-Lisowski, K. (1948) 'Contributions to a Study in Irish Folklore', *Béaloideas* 18, pp. 142–99.

Nagy, N. F. (1981/2) 'Liminality and Knowledge in Irish Tradition', *Stud Celt* 16/17, pp. 134–43.

—(1985) *The Wisdom of the Outlaw: the boyhood deeds of Finn in Gaelic narrative tradition*, Berkeley, California.

Navarro, A. de (1928) 'Massilia and Early Celtic Culture', *Antiquity* 2, pp. 423–42.

Neumann, E. (1955) *Die Schicksal in der Edda*, I (*Beitr deut Philol*, 7), Giessen.

Nilsson, M. P. (1920) *Primitive Time Reckoning (Skrif Human Vet Lund* I), Lund.

—(1938) 'Julen' *Nordisk Kultur* 22, pp. 1–63, Stockholm.

Nordal, S. (1978) *Vǫluspa* (ed.), trans. B. S. Benedikz and J. McKinnell (*Durham and St Andrews Med Texts*, 1), Durham.

Nordland, D. (1949) 'Ormegarden', *Viking* 13, pp. 77–121.

Nutt, A. (1897) 'The Celtic Doctrine of Rebirth', *The Voyage of Bran Son of Febal*, II (ed. K. Meyer).

O'Curry, E. (1873) *On the Manners and Customs of the Ancient Irish*, ed. W. K. Sullivan, II, London.

O'Duigeannáin, M. (1938) 'On the medieval sources for the legend of Cenn (Crom) Cróich of Mag Slécht', *Essays and Studies presented to Professor Eoin MacNeill*, ed. J. Ryan, Dublin, pp. 296–306.

Ogilvie, R. M. (1969) *The Romans and their Gods in the Age of Augustus*, London.

Olrik, A. (1902) 'Om Ragnarok' part 1, *Aarb nord Oldkynd*, pp. 157–291.

—(1913) *Ibid.* part 2, *Danske Stud*, pp. 1–283.

—(1922) *Ragnarök, die Sagen vom Weltuntergang* (trans. W. Ranisch), Berlin.

Olsen, O. (1965) 'Hørg, Hov og Kirke', *Aarb nord Oldkynd*, Copenhagen.

—(1970) 'Vorchristliche Heiligtümer in Nordeuropa', *Vorgeschichtliche Heiligtümer und Opferplätze in Mittel- und Nordeuropa*, ed. H. Jankuhn (*Abhand Akad Wiss Göttingen 74*), pp. 259–78.

O'Rahilly, T. F. (1976) *Early Irish History and Mythology*, Dublin.

O'Riórdáin, S. P. (1957) *Tara, the Monuments on the Hill* (2nd ed.), Dundalk.

Ørsnes, M. (1970) 'Der Moorfund von Ejsbøl bei Hadersleben', *Vorgeschichtliche Heiligtümer und Opferplatze in Mittel- und Nordeuropa*, ed. H. Jankuhn, (*Abhand Akad Wiss Göttingen*), 74, pp. 172–87.

O'Sullivan, A. (1968) 'Verses on Honorific Portions', *Celtic Studies: Essays in Memory of Angus Matheson*, ed. J. Carney and D. Greene, pp. 118–23.

Owen, G. (1981) *Rites and Religions of the Anglo-Saxons*, London/New Jersey.

Oxenstierna, Count E. (1956) *Die Goldhörner von Gallehus*, Lidinge.

Page, R. I. (1973) *An Introduction to English Runes*, London.

Paulsen, P. (1967) *Alamannische Adelsgräber von Niederstotzingen (Veröff Staat Amtes Denkmalpfl Stuttgart*, A, 12), Stuttgart.

Phillips, E. D. (1965) *The Royal Hordes: Nomad Peoples of the Steppes (Libr Early Civilizations)*, London.

Pierrefeu, N. de (1955) 'Irmunsul et le livre de pierre des Externsterne en Westphalie', *Ogam* 7, pp. 363–86.

Piggott, S. (1962) 'Heads and Hooves', *Antiquity* 36, pp. 110–18.

—(1968) *The Druids*, London.

Powell, T. (1958) *The Celts (Ancient Peoples and Places* 6), London.

Radin, P. (1956) *The Trickster: a study in American Indian Mythology*, London.

Radner, J. N. (1983) 'The significance of the Threefold Death', *Celtic Folklore and Christianity* ed. P. R. Ford, (*UCLA Cent Comp Folklore and Mythology*), Berkeley, California, pp. 180–200.

Rees, A. and B. (1961) *Celtic Heritage*, London.

Reinach, A. (1913) 'Les têtes coupées et les trophées en Gaule', *Rev Celt* 34, pp. 38–60, 253–86.

Rodwell, W. (1980) 'Temple Archaeology', *Temples, Churches and Religions: Recent Research into Roman Britain*, ed. W. Rodwell, BAR (Brit. ser.), 77 (i), pp. 21–41.

Roesdahl, E. (1982) *Viking Age Denmark* (trans. S. Margeson and K. Williams), British Museum, London.

Ross, A. (1967) *Pagan Celtic Britain*, London.

—(1968) 'Shafts, pits, wells – sanctuaries of the Belgic Britons', *Studies in Ancient Europe*, ed. J. M. Coles and D. D. A. Simpson, Leicester, pp. 255–85.

—(1970) *Everyday Life of the Pagan Celts*, London.

—(1979–80) 'Chartres: the *Locus* of the Carnutes', *Stud Celt* 14/15, pp. 260–9.

Rydberg, V. (1880) *Teutonic Mythology* (trans. R. B. Anderson), London.

Sandars, N. K. (1968) *Prehistoric Art in Europe* (*Pelican History of Art*), Harmondsworth.

Sacken, E. von (1868) *Das Grabfeld von Hallstatt*, Vienna.

Sauvé, J. L. (1970) 'The Divine Victim', *Myth and Law among the Indo-Europeans*, ed. J. Puhvel, Berkeley, California.

Schmidt, A. F. (1932) *Danmarks Kæmpesten* (*Danmarks Folkeminder*, 39), Copenhagen.

Schove, D. J. (1950) 'Visions in N. W. Europe . . . and dated Auroral displays', *Journ Brit Arch Ass* 13 (ser. 3) pp. 34–49.

Scott, R. D. (1930) *The Thumb of Knowledge*, New York.

Sharpe, R. (1979) 'Hiberno-Latin *Laicus*, Irish *Láech* and the Devil's Men', *Ériu* 30, pp. 75–92.

Siikala, A. L. (1978) 'The Rite Technique of the Siberian Shaman', *FFComm* 22, pp. 143f., 274–5.

Simpson, J. (1962) 'Mimir: Two Myths in One', *Saga-Book Vik Soc* 16, pp. 41–53.

—(1965) *The Northmen Talk: a choice of tales from Iceland* (trans.), London.

—(1966) 'Otherworld Adventures in an Icelandic Saga', *Folklore* 77, pp. 1–20.

—(1972) *Icelandic Folktales and Legends* (trans.), London.

—(1979) 'The King's Whetstone', *Antiquity* 53, pp. 96–100.

Sjoestedt, M. (1982) *Gods and Heroes of the Celts* (trans. M. Dillon), Berkeley, California.

Smith, D. (1962) 'The Shrine of the Nymphs and the Genius Loci at Carrawburgh', *Arch Ael* 40 (ser. 4), pp. 59–81.

Smyser, H. M. (1965) 'Ibn Fadlan's Account of the Rus', *Medieval and Linguistic Studies in honour of Francis Peabody Magoun Jr*, ed. J. Bessinger and R. P. Creed, London.

Sprockhoff, E. (1954) 'Nordische Bronzezeit und frühes Griechentum,' *Jahrb Rom Germ Zent Mus Mainz*, pp. 28–110.

Sternberg, L. (1925) 'Divine Election in Primitive Religion', *Congrès Intern Amer* 21, Goteborg, pp. 472–512.

Stevens, C. E. (1976) 'The Sacred Wood', *To Illustrate the Monuments, Essays ... presented to Stuart Piggott*, ed. J. V. S. Megaw, pp. 240–4.

Ström, A. V. (1966) 'Die Hauptriten des Wikingerzeitlichen nordischen Opfers', *Festschrift Walter Baetke*, ed. K. Rudolph *et al*. Weimar, pp. 330–42.

Ström, F. (1942) *On the Sacral Origin of the Germanic Death Penalties* (*Kungl Vitt Hist Antik Akad Handl*, 52), Stockholm.

Strömbäck, D. (1935) *Sejd: textstudier i nordisk religionshistoria* (*Nord Text Uppsala*, 5), Stockholm/Copenhagen.

—(1975) *The Conversion of Iceland*, trans. P. Foote, *Vik Soc North Research*, Text Series 6, University College, London.

Struve, R. W. (1967) 'Die Moorleiche von Dätgen', *Offa* 24, pp. 33–76.

Talbot, A. (1982) 'The Withdrawal of the Fertility God', *Folklore* 93, pp. 31–46.

Thevenot, E. (1955) 'Sur les traces des Mars Celtiques' (*Diss Archaeol Gardenses*, 3), Bruges.

—(1968) *Divinités et sanctuaires de la Gaule*, Paris.

Thurneysen, R. (1921) *Die irische Helden- und Königsage*, Halle.

Tierney, J. J. (1960) 'The Celtic Ethnography of Posidonius', *Proc Roy Irish Acad* 60, pp. 189–275.

Toynbee, J. (1957) 'Genii Cucullati in Roman Britain', *Coll Latonus* 28, pp. 456–69.

Turville-Petre, G. (1963) 'A note on the *land-dísir*', *Early English and Norse Studies presented to Hugh Smith*, ed. A. Brown, P. Foote, London, pp. 196–201.

—(1964) *Myth and Religion of the North*, London.

—(1966) 'Dream Symbols in Old Icelandic Literature', *Festschrift Walter Baetke*, ed. K. Rudolph *et al.*, Weimar, pp. 343–54.

—(1976) *Scaldic Poetry*, Oxford.

Vierck, H. (1967) 'Ein Relieffibelpaar aus Nordendorf in Bayerisch Schwaben', *Bayer Vorgesch Blätt* 32, pp. 104–43.

Vouga, P. (1923) *La Tène* (Comm. des Fouilles de la Tène), Leipzig.

Vries, J. de (1930) 'Ginnungagap', *Acta Phil Scand*, pp. 41–66.

—(1932–3) 'Über Sigvats Álfablót-Strophen', *Acta Phil Scand* 7, pp. 169–80.

—(1935) 'Bilrost en Gjallarbrú', *Tija Nederl Taal Letterk* 54, pp. 77–81.

—(1952) 'La valeur religeuse du mot germanique irmin', *Cah Sud*, pp. 18–27.

—(1956–7) *Altgermanische Religionsgeschichte* (2 vols) (*Grund Germ Philol* 12) 2nd ed., Berlin.

Vyncke, F. (1968) 'La Divination chez les Slaves', *La Divination*, ed. A. Caquot and M. Lerbovici, I, Paris, pp. 303–31.

Ward, D. J. (1970) 'The Three-fold Death; an Indo-European Trifunctional Sacrifice?' *Myth and Law among the Indo-Europeans*, ed. J. Puhvel (*UCLA*

Cent Comp Folklore and Mythology 1) Univ of California, Berkeley.

Wasson, R. G. (1971) *Soma: Divine Mushroom of Immortality*, New York.

Watson, A. (1981) 'The king, the poet and the sacred tree', *Ét Celt* 18, pp. 165–80.

Wightman, E. M. (1970) *Roman Trier*, London.

Wilson, D. R. (1980) 'Romano-British Temple Architecture', *Temples, Churches and Religions: recent research into Roman Britain*, ed. W. Rodwell, *BAR* (Brit. ser.) 77 (i), pp. 5–30.

Wood, J. (1982) 'The Folklore Background of the Gwion Bach Section of *Hanes Taliesin*', *Bull Board Celt Stud* 29, pp. 621–34.

Woolmer, D. (1967) 'New Light on the White Horse', *Folklore* 78, pp. 90–111.

Index

259

Norns, 96, 164

Norway, early churches in, 34–5; folklore, 52, 79; pillars from, 23, 135; sacrifice in, 54, 55–6 *see also* Oseberg, ship-burial at,

Núadu, 178, 193, 203, 212; sword of, 177, 208

nuts, 117, 175, 179; source of inspiration, 86, 180

Nydam, offerings at, 27, 63, 132

oak, 170, 179; associated with Thor, 37, 135; forests, 24; place of sacrifice, 37

oaths, 201, 225

Oberflacht, cemetery at, 9

Odin, 10, 105, 174, 207–8, 212; ancestor of kings, 129, 221–2; cult of, 40, 42, 66, 70, 100–01; death of, 142, 192–3; god of inspiration, 14, 26, 44, 60, 77, 121, 143, 149, 155, 162–3, 173, 218; of warriors, 24, 56, 69, 70, 80, 81, 83, 86, 88f., 92f.; link with birds, 58, 87, 91, 98–9, 136; sacrifice to, 59, 65 66, 67, 98, 170; trickster, 175–6, 225–6; Valhalla, 45, 46, 89, 90

Oengus, the Mac Óc, 123, 127, 142, 206, 212

Ogam, 148, 157

Ogmios, 203

Olaf of Geirstad, 122

Olaf Haraldson (St Olaf), 40, 115, 122, 141

Olaf the Peacock, 138, 141

Olaf the Quiet, 41

Olaf Tryggvason, 43–4, 61, 116, 149, 158, 185–6

Olrik, A, 190, 193

O'Rahilly, T. F., 178, 196–7, 214

Orange, Arch of, 71

Orkney, 8, 114, 189

Orosius, 62

Oseberg, ship-burial at, 9, 65, 117–18, 183; tapestry from, 202

Ostrogoths, 6

Ottar the Simple, 50

Partholon, 124

Paul the Deacon, 120

Percht, 111

Petrossa, treasure from 34

Pfalzfeld, pillar from, 72, 129

pig, cooked at feast, 46, 48, 207; head of,

48, 49; pig-sty, 141; restored to life, 46 *see also* boar

pillar, as symbol, 21f., 25, 170, 224; from hall, 2, 23, 135, 136; head on, 72, 74

Polybius, 89

Polsidonius, 7, 156; on feasting, 40, 48; fighting, 71–2; religion, 60, 126, 131, 188

priests, 68, 150, 156, 157–8, 225; priestesses, of Cimbri, 226

Procopius, 40, 64, 191

Prose Edda, see Snorri Sturluson

Queen's College, Oxford, 51

Ragnarok, 1, 171, 172, 175, 188f., 211, 212, 226; approach of, 77, 143

Ragnhild, Queen, 141

Ralaghan, figure from, 17

rams, 56, 211

Ran, 210

ravens, 58, 86–7, 90–1, 96, 98, 136, 202; banner, 98

rebirth, 122f.

Regin (gods), 202; the Smith, 155

Regner, 85, 94

Rhiannon, 53, 114, 130, 210

Rigveda, 54

Rígsþula, 87, 174, 211

Rimbert, 154

ring, neck, 17, 27, 131, 209; of Odin, 131, 175

rock-dweller, 103

Romans, attitude to barbarians, 5, 7, 16, 131; battles with, 28, 59, 64, 73–4, 76; religion of, 97, 108, 198, 200–1, 207, 220; symbols, 48, 169; temples, 10, 28, 30

Roqueperteuse, temple at, 28

Rudolf of Fulda, 22

Rude Eskilstrup, figure from, 17, plate 4b

runes, 58, 85, 86, 148, 153, 158, 164; Runic Poem, 119–20; inscriptions, 10, 158

Rus, 18, 36

Rydberg, V., 197

sacrifice, 12, 36f., 134, 156; animal, 31, 40, 45f., 58, 59, 95, 138, 161–2; human, 58f., 184; in water, 26, 131–2

St Anskar, 122, Life of, 154

St Augustus, 125